More Praise for Gary Jennings

"Jennings has the essential knack of a historical novelist. He can breathe life into the dust of history."
—*The Washington Post*

"Jennings is noted for his exhaustive research. What he does best is write enjoyable adventure stories."
—*The Tampa Tribune & Times*

"Jennings's strength lies in his painstaking research and his authentic detail."
—*The Seattle Times*

"Jennings is the best among our historical novelists."
—*The New York Times*

Praise for *Aztec Autumn*

"If you can't make it to the latest summer blockbuster film, *Aztec Autumn* is the book equivalent."
—*The San Francisco Chronicle*

"*Aztec* addicts will have to read the sequel."
—*The Washington Post*

"Fascinating. . . . Guided by exhaustive research into practically every facet of life in sixteenth-century Mexico."
—*The New York Times*

"A plum pudding of historical information and detail set unobtrusively into brilliant plotting and offbeat remarkable digressions."
—*The San Diego Union-Tribune*

D1007301

Books by Gary Jennings

Aztec (1980)
The Journeyer (1984)
World of Words (1984)
Spangle (1987)
Raptor (1992)
Aztec Autumn (1997)

GARY JENNINGS

THE ROAD SHOW

SPANGLE VOLUME I

A TOM DOHERTY ASSOCIATES BOOK
NEW YORK

for Jacob Van Dyken, M.D.

This is a work of fiction. All the characters and events portrayed in this book are either products of the author's imagination or are used fictitiously.

THE ROAD SHOW: SPANGLE VOLUME I

Copyright © 1987 by Gary Jennings

A Forge Book
Published by Tom Doherty Associates, Inc.
175 Fifth Avenue
New York, NY 10010

Forge® is a registered trademark of Tom Doherty Associates, Inc.

ISBN: 0-812-56471-5

First Forge edition: February 1999

Printed in the United States of America

0 9 8 7 6 5 4 3 2 1

⋯⟹ AMERICA ⟸⋯

1

I'D SAY WE'VE SEEN the last of the elephant, eh, Johnny?" said one of the soldiers in blue.

"Reckon that's so, Billy," said one of the soldiers in gray. Then he looked mildly surprised. "Hey, you Yankee fellers say that, too? About the elephant?"

"All the time, or used to," said the Union soldier. "Feller said he was going to see the elephant, it meant his outfit was off to tangle with you Rebs."

"Sure enough, same with us Cornfeds. I'm sorry we lost this war, but I ain't sorry I won't see that particular elephant no more."

"Me neither. What say to a smoke, Johnny?"

"Lordamighty, Billy Yank! You got tobacco?"

"Some. You got a pipe?"

"About all I have got." The Confederate soldier shifted the several horses' reins he was holding, so he had a hand free to scrounge in his pocket. "We been smoking and chewing raspberry leaves. When we wasn't brewing 'em up for mock tea. Imagine that? And all this part of Virginia hereabouts used to be prime tobacco country.''

"Here y' go. Connecticut shade-grown broadleaf. Stoke up.''

Several others of the enlisted men now unbent from the stiff parade-ground "stand to horse" postures they had been maintaining. They mingled, blue and gray together, and handed back and forth the reins they variously held so they could pack their pipes or cut quids. They were on a grassy knoll off to one side of a triangular acre of bare ground, just down the road from the village courthouse, and they were tending the mounts of the numerous Union and Confederate officers overseeing the final stacking of arms.

Those officiating generals and colonels at the edge of the ceremonial ground did not yet relax, but stood as straight and somber as if they were attending a military funeral. Which, in a way, this was, even to the melancholy music the Union band was playing—the more doleful of the campfire songs favored by one army or the other—the Confederates' "Lorena," the Yankees' "Tenting Tonight on the Old Camp Ground." Out in the fields beyond the drab Yankee tent city that had sprouted beside the village, the remnants of the Confederate Army of Northern Virginia were gathered in formation. Now, on command, those men marched by companies to the verge of the triangular bare ground and, on command, by squads stepped forward into it. The movements were done solemnly, but grudgingly and therefore sloppily, with the men all out of step and their lines never dressed.

In the triangle, they did not stack any of their arms in approved tripod fashion, but merely dropped their rifles, muskets and carbines—and the pistols and sabres of the cavalrymen—in a heap for the waiting Union armorers to bundle away. When each squad had disarmed, it abandoned all semblance of order and, without waiting for any command of "Dis-missed!" the men ambled separately wherever they chose. Some stayed to watch for a while. Others went to gather up whatever belongings they still possessed, and then simply went away. Some departed with broad grins on their faces, some with tears. Off in the distance, on the other side of the Appomattox River, the Confederate artillery's heavier weapons were being trundled by horse teams into one collection area.

There were several civilian spectators also on the scene, most of them reporters from northern newspapers. But one was an old woman, a local resident. She stood, gumming an unlit corncob pipe, all that morning on the rickety porch of her clapboard cabin at one side of the acre of stacking ground. A small white cat, evidently hers, strolled here and there, sometimes rubbing and purring against the old woman's bare feet, sometimes against the scarred leather boots of the generals and colonels, sometimes against the fetlocks of the officers' waiting horses. Meanwhile, the orderlies of those officers had lit up and were puffing gratefully, or were chewing and spitting luxuriously, and now they amiably began chatting about the horses they were tending.

"This-here big black beauty," said a Union sergeant, "is General Sheridan's charger, Winchester. And that gelding, Johnny—that's General Lee's famous gray, ain't it? The one named Traveller?"

"That's him. Been called Traveller ever since Uncle Bobby has owned him. Named Jeff Davis afore that. And my own name ain't Johnny Reb—not after today it ain't. It's Obie Yount."

"And I won't be Billy Yank no more neither, Sergeant Yount. I'm Raymond Matchett."

"Pleased to make your acquaintance, Sergeant Matchett. And I thank you for the smoke. This does taste mighty fine."

Around those two men, other sociable conversations went on, overheard in snatches.

"... Yessir, used to be in the United States Army myself. And when I joined this-here Secesh Army, you know what happened? I went to visit some old U.S. Army friends, and they very rudely *turned their backs on me*. At

First Manassas, that was. Them friends turned all the way back to Washington, D.C.''

"I believe it, Johnny, 'deed I do. All the time I been in this war, our officers been telling us, 'Men, them Rebs is *retreating?*' But every damn time it turned out that them Rebs was retreating at us!''

"... Hell, yes, Johnny, just like you, I'm craving to get home to my gal and, hell, yes, do that. But I never in my life heard it called *doodling* a woman.''

"Ain't surprised, Billy. It's kind of a private word. My wife is a piano teacher, see, and we used to call that 'making music.' But after the war begun, her and me thought up a new name. Now we call it 'playing Doodle without the Yankee.' ''

"... Just offhand, Sergeant Yount, I'd take you to be too big and ugly and ornery-looking to be doing wagon-dog duty as an orderly.''

"You're right, Sergeant Matchett. I'm only here because my colonel is, and he ain't no pigeonhole officer either. Colonel Zack and me, we're cavalry. It's just that General Lee wanted our side to make a presentable showing here at the surrender, so the officers he brung are them few that owned uniforms which wasn't all in tatters. This claybank horse here is Colonel Zack's mount, Thunder. This one of mine here, I named him Lightning, so they'd go together proper. Thunder and Lightning.''

"Lightning?" said a Union corporal standing nearby. "That's a Percheron brewery horse!" He laughed. "No offense, Sergeant, but oughtn't you to call him something more suitable? Like Leviathan?''

"Don't go throwing off on him, sonny," Yount said affably. "I got this brute from your side. From some Yankee farmer up towards Gettysburg, after my own got shot out from under me.''

"Well, now that I've took a good look," said the corporal, "the horse ain't a *hell* of a lot heftier than you are. Big horse for a big man. So them's Thunder and Lightning, eh? I kind of admire that notion.''

"This-here horse of Sheridan's used to have another name, too. Rienzi," said the Union sergeant. "Little Phil changed it to Winchester, because it was from the town of Winchester that the general started the last Valley campaign, and won it."

Yount growled, "Little Phil Sheridan calls it a campaign, huh? Everybody in the Shenandoah Valley called it the Burning."

"You were there?"

"Me and my colonel both. He was only a captain then, Captain Edge, and that was only—Christ, that was only last autumn. We was there with the Thirty-fifth Cav. That time, we saw the elephant at a place called Tom's Brook."

"Me, I wasn't ever in the Valley," said Sergeant Matchett. "But I recollect hearing something about the Thirty-fifth Virginia." He scratched meditatively in his beard. "Wasn't that the battalion nicknamed the Comanches? And wasn't it—?"

"Disbanded right after that engagement," Yount interrupted abruptly. Then, as if to smooth over his brusqueness, he grinned and drawled, "I've always wondered why we call it that."

"What? Comanches?"

"No. Seeing the elephant."

The Yankee corporal said, "Come to think on it, I don't rightly know, either. It used to be a city folks' saying— 'I've seen the elephant!'—meaning you can't fool me; I've been around. Nowadays it means I've seen action; I'm no green recruit. But I don't know how it came to mean that."

"I never heard any soldier say it down in Mexico or out in the Territories," said Yount. "Never heard it used so until this war commenced."

Sergeant Matchett exclaimed, "You was in Mexico?"

"Me and Colonel Zack both. And back then, we was both just *troopers*, no rank at all. When we was still . . ." Yount coughed and looked down, past his bush of black beard, at his shabby garb of gray and butternut. "We was both wearing blue then. Well, hell, so was Jeff Davis and Robert E. Lee.''

''Why, so was I! Mexico, I mean. Went in with General Scott at Veracruz.''

''We went in earlier, at Port Isabel, up north.''

The corporal, who had known only this one war, looked from sergeant to sergeant, respectfully silent.

''If you was in the northern campaign, then you probably didn't get into the action at Cerro Gordo. Or Chapultepec?''

''No. We fought at the Resaca. Monterrey. Buena Vista . . .''

The two newly met, once-allied veterans were still swapping the names of battlefields far from Appomattox Court-house—far from Virginia, far from this war—when this war ended. Someone barked, ''Atten-*hut!*'' and every enlisted man, in blue or gray, snapped to statue stiffness. All the Confederate arms were stacked, the Confederate army surrendered, and now the generals and colonels in blue and gray came to collect their horses. Colonel Edge, not the youngest of the officers, but the only one not wearing a beard or mustache, came and took Thunder's reins from Sergeant Yount.

There was a considerable noise of jingling harness, creaking leather and shuffling hoofs, as the officers and men mounted. Yount leaned across from his great Percheron and asked confidentially, ''You sure, Colonel Zack, you don't want to fight no more? I'm game if you are. There's other Cornfed armies south and west of here that ain't quit yet.''

Edge said quietly, ''I've given my parole not to fight any more.''

''Well, I ain't gave no parole yet. A lot of the men ain't bothering, and the Yanks don't give a damn. They know as well as we do, them certificates is just so many ass wipers.''

Edge took out and looked again at the flimsy slip of paper he had been accorded in exchange for his word of honor. In smudgy print and scrawled handwriting, it informed all whom it might concern that "The Bearer, *Lt. Col. Zachary Edge, CSA*, a paroled prisoner" now had the United States Army's "permission to go to his home, and there remain undisturbed."

Yount said, "You being an officer, you still got a carbine, a revolver and a sabre. They outweigh that piece of privy paper. And we both got horses—like Devil Grant said, to use for the spring planting. But a lot of these men you see leaving here ain't scooting for home to farm. They're heading south to see can't they meet up with General Johnston in North Carolina, and fight alongside him."

"They won't, though," Edge said dispiritedly. "The news that Lee has surrendered will get there before they do. Old Joe will quit, too. So will Taylor and Smith and the others. They've got no choice, with Lee out of the war. Obie, it's all over."

Yount raised his bulky shoulders high, then let them sag. "Where are you going, then? You don't aim to hitch Thunder to a plow and start spring planting here in Appomattox County?"

"No. I reckon, just as it says here, I'll go to my home and there remain undisturbed." Edge tucked the paper in a tunic pocket, turned in his saddle and checked the secureness of his bedroll and pack behind the cantle.

"Come on, Colonel Zack," Yount said plaintively. "You know damn well you ain't got no home, no more'n I do, outside a barracks or a cantonment or a bivouac. Long as we've knowed each other, you and me, we ain't done nothing but soldier. Near twenty years of soldiering."

"There won't be much call for our soldier services, Obie, not for a long while. We'd better learn new trades."

"What, then? Where?"

"I can't tell you what to do. I'm not your troop commander any more. As for me, I figure I might as well go on back where I came from, be it home or not."

"Back to the Blue Ridge?"

"Yes."

"You'll go and be a hillbilly again? And me back to a mill town in Tennessee? We split up, after all these years?

"No need to split up right now, anyway. Both places are west of here." Edge kneed Thunder to a walk, turning in the direction of the courthouse, where now was flying the United States flag.

Yount hastily checked his own gear and spurred his big Lightning to a reluctant and ponderous trot. The horse had to shoulder its way through the crowds of other horses, soldiers and vehicles of all sorts, so Yount didn't catch up to Edge until they were both out the other side of the village and on the packed-earth Lynchburg Pike. As they rode side by side past falling-apart worm fences and falling-down tobacco barns, the commotion and music of Appomattox—where the Yankee band was now playing a funereal rendition of "The Bonnie Blue Flag"—faded behind them.

Only then did Yount speak again, and gloomily. "You know what we are now, Colonel Zack?"

"I know what I'm not, and that's a light colonel, CSA. And you're not my troop sergeant any more. So let's scrap the ranks and go back to the way we first knew each other. Zack and Obie."

"All right by me. You know what we are now, Zack? What we are *right this minute* is history."

"Maybe so. More likely our history is all behind us. I reckon we ought to be grateful that we lived through it."

"Trouble is, we got to go on living. How do you calculate to earn a living in the Blue Ridge Mountains?"

"Well, it's been nearly a year since Hunter and his vandals burned down VMI. By now, I'd hope somebody has started rebuilding it, and it's only right that I should lend a hand to my old school. They'll need all the hands they can get. Yours, too, if you don't favor going on to Tennessee. And once it's rebuilt, it'll need professors and instructors again. Maybe I'll qualify. If I do, maybe I could get you taken on as a drill sergeant."

"Me? Teaching cadets at the Virginia Military Institute?'' Yount went from gloom to wonderment to radiant cheerfulness. ''Say, now, that would be some pumpkins!''

''We can go and see.''

After all the hubbub of the commingled armies was behind them, they rode through an eerie silence and emptiness. They came to no sizable communities west of Appomattox, and the few farmhouses they passed were shuttered and smokeless, and there was no one else on the road except an occasional other soldier in gray, like themselves, riding or trudging somewhere homeward. The word had gone abroad, less than a week ago—when Lee's army pulled out of its long besiegement at Petersburg, to make a desperate dash for a new stronghold at Danville or Lynchburg—that it would have to come this way, and that Grant's armies were sure to pursue. So every inhabitant of these parts had grabbed up everything he or she could lift and had got out of what was bound to be a battlefield. As things turned out, the battling had stopped short of here, but there was no one around to hear that news.

Edge and Yount had not taken to the road until well after noon, so the early April twilight was soon upon them. They took shelter for the night in a deserted hamlet, in a ruined and vacant but still partially roofed frame building that, according to the dim signboard still over the doorless doorway, had formerly been the Concord Township School House.

They awoke the next morning to a gray, chilly and drizzly day, the rain not enough to make them stay put, but enough that the red-dirt road soon became a sticky red clay. That slowed the horses, so they made no more progress in a whole day of riding than they had done on the previous afternoon. A while before dusk, they came upon another vacant roadside building, also with a sign: GILES'S STORE. It was empty not only of Gileses but also, as Yount made sure to ascertain, of any kind of stores. The discouragement was enough to disincline them to stop there for the night, and they pushed on. This proved to be a mistake because, after only three or four more miles, the rain began to come down harder, and at the same time Lightning began to limp.

"Cussed animal," Yount grumbled. "Out of all this muck, you manage to pick up a stone."

A little way ahead, there was a wooden bridge visible through the rain, so they kept going until they were on its boards and out of the red mud. Yount dismounted, knelt, took up the hairy barrel hoof on his barrel thigh and began prying at it with his belt knife, meanwhile continuing to grumble:

"Folks around here are great ones for putting up sign-boards." There was one attached to the bridge railing, identifying the stream underneath as Beaver Creek. "Got to keep reminding themselves who they are, and where."

"We should have stopped at that last sign," said Edge. "This rain won't let up for a while. I vote we get under the bridge and make a camp. There ought still to be some dry wood down there."

So they did, and there was, and they soon had a small fire going. They sat on either side of it in the gathering twilight, Edge heating over the flames a pan of sagamite, the cavalryman's iron ration of mixed cornmeal and brown sugar.

"I remember another Beaver Creek on the map," said Yount. "We crossed it coming from Petersburg. No, I recollect now, that one was Beaver *Pond* Creek."

"Oh, hell, there must be more Beaver Creeks in Virginia than there are Baptists," Edge said idly. "I've never seen a real live beaver in the wild, though." He chuckled to himself. "But I've seen many a wild Baptist." When Yount made no comment, Edge glanced up at him. Yount's eyes were wide and his mouth hanging open, a gap in his black beard. Edge said, "Why in the world should that remark surprise you so?"

"Beavers and Baptists be damned," said Yount, in a hushed voice of reverent awe. He was still staring intently, but not at Edge—over his shoulder, past him, down the creek bank. "Just yesterday . . . me and some fellers was talking about seeing elephants. And now, all of a sudden— by Jesus, Zack—right yonder is one!"

2

"MASSA FLORIAN!" came a distant but distinctly agonized wail from somewhere beyond the curtain of rain. Then the wailer materialized out of the wet twilight, a short and scrawny brown-skinned man. He came running barefoot toward the wagon train, his big turban askew and his gaudy robes flapping. "Oh, Lawdy, Mas' Florian!"

"Confound it, Abdullah!" snapped the more plainly garbed driver of the leading vehicle, a rockaway carriage. "Every time you get flustered, you forget to address me as Sahib."

As he came up to the carriage, the brown man panted, "I ain't flustered, Mas' Sahib, I got skeered."

"Damn it all, not *Master* Sahib, just . . ." Florian stopped, heaved a gusty sigh and shook his head. He reined the carriage horse to a stop. The four wagons in line behind also stopped, and all began quietly but perceptibly settling into the red mud of the road. "Now tell me calmly, Abdullah. What frightened you? And where is Brutus?"

"She yonder." He pointed a wavering brown finger up the road toward the wooden bridge with the sign: BEAVER CREEK.

"Hannibal Tyree, you cowardly black good-for-nothing!" said a pretty blonde woman, who leaned suddenly out the side opening of the rockaway. "You ran off and left poor Peggy all by herself?"

"I *wish*," Florian said fervently, through gritted teeth, "now that we're on the road again, Madame Solitaire, I wish to God we could all get back in character, and remember what character we're each of us in."

"Oh, piss on that," said the pretty woman. "If Hannibal's lost that bull, we might as well get off the road again and back to oblivion.''

"Peggy she all right, Miz Sarah," the Negro assured her. "She got all foah feet in de creek yonder. She spouting water wid her trunk, happy as kin be.''

"Then what is the trouble, Abdullah?" asked Florian.

"Spied two men a-hiding unner dat bridge, Mas' Florian. Sojer men! Jist happened to look, seen 'em crouched and waiting. *Rebel* sojers. Now dat de waw is ovuh, dey prob'ly turned bummers. Y'all drive 'cross dat bridge, dey spring up and *whoooey!*" He turned to say reproachfully to Madame Solitaire, "I ain't no cowardy nigger, Miz Sarah. I come running to warn y'all.''

Another two men and a half, from the other wagons, had come up in time to hear the warning. The half, a man about four feet high, said sourly. "The linthead showed some sense for once. It was only that rube on the road said the war was finished. Maybe it ain't. I kept telling you, Florian, we'd be taking a Christly risk, coming out this soon.''

One of the two taller men—this one not really tall, but slim and lithe, and elegant-appearing despite his wagon-driver attire—said more temperately, "Oh, I don't know. In this dismal desolation, it may be better to get shot, une fois pour toutes, than to perish of slow starvation.''

The other, a beefy man whose head was totally hairless except for a fierce walrus mustache, bluntly asked Florian, "Vas ve do, Baas? Ve go chump dem first? Feed dem to de cat?''

Florian considered, then got down from the carriage seat and said, "Well, it may be that they're laying for prey. But right now, I'll warrant, they're goggling bug-eyed at that unexpected elephant, and making the teetotal pledge to God and each other. We won't take chances, though. Abdullah, you said Brutus is in the creek. Which way from the bridge?''

"Left side, Sahib Florian," said the Negro, quite collected now. "Upstream of dem two bummers.''

"All right." To the woman inside the rockaway, Florian said, "Dear lady, would you hand me our firearm?" She gingerly poked out to him an old and antiquated under-hammer buggy rifle. "I'll go first, men, and down the left bank to where Brutus is. So you, Captain Hotspur and Monsieur Roulette, sneak down on the right side of the bridge. If those lurkers jump me, you dart under the bridge and take them by surprise."

The bald man cracked his knuckles and said, "Ja, Baas." The slim man only shrugged languidly. The near-midget protested, "Hey, Florian! I don't count for shit, do I?"

"Tim, Tim," Florian said soothingly. "You'll be the most necessary of us all. You can tread lightly, so you walk right onto the bridge itself, and they won't hear you. And here, you take the firearm. If you see us all about to tangle, you can get off the one shot. Please make it a good one."

The little man took the rifle, almost exactly as tall as he was, and wickedly bared his little teeth.

"But don't jump them first," Florian said to everybody. "Give me the chance to introduce myself. They may be harmless tramps and—who knows?—they may even have some victuals to share."

However, as he made his way through the wet under-brush and sniffed the caramel-smelling campfire smoke in the air, he muttered unhappily, "No, they won't, damn it, not if they're reduced to eating sagamite."

He halted behind the last dripping screen of creekside foliage and, dripping abundantly himself, peered through at the two gray-uniformed men, a few yards away. They were standing in the shallows right beside the elephant, the water near their boot tops. As they regarded the animal, one of them reached out to stroke its trunk, at which Bru-tus, seeming pleased, voluptuously raised and flexed and curled the trunk. Florian glanced downstream, saw the small campfire aglow beneath the bridge and, beyond that, two horses browsing on the shrub they were tethered to.

Florian's eyes lighted, and he said under his breath, this time not at all unhappily. "Well, well, well . . ."

Then he stepped boldly out toward the men and the elephant, and with great joviality called, "Good evening, good sirs!"

They gave no start of guilt or alarm as they turned, but one of them casually laid a hand on the big black holster at his belt.

With a seigneurial gesture, Florian said, "Allow me to present to you, sirs, *Big Brutus, Biggest Brute That Breathes!*" The men nodded civilly enough, to him and then to the brute. Florian addressed the one with the holstered pistol and with the two stars embroidered on his tunic collar. "Do you know, Colonel, what it signifies when you stroke the trunk, as you just did, and the elephant curls it in respectful salute, as Brutus just did?"

Edge said soberly, "No, sir, I do not."

"It means—according to a venerable circus tradition— that you will someday succeed in owning a circus of your own."

That made Edge smile. And the smile made Florian regard him with some puzzlement. The Colonel's face, in repose, was personable in a craggy kind of way, like a benign rock sculpture. But his smile was ineffably sad, and made his face almost ugly.

The two soldiers sloshed out of the water to join the man on the bank, and Yount said, "Circus, hey? That explains it. Mister, I thought I was going crazy. Maybe I still am. Of all the things I might expect to see coming along on the heels of a war, a circus sure ain't high on the list."

"*Florian's Flourishing Florilegium of Wonders.* I have the good fortune to be that very Florian, owner and director of the enterprise." He stuck out his hand.

Edge took it, and noticed that the circus owner had a peculiar grip: it included a sort of extra pressure with his forefinger and thumb against the recipient's palm and knuckles. Maybe, thought Edge, it meant something among circus people, or in whatever foreign country this

Florian haled from; he spoke English with too nice a precision for it to be his native tongue.

"A pleasure, Mr. Florian." Edge's uglifying smile was gone, and he looked pleasant again—but he did not act so. While he held onto the circus owner's right hand, his own unencumbered left hand undid his holster flap, drew the long pistol and thumbed back its hammer with an ominous triple click of steel moving against steel. "Sir, you'll do me the favor of standing still, right where you are."

"Oh, misery," sighed Florian, as Edge let go his hand and moved one step back from him, still pointing the revolver at his vest buttons. "Of a Yankee, sir, such behavior would not much astonish me. But I did not know that Southern officers ever fell from gentility to rascality. I hoped you'd prove friendly."

"So I will be, sir, as long as you don't move left or right. Where you're standing, you are the shield between me and some other friends of yours. There's one up on that bridge and two beyond it. In this bad light, I might not hit all of them, sir, but I promise I can't miss you. Obie, go get the carbine."

"Wait," said Florian. "My own fault, sir. We hoped you would be on the square, but we couldn't be sure you were not bummers lying in ambuscade. If I may raise my voice, I will call those men peaceably in to meet you."

"You may give a call, sir. I recommend that you be persuasive."

Florian turned his head ever so slightly, and shouted, "Friends it is, men! Tim, come down with the gun reversed. Best, kapitein, komt u en ons ontmoeten. Soyez tranquille, Roulette, et venez ici."

After a moment, they could hear the scrabbling noise of the others approaching through the underbrush. Edge nodded approvingly, and recited. "Jamais beau parler n'écorche la langue," but he did not yet lower his pistol. "What was the other language?"

"Dutch," said Florian. From one frayed sleeve of his coat he plucked a fine lawn handkerchief, to pat his brow.

"Actually the captain speaks the very crude Cape Dutch, but he comprehends the real thing. More readily than English."

Yount said suspiciously, "Then you and your friends ain't Yanks nor Secesh neither one?"

"My dear Sergeant, any circus is a menagerie of nationalities. I myself am an Alsation . . ."

"I meant your political sympathies, mister."

"And we try never to inquire into another man's politics or his religion or any of his other superstitions. Here come my colleagues. If I may introduce you, sirs?" He waited until Edge reholstered the revolver. "In order of arrival, if not of stature, this is Tiny Tim Trimm, our world-renowned midget and hilarity-provoking clown, who doubles in brass as our cornet player."

The little man came dragging the buggy rifle at trail, and nodded grumpily, as if he resented not having had excuse to use the weapon.

Yount remarked, "I've seen smaller midgets."

Tim Trimm glared at him with eyes like those of a fish, colorless, and with that same hard, scaly sort of surface glaze. He snarled, "You can kiss my midget pink ass!"

Florian hastily said, "And this is Monsieur Roulette, champion acrobat, tumbler and ventriloquist."

"Enchanté," said the slim man, unenchantedly.

"And this is Captain Hotspur, our nonpareil equestrian, fearless lion tamer, expert farrier, cartwright and trustworthy wagon-master to our entire train."

"Goeie nag," said the bald man, then, in translation, "Gut evening, meneers."

"You will have perceived, sirs," said Florian, "that in our circus each man in his time plays many parts . . . as another great showman once observed."

"You-all sure do have fancy names," Yount said admiringly.

"Les noms de théâtre." Florian flipped a dismissive hand. "Most of us find our noms de baptême unsuited to what we are these many years later in life. For one in-

stance, Jacob Brady Russum's baptismal name is longer
than he is, so we redub him more aptly Tim Trimm.''

"En nee gut for hotspur horse rider, my name," said
the captain, humorously waggling his mustache. "Ignatz
Roozeboom.''

"Hélas," said Monsieur Roulette. "My name is regret-
tably an only slightly fancified version of my real one.''
He held out to Edge a manicured hand from his draggled
cuff. "Jules Fontaine Rouleau, late of New Orleans, and
a malheureusement far way downhill from there. No doubt
my people back home devoutly wish I would take a permanent alias. Even one like Ignatz Roozeboom.''

To the company at large, Edge said, "We're pleased to
meet all of you. I am Zachary Edge and this is Obie
Yount.''

"Well," said Florian, "we wayfarers met suspicious of
each other, and now that is over, thank goodness. Also the
rain is tailing off. But we are all wringing wet and the
night is upon us. Brutus seems happy enough here, but I
suggest that the rest of us adjourn to shelter in the wagon
train. And you, Colonel Edge, Sergeant Yount, maybe you
would like to sup on something better than sagamite?''

Those two looked at him as they might have regarded
a mirage. The circus men also looked at him, and even
more incredulously.

"Thank you, but, to tell the truth," said Edge, unwilling
to be taken for a cadger, "we had a pretty good meal night
before last. Some Yankee boys shared some with us.''

Likewise trying to appear self-sufficient, Yount added,
"And we had an onion, for a while." Then he weakened.
"But it's been damned short commons for a damned long
time.''

"Ja!" Roozeboom said feelingly, still staring at Florian.

"Yes, yes," said Florian. "With us, too, it's chicken
one day, feathers the next. But you lads won't say no to
a pork chop tonight?''

"Hell, no, we won't say no!" Yount blurted, to forestall
any polite demur from Edge.

As those two went to fetch their horses and other belongings, Rouleau said, "Pork chops?" as lusciously as if he could taste them, and Roozeboom continued to glare—with the space above his eyes, where his brows should have been, contracted into a frown.

Florian ignored them and said to the small man, in an urgent undertone, "Run on ahead, Tim. Tell Madame Solitaire to prepare her wagon for company, and to start a fire under the chops. She'll know what you mean."

Trimm protested wrathfully, "The last time *we* had pork chops was the day we left Wilmington. Ever since, the rest of us have been living on mush and molasses. And damn you, Florian, you and that yeller-haired bitch have been having chops all along?"

"Shut up and scamper. That last time you gorged, Madame Solitaire and I put our two chops away, to save them in hopes of just such an opportunity as this. Don't you see what those soldiers have got? Two capital horses! Go on, you vile homunculus, and do as I say!"

Trimm went, but still fizzing mutinously. The others waited to accompany Edge and Yount from the creek up toward the road again. Roozeboom, walking beside Edge and his Thunder, observed, "Goeie pards, your two horses, meneer. Dey nee have fear of olifant?"

"The matter never came up before," said Edge, with good humor. "I reckon a war horse gets accustomed to surprises."

Florian apparently thought it best not to show too much interest in the horses. He changed the subject. "Aren't you a trifle young, Zachary, to be a lieutenant colonel?"

"No, sir. These last months, promotion kept pace with attrition. Johnny Pegram was a brigadier general at twenty-three and dead just two months ago. I'm thirty-six."

"And alive. Well, it did look to me as if you know how to handle your weapons."

Edge shrugged. "I'm alive."

"I was a little astonished to see that you shoot left-handed."

"Either hand. But I'm right-handed by nature, I prefer to shoot that way."

"You drew your pistol with your left hand."

"Because the cavalry holster is made the way it is. See? Belted on the right hip, pistol butt sticking forward. That's because a cavalryman is expected to use his sabre most often. And you draw the sabre with your right hand from over here, on the left of the belt."

"Ah. The pistol is supposed to be only a second resort."

"Supposed to be. So you learn to draw it left-handed and shoot that way, if you have to. Or flip it to your right hand, if you've got time."

"And you, are you accurate with it either way?"

Edge dryly repeated, "I'm alive."

"Allow me to introduce you, messieurs," said Florian, as they got to the top of the creek bank, "to another valued member of our troupe. This is Abdullah, our irreplaceable juggler, drummer and bull man."

"Bull man?" echoed Yount.

"Abdullah is in charge of Brutus, whom you met first of all."

"The elephant? A bull?" said Yount. "I ain't no expert on that breed, Mr. Florian, but I'd reckon even your midget has got more pecker than your Brutus does. Might you be mistaken in supposing it a male critter?"

Florian laughed. "Brutus is a cow, true. And the name she comes to when called is Peggy. Practically all circus elephants are females. Easier to handle. Nevertheless, all circus folk call all elephants bulls. Just another old tradition, like the extravagant names."

"Yessuh," said the Negro to the newcomers. "My real name be's Hannibal Tyree."

They said hello, and Edge remarked that the young man's real name seemed suitable enough for an elephant handler.

"Again, true," said Florian. "You clearly have studied history. But the lad is hardly the right color for a Hannibal. Even more unfortunate, we don't have any armor to dress him as a Carthaginian. But his color *can* pass for Hindu, and an Abdullah requires only some scraps of bright cloth for costume. You will learn, my friends, that a circus, like a woman, lives by artifice and contrivance. We work things out as we go along.''

They had come by now to the wagons still standing disconsolately in the darkening night, and rather deeper in the mud. The remainder of the circus troupe had managed to find wood for a fire. They stood around it, bundled in shawls and horse blankets, their eyes yearningly fixed on the frying pan that the pretty woman was holding over the flames. The pork chops, just starting to sizzle in that pan, were also the first thing Edge and Yount looked at.

''Good for you, me dear!'' Florian said heartily. ''Some provender for our guests.''

The woman gave him a good-humored look; the others of the troupe did not. Yount said indistinctly, because his mouth was watering, ''Ain't y'all eating?''

''The rest of us,'' Florian said very distinctly, ''have already dined.'' A subdued growl answered him, whether from someone's throat or belly was indeterminable. Over it, Florian went on, ''Let me finish introducing you around. The charming lady doing the cooking is our Madame Solitaire, équestrienne extraordinaire.''

She gave them a smile, and it wavered slightly when Edge smiled back. The woman had dark blue eyes and curly, short hair of an antique-gold color. Up close, her pretty face could be seen to have weathered somewhat, and Edge supposed her to be about his own age. She shifted the frying pan to her left hand to shake the strangers' hands with her right; it was as callused as theirs were.

''The bonny young wench is Madame Solitaire's daughter, Mademoiselle Clover Lee, who is learning her mother's art as an apprentice rider.''

The girl was thirteen or fourteen years old. She had her mother's cobalt eyes, luminous young skin, and her long, wavy hair was a cascade of even brighter gold, the color and flowingness of a satin cavalry sash.

"The dowager lady," said Florian, "is our farseeing soothsayer and all-seeing wizardess. I am not quizzing you, gentlemen. Perhaps you have sneered at palm readers and other such humbugs on other shows, but I guarantee you this is the genuine article. Some of her prophecies have astounded even me, when they so accurately came to pass, and I am the consummate cynic. I might also mention that the lady's name is no circus coinage; it is what she calls herself. Gentlemen, I have the privilege of presenting Magpie Maggie Hag."

"Good evening—er—ma'am," said Edge.

The old woman's dark face was a tight-tied knot, all wrinkles and puckers and creases, deep within the hood of an ancient cloak. Edge expected her voice, if she had one, to come creaky and feeble from in there. He was surprised when it came, as deep and resonant as a big man's, saying, "Mucho gusto en conocerles."

Yount, not at all taken aback, replied politely in the same language, "Igualmente, señora."

"Why, Mag," said Florian. "It's been a long time since I've heard you speak in one of your old tongues. Why now?"

"Because they speak it," she rumbled.

"Ha! You see?" said Florian. "Knows all, tells all. Well, now you have made the acquaintance of our whole troupe. Oh, except for the Wild Man—back there in the shadows."

They leaned and peered. The lurking one appeared to be nothing but a loutish youth of uncommonly unappealing looks. He had a tangle of long but scanty and colorless hair, slanted eyes, vestigially tiny ears and a repellently protruding tongue too big for his mouth.

"Don't bother to say hello," Florian said carelessly. "He'll take no notice, and he can't reply. We dress him up as a savage and bill him as the Wild Man of the Woods, but he's only a run-of-the-mill idiot."

To the women, Edge, said, "I'd like to beg your pardon, ladies, for our coming among you bearing arms. I know it's inexcusable manners. It's just that these weapons are about the only valuables we have left to our name."

The basso voice spoke again. "They soon serve you better, gazho, than ever before."

"Uh, well . . . thank you, missus . . . ma'am . . ."

"Magpie Maggie Hag I am, and so you may call me."

Edge was incapable of addressing any grown woman by a nickname, especially a beldame apparently two or three times his age. So he bowed and turned away, to look at what Florian had described as the "wagon train," and regarded it with wry amusement.

The train consisted of five vehicles. The cooking fire's light was sufficient to show that they had all seen better days, and a multitude of bad days since. Their onetime coats of blue paint and multicolored lettering were faded and peeling, disclosing sprung seams and gaping cracks stuffed with rags. Not two wheels on any wagon were in true, and few even leaned in the same direction, and a number of their spokes wore splints tied on with rawhide thongs. At the head of the line was the dilapidated rockaway riding carriage. The next three were high, heavy, slab-sided closed vans. The last, hard to make out in the darkness, seemed to have barred sides, like a jail cell. There was a decent enough horse, a white one, between the shafts of the rockaway, and another, a light dapple gray, to draw the first wagon. The next wagon in line was attached to a drayhorse that had once been as massive as Yount's Lightning, but now was an immense rack of ribs and knobby joints. The next wagon had no shafts or tongue at all, but a complex cat's cradle of leather traces, ropes and whipple trees, patched together to enable it to be drawn by two very small, shaggy and dejected-looking animals.

"*Jackasses?*" said Edge.

"Disdain them not," Florian said airily and without embarrassment. "The little beasts have served loyally, hauling that museum wagon. They also inspired me to make up one of the few poems I have composed in my life. I have been saying it over and over to myself, over the weary miles:

> Far have we traveled,
> And slowly time passes.
> Tired are our feet
> And tired are our asses.

"Florian's Flourishing Florilegium ..." muttered Yount. He was puzzling out the ornate and once brilliant legend on the side of the nearest wagon. "Southern Men, Southern Horses, Southern Enterprise ... A Southern Show for Southern People!"

"To be honest," said Florian, "I borrowed that line from Mighty Haag." Edge and Yount nodded, though uncomprehending. "It went over well in North Carolina, where we've just come from. However, in real Bible-thumping-bumpkin land, I generally make it 'A Clean Show for Moral Folk.' It is usually necessary to overcome the typical intolerance of the provincial intellect for anything new or foreign. But come, friends! Let Captain Hotspur take your horses. While your supper is cooking, let us go inside this wagon and"—he nudged Edge with an elbow—"take on some wood and water, eh?"

They got inside by climbing a little stile, hinged to let down from the wagon's sagging rear, and then opening a narrow door in the wagon's back wall. The interior had only a constricted open aisle down its middle, because on both sides were shelves and racks and uprights from floor to ceiling, provided with many hinges, hasps, hooks, sliding bolts—all sorts of hardware, all of it rather rusty—so the sections of apparatus could be variously let open or stowed tight or made to do double duty, and every opening in that woodwork bulged with rolls of canvas, painted poles, coils of heavy rope, unidentifiable other gear. A coal-oil lantern was already alight and dangling from a ceiling hook. The atmosphere inside the wagon was pungent but not offensive, compounded of several major smells: old smoke, warm hay, feminine perfumes and powders, animal odors—and several minor ones: grease-paint, mildew, dried sweat.

Florian said, as he went stooping and searching for something, "Pull down that section there, Obie. It's a bunk you two can sit on. This is normally the tent wagon and the women's quarters, but I told Madame Solitaire to prepare it for guests and—ah, yes, here we are."

He stood up, holding a half-full bottle and three tin cups. Edge unbuckled and laid aside his belt and holstered pistol. Yount fumbled with latches and cautiously eased down one blanketed bunk shelf for himself and Edge, while Florian deftly let down another for himself across the narrow aisle, deftly uncorked the bottle and deftly poured. The guests took the proffered cups, and Florian, with his, made a gesture of toasting.

"Well met, gentlemen. Here's to you."

The guests murmured replies, drank, flinched, shuddered and meditated. After a moment Edge inquired, "Ought we to be drinking up your horses' liniment?"

"I admit it's not Overholtz rye," said Florian, looking a little hurt. "Wilmington city was fairly well provided with the luxuries of life, but not many of them percolated down to us. Still, this is whiskey of a sort, and not everybody in Dixie is drinking whiskey of any sort tonight."

"Amen!" said Yount, holding out his cup for a refill.

Edge said, "Was Wilmington your last stopping place?"

Both Edge and Yount, though they had not exchanged a word about it, now strongly suspected the real reason for their being so cordially received: that he would try to talk them into parting with their horses. So they sat back and studied Florian as he talked. What they saw was a small, compact, slightly plump man in a maroon frock coat and gray shoe-loop trousers that once had been exceptionally natty and now were stained, patched and threadbare. The lapels and turnback cuffs of his coat still bore remnants of what had been an expensive job of gold-thread embroidery. Florian's brown eyes were bright and lively, and he didn't seem to be much over sixty, but his hair and his neatly vandyked little beard were silver-white, and his ruddy face had been deeply stamped and rutted by the tread of his years.

"Wilmington," he said, not fondly. "It looked like Wilmington would be our last stopping place forever." He sloshed more whiskey into their cups. "Five years ago, when it was clear that a war was going to break out any day, practically every circus in North America hurried to make one last tour before the roads were barred. We owners and directors all convened at the Atlantic House in Philadelphia, to agree on which of us would go north, west or wherever. For a particular reason, I chose south, and here I've been ever since. Even the shows that got back safe and sound to their northern grounds haven't had an easy time of it over these last years, so I've heard. Dan Rice put his show on a boat, and he's been not very profitably working up and down the Ohio River. Spalding and Rogers took ship to South America to wait out the war. Howes and Cushing to England. Maybe some others got stuck behind the lines, the way we did; I don't know."

He paused to sip at his whiskey. Yount asked, "Can we smoke in here?" Florian bobbed his head, so Yount got out the last of the tobacco he had scrounged from that Connecticut Yankee. He and Edge filled pipes and lit up, and asked what was the particular reason that had brought Florian south.

"I wanted to acquire some good freaks. In America, North Carolina is the best source for them."

"Is that a fact?" said Edge. "Why?"

"Hell, man, up there in the Great Smoky Mountains those Tarheels have been inbreeding for centuries. Why else do you think the North Carolinians are called Tarheels? Because they stick where they are. Those hillbillies never move five miles off their home mountains in their whole lives, so they've got nobody to marry but one another. When sisters and brothers and cousins have been inter-marrying for generations, all they generate is Wild Men, Pinheads, Three-Legged Wonders, Bearded Ladies, you name it. And they'll gleefully give them away free gratis.''

"I just bet," said Yount.

"So that's why I decided to head south. And immediately half my show walked out on me. Ten or twelve artistes and numerous animals they owned. Those performers just would not venture southward under the prevailing uncertain circumstances. That didn't surprise me much. In fact, I was considerably surprised and pleased that Abdullah consented to come, since he'd been freed only a few years before, from a Delaware plantation. And I wasn't too much bothered by the defection of those others. A smaller troupe was easier to transport, and still it was a good enough show to draw the yokels.''

"You came with just what circus you've got now?" Edge asked.

"Yes. Except that we had better road stock than jackasses, and the wagons and gear and costumes were all in good condition and sparkling trim back then. We made a sufficiently awesome impression on the Tarheels. Better than they made on us. Which is to say that they were, for once in history, dismally short on freaks. All we picked up was that mediocre idiot. So there we were, working our way through the Smokies, and as remote from civilization as those hillbillies. We didn't even hear that the war had started until it was well under way. When we did, we came hellity-split out of those mountains. Made a dash for the coast, hoping to get a ship. We made Wilmington all right, and that was the end of our luck.''

"Ought to've been grateful you had that much," grunted Yount.

"Oh, we were indeed. Wilmington was a Confederate seaport—but even so, all through the war, it was a sort of little Switzerland between the belligerents. Both sides seemed tacitly to have decided on that. The Union warships blockaded the port, but only in a halfhearted way, so there was constant traffic through it—to and from both sides. It was the Confederacy's best access to foreign trade. And it served the Union as a channel for slipping in spies and provocateurs, for arranging prisoner-exchange agreements, that kind of thing.''

''If so many other things were going in and out,'' said Edge, ''why couldn't you?''

''For one reason, blockade runners don't use craft big enough to ship an elephant. For another, they had their pick of far better-paying cargoes. Going out of Wilmington, the runners could take cotton, tobacco, hoarded gold and jewels, passengers eager to pay any price—foreigners who'd got caught over here, wealthy southern planters and their families fleeing abroad, young southern gentlemen not caring to put on a gray uniform . . .''

Yount snorted in disgust, then said, ''But it couldn't of been the worst place in the world for you to be stuck.''

''No, no, not at all. A lot of the goodies going in and out clung to Wilmington's fingers, so to speak. The city lived royally, compared to most of the South. Not that *we* could afford many of the good things. But the gougers had to spend their loot somewhere, so they spent it on entertainment. Throwing gala balls and dinners, going to the theater, to the racetrack—and to the circus, which was us.''

The three men sat silent for a minute, listening to the circus outside making ready for the night. There were muted whinnies as the horses and asses were unhitched and let loose to graze. There were some louder moos that suggested cows, but were apparently the noises of the Wild Man. There was shuffling and clatters and a rumbling of the gypsy's voice that sounded like conjurings in some unintelligible tongue. And once there came the light, young laugh of a girl.

Florian resumed, ''We couldn't add to the troupe or even keep up our equipment while we were in Wilmington; the blockade runners didn't import circus gear or performers. Cloth was too expensive for us ever to afford new costumes. But we kept our tickets cheap to keep folks coming in time and again. And by changing our acts and our program at intervals, we managed to show the folks some diversity. Every one of our people changed names so many times—that's why I am being insistent now: that they resume and remember their original characters. Well, that's it. We didn't thrive, God knows, but we survived.''

''And now?'' said Edge.

''Now we damned well *want* to thrive. We've had enough of poverty and misery and making do. Making the horses and poor Brutus learn to live on corn shucks. Feeding poor Maximus any guts and tripes we could scavenge, and the feet of the chickens we stole for ourselves, and any stray pet dogs and cats we could catch in the alleys.''

Yount asked, ''What's Maximus?''

''Our circus cat.''

''You fed a cat *cats?*''

''Cat is the circus word for feline—lion, tiger, leopard, whatever. Maximus is a lion. That reminds me . . . if you'll excuse me a moment, Zachary and Obie?'' He opened the door, stuck his head out and called loudly, ''Captain Hotspur!''

When Roozeboom appeared at the foot of the little stair, Florian spoke at some length in Dutch, except that the name Maximus occurred a time or two. Roozeboom replied, ''Ja, Baas,'' and went away again.

Florian shut the door and continued, ''Let me give you an instance of the troubles we've seen. These last days, coming inland from Wilmington, we've put on a show in every crossroads community on the way. I mean, here we are, in Backwater Junction, North Carolina: we might as well set up and perform. And here are some Backwater people to watch, and maybe they've got a spare copper or a turnip to pay us with.''

He paused and chuckled richly. ''No, I'll be honest. Circus folk will put on a show wherever there are people to watch. Admiration is our sunshine. We are like birds—we would sing and preen and strut in any case, and so any

paying audience just adds extra warmth to the sunshine.''
He chuckled again, then sobered. ''Well, North Carolina
is swarming with tramp darkies—freed or run away—so
we would give them a meal of whatever we had, in
exchange for their running on ahead to the next town, during the night, and posting our paper.''

Edge and Yount looked blank.

''Putting up our circus posters on walls and trees—
sticking them up with flour-and-water paste. We'd give
them a little pail of it to carry along with the paper. Well,
we kept coming to new towns and seeing no paper, and
the people not aware we were coming. What it was, the
darkies were throwing away the posters and *eating the
paste!* That's how bad things have been.''

''Do you think things are any better here?'' Yount
asked, with a harsh laugh. ''Mr. Florian, for the past ninety
miles or so, you've been inside the Commonwealth of Virginia. You talk about people and coppers and turnips—
hell!—we ain't even seen a loose *darky* in the last two
days.''

Florian looked glum. ''We had no choice; we had to get
out of Wilmington. The Federals finally invaded and took
over, five or six weeks back, and the good life, so-called,
came to an end. It was clear that the whole war was fast
coming to an end. We didn't want to risk being marooned
in Dixie for however long the Union decides to keep the
Confederacy under severe martial law. Right now, we're
aiming for Lynchburg.''

''Just a short day's ride from here,'' said Yount.

''And it's a sizable burg,'' said Florian. ''Big enough
that it might provide some badly needed sustenance for us.
Then we'll keep on north. On the way, maybe recruit new
acts, find new gear to replace our worn-out stuff. If we
can only get across the Mason-Dixon line . . .''

''When you came out of Wilmington and headed this
way,'' said Edge, eyeing Florian curiously, ''you were
aiming straight across General Lee's intended route of
march. Right this minute you might have been in the very

middle of a shooting war. What fool kind of thing was that to do?''

''A gamble, yes, but a shrewd one, I thought. And so it proved. You see, we got word in Wilmington as soon as your army pulled out of Petersburg, and the word was that your men were deserting by the thousands from that moment on. The end had to come soon. I figured Lee's march would stumble to a stop, well before we crossed its route.''

''I see,'' Edge said somberly. ''Well, we realized the end was imminent when General Lee didn't issue any order against straggling. It was the first time he ever neglected to do that, and we knew it was deliberate, and everybody knew what he meant by it. We left Petersburg with something like twenty-seven thousand men, and they just melted away. At Appomattox, as best I could count, we had about eight thousand left to surrender. Yes, you judged right, Mr. Florian. I hope you keep on being right.''

''If I could boast a Latin family motto, Zachary, I daresay it would be . . . let's see . . . 'In mala cruce, dissimula!' Rough Latin, maybe, but it says it: 'When in a bad fix, bluff!'''

There was a kick at the wagon door, and a voice announced blithely, ''Flag's up!''

Florian leaned to unlatch the door. Madame Solitaire stood smiling on the little stile, holding two steaming tin plates. Each bore a single, very small, fried pork chop, a dab of cornmeal mush and some anonymous greens and a tin fork apiece. They sat looking at the plates and politely hesitating and audibly gulping.

''Well, go on, eat!'' said the pretty woman. ''Don't wait for me. I've already had mine. We all have. Florian said so, didn't he?'' She threw him a mocking glance.

So the two men pulled out their belt knives and pitched in, trying not to look voracious about it. Edge cut for himself a tiny fragment of pork, forked it into his mouth, chewed it for a savoring long time, swallowed, paused in appreciative deliberation and said, ''Mighty fine, Madame

Solitaire, and mighty welcome, and mighty hospitable of you folks.''

"If you're going to make speeches at me while you eat, call me Sarah—it's shorter, and you can eat a lot faster. My real name is Sarah Coverley.''

"Please, Madame Solitaire,'' Florian objected mildly. "I am trying to teach them circus ways.''

"Oh, balls,'' she said, and the two men's eyebrows went up. "*I'm* circus, but I can't remember all the names I've had for all the ways I've performed. Princess Shalimar in harem gauzes, Pierrette in a clown suit, Joan of Arc in pasteboard armor, Lady Godiva in nothing at all . . .'' The two men's eyebrows practically merged into their hairlines. "Will you two stop stopping? Go on and eat while it's hot.''

Florian commented, "They may be hesitating over the taste of it. I'm sorry, lads, but that's how Nassau pork is. Coming all that way from overseas, it does tend to get a little greenish.''

"No, no, it's fine!'' Edge said, and cut another minuscule bite. He chewed as thoroughly as if it had been an entire ham, swallowed and spoke again. "If your name is Sarah, ma'am, I reckon your little girl is not Mam'selle Whatever-it-was.''

"No, she's Edith Coverley, but *her* stage name came sort of naturally. See, when she was only a teensy squirt, first learning to talk, she couldn't pronounce that name Coverley. Best she could do was Clover Lee. So she just kept it as she grew up.''

"It *is* a nice name,'' said Yount. "And Mr. Coverley, what's he called?''

" 'The late,' I hope, if he's in hell where he belongs. I haven't laid eyes on the son of a bitch since I notified him that Clover Lee was on the way.''

Yount's eyebrows did some more twitching, but Edge hastened to say, "From your name, I take it you're not a foreigner.''

"To you I probably am, Reb,'' she said mischievously.

"I'm from New Jersey. Now shut up and eat. I'll be back for the dishes when you're done. Florian, pour them some more of your snake piss, to cut the taste of that pork."

She went out, and Florian did as he was bidden. Edge drank from his freshened cup and said:

"I was just trying to sort out the menagerie of nationalities you spoke of. It seems to me that most are Americans. That lady and her daughter, the Louisiana gentleman, the Tarheel idiot. I reckon you could stretch a point and call the elephant darky an African. You said you're Alsation, and the lion tamer is Cape Dutch. But the midget— from his lovable disposition and his cultured speech, I'd guess Deep South poor-white trash."

"Yes, Tim's just a Mississippi mudcat. But most circus people talk rough—you heard Madame Solitaire. If Tim talks filthier and louder, it's because he's talking *taller*. Of course, that's about as hopeless as a cross-eyed man trying to look dignified."

"The old dowager lady ain't American, Zack," Yount pointed out. He said to Florian with some pride, "We picked up a good deal of Spanish down in Mexico."

"But the old lady is no Mexican," said Edge. "She speaks her 'c' with a lisp. That's European Spanish."

"Right," said Florian. "Maggie's a Spanish-born gypsy." He looked at Edge long and thoroughly. "So you know Spanish well enough to spot the real Castilian. And down there at the creek you spoke to me in French."

Edge said deprecatingly, "A textbook proverb. My French has gone rusty, I'm afraid. I tried to keep it up— spoke it sometimes with General Beauregard. He's from an old New Orleans Creole family, like your Rouleau gentleman."

"And you?"

"I'm not. Not a gentleman, not anything. No old family, no exotic birthplace. Never been abroad, except for Mexico and the Territories. I'm just a Virginia hillbilly."

"I meant where did you learn French?"

"At the 'I'—when I was a rat."

Florian blinked. "I beg your pardon?"

"Well, you've been flinging circus slang at us all evening. I thought I'd retaliate." He smiled, and Florian blinked again, at the change it made in Edge's face. "A rat is what a new cadet was called at the Virginia Military Institute—the 'I:' That's where I learned French. One of the first books we had to crack there was the *Vie de Washington*."

Florian continued to look keenly at him. "So you have some French and some Spanish. Any other languages, Zachary?"

"Well, I read Latin, of course."

"Of course. I'd expect that of any Virginia hillbilly."

"You know what I mean. We had to study Latin at VMI. Major Preston taught it, and he was a good teacher. Hell, all our teachers were top-notch. One of them you've probably heard of—Stonewall Jackson. Not that he was called Stonewall then. We called him Professor, and we took care to say it respectfully. He was pure-poison pious and strict. Anyhow, I was well taught, and I've tried to hang onto what I got there. I don't mean I could sit here right this minute and construe a passage in Tacitus, but . . ."

"But you have some Latin, some French and some Spanish. Quite a cultivated man, you are. You could easily make your way all over Europe. Have you boys ever thought of going to see it?"

Edge stared, smiled his woebegone smile, shook his head and sighed. "Europe? Mr. Florian, there's about as much chance of us going to see Europe as there is of it coming to see us."

Florian laughed, but went on sincerely, "Again I say that I am not quizzing you, friends, I am dead serious. Europe is where I came from, where I got my early circus experience. That's where I intend to go back to just as soon as I can, and take my circus there. The United and Confederate States are going to be suffering turmoil and deprivation for a long time yet. If I hope to recoup my

fortunes, and increase them—and everybody else's on the
show—Europe is the place to do it. We shall forge on
through this impoverished southland until we get to some
northern cities where there is more money to be made, and
make enough of it to take ship for England or France.
What do you lads say to coming along?''

Edge said, with sardonic amusement, ''All this while,
I've been expecting you to make us some kind of offer for
our horses.''

''Well, ahem, yes. I'd like to have them, indeed I would.
And when we first met, they were all I had eyes for. But
now I'd like to have you two along with them.''

Yount said unbelievingly, ''Ain't you already saddled
with enough poor-whites—and other colors—counting on
you for support? Why in blazes would you want two more
that can't earn their keep?''

''Because I think you could, Obie. Earn your keep and
more. I told you I hoped to be adding new acts as we go.''

''Acts? Hell fire, mister, I ain't no actor! All I know is
soldiering. Why, the notion is pure moonshine. Me, at my
age in life, running off like a schoolboy truant to join a
circus?''

''No actor was ever an actor until he started acting. And
nobody ever knows what extraordinary things he may be
capable of, until he tries something out of the ordinary.
That's what the circus is, Obie—a stretching of the limits
of the possible, a defiance of the strictures of the commonplace, a realization that the impossible *can* be possible.''

''Well, mebbe so,'' Yount mumbled, overwhelmed by
the rhetoric. ''But it ain't for everybody.''

''When I first met Hannibal Tyree, he was shining shoes
on a Pittsburgh street corner, and he never figured to be
anything but a Negro shine-boy for the rest of his life. I
came along. I saw the way he flipped those shoe brushes
and slapped that shine rag in cakewalk tempo. Result? Today he is an artiste, a competent juggler, and a bull man
besides. As long as there exists a circus on this planet,

Abdullah won't lack for gainful employment at a job he enjoys . . . and he'll have admiration . . . and a measure of celebrity. He may never be a star turn like Léotard or Blondin or the Siamese Twins, but he'll never be just a lowdown nigger again. Sergeant, what's the heaviest thing you ever lifted?''

"Uh, what?'' Yount started at the unexpected question, and stammered, ''Why . . . heavy thing? Jesus, I don't know. Heaving an artillery caisson out of a mudhole, I reckon.''

"All by yourself?''

"Uh huh. See, it was like this—''

"Never mind. I just wanted you to realize. That's something not everybody could do. Now, I doubt that you could lift Brutus off the ground, but I wouldn't give odds that you can't lift that Percheron of yours. You certainly *look* like a strongman, and that's how I'll bill you. How does *The Quakemaker, Strongest Man on Earth* sound to you?'' Yount gawked at him, stupefied. "As for you, Zachary, I've been thinking: something dignified, along the lines of Colonel Deadeye or Colonel—''

"No,'' Edge said flatly. "Don't squander your powers of persuasion on me, Mr. Florian. Anyway, I'm not a Colonel Anything any more. As soon as I can lay me down to sleep someplace warm enough to take off this tunic, I'm going to pick the damned embroidery off the collar so nobody'll mistake me again for what I'm not.''

"Don't be a simpleton,'' said Florian. "At least you came by those two stars honestly. Hell, after this war, every measly militia man who spent his whole military career in the Saltpeter Corps—if he got even a brevet rank for it—will insist on being addressed as Major or Colonel to the end of his days.''

"Let him, I don't give a damn. He can't outrank me. There are no ranks in civilian life.''

"Anyway, Zachary, I was talking of a stage name. In everyday civilian life, outside the pavilion, you can call yourself what you like.''

"Everyday civilian life is exactly what I'm going back to, thank you. Not a circus life of doing tricks for anybody who's got the price of admission, and deluding myself that that's celebrity."

There was a thump at the door again, and this time Sarah Coverley let herself in without waiting. She said cheerily, "The troops all fed? And what's this—nobody drunk yet? What kind of Southern gentlemen—?" She stopped and gazed around at them: Edge looking adamant, Yount looking uncomfortable and Florian apparently pondering deeply. "Did I interrupt devotions, or what?"

Florian shook his head and said to nobody in particular, "I was trying to think of some civilian occupation that does *not* consist of doing tricks for whoever will pay for them. And a civilian occupation that is *not* arrayed according to rank."

"Ah, you gents are playing at conundrums," said Sarah. "Do I get a turn?"

"Be quiet," said Florian. "Tell me, Zachary, what occupation are you going back to?"

"I don't know. Maybe I'll have to turn bandido or filibustero, like the leftovers from most wars. But I'm hoping that maybe I can get on the faculty of VMI. Teach cavalry tactics or something. Hell, after nineteen years in one uniform or another, I ought to be able to give the rats something worth their while."

Florian jumped to his feet and said loudly, in disbelief, "A man in the absolute prime of life, a veteran of nineteen years of manly action in the wide-open outdoors, and you're going to dwindle into a *schoolmarm?* A dusty, desk-bound, time-serving, nose-wiping warder of green and pimpled recruits? For that, you'd forgo the opportunity I am offering you? To stay on horseback, to go on using your skills and your weapons and your experience. To enjoy all manner of excitement and adventure, to be a man among men—*and* among gorgeous women like Madame Solitaire here—*and* to see the world into the bargain. Solitaire, tell Zachary what a fool he is!"

"What a fool you are, Zachary," Sarah said, biting back a grin.

Florian said, "Gentlemen, I offer each of you thirty dollars a month. And peck, of course." He indicated the plates the two men had cleaned. "Obie, you to be the Circus Strongman. Zachary, you to be our Exhibition Shootist. You heard what Magpie Maggie Hag said—that your weapons will serve you better now than ever before. For each of you, thirty dollars and peck. And prospects, gentlemen, *and prospects*. The prospects of advancement to positions of responsibility and unimpeachable respectability. Prospects of—"

"Of performing before the crowned heads of every country on the globe!" Sarah took it up as if she was reciting a speech heard often before, and now she was not hiding her grin. "Prospects of meeting and dazzling the wealthiest and handsomest young counts and dukes and even princes. Why, you could marry some European nobleman so far above your station, so far beyond your wildest New Jersey dreams . . ."

She desisted, for they were all laughing.

Florian took advantage of the moment to bring forth his bottle again. "Here, lads, have another dram of this dyspepsia."

"Thank you," said Edge. "But I still have to decline your offer, sir. It would actually mean a considerable comedown for me. My present wage is ninety dollars a month, all found."

"And when did you last get paid?"

"Oh, well."

"If you had a thousand of those Confederate butt-wiper dollars right now, you'd be lucky to exchange them for one Federal ten-dollar gold piece."

Yount exclaimed, "You're offering thirty a month in gold?"

"Yes, by God, I am. Gold, sterling, whatever is the specie of whatever realm we're in. Of course, you understand that it must be promissory for the time being. I think

I've made plain to you the current situation. We are all of us working on speculation, as it were. However, strict account will be kept, and all obligations honored in full.'' While he went on talking to Yount, Florian gave Sarah a look, and she nodded almost imperceptibly in reply. ''So, Obie, let's you and me step outside and discuss this, and we'll also decide where you two might spread your bedrolls tonight. In the meantime, Zachary, would you kindly lend Madame Solitaire a hand with clearing away the supper utensils?''

He was gone, with Yount in tow, and the door closed behind them, before Edge could ask why the woman should need assistance in gathering up two small plates, two forks and three cups. She didn't even pick them up. She picked up the bottle instead, held it to the lantern, then divided its remaining inch or so of liquor into two of the cups and handed one to Edge.

''Let us drink,'' she said, ''to you being such a fool that you don't want to bedazzle a duke.''

''Is that what you want to do sometime?'' he asked, as they clinked cups and drank.

''Sure, why not? I've bedazzled lesser notables, and not just in the circus ring. Aren't you dazzled, Zachary?''

''Is that what you want me to be?''

''Yes,'' she said, and seemed to wait. She added, ''I am extremely susceptible to compliments.'' When Edge responded only with a boyish flush to his face, she added, ''I am a widow—of sorts—and I frequently suffer from the widow's complaint.''

Exposed to so much feminine frankness unprecedented in his experience of women, Edge could only say, ''What is that complaint, Ma'am?''

''Suppressed flirtation. If it should break out in boils, I could not sit a horse. I've got to think of my art and my livelihood.''

Edge recklessly suggested, ''Better not suppress it, then.''

''I try not to. And right now the other ladies are doing

their best to help me not to. Old Maggie and my Clover Lee are bedding down tonight in the property wagon—the white men's quarters—and they've booted the men out to sleep on the ground with Hannibal and the Wild Man and your sergeant. So you and I can have this wagon to ourselves. These bunks are not exactly commodious, but we can pile the bedding on the floor.''

Edge cleared his throat. ''I'm not at all averse, Madame Soli—''

''That's big of you. You're supposed to be as dazzled as a duke. And do call me Sarah, or we'll never get past these kittenish preliminaries.''

Edge said patiently, ''Sarah, I was only trying to remark, with apologies, that I haven't had this uniform off in I can't remember how long.''

She shrugged. ''Leave it on, then. Do you only perform by the manual of drill?''

''I mean, goddamn it, woman, *I need a bath!* Can you let me borrow a piece of soap? I'll slip down to the creek.''

''Oh. Well, if we're going to be duke-and-duchess fastidious about this, I ought to have one too. I'll come with you.''

''That water'll be cold. You may be a horsewoman, but I doubt that you've got the hide of a cavalryman.''

''You can feel it all over, and tell me.'' Still carrying her cup of whiskey, she reached for the door. ''Come on. You can even satisfy your cavalryman's curiosity. About whether this filly's tail matches her mane.''

''Wait a minute. I want to ask—are you Florian's woman?''

She tossed off the dregs in her cup. ''When he needs one.''

''And when he needs somebody persuaded of something, he uses you for that, too?''

''That's not very flattering, Zachary. To yourself or to me, either one.''

''I just wouldn't want you to do something under duress, and find out afterward it went for naught.''

"Oh, crap. Now you're being the gallant Southron. Maybe there was a time when I wanted to be wanted. Now I'm satisfied just to be needed."

"Damned if I'm acting gallant, when I'm saying straight out that I *don't* need you. I mean, I don't need a woman so bad that tomorrow I'll join this road show out of gratitude or guilty conscience."

"Why don't we both simply shut up and let nature take its course? You never know, you may be so smitten that you'll join out, just hoping for more of me."

"You really reckon that you'll bedazzle me, Sarah? That you're so irresistibly good-looking? Or so talented in that way?"

She shrugged again. "The looks may have gone downhill over the years, but the talent could only have increased, right? . . . Don't do that."

"Do what?"

"Smile. Don't. You're a much handsomer man when you don't smile."

"Well, I don't often. I don't find many things nowadays to smile about. I thank you for giving me cause to smile, just then—but if you say so, I'll try not to."

"Good," she said, and sighed a little. "So will I."

But later, in the dark, she did smile, and so did he.

3

AT THE sound of a shot very close somewhere, Edge came instantly awake and flung off the blanket that covered him. He was not quite awake enough to be aware of where he was, but he had recognized that the sound was not of friendly fire. It had been a rifle shot, but of a lighter-calibre weapon than his own familiar carbine. In the dark, he grabbed for his revolver, left within easy reach whenever and wherever he went to sleep. Instinctively he made for the nearest light in the darkness, a rectangular bright sliver indicating a closed door. He burst through that door, pistol foremost, and was in the full sunlight of a mild April morning where he was greeted by an uproar of shouts, laughter and at least one piercing feminine screech of outrage. Edge realized that he was standing at the top of the little stair leading from the circus wagon in which he had slept, and that he was standing there buck naked, unaccoutred except for the revolver in his hand.

"Colonel Zack!" cried Obie Yount, scandalized. "You're out of uniform!"

"Superb entrance, Zachary!" caroled Sarah Coverley, already dressed and outdoors.

Jules Rouleau began to sing, in a syrupy way, the refrain of "Oh, Wake and Call Me Early, Call Me Early, Mother Dear."

"Hey, Colonel!" yelled Tim Trimm. "At least stick on your stars and braid!"

Even the elephant let out a mocking trumpet blast, and the outraged screech sounded again, from a middle-aged woman upon a lattice-sided tobacco wagon that had not been there the night before. She would only have had to turn her head and the immense coal-scuttle bonnet she wore would have blocked out any unwelcome sight. Instead, she dramatically flung her apron up over her head.

At least assured that nobody was under armed attack—though that did not much palliate his hideous embarrassment—the red-faced Edge popped back through the door and slammed it shut.

"Well, I never!" wailed the woman, from under her apron. "And in front of a good Christian woman and her innocent chillun! Oh, I had heerd of sich goings-on amongst you traveling folk, but never did I think to see the day—"

"Pay it no mind, Mrs. Grover," said Florian.

"He's gone now, Maw," said the middle-aged man beside her on the wagon seat, and spat tobacco juice over the wheel. "You kin unkiver your head."

Florian solemnly explained, "A case of what the military surgeons call soldier's heart—a nervous disorder brought on when a man has endured long service under fire.''

"Lots of our sojers suffer from it, I hear," Mr. Grover said sympathetically. "You hadn't ought to of let that gun be shot off, without warning the poor feller."

"Too true, sir. Now as I was saying, you folks will be in Lynchburg this afternoon, before we can get there, so we'll gladly reward you for doing us a favor."

The tobacco wagon had come along the road from the east and was waiting for the circus to clear the way for it to pass. Florian had already ascertained that Mr. and Mrs. Grover and family were refugees who had fled Lynchburg in expectation of its soon being under siege. Now that the war was over, they were going home again. Their wagon carried no tobacco, but was heaped and hung with all their household belongings, including numerous children. While the Grovers' collective attention was on the elephant and the other exotica roundabout—and, briefly, Zachary Edge's contribution to the spectacle—Tiny Tim Trimm and Magpie Maggie Hag were uobtrusively but industriously filching from the wagon every small item within their reach that was concealable in the gypsy's many layers of voluminous skirts.

"Just take these posters and this paste along with you," said Florian, handing them up to the woman. "Stick them anywhere you can—walls, trees, shop windows."

"They ain't nasty things, are they?" Mrs. Grover asked, looking disapprovingly at the rolls of paper on her lap. "Like that-there sojer's hard we jist seen?"

Florian turned away to cough for a minute, then said, "Madame, read the poster yourself."

She said primly, "I don't never read nothing 'cept the Good Book. Rev'rend Jonas bids us avoid everything what's unnecessary or unwholesome."

"You would avoid laughter, madame? Pleasure?"

"Rev'rend Jonas says laughter is seldom necessary and pleasure is seldom wholesome. So I don't never read nothing 'cept—"

"This is a perfectly respectable advertisement of our show. Perhaps you'll allow me to read it to you . . ." Flapping open one of the rolled sheets he still held, Florian began to do so, with appropriate gestures, vocal modulations from piano to forte, occasional suspenseful pauses and distinctly audible capitals and italics.

" 'FLORIAN'S FLOURISHING FLORILEGIUM! Combined Circus, Menagerie, Educational Exhibition and Congress of Trained Animals! . . . Recently acclaimed at Niblo's Garden in New York City! . . . Crowned with *new Laurels of Success* in the Capitals of Europe and South America! . . . To be *Presented Here in Pavilion* . . . TO-MORROW!' "

"Hooray!" cried all the little Grovers.

". . . 'Under the auspices of an enlightened management whose sole aim has been to form a COMPLETE MODERN COTERIE comprising the *Male and Female Elite* of the Equescurriculum . . . and the *Crème de la Crème* of Acrobatic and Gymnastic Artistes, Coryphées and Vaulters, who, in their Astonishing Feats of Agility, defy the Earth's Own Gravity!' . . ."

"My!" breathed Mrs. Grover.

". . . 'Plus the most MAMMOTH MENAGERIE of the Treasures of Zoölogy ever presented to a Discerning Public, including the *Man-Eating African Lion*, MAXIMUS, King of Beasts, trained and commanded by the daring Captain Hotspur . . . and BRUTUS THE ELEPHANT, the veritable *Behemoth of Holy Writ*, captured by his present keeper, Abdullah the Hindu Hunter, in the jungles of far-off Asia!' . . ."

"Is that a fact?" said Mr. Grover, staring at the elephant even more admiringly than he had been doing.

". . . 'And all the other *Unique Attractions* which make up this WORLD-FAMOUS CONVENTICLE OF WONDERS!!!' . . ."

Florian glanced up and saw Edge standing nearby, dressed now, regarding the scene from under a skeptically cocked eyebrow.

"Well, ahem, there's a good deal more of just plain description like that, so I won't read it all. But do listen to this part: 'It is *too true* that very few of today's traveling establishments are suitable for ladies and families to visit. A laudable exception is Florian's GREAT MORAL EX-HIBITION, wholly free from indelicate sights, sounds or allusions, and dedicated to the upholding of *Virtue and Piety*.'"

"It all does sound right respectable," said Mrs. Grover.

"Beats me why world-famous folks like you-all would *want* to spread yourselves in poky old Lynchburg," said Mr. Grover, spitting juicily again. "What's it cost?"

Florian read again from the poster: "Notwithstanding the enormous outlay attendant upon such a SHOW OF SPLENDORS, the admission price is fixed at the trifling figure of only twenty-five cents; children under twelve and servants only ten cents . . .'"

"Fergit it, mister," said Mr. Grover.

Florian hastily took out a thick mason's pencil, scribbled on the poster and read the emendation: " '*Or* twenty-five dollars and ten dollars in Confederate scrip. *Or* barter in kind acceptable.'"

"That mean groceries?"

"Any local produce or commodities."

"Ain't much *in* Lynchburg 'cept a little tobacco."

"Well—heh heh—believe it or not, yonder behemoth enjoys a plug when it's offered."

"What, the Beast of Holy Writ? *Chews tobacco?*"

"Learned it from an Old Testament prophet, yes. But it will cost you good Grovers nothing at all to see our ex-travaganza. Merely post those papers today and, when you present yourselves at the Big Top tomorrow, I will per-sonally hand to you and every one of your fine children a free ticket to the best seats in the house."

"Hooray!" all the little Grovers cried again.

"I don't know as the Rev'rend Jonas would approve of us having dealings with show folk," mumbled Mrs.

Grover. "But I reckon we cain't disapp'int the chillun. We'll do it, mister."

Roozeboom and Yount had by now moved all the circus vehicles to one side of the road. Mr. Grover clucked to his horse and the tobacco wagon clattered across the bridge over Beaver Creek.

Edge said to Florian, "I never heard such a pack of lies as you dealt to those poor hicks."

"Lies? Nothing of the sort. Only a trivial adornment of the truth, here and there."

"You and your posters make this outfit sound like something the Caesars dreamed up to embellish Rome." Edge looked around, with amused contempt, at the derelict wagon train and its shabby crew. "Aren't you kind of raising people's expectations too high? When they see what little you've really got to show them, you might just get stoned out of town."

"Not so, my boy," Florian said kindly. "You will learn that most people see exactly what they expect to see. If that constitutes deception, it is no fault of mine. Blame the deficiencies of the average human mentality."

"Want some breakfast, Mr. Florian, Mr. Zachary?" The golden daughter of Sarah Coverley came up to them with two tin plates, each bearing a very narrow wedge of some brown substance.

"Why, thank you, Clover Lee," said Florian. "This is a delightful novelty—breakfast! What is it, anyway?"

She giggled. "I know it looks like a piece of a cow flop. But it's sweet-potato pie. Tiny Tim snuck it off those folks' wagon. Not much to go around, but it was the only eatable he could snatch. Anyhow, Tim mainly wanted the baking pan it was in. For his act."

"My compliments to the chef de filouterie." Florian turned to Edge, who was glowering at the plate he held. "Say thank you, Zachary. Or if it troubles your conscience to eat someone else's pie, we can give it to someone else."

"No, no," mumbled Edge. "Thank you, Clover Lee."

With two fingers, he put the tiny moist brown fragment in his mouth.

"Enjoy it, Mr. Zachary," the girl said brightly, and then, just as brightly, "Did you enjoy my mother?"

Edge choked on his pie.

"Of course he did, my dear," said Florian. "Anyone would, don't you fret. But run along now. Never interrupt the grown-up talk of your elders with childish prattle."

She sauntered away, and Edge said, "I'd hate to hear that kid talk any *more* grown-up."

"Yes, well, a child raised in a circus does tend to be somewhat precocious. Monsieur Roulette, who tutors her in her lessons, tries mightily to instill some good manners at the same time. But I suppose even the best education doesn't discourage a young girl's natural curiosity about things like sex and—"

To steer the conversation away from that very thing, Edge interrupted, "I take it thievery is not discouraged, either. That pie was probably intended to be a homecoming feast for that Lynchburg family."

Florian said tsk-tsk. "Really, Zachary. We sometimes have to live by foraging, just like your cavalry. Are you pretending that your men never conveyanced anything from the civilians?"

"I don't recollect that we ever pilfered from somebody who was already doing us a favor at our request."

"You heard what Clover Lee said. Tim did not steal the pie. The pie just happened to come along in the pie tin he wanted for a prop in his act."

"He props himself on a pie tin?"

"Prop. A property. A gimmix. A tool. Something he employs to enhance his act."

"How the hell could a pie tin—?"

"I don't know and I won't ask. It is considered impolite to be too inquisitive in such cases. I'll just have to wait and see what Tim does with the baking pan in the show. You can too, if you like, since you and Obie are going our way. As a matter of fact, he has very kindly offered his

Percheron as a draft horse for us, as far as Lynchburg. Perhaps you'd also volunteer yours, and ride along with us? Stay to see our performance? As our guests, of course. Will your charger work in harness?''

"He won't like it, but he'll do it. In his time, Thunder has pulled caissons, ambulance—even a cold-meat wagon, once. All right, yes, you can hitch him up. I reckon I owe you that."

"Me? Or Madame Solitaire?"

Edge gave him a very chilly look and said, "I owe you for drinks and food and general hospitality, Mr. Florian. You'd have to ask Sarah if she feels *she's* owed anything. Or let her daughter ask, since you and the brat both seem to share natural girlish curiosities about such things."

Florian stepped a pace back and raised his hands. "I stand deservedly admonished. Now come, you'll want to supervise Captain Hotspur's harnessing of your horse."

But Roozeboom was busy with something else: skinning and quartering a dead animal. Magpie Maggie Hag was assisting, to the extent of holding a mug to catch some of the spilled blood. Yount and Rouleau also stood by, Yount keeping hold of the Wild Man, who mooed and blubbered and laughed, seeming eager to lend a hand in the dressing-out.

Edge saw the old underhammer rifle lying to one side, and said, "So that's what woke me up. You shot one of the jackasses."

Florian said, "They aren't needed, now that we've got Obie's horse to haul the tent wagon. We'll lead the other ass. And if your Thunder will draw the cage wagon, Brutus can be excused from that task for a while. The elephant has work to do when we get to the pitch. We try not to make the bull labor on the road unless it's absolutely unavoidable. That's the most valuable animal in this whole train."

"That little jackass might not have been valuable, but he was still sound," Edge said. "Just last night, you told us how loyally those burros had worked for you. And this

morning, by way of thanking them when their work is
done, you shoot one of them.''

Florian looked chastened, and for once he did not seem
to be acting. In fact he winced from Edge's angry scowl
and dropped his own gaze to his scuffed shoes, saying
nothing at all. So Jules Rouleau spoke:

"Zachary, ami, you might not know it to look at me
now, but I too was once an advocate of chivalry, of nob-
lesse oblige, the beau geste and all that. I have had to learn
expediency and compromise since I joined out with the
circus, especially in recent years. Step over here and let
me show you something.''

He led Edge to the wagon barred like a jail cell. It was
simply a big cage on wheels, measuring about four feet by
ten, composed of vertical iron bars along the sides and at
the back, where there was a barred gate for access. Up
front, there was solid wood between the driver's seat and
the cage, and the whole top was wood with a bit of gin-
gerbread overhang, for some slight protection against the
weather. Edge looked in, at what might have been a large,
tan, crumpled and rather moth-eaten fur rug.

"That is Maximus," said Rouleau. "King of the Great
Cats, His Majesty Maximus.''

"Is he sick?''

"He is old. And he is famished. Tell me, Zachary. That
piece of pie you ate, did it fill you up? Or are you still
hungry?''

"Hell, yes, I'm hungry. I've been hungry for most of
the last four years.''

"Aussi moi-même. Yet you and I are young, so it is a
miserable condition, but it is not intolerable. We know we
won't starve. If it gets bad enough, we will cadge or steal.
But suppose you were extremely old and weak, and helplessly penned up, and dependent on others to feed you.''

Edge said nothing.

"Maximus depends on us. And we depend on him, for
he is worth any three or four of us as an attraction for the
canaille. No ticket-buying Reuben will ever properly ap-

preciate *anything* another human being may do in the ring, however spectacular, but he will gawk avidly at this poor, sad, aged African lion. So we depend on Maximus, and all the cat asks in return is that we feed him when we can.''

''What would you have fed him if the jackass hadn't been expendable?''

''Je ne sais quoi. But I can assure you of one thing. If all the rest of us were prosperous and well fed, and it was only the little *ass* that was going hungry, Florian would cut off his own hair and beard for hay for it. As things stand, the lesser must be sacrificed for the greater good, and Maximus desperately needs meat. Your scolding of Florian was unnecessary. He already feels bad enough. He is a good circus man, and every good circus man is kind to his animals above all else. Same way a good carpenter takes good care of his tools. In this case, Florian was being kind in the only way possible.''

''I didn't mean to sound like some meddling little old lady,'' said Edge. ''God knows a cavalryman doesn't get sweet notions about animals, because God knows the horse is probably the stupidest animal there is. But a cavalryman does learn respect for sound horseflesh, and he won't mistreat it. That's not little-old-lady sentimentality, and I'm not sentimental about anything else in the world.''

Rouleau gave him a sidelong look. ''Oh, a cavalryman has to sound manly and gruff, of course. But you can't make Jules Fontaine Rouleau believe that Zachary Edge doesn't have a sentimental regard for some things.''

''What, for instance?''

''That, if nothing else.'' He reached and touched Edge's sleeve. ''The gray uniform. The lost cause.''

''Oh, hell,'' Edge muttered. ''There was a time once when I believed babies were brought by the stork. Are you going to throw that up to me, too?''

''Florian said you had worn a uniform for nearly twenty years. The gray one has existed for only four years or so.''

''But there was a Virginia a hundred and fifty-some

years before there was a United States of America. So all right, I'm a Virginian, and yes, I turned my coat.''

"And you don't call that sentimentality.''

"Call it what you like. I don't have it any more. The cause is lost. As dead now as Sam Sweeney's banjo. I won't spend the rest of my life weeping over it.''

"Do not sound so defensive. I was not accusing you of any unmanly weakness. As I said, I too was once a person of some sensitivity and much sentiment. The circus is not a cruel place, but it is a demanding one. It demands much of all of us. I would like to think that I still possess sensitivity. But, for the good of the troupe, I learned to subdue sentiment. Every kind of sentiment." He looked away. "Sweet notions. Lost causes."

"Maxi-*moose!*" bellowed Roozeboom, as he came with a reeking and dripping blue-red haunch of meat. The crumpled fur rug responded to its name, or to the smell of the raw meat, by raising one end of itself, revealing that to be an immense head with a matted mane and rheumy eyes. Roozeboom said tantalizingly, "Was gibt es zum Festessen? Ha *ha!* Fest-*Esel!*" and shoved the haunch between two of the iron bars.

"Captain Hotspur makes a play on words," said Florian, joining them at the cage. " 'Festessen' means a feast of eating. 'Esel' means ass. You noticed that he spoke German to the cat, not Dutch?"

"I wouldn't know the difference," said Edge.

"An old European circus tradition. Whatever a cat trainer's nationality, he addresses and gives orders to his animals in German. Mainly, I suppose, because the German language seems to have been *made* for command. A Russian trainer once pointed out to me how it would take him at least two Russian words to give his tigers a command that could be given in German with one—and might have to be given in a hurry. A syllable's fraction of a second can mean life or death when you're working lions or tigers."

Maximus did not leap for the meat, or even stand up.

As if unable to believe either his trainer or his own nose, he only slowly raised his front end on his forelegs, and wearily dragged himself to where he could lick the offering with his vast tongue, then wonderingly mumble it with his capacious lips. But that first taste seemed to revive and cheer him considerably. He curled back the lips, showing a mouthful of teeth that were yellowed and blunt, but still formidable in number. And, with a muted growl, he began to tear hungrily and gratefully at his meal.

Edge asked, ''Why was the old gypsy collecting the blood? Does she do some kind of witchery with it?''

''No,'' said Florian. ''She was doing that for Captain Hotspur. He uses it in his act.''

''And I forgot—I shouldn't be the inquisitive Reuben,'' Edge said. ''I apologize. And I'm sorry I sounded off at you back there, Mr. Florian. An outsider shouldn't meddle in things he can't possibly know from the inside.''

''I was only worried that you might retract the offer of your horse. I promise we won't feed him to the menagerie.''

''Let's go hitch him up, and the others, and ride on to Lynchburg. I want to see your show.''

It was a pleasant road from Beaver Creek onward, and dry now. The area was one of the few in Virginia that had not been fought over during the war, so, except for many farm fields left fallow for lack of hands, there was no ruination to be seen. The road ran alongside the broad, brown, swift-flowing James River. It was bordered by early-blooming wild flowers and overhung by willows and sycamores just coming into bright spring green. As the road got within a few miles of Lynchburg, it changed from mere packed earth to a corduroy of well-laid transverse logs.

There were more people to be seen now. On the road, in the fields, on house porches, around roadside inns and stores, the people all paused in their occupations to stare, with more head-scratching bewilderment than they prob-

ably would have shown if the wagons had been bringing
Devil Grant or Vandal Hunter or any other of the Yankee
conquerors. Most of the folk must have seen circuses on
the move before, but not in recent years. And, as Yount
had remarked, a circus could hardly have been one of the
first things they expected to see traveling from the direction in which there had lately been warfare, devastation
and desperation. Indeed, the circus looked as if it had never
heard of the war: the horses ambling, the wagons trundling
slowly, the riders aboard looking lazy and carefree.

As usual, the rockaway led the train, drawn by the
show's white ring horse. Florian was wearing a high silk
hat, not much dented, and the rest of his spiffy attire did
not show its decrepitude from a distance. Beside him sat
a Confederate officer garbed in gray dress that likewise did
not, to the spectators, proclaim its age or the fact that it
was Edge's one and only uniform. The weather curtains
of the carriage were rolled up, exposing its interior, and
its two pretty female occupants frequently leaned out to
wave at the oglers, and their yellow hair shone in the sunshine.

Ignatz Roozeboom's bald head gleamed almost as
brightly. He was driving the next wagon, with the Wild
Man beside him, bundled in shawls to hide his uniqueness
from nonpaying spectators. They were on the cage wagon,
pulled by Edge's handsome claybank Thunder, which kept
snorting and sneezing at the ammoniac smell of Maximus
so close behind. Inside the cage, the lion was in its favor-
ite—or only—position, lying down.

The next three wagons were the closed vans, not revealing what marvels they might hold, but they were the
painted ones. And the April sunlight picked out what colors they still flaunted, and made the colors bright, and sparkled the traces of gilt on the garish lettering that
proclaimed the Florilegium's name and character. One was
the property wagon, drawn by the gaunt and shambling
cart horse and driven by Jules Rouleau, no distinctive
sight, dressed as he was in common country overalls. Next

came the tent wagon, driven by Yount because his own big Lightning was hauling it, and it was trailed by the remaining ass on a lead rein. Next came what Florian had called the museum wagon, drawn by the circus's other ring horse, the dapple gray, and driven by Tim Trimm. To onlookers, Trimm's littleness was not much apparent up there on the high seat, especially because of the even littler dark thing on the seat beside him: the hooded, draped, clenched and mysterious-looking Magpie Maggie Hag.

But if the wagon part of the train was not flagrantly spectacular, the last part made up for it, because the last was the majestically slow-striding elephant. Peggy was swathed in a great blanket of scarlet velvet which, glowing in the sun, did not show its naplessness. With the grand animal, sometimes stalking beside it, sometimes perched aloof on its lofty neck, came the exceedingly foreign-looking brown man in turban and robes. His face was set as stern and determined as if he were the real Hannibal, and as if this gently rolling Virginia piedmont were in fact a craggy pass between ponderous Alps and his elephant only one of hundreds, and sleepy Lynchburg yonder really an apprehensive and cowering Capua.

Though Florian led the wagon train at a leisurely pace, it arrived in the outskirts of Lynchburg before dusk, and he decided against going very far into town. The dark-leaf tobacco growers who had built the city for their auction-market center had set it prettily on a cluster of small but steep hills. That made its cobbled streets not so pretty to the teamsters and draft animals of the tobacco wagons that had to go up and down them. But the city looked good to the circus people, as they came into it along Campbell Court House Road, because the Grover family who had preceded them had kept their promise: the Florilegium's black-printed buff posters were visible on posts, trees and building walls.

Edge asked, "Did you get all those papers printed down in Wilmington?"

"No," said Florian. "Had a good supply left from be-

fore we came south. That's why they describe a number
of acts and attractions no longer with us. But so grandiloquently that I can't bring myself to cross them out.''

The wagon train rounded Diamond Hill and kept to the
outer reaches of the city until it came to a railroad and
warehouse district near the river. When Florian saw a commodious empty lot off the street, he turned the carriage
into it. The rest of the train followed, from the cobblestones into the weeds. Between the farther extent of the
lot and the banks of the river stood some derelict railroad
sheds, and among them wound rusty rails on which stood
long-sidetracked boxcars and platform cars. During the
past year or more, as the fortunes of war and the battle
lines had shifted, the South Side Rail Road had had either
no goods to carry or no hope of carrying them through the
blockades to where they might have been of use and profit.
Nevertheless, this neighborhood still smelled faintly but
distinctly of old engine smoke and steam-heated iron boilers.

When Florian stopped the carriage, and the horse immediately began grazing among the weeds for something
edible, Edge said, ''You don't ask anybody's permission
to set up here?''

''If this run-down acreage has an owner, he'll show up
soon enough. Or the city fathers may send a policeman to
demand a fee for the pitch. But usually, these days, a few
free tickets will suffice.'' He handed Edge the rockaway's
reins and said, ''Keep the carriage here, out of our way.''

He hopped nimbly from the seat, stowed his silk hat and
frock coat under it and began to pace the length and depth
of the lot, occasionally bending down and cocking his head
to check for irregularities in the ground. Then he yanked
a clump of weeds to leave a bare spot, and shouted,
''Gumshoe here!'' he walked a dozen or so long paces
toward the rear of the lot and shouted, ''Backyard!'' Then
he came toward the street side of the lot again, shouted,
''Front door!'' walked a few more paces and shouted,
''Red wagon!''

Every other member of the company had gone into action at the same time Florian had, and just as purposefully. The scene became one of confusion, but organized confusion. Sarah and Clover Lee got out of the rockaway, carrying pots and pans. Roozeboom handed the reins of his cage wagon to the Wild Man and got down, carrying something bulky in his arms. So he was right there when Florian shouted "Gumshoe here!" and he dropped the thing on the ground at that spot. As well as Edge could see, it was no kind of shoe, but a large, thick round of log, with a heavy spike jutting up from it to near knee height. Roozeboom got onto the cage wagon again and drove it to the place where Florian had shouted "Front door!" Meanwhile, Jules Rouleau was driving the property wagon past the gumshoe thing, and stopped the wagon a good distance beyond that, where Florian had shouted "Backyard!" Hannibal Tyree had stripped the immense red cover off Peggy and was carefully folding it for stowage. By the time Florian shouted "Red wagon!" Tim Trimm had the museum wagon there to stop on the spot.

Now the Wild Man scrambled down from the cage wagon's seat, and under that wagon, and began letting down some canvas flaps there, to hang like curtains from the cage bottom to the ground all around. Hannibal had got a heavy leather strap from somewhere and was buckling it like a collar around Peggy's big neck. Magpie Maggie Hag got down from the museum wagon, which had its rear toward the street, whence presumably the circus's patrons would approach. She opened two doors there, throwing open the whole back to reveal a sort of shallow booth where a ticket seller could sit behind a high counter.

Hannibal, Trimm, Rouleau and Roozeboom converged on the tent wagon, which Yount had simply brought to a halt some way in from the street. They unlatched its door and began dragging out the gear compactly stored in there—rolls of canvas, various metal objects, a great deal of rope and numerous tackle blocks, and three long, thick, smooth-rounded poles. Each of those was painted red, except for a narrow blue band near its middle, marking the balance point, so a man could seize the heavy pole there and carry it most comfortably.

Edge was half inclined to join the workers and lend a hand. But he was an old campaigner, veteran of many a tenting ground and redoubt construction, and he had too often seen hard work made harder by the awkward efforts of a new recruit pitching in among practiced professionals. Also, when Roozeboom bellowed something like, "Off-loaden de stabs out of de vay!" or Hannibal called something like, "Hyar come de bail ring!" Edge had no idea whether it was some circus jargon he couldn't possibly know, or just their native accents which he couldn't decipher. So he sat where he was and watched.

Hannibal lugged a heavy hoop of iron, as big around as a wagon wheel, and laid it on the ground so it encircled the thing called the gumshoe. Trimm, Rouleau and Roozeboom each brought one of the three red-painted poles and laid them nearby, end to end, while Hannibal ran again to the tent wagon and fetched two metal cylinders, open at the ends. The men fitted them like sleeves onto the separate poles to join them into one continuous pole, or mast, some forty feet long, that tapered from waist-thickness at one end to thigh-thickness at the other. In the thick end a hole was visible, drilled straight up into the pole's interior. Hannibal now fetched the elephant, while the others secured pulleys to both ends of the long pole, and reeved ropes several times back and forth between them. Another rope they uncoiled to reveal that it ended on a large metal hook, and Hannibal slipped that into the elephant's collar.

He said loudly, "Peggy, mile up!" and the elephant began very slowly to walk away from the group of men, while they snubbed the thick end of the pole. As Peggy's tugging brought the thinner end up off the ground, the men hefted the thick end so the hole in it went up and onto the point of the gumshoe's heavy spike. The elephant continued to draw on the rope, and the pole rose, all its pulleys and ropes rattling, until it was at the vertical, when its butt end slid down firmly on the length of spike. Hannibal yelled, "Tut, Peggy!" and the elephant stopped, leaning to keep the rope taut and the mast held steady at vertical. Edge now could perceive the function of the gumshoe. That high pole could have been stood on the bare ground, but if the ground were soft—and a sudden rain might make it so at any time—the pole would sink, without the gumshoe to provide a wider base for it.

While the other men had been engaged with the pole, Florian was kicking open the bundles of canvas laid nearby, and they unrolled to become tremendous triangles. Elsewhere, Yount was helping Sarah kindle a campfire with some dead weed stalks, and Clover Lee and Magpie Maggie Hag were moving about the lot, bent over, apparently in search of more substantial burnables. Of the whole troupe, only the Wild Man was not in sight. The elephant stood staunch at her station, and in the cage wagon even the lion Maximus seemed to have revived somewhat from his customary comatose state. Edge could hear from there a hollow grumbling and low roaring, accompanied by clinking and clanking, as if the lion were struggling against iron fetters.

When the workers were satisfied that the tall pole was firm and that its hanging pulley ropes were clear of tangles, they turned to the next job. Trimm and Hannibal joined Florian, and those three arranged the immense canvas triangles side by side on the weedy ground, so they surrounded the gumshoe like slices of a pie. Then the men produced lengths of light rope and, running them through brass grommets in the canvas edges, began to lace the slices one to the next, as if they were making an unbroken crust over the weed pie beneath. Meanwhile, Rouleau and Roozeboom were making repeated trips to the tent wagon, bringing smaller poles—these painted blue, only armthick, about twelve feet long, each with a short iron spike at one end—and laying them spoke-wise around the perimeter of the canvas on the ground.

When the canvas sections were all laced together in a

circle, the piecrust had a hole in its center just the size of
the iron hoop still lying at the base of the upright mast,
encircling it. The canvas had more grommets around that
hole which the men employed to lace it securely to the
iron, and then the ring was fixed to the pole's pulley ropes.
The men came off the canvas, walking delicately so they
stepped only on the laced portions of it. Hannibal brought
with him the end of another rope, this one running under
the canvas from the pulleys at the center pole's base, and
he attached that line also to Peggy's leather collar.

Florian and Roozeboom lifted up the outer rim of the
canvas piecrust, a bit at a time, so Rouleau and Trimm
could take the blue poles, insert their spike ends into still
more grommets at the canvas's edge, then wedge the poles
upright between canvas and ground. When the men had
done circling the canvas, it was no longer like a piecrust,
but hung like a vast, limp, wrinkled saucer, its inside at
the base of the center pole, its rim supported some twelve
feet above the ground by the ring of outer poles.

While Florian gave the result a looking over, the others
made several more trips to the tent wagon, bringing unpainted wooden stakes about four feet long, sharpened at
one end, flat and splayed at the other. They also brought
three heavy sledgehammers, and now they put on a vir-
tuoso performance as pretty as any Edge expected ever to
see inside the pavilion.

Trimm held erect one of the stakes, about eight feet
outside the nearest blue pole, and Roozeboom tapped it
with his sledge to start it into the ground. Then he, Rouleau
and Hannibal swung their sledges all together and repeatedly, so rapidly that they were a flickering blur, all ham-
mering the one stake, but with such perfect timing that the
blows were like the staccato stutter of a Gatling gun, and
the stake sank as if into butter, until only a foot of it remained above ground. The men went around the circle of
the tent, pounding home one stake after another, one stake
to each blue pole, and their rhythmic tempo never faltered,
a swing never missed its mark or collided with another

sledge. Florian came along after them, with some more lengths of rope, these each with a loop spliced in one end. He tossed a loop over a support pole's spike protruding above the canvas, guyed the rope down to the ground spike, secured it there with the simple but reliable round-turn-and-half-hitch, and went on to do the same at the next pole and stake.

When that phase of the work was finished, the result looked less like a saucer and more like a spider: its canvas body sprawled among uplifted leglike side poles, each with a strand of web running to the ground. Florian again gave everything a close appraisal, then he and the others congregated around the elephant. Hannibal untied from the leather collar the rope with which Peggy had raised the center pole, and the men took hold of it to keep that pole steady. Hannibal again called, "Mile up!" and the bull again began slowly to walk, drawing only the rope that ran from under the canvas. The pole's numerous pulleys creaked, and their ropes rattled and twanged, and the iron hoop slowly ascended into view above the upturned canvas rim, bearing with it the center and the whole weight of that canvas. When the hoop touched the pole's top pulley, Roozeboom called, "Ja, klonkie!" and Hannibal instantly commanded, "Peggy, tut!" to halt her.

And now the canvas had ceased to look like a spider or a saucer or a piecrust. It was a shapely, round, pointed, dun-colored tent roof, some seventy feet in diameter, its peak about thirty-five feet above the ground, its slopes gently billowing and rippling in the evening breeze.

"C'est bon," said Rouleau. "All right, tie off the bail ring."

It was Tim Trimm who complied, no doubt because he was the lightest in weight. He shinnied up one of the side poles onto the roof of canvas, then scurried up the slope along one of the laced seams. At the very peak, he did some strenuous lashing of ropes around the iron hoop— the "bail ring," Edge decided—and the pole tip and pulleys, to hold everything firm up there. Then he just let go and slid down the slope of the canvas, whooping excitedly, swooped off the edge and was neatly caught in the stout arms of Roozeboom.

The tent's blossoming into recognizable shape was greeted by a scattering of cheers and applause. Edge turned and saw that a score or so of Lynchburgers had gathered at the street side of the lot. Most of them were children and most of those were black, but there were some adult males, all elderly. Florian was quick to take advantage of having an audience, calling to them:

"Welcome to the Big Top! And thank you, gentlemen and young folk, for your kind reception!" he spoke aside to Rouleau, "Get on with the sidewalling. But it'll be dark soon, so we'll save the ring and seats until morning." He raised his voice again to the onlookers: "Performance tomorrow, good people!" and, as he spoke, he was hurrying to the rockaway. There he put on his frock coat and top hat and snatched up one of the rolled circus posters. "Yessirree! Come one, come all!" Now properly attired, he strode over to the little crowd, still speaking in a loud voice but conveying a confidential tone.

"Performance tomorrow at two o'clock! However, since you fine folks are clearly the most eager and appreciative circus lovers in this fair city, we shall repay your good will with some of our own." The children goggled; the men looked interested but wary. "Tomorrow at show time there is certain to be a crush of people elbowing for the best seats. But, since you folks were the first to welcome us, we shall not only permit you to reserve your seats right now, we will offer them to you at *half price!*"

The men and children looked glum and embarrassed, and shuffled a little away from him. Florian flapped the poster to unfurl it, got his mason's pencil from a pocket and, with a flourish, scrawled on the bottom of the paper.

"Regard that, friend!" he said, shoving the poster in the face of the nearest white man. "You see what the regular price is? See also how I have slashed it precisely *in half!*"

The man mumbled, "Cain't read, mister."

"Right! As you say, sir, an incredible offer! Instead of the usual price of just two bits for you gents and just one thin dime for you tads—*instead* of that, I have cut the prices to twelve and a half cents and five cents respectively. Merely step over to the ticket wagon yonder''—he waved toward the museum wagon, where Magpie Maggie Hag had magically appeared inside the booth—"and our Chief Cashier will gladly dispense tickets to you gentlemen for only *one bit*, tickets to you children and persons of color for only *five pennies!*"

There was some more glum and embarrassed shuffling. "Or barter in kind acceptable!"

The men looked dolefully at each other; so did the children. Edge shook his own head sympathetically and turned back to where the tent was still being worked on. Hannibal was under it, at the center pole, warping onto cleats there the ends of the ropes that had done the raising of pole and roof. Roozeboom was going about the outside, checking the ropes from roof to stakes, here and there tightening one or easing another to get the tension equal all around, then giving every rope an extra half hitch and tidily belaying the loose end so it would not be tripped over. Trimm and Rouleau were unrolling yet more canvas, twelve-foot-wide lengths of it that they hung from under the roof eaves and pegged to the ground. Peggy the elephant, released from duty, was desultorily plucking up weeds with her trunk, putting them in her mouth, spitting out most of them, occasionally and not very zestfully eating one.

"You have seen the mighty pachyderm putting up the Big Top!" Florian continued to harangue the onlookers, now with rather a cajoling voice. "Tomorrow come and see him at play—*Brutus, Biggest Brute that Breathes*— doing impossible tricks and imposing feats of strength at the command of his genuine Hindu master!"

When the canvas lengths were hung and pegged, the tent was walled all around, except in two places. At the side farther from the street a gap was left—for the performers to go in and out by, Edge presumed—and beyond it in the "backyard" was parked the baggage wagon. Opposite that opening, in the nearer wall, was the "front door" through which the patrons would enter after they had first stopped to pay at the ticket booth and then, between it and the entrance, had stopped at the cage wagon to admire the lion.

"King of the Great Cats, *His Majesty Maximus!*" cried Florian. "You can hear him, folks, roaring for raw human flesh, which is the only meat Maximus will eat! Tomorrow come and see the daredevil Captain Hotspur actually climb inside the cage and try to subdue that bloodthirsty beast!"

Edge saw that Yount was unhitching his Lightning and the little jackass, and back behind the tent Hannibal was loosing the other dray horse. So Edge got down from the rockaway and went to unharness Thunder from the cage wagon. He paused to look back toward the street when he heard Florian cry encouragingly:

"That's right, sir. Step on over to the booth. You too, lad." he raised his voice to shout, "Madame Bookkeeper, be so kind as to issue tickets to our first two patrons! Best seats in the house, make sure of that!"

Edge grinned in some surprise. Indeed, a gray old man and a towheaded boy, both wearing faded overalls, both looking sheepish but radiant, were crossing the lot to the wagon. The other men and children were watching them wistfully, and a few more rummaging deep in their pockets. Edge went on to the cage wagon to attend to Thunder, and got another surprise.

His Majesty Maximus was evincing no more vivacity than Edge had previously seen in the animal. He was lying on his side, his eyes closed, only his barrel ribs moving as he softly snored. The jangles of iron fetters and the hollow roars of bloodthirst were coming from *under* the cage. Edge bent and lifted the canvas that had been let down for a curtain below the base of the wagon. In the space underneath squatted the Wild Man, diligently shaking a length of rusty chain, and making more or less his normal vocal noises, but with his head invisible inside a zinc bucket that amplified and made the sounds passably leonine and ferocious.

"It's his only real talent," said Florian, coming up just then. He was patting his moist forehead with his handkerchief, as if his exhortation to the onlookers had been the hardest work he had done all afternoon. "And the poor idiot loves to do it, so don't look so disapproving."

"I swear . . ." Edge said softly, and shook his head. He dropped the canvas and stood up. "I see you sold some tickets."

"Only two, alas. The other gawkers were just the usual lot lice."

"What did those two pay you with?" Edge started undoing Thunder's harness.

"The old gent was carrying quite a wad of Rebel dollars, and he handed over thirteen of them. Said he'd been saving up for his funeral, but he'd rather see a circus any day than get buried. The boy had just come from the river. He was taking this home, but decided to part with it." Florian held up astring on which hung a medium-size dead catfish. "The lad went back to the river to see if he could catch another for the home folks before suppertime."

"A fish? What are you going to do with a fish?"

"Eat it, man! Did you think I was going to have it perform?" Florian laughed. "I grant you, though, I did do that once—with dancing turkeys."

"Dancing *turkeys*," Edge repeated.

"We, ahem, acquired a small flock of them. Took them along as provisions on the hoof, you might say, so while they lasted, we presented them as dancing turkeys."

"*Dancing* turkeys."

"Stand any turkey on a sheet of hot iron, and watch."

Edge shook his head again, and went on with the unharnessing, and said, "So now, for some worthless Confederate paper and a catfish, you gave those folks the two best seats in the house?"

"Well, two seats. Come along now. The flag is up—or it would be if we had a cook tent to hoist it on. We'll toss this mudcat into the nettle soup and it ought to make a delectable—"

"Nettle soup?"

"Old Mag is adept at living off the land. She was collecting the ingredients while we put up the pavilion. Nettles and wild onions. Not bad soup at all, you'll see. But it will be better with a dash of fish meat."

Edge stared at him. "These people of yours haven't eaten a bite since that sweet-potato pie this morning. And that was *just* a bite. They've traveled the livelong day, and now they've been working like niggers. And you're going to feed them nettles and catfish juice?"

"We eat what we have," said Florian. "The ass meat has to be kept for the lion"

"I swear," Edge said again, "I don't think I've ever come across such a scruffy outfit in my entire life. I've seen the Mexican militia and the Texans of the Big Thicket and I've heard all the jokes about the Yankees' pitiful Oneida Cavalry. But for sheer hangdog miserableness, I'm damned if you people don't beat them all—come day, go day, God save Sunday!"

"You are overwrought," Florian said kindly. "From hunger, no doubt. Tether your horse over there with Snowball and Bubbles and come and dine."

When they joined the others around the fire, Florian went to the far side of it and gave the fish to Magpie Maggie Hag. Yount hailed Edge with enthusiasm. "You watch the putting up of that monster tent, Zack? Wasn't that a pretty piece of work?"

Edge snorted. "Many a time, Obie, you've watched the reserves do maneuvers in peacetime, just as pretty and busy and self-important. And what was all their fuss ever worth?"

"Zachary, you sound like you don't think much of us," said Sarah Coverley. She gave him a wicked grin. "And I tried so hard to make a good impression."

"Mother!" Clover Lee exclaimed, as if scandalized, but then she giggled.

Edge said he was only trying to maintain a trace of common sense, which commodity seemed in short supply hereabouts. "Yesterday, your Mr. Florian yonder described himself as the comsummate cynic. Never had I heard a man more wildly misread his own character. I've been trying to decide whether he's the world's most hopeful optimist or its most blithering nincompoop."

Sarah said quite sharply. "Lots of know-it-alls have refused to believe that Florian would do what he set out to do, and he has confounded them time and again. It's true enough that we're supping on pucker-water soup tonight." She started angrily slinging tin bowls around to the company. "But if Florian says we'll someday be dining on caviar and champagne, we don't laugh or jeer. We get our faces *set* for caviar and champagne."

There were only enough of the tin bowls for the regular troupe; to Edge and Yount she gave bowls of cheap chinaware. At that, Tim Trimm scowled and said testily, "You horseshit-kickers be careful of them good dishes. They're props for my act. You break one, you better watch out!"

"Ja! Make Tim mad, he *sting* you," Roozeboom said with a rumbling laugh.

"Little man," said Yount, "you're as mean as snot."

Tim gave him an ugly look and stalked off to the fire, perhaps to provoke the pot to the boil. Rouleau said to Yount, "Don't be misled by the defects of his personality. In the ring, in front of an audience, Tim is a passable joey."

"He is, huh. What's a joey?"

"Circus word for a clown."

"Ah," said Yount, and pridefully displayed his erudition. "Named for Joe Miller's Joke Book, I reckon. Our chaplain had one of them books, to spark up his sermons with."

Rouleau laughed at that and said, "Good guess, ami, but no. Named for Joe Grimaldi, the first clown—or at least the first famous one—in England, maybe fifty years ago."

Magpie Maggie Hag was just now crumbling the skinned catfish into her iron kettle, so the deplorable meal was not quite ready, and—this being the first time Edge had been among all the circus fold in close company—he was suddenly aware of how unwashed and unclean they smelled, as bad as so many soldiers together. He himself had had at least a cold dip and a quick shave the night before, but his uniform and undergarments no doubt contributed to the general odor. Anyway, he carefully set down his bowl and ambled away to fresher air. He left the lot and crossed the cobbled street, to take a closer look at one of the Florilegium's posters pasted on a telegraph-line pole over the way.

The paper was common buff-colored newsprint, densely covered with a hodge-podge of different sizes and styles of type, from swaggering big bold black to mincingly elegant scripts. Among the clutter of words were muddy woodcuts. Some showed ill-drawn apes and elephants, and improbable creatures like unicorns and mermaids. Others depicted improbable events: a gentleman in striped drawers wrestling barehanded with a writhing heap of lions and tigers, and a dainty lady balancing on one toe on the withers of a horse weirdly levitating entirely off the ground, its legs extended fore and aft. The printed matter was equally improbable, describing performers and performances that Florian had once had in his Florilegium, or maybe only had wished he had:

"MLLES PEPPER AND PAPRIKA, charming Volantes and Figurantes, doing breathtaking *aeronautic Oscillation* on the Vertiginous High Pole, dizzying exploits to make strong men gasp!

"ZIP COON and JIM CROW, the two Comic Mules, never failing to convulse the Audience with their *Knock-about Humor!*

"ALLEGORICAL TABLEAUX of Living Pictures formed by *Beautiful Young Ladies*, personifying Liberty Triumphant over Tyranny . . . the Queen of Sheba at King Solomon's Court . . .''

"Or barter in kind acceptable," said a voice at Edge's elbow, and he turned. Another Lynchburger in overalls was peering at the poster in the deepening twilight. "Says so, there at the bottom. You reckon, Cunnel, they'd take a couple sacks of smokin' tobacco fer a couple of tickets?''

"I'll personally see to it that they do." Edge steered him across the street to the campfire, where Florian was more than happy to interrupt his slurping of nettle soup to effect the exchange.

Edge let Magpie Maggie Hag ladle some of the soup into his bowl too—only a meager portion, not because it tasted awful, which it did, but because he felt he ought not to deprive the men who has worked so hard. After he had got the soup down, Edge took off his tunic and, with the point of his belt knife, began picking the curlicue braid off the cuffs and the embroidered stars off the collar. The gypsy's cooking kettle was soon scraped empty, though none of the partakers could have been anywhere near full. So Florian next produced a paper bag and handed it around.

"Dried apples for afters," he said. "Get some of these inside you and the soup will swell them up. You'll swear you've just had a nine-course meal."

Then he passed around the newly acquired tobacco, and he and most of the other men—and Magpie Maggie Hag—packed pipes and lit up. After the indolent smoking session, everybody began preparing for an early bedtime. The Negro Hannibal, who customarily slept under one of the wagons with the Wild Man, solicitously led the idiot inside the pavilion for this night, and carried in pallets and blankets for them both. Because the night promised to be a mild one the white men also decided to sleep in there instead of in a wagon. So Edge and Yount, too, lugged their bedrolls inside the tent and spread them on the cush-

ioning mat of weeds. Soon everybody was asleep, except
Edge.

There was a moon, and the worn old canvas did not
much impede the light of it. The whole tent interior
glowed a sort of dreamy blue-white, with brighter patches
here and there, where the canvas was particularly threadbare. No one else awoke to admire the effect, or to de-
plore it, but Edge lay wide-eyed. He had once, in
Richmond, seen a military observation balloon inflated—
growing from a flaccid pile of fabric to the immensity of
a wineglass elm tree, the cloth rippling and dimpling and
billowing as it grew. Now he could almost imagine himself *inside* such a thing, vast and empty, translucent to the
moonlight, whispering and sighing and chuckling in the
soft night breeze.

Though he was dressed only in his long underwear,
Edge got up and went outdoors, for another look at the
Big Top's outside. It now looked like a pavilion indeed,
like a fairy-tale rotunda built of moonbeams and spindrift
and held to the ground only by a web of gossamer threads.
None of the tent's worn places or patches or seams showed
in the bluish half-light, and even its ordinary peaked
roundness seemed blurrily mysterious of outline as it
gently quivered and swelled and ebbed. Edge heard some
quiet noises from the far side of the big tent, and he went
around it to where the baggage wagon was parked near
the back-door gap in the tent wall, and he saw a prettier
sight yet.

The elephant was back there, chained by a clamp around
one hind foot to one of the tent pegs, but with a decent
length of chain, so it did not hinder what the animal was
doing. And the great beast, mumbling softly, talking to
herself, was doing some peculiar things. As Edge watched,
she lifted one front foot, placed it on the splayed top of a
tent stake, took it down, put the other front foot atop a
different stake, then put both feet on both of the stakes so
her upper body was raised. Then she lowered herself to
ordinary standing position, and stood thus as if mediating.
Then she knelt on both hind legs, keeping the front ones

stiff, so her back was steeply inclined. Then she stood up and meditated some more.

Edge wondered if the animal had perhaps eaten some kind of locoweed during her browsing of the unfamiliar ground. There was some elephant dung about, but it gave off no offensive aroma; it smelled fresh and garden-y and not at all unpleasant.

Now, quite suddenly, the elephant let her hind legs slide forward under her, sat back on her tremendous rump and raised her front feet, sitting erect, so she towered as high as the tent eaves. She waggled those front legs, playfully pawing the night air, then raised her trunk and curled it and whuffled softly through it what would have been a trumpet blast if she had really blown. And Edge realized what the elephant was doing. All by herself, without goading or command, all alone in the moonlight, the bull Brutus, Biggest Brute That Breathes, was rehearsing her circus act for tomorrow.

4

BECAUSE EDGE had been the last to get to sleep, he woke to find work going on all around him. Florian, Roozeboom and Rouleau were bringing into the tent armloads of planks and oddly shaped other pieces of wood, and piling them close around the curved canvas walls. Obie Yount and the Wild Man were on hands and knees on the ground, working under the officious direction of Tim Trimm, all three of them yanking up the weeds and other growth to provide a clear floor for the middle of the pavilion.

"Rise and shine, Zachary!" Florian called, when he saw Edge sit up. "The boys went down to the river at dawn, and they got some decent fish for breakfast. Maggie's keeping one warm for you."

Edge hurriedly got into his clothes, rolled up his bedding and took it outside, out of the way. At the lion's wagon, Hannibal was using a long-handled hook, which he ordi-

narily employed for guiding the elephant, to poke gingerly
through the cage bars and scrape out the lion dung from
the floor of the wagon. Maximus himself was awake for a
change, pacing up and down the cage, stepping daintily
over Hannibal's scraping hook.

Sure enough, Magpie Maggie Hag had a fish fried and
waiting for Edge on a tin plate, while she worked at cleaning the others' used dishes with a handful of sand. Edge
thanked her sincerely and ate his breakfast with wolfish
appetite, though it was only a small carp and as tasteless
and textureless as all river carp. He could tell, from the
well-cleaned but identifiable bones on the used plates, that
the earlier diners had eaten catfish and suckers, much tast-
ier fish, but he could hardly complain because the last one
awake got the leavings.

"Now, gazho," Magpie Maggie Hag said, in her deep
voice, "you go help with the tabernacle."

Edge gave her a look askance. "Godamighty. Florian
calls it a pavilion and a Big Top. You call it a tabernacle.
All it is is a tent."

"Tacho, gazho. You see the words 'holy tabernacle'
these days, you think a big church, no? Or saint's tomb,
no? But you see word 'tabernacle' in Bible, all it meant
then was hut or tent, easy to move around. Me, I know.
My people, the Romani Kalderash, they have lived always
in tabernacles."

"If you say so, ma'am." Edge obediently went to the
tabernacle and inside it.

There, Florian was directing Rouleau, Trimm and a volunteer, Obie Yount, in the putting up of the spectator's
seats. Those consisted only of long planks laid across the
stair-step notches of stringer boards that slanted from high
on the tent walls down to the ground. Each of the stringers
was supported at its high end by a fork in the end of an
ordinary upright sapling, and a small toe peg was driven
into the earth at the stringer's lower end to keep it from
sliding. When the seat planks were laid, they made a semi-
circle of five tiers from the tent eaves to near the ground,

around each curve of the pavilion from front door to back door. Edge calculated that, if people really crammed in and sat tightly together and let their feet dangle unsupported, the tent would seat a capacity crowd of about five hundred. But he remarked to Florian that the whole arrangement looked pretty precarious.

"We rely on the natural laws of physics," Florian said equably. "Right now, the laws of friction and inertia are holding everything together. When the people come and sit on the planks, the law of gravity will hold everything more securely. Of course, if any crowd gets really excited and starts to bounce around, the whole works *can* come clattering down."

"Must be a continual worry," said Edge.

"Worry?" Florian repeated, as if the concept had never occurred to him. "Why, my dear Zachary, that would mean we had put on a truly thrilling show!"

Toward the middle of the now bare ground inside the tent, Ignatz Roozeboom was working at something else and getting some help from the Wild Man. To the center pole Roozeboom had tied a long string with a spike on its far end, and he had walked on his knees around the pole at the extent of that string, scratching the spike on the earth, to inscribe a circle somewhat more than twenty feet in radius, centered on the center pole. Then, with a short spade, he had started digging up the earth in a narrow band around that mark—then had given the spade to the idiot, who was continuing to dig around the circle. Roozeboom now was firming that loose soil with his hands into a little parapet enclosing the ring, about a foot high and a foot thick.

"American-style ring," Florian said, with a disparaging sniff. "In Europe, every respectable traveling circus carries a nicely painted wooden ring curb in portable segments. We'll have one, too, by damn, whenever I can afford it."

Edge said, "Mr. Rooseboom—I mean Captain Hotspur—seems mighty fastidious about the dimensions of his work."

Florian looked at Edge in amazement. "Lord, I thought *that* was something even a rube would know about. Every circus ring everywhere in the world, Zachary, is precisely the same size. Forty-two feet across, ever since the Englishman Astley started the first modern circus, and decided on that diameter. It *has* to be standard everywhere, or how could the horses and other animals be trained? And then be traded about and perform in one circus after another? There'd be ungodly confusion if all rings weren't the same size."

"Oh," said Edge.

"Not just for the animals. For the performers, as well. A bareback rider's horse, at performing pace, takes exactly twenty-two steps to go once around the ring. The horse knows that, and so does the artiste, and so does the band of musicians, if there is a band. So the horse and rider know just where each of them is during each trick—every step of the horse, every movement of the rider—and the band music can keep perfect tempo, too."

"I reckon I must be a real rube Reuben," said Edge. "Something like that, I should have figured out for myself. In the peacetime cavalry, we've done dressage and other sorts of fancy riding, where you have to keep close count and all that. Sometimes with a brass band playing."

"One of these days I'll have a band," said Florian, more to himself than to Edge. "Someday I'll have everything just right. Decent seats, and with real jacks instead of saplings to level the stringers." He looked about the tent and then looked up. "And a decent pavilion, too, by God. A really *big* Big Top. And it'll be called the Big Top because it's the biggest, not just the only one. There'll be another top for the menagerie, and one for a sideshow. And we'll have horses that are matched and gaited, and grained every day. Not just the ring horses, but the wagon stock too. And we'll have the fanciest of spangled dress, and nickelplated rigging, and plenty of slum to peddle at intermission . . ."

Edge noticed that he had started that soliloquy saying "I," but soon was saying "we."

". . . and we won't be playing high-grass stands like this poor burg. We'll have a sharp advance man out in front of us, and he'll head for the smokestacks—the big, prosperous cities—and he'll arrange for the stand and the animals' feed and our own provender and all kinds of first-class publicity. We'll be a real low-grass show— won't play any city that won't mow its courthouse lawn for our pitch. And we'll parade into every town in full dress, right down Main Street. Not just the band playing, but a steam cally-ope besides!"

"A cally-ope?" Edge echoed.

"Ah, I was forgetting. You had a classical education. Yes, the steam organ was named for the foremost of the nine Muses, and it should properly be pronounced calliope. But every American circus man pronounces it cally-ope. And it was invented by an American, so who am I to correct the name? Anyway, I intend to have one of the things, and play it full blast."

As if to mock him, a single, forlorn drum began boomp-boomping outside. Florian left the tent and Edge followed, to see Hannibal Tyree dressed in his Hindu turban and robes, seated on top of Peggy's neck, banging a big bass drum that rested on his thighs and was secured by a strap around his back. Peggy was again wearing the scarlet, once-velvet covering, but Hannibal had reversed it. This side of the big blanket bore, on either flank of the elephant, tarnished letters that had once been gilt, commanding COME TO THE CIRCUS!

The Negro paused in his thumping to shout cheerfully, "We's ready to go whenever you say, Mas' Florian!"

"*Sahib* Florian, damn it, Abdullah!" From a vest pocket, Florian took out and consulted a battered tin watch. "Well, it's nearly noon and we're nearly ready, so you might as well start. Make as many streets as you can, but make sure you can find your way back here."

Hannibal nodded, called, "Shy, Peggy!" and the bull made a smart right turn, to shuffle briskly across the lot to the street. There Hannibal ordered, "Come in, Peggy!"

and the elephant made a smart left turn, to go toward the center of town. Hannibal resumed his pounding of the drum to punctuate the words he began shouting. "Follow me to de circus! Down by de railroad yards! Follow me to de Big Top!"

"He'll do that up one street and down another," said Florian.

"Won't he stampede every horse in town?"

"The children will crowd around as soon as they spot him. And they'll be happy to run ahead and yell 'Hold your horse!' By the time Abdullah returns, he'll come like the Pied Piper, leading all the kids that exist here. I trust their older folks will follow after."

"They might not," Edge observed. "They *might* think he's recruiting for the Union Army." The drum was painted on both drumheads: U.S.A. IIIrd DIV. HQ. BAND. "It would be kind of ironic if your black man got lynched in Lynchburg."

"Um, yes," said Florian. "The Yankees, ahem, misplaced that drum and sticks down in Carolina. If ever I came across some paint, I'll put our name on it."

Edge, feeling guilty that he had done nothing at all to deserve his having been given breakfast, went back into the tent to help Roozeboom with the ring curbing. Yount, having earned his peck by helping to put up the seats, had thereby worked off the meal and was hungry again. He suspected that everybody else was, too. So he said to Sarah Coverley:

"If you'll lend me that hook and line again, I'll go back to the river and try to catch us something else to eat before it's time for the show."

"Don't trouble, Sergeant," she said kindly. "We can ignore our gut rumblings if you can. Florian has predicted that we'll have a real straw crowd, bringing bushels of good things for us to eat."

"A straw crowd?"

"Overflow attendance. Too many for the seats, even, so some have to sit on the straw. On the ground. Anyway,

Obie, we've probably scared off every fish in the river. We've been going down there, by ones and twos, for a quick sponge bath before we dress. It's my turn at the sponge now, so excuse me.''

Yount sat down on an upturned tub—the circus women's wooden washtub, half of what had once been a flour or whiskey barrel—and watched those troupers who were not off bathing. One who clearly bathed very seldom was the Tarheel idiot, whom Hannibal, before departing on the elephant, had dressed in his Wild Man outfit. That consisted of a few skimpy animal skins draped around him in only sufficiency enough to avert public complaint, plus some lengths of very stout chain hobbling his ankles and wrists, and some campfire char daubed here and there like war paint on top of his natural dirt. The Wild Man spent a little while leaping about and jangling and making faces, apparently getting into character, then crawled under the canvas below Maximus's wagon and began again to grunt and roar inside his bucket, supplying the bloodthirsty noises for the lion sedately pacing up and down the cage.

Closer to Yount, Florian was doing his dressing, which meant only brushing his black top hat and maroon frock coat, and scraping some traces of animal manure off his boots and the stirrup ends of his trousers. Magpie Maggie Hag also did not have to dress for her rôle, beyond the cowled cloak and layers of skirts she already and always wore. So Florian said to her:

"Mag, there are some more rubes stopping along the street to give us the eye. Just in case they're not all lot lice, why don't you take your place in the red wagon now?''

She went to do that, and Yount got up from his tub to inquire of Florian why he referred to a "red wagon" that was no redder than any other wagon on the lot.

"Another circus tradition, Obie. I assume some circus at some time first painted its ticket wagon red for the sake of visibility. Ever since, the office and cash-box wagon of every circus has been called the red one, whether it is or not."

"Oh. Well, another thing. Couldn't your red wagon have been built more convenient? Look yonder. You can barely see the old gypsy woman up behind that high counter. Anybody that wants a ticket from her really has to stretch. Don't that discourage business?"

"More tradition, Obie, and more than tradition. It is set high that way not to discourage the patrons, but to encourage the walks."

"The walks?"

"The walkaways. People who walk off without scooping up all the change they've got coming. There's always crowding around the ticket booth, and everybody wants to hurry along for a good seat. So they may fling up a bill and just make a snatch for their tickets and their change. With the counter above eye level like that, you'd be surprised how many walks leave a few coins behind."

Yount said he'd be damned, and went to sit on the tub some more. Florian strolled over to the wagon under discussion and unlatched and let down the side panels of it forward of the ticket booth. That disclosed the body of the wagon to be another sort of cage, only with wire netting instead of bars enclosing it. Yount remembered that the "red wagon" had also been referred to as the "museum wagon," so he got up again and went to see what it contained.

Not much.

The cage had a dirt floor and a branched section of dead tree pretending to grow from the dirt up to the roof. There were several animals standing or lying about the floor of the cage, and a few—including a snake—climbing about on the tree, and a number of birds in the branches. But all of them were as dead as the tree, and they had been so inexpertly embalmed and stuffed, and so gnawed by moths and mange, that they looked deader yet. The largest creature was at least a minor curiosity: a calf with two muzzles growing from its head, so it had two mouths, four nostrils and three glass eyes. The other animals and birds had been normal enough when they were alive, and none of them uncommon in these parts: a woodchuck, an opossum, some chipmunks, one skunk, a mockingbird, some cardinals and hummingbirds. Even the snake was an ordinary gray and brown, yard-long North American milk snake.

Yount said, "Excuse me, Mr. Florian, but there's not much of anything here that every person in Virginia ain't seen running around alive—and prob'ly cussed it for a varmint. Even a calf like that ain't nothing too out of the ordinary to a dairy farmer. A dairyman also won't appreciate looking at a milk snake—and, by the way, milk snakes don't climb trees."

"Thank you, Obie," said Florian, sounding not at all downcast by the information. "True, these species may be undistinguished, but each of these *specimens* has some unique story connected with it. And when I relate those edifying stories, the rustics see the creatures through new eyes. Also, I might as well confide, I collected these exhibits not so much to amaze American audiences as those in Europe, when we get there. The hummingbirds, for example."

"Mr. Florian, even foreigners won't be amazed by hummingbirds. I've seen more of them in Mexico than here."

"You'll never see one in Europe, unless in a museum. They simply do not exist over there. No European ever saw or heard of a hummingbird until sometime long after Columbus, when the naturalists began to bring over specimens. Same with the opossum, and several others of these items. So my little museum will interest our European audiences, you may depend on it."

Yount said again that he'd be damned, and returned to his tub to mull over the wide-ranging education he was acquiring here.

Inside the tabernacle, Edge and Roozeboom finished tamping the earthen ring curb, and Roozeboom hurried out through the backyard to take his turn at the river and then in the property-wagon changing room. Edge went also to

wash and shave, and he got back to the lot just as Tim
Trimm emerged from the prop wagon, wearing his performing garb. It would have been no extraordinary costume for any ordinary man: merely a farmer's frazzled
straw hat, plaid shirt, well-worn bib overalls and old gum
boots, but all of a size that they made him look considerably tinier than he was. He could easily have put both
legs into just one of the boots, and the straw hat came
down below his nose. What little of him was visible between hat brim and boot tops was engulfed in voluminous
folds of shirt cloth and overall denim, and the shirt's cuffs
hung nearly to the ground. It was a costume that Tim had
certainly assembled on the cheap—possibly free, from
some cornfield scarecrow—but it was effective. Even
though Edge detested the little wart, he couldn't help
chuckling at the sight of him.

"You shouldn't laugh, Colonel Zachary," said Clover
Lee, who was already dressed for the ring.

"Why not, mam'selle? He's a clown. Aren't people supposed to laugh at him?"

"I mean *you* shouldn't laugh. You look nicer when you
don't."

Edge sighed. "So I was told by your mother, too. You
are your mother's daughter, all right."

"Not altogether. Whatever she says to a man, she's flirt-
ing. When I say something, I mean it seriously."

Anyhow, in Edge's opinion, Clover Lee was her
mother's daughter at least in the matter of good looks, and
she bade fair to outdo her mother in that respect. Granted,
right now—dressed in flesh-colored tights from neck to
wrists to feet, with a faded crimson torso-garment over the
tights, and a gauzy tarlatan frill sticking out like a shelf
around her hips—Clover Lee looked like a young stepladder, all legs and angles. But if she ever got enough to eat,
her body would blossom and, with her pretty face, the
bright blue eyes and the waist-length hair of golden satin,
she gave promise of being a stunning beauty.

A pity she couldn't be better dressed, thought Edge. The

flesh-colored tights had permanent large knees and elbows pouched in them, and the cloth was much darned at those bulges. Elsewhere her costume sported patches—minutely and painstakingly applied, so they were visible only up close, but patches nevertheless. And in other places the costume showed snags and pulls and small rips that had not yet been patched. At this moment, for some reason, Clover Lee was patting herself all over with a wet sponge. Edge asked why.

"Oh, this is the first trick every artiste learns," she said. "Put on your fleshings"—she rubbed the sponge along one leg of her tights—"and your léotard"—she ran the sponge over the little bumps her breasts made in the body garment—"and then damp them all over. When they dry, they cling tighter to your body."

"And I reckon that helps your agility in the tricks."

She stared at him for a moment before smiling the smile of a woman of the world.

"My, but you are an innocent, aren't you, for a colonel? It makes the fleshings look more like real skin, *naked* skin. Do you suppose the yokels truly come to see circus women do tricks? They come to watch us shameless, scandalous circus women expose ourselves. The men eye us to see how much of us they can catch a glimpse of. And the women only watch to see how much we'll dare to show of ourselves, so they can disapprove. Hell, if I was as good a rider as my mother—or even the Great Zoyara—the rubes would never realize it. But if they think they've had just one peek up my bare legs, right to where my legs join, then the gawkers go home believing they've had their ticket money's worth. And I don't even have shapely woman's legs yet—let alone anything real interesting up where they—I told you, Colonel Zachary, you look nicer when you're not grinning."

"I'm sorry. I was just thinking again: you sure are your mother's daughter, no doubt about it."

Their colloquy was interrupted by a sudden blare of horn music, not very well played, but recognizable as the

opening bars of "Dixie Land." Edge sought the source of
the sound and found it inside the tent. Tim Trimm was
playing a cornet, holding its bell out the front door of the
pavilion while he kept his costumed self behind the canvas
and invisible to passersby. The cornet was recognizable,
by its carrying strap, as having once been the property of
an army band.

Edge stood and listened until the cornet wailed away the
last "Look awa-a-ay . . ." Then he winced as it launched
into "Listen to the Mockingbird" with a tooth-jarring bad
note that no mockingbird would have tried to mock, and
he departed the tent again for the backyard. Roozeboom,
Rouleau and Sarah Coverley were also dressed by now,
and had become Captain Hotspur, Monsieur Roulette and
Madame Solitaire.

The captain had donned a wide-awake hat, a tunic with
vast epaulettes and roomy side-stripe trousers. Except that
he wore soft shoes instead of boots, his costume was a
quasi-military uniform that obviously had been accreted
from castoffs of Yankee blue and Rebel gray, all dyed now
to a uniform purple unlike the uniform of any army in the
world. The monsieur and madame each wore the second-
skin tights that Clover Lee had called fleshings. Over his,
Roulette wore underwear—an ordinary "combination"
suit of short-sleeved top and knee-length drawers—in wide
stripes of yellow and green. Over her tights, Solitaire wore
a vest spangled with some silvery things like fish scales,
and about her waist a translucent skirt of stiff silvery tulle
that reached to her knees. Edge thought the glittery top
showed off her handsome bosom just fine, but the skirt
might deprive the yokels of some of their Peeping Tom
pleasure.

He did not approach her, because she and the two men
were busy, bringing things out of the property wagon.
Monsieur Roulette lugged into the Big Top a short ladder
and something that looked like a small child's teeterboard.
Captain Hotspur and Madame Solitaire carried in some
lengths of thick pink rope and some things like children's

rolling hoops, only frilled with all-around ruffs of pink crêpe paper. Edge got out of the way, ambling on around the outside of the canvas wall toward its front door. He passed the two tethered ring horses, the white and the dapple—bareback except for a single girth band—and saw that somebody had braided colored ribbons into their manes and tails, and dusted their backs with rosin powder, and put on them bridles with extra-long reins, check-straps from jaw to girth, and head plumes that waved above the horses' ears.

When Edge got around to the front of the lot, he saw quite a number of Lynchburgers, white and black, male and female, grown-ups and children, standing along the street, wide-eyed and open-mouthed as they listened to the invisible Trimm, who was now raucously playing "Goober Peas," and to the invisible idiot roaring and jangling his proxy lion noises from under the cage, and to the very visible Florian, who was alternately bowing and stretching a-tiptoe, and waving his hat, and all but prancing, and loudly exhorting:

"Come one, come all! Come to the circus, where everybody is a child again, just for a day! Ladies and gentlemen, young folk and colored folk, even before the performance begins, you will fix your admiring gaze on our zoölogical and ornithological museum of rare creatures captured in the wild. Then approach as near as you dare to the den of the man-eating African lion, king of the jungle. Inside the Big Top, you will first thrill to the music and spectacle of the Grand Entry and Promenade of the entire circus troupe. Then—"

He broke off as the first townies to shake loose of their timidity—an elderly and shabbily dressed man and woman—approached him offering something in outstretched hands. Whatever it was, it was not money. Florian examined it, and turned and shouted to the red wagon, "Madame Treasurer, two full-price tickets for our first two discerning patrons of the day!" Then turned back to continue haranguing the onlookers:

"Come one, come all! You will disbelieve your own ears when the renowned Monsieur Roulette, master of engastrimythism, projects his voice into remote parts of the arena and engastrimythizes even inanimate objects . . ."

Yount came up to Edge and said admiringly, "Man, he sure can wrap his tongue around some heavy-artillery words, can't he?"

The people were coming, some singly, but mostly by couples and families, from the street toward the red wagon, and some appeared to be paying at the booth with cash money. But the greater number of them had to pause on the way, to have their barter offerings appraised by Florian. As well as Edge and Yount could see, he did not spurn anything presented and did not turn anyone away, but waved them all on to the ticket counter. Only a number of ragged children, with nothing whatever to offer for admission, remained at a distance.

Maximus and the Wild Man clearly knew their circusday procedure. As the first patrons received their tickets and made their first stop to peer into the museum part of the red wagon, the idiot scrambled out from under the cage wagon and disappeared toward the backyard, leaving the lion to do his own rather poorer vocal imitation of a bloodthirsty man-eater. Now, besides pacing, Maximus was occasionally baring his teeth and emitting a hoarse, coughing grunt. But that seemed enough to impress the visitors. When they came to his cage, they stood at a respectful distance from it and eyed him with awe, and pointed him out to each other, and in hushed voices discussed his various leonine characteristics.

At a moment when there was quite a cluster of people at the ticket booth and Florian could take a break from his orating, he trotted across the lot and said to Edge, panting slightly, "Would you do me a favor, Zachary? Your uniform looks enough like a doorkeeper's—"

"I thank you kindly. So does the Confederate States Army."

"Yes. I wonder if you would do me the kindness of

taking tickets at the front door. Don't tear them, just collect them, so we can use them again. Direct the darkies to the upper boards on the left. The whites sit where they please." Not waiting for Edge to accede, he added, "Ah! I see you are wearing your gun belt."

"Sorry. I didn't know any safe place to leave it, so—"

But Florian only raised his voice to address the rubes at the cage wagon: "Be not afraid, ladies and gentlemen! Just in case that vicious lion *should* break out of the cage"— the rubes all took a step away from it—"we have always in alert and armed attendance the noted English explorer of Africa and hunter of big game, Colonel Zachary Plantagenet-Tudor here—"

"Jesus."

"—And at the first sign of any danger, you may depend upon the colonel and his trusty six-shooter to dispatch the beast before he can mangle and maim any significant number of bystanders. Thank you, ladies and gentlemen. Now enjoy the exhibits. The show will commence shortly." And he strode back to his post near the street, leaving the people looking with even more respect at old Maximus, and with almost as much at Edge.

"By damn," Yount said, still admiringly. "That man can manufacture some advantage out of anything that catches his eye."

Edge gave him a look and left him, to go and stand beside the front-door gap in the tent, and flinch at Trimm's tootling of "Get Along Home, Cindy." Yount went the other way, to help Florian handle the arrival of still more patrons bearing barter goods. The crowd increased when, in a little while, Hannibal returned aboard Peggy and leading, as predicted, a retinue of children, all of them cheering and whooping and trying to imitate the elephant's ponderous walk. Not far behind them came the first of a train of wagons, carts, buckboards and buggies bringing older folk and whole families. And after them came still more, afoot.

"Begod it *will* be a straw day!" Florian exulted. "Do

you know what, Obie? Besides the edibles and usables and shinplaster Secesh paper, I've actually taken in seventy-five cents in good, hard, sound Federal silver coinage!'' he called to Hannibal, as the Negro swung down from the bull's neck to her flexed trunk to her upraised knee to the ground, ''Abdullah, rejoice! One lady traded me six china soup plates for tickets. So you and Tim can afford to smash one or two, if you like, when you do the mimic-juggling turn.''

Hannibal beamed happily and, well in character now, called back, ''Amen to Allah, Sahib Florian!''

The bargaining and bartering and dispensing of tickets went on, Yount running the received goods to the tent wagon for storage, while Hannibal and his drum joined Trimm and his cornet to play inviting music like ''Nobody Knows What Trouble I Seen,'' and Edge stoically accepted the grubby bits of pasteboard from the people entering. When one female patron remarked in passing, ''Gotcher clothes on today, I see,'' Edge smiled sheepishly, recognizing Mrs. Grover.

Eventually, and just about at the promised two o'clock, the outside lot was empty—except for the many vehicles left by the railroad sheds, a good distance away, so their horses and mules would not be spooked by the smell of lion or elephant—and every board seat inside the Big Top was groaning under the weight of expectant spectators. With so many people inside it, the pavilion had become rather warm and humid. The sun, high now, sent bright yellow shafts poking down through the dusty twilight of the interior, a large beam like a spotlight from the bail-ring aperture in the canvas at the top of the center pole, and thinner rays by way of the dozen or so unintended holes elsewhere in the roof.

Down by the red wagon, Florian graciously dismissed Yount to go and find a place to watch the show—''So you'll see it all, right from the come-in spec''—then he looked around with great satisfaction. In all of what he could see of Lynchburg, there was not another prospective patron in sight, except the several scruffy children still standing empty-handed and wistful on the cobbled street yonder. He beckoned to them. They came warily, as if expecting to be scolded, and they were.

"You brats don't show much gumption!" Florian barked. "When I was your age and size, I'd have sneaked under the sidewall long before now. What's the matter with you?"

A girl with a dirty face mumbled. " 'Twouldn't be right, suh."

"Claptrap! Think you're buttering up your Sunday School teacher? Come on, sis. Which would you rather be? Righteous and melancholy or sinful and joyous?"

"Uh, well . . ."

"Don't tell me. Go now and be joyous. When you grow up, try to be sinful." As he started around to the backyard, he shouted to Edge, "No tickets, Colonel, guests of the management! Let them pass!"

The children filed through the front door at a funeral shuffle, still wary, looking wall-eyed a the big holster on the doorkeeper's belt and the big, bearded Yount beside him. But, once within the portals, they scattered and scampered, giggling delightedly, and scrunched room for themselves somewhere on the crowded tiers, and the show began.

5

THE GRAND entry and promenade consisted of most of the troupe coming in through the back door and marching three or four times around the pavilion between the banked-earth ring and the spectators' seats. It was led by Florian, walking with a swagger and flourishing his top hat. Behind him came the white horse Snowball with the glittery Madame Solitaire riding sideways on its bare back, facing the crowd, then the dabble-gray Bubbles with Clover Lee doing the same, both the steeds stepping high and

prettily and nodding their heads so their plumes danced.
Behind them marched the purple-suited Captain Hotspur,
his fringed epaulettes flopping at each step. Behind him
came Monsieur Roulette, sometimes lightly bounding
along, sometimes throwing somersaults and cartwheels.
Brutus brought up the rear of the procession, bearing both
Tim Trimm and Abdullah on her back, and walking with
a sort of rocking-horse gait so as not to overmarch the
marchers in front of her. Tim was playing on his cornet,
and Abdullah drumming in time to it, a sprightly tune that
was recognizable as having originally been "God Rest
You Merry, Gentlemen." Everybody in the parade except
Tim and the animals—and Roulette when he was head
over heels—was singing new words to that old music,
singing lustily but sounding feeble in the cavernous space
under the canvas:

> All hail, you ladies, gentlemen,
> Let nothing you dismay!
> We're here to cheer you in your seats
> On this fine circus day . . .

"You reckon Florian wrote them words?" Yount asked
Edge.
"If he did, he ought to be ashamed. 'Cheer you in your
seats,' good God."

> And bring to you some gorgeous sweets
> We hope will make you say . . .

The words and meter might have been atrocious, but the
tune was familiar enough to everybody in the stands, so
that, before the troupers and had completed their second
circuit of the arena, the entire audience was humming or
whistling and clapping hands along with the song. What
had begun as a piping bleat-and-thump of drum, horn and
voices became a music as clamorous as if it were being
played by a full brass band:

O-oh, grand it is, that ci-ircus joy
For girl and boy
O-oh, gra-a-and is that ci-ir-cu-us joy!

The song evidently, mercifully, had no other verses; it got repeated several times as the company circled the tent. Then, at the peak of the spectators' participation, while they were still enjoying being performers themselves, Florian led the procession out through the back door. The last tailing off of the noise was Captain Hotspur's "... Dot cir-coo-oose choy!"

And immediately Florian, alone, frisked back into the tent, shouting, "Welcome, ladies and gentlemen, boys and girls, to *Florian's Flourishing Florilegium of Wonders!* To commence today's performance, allow me to introduce to you the first of our Educational Marvels—a mite-y artiste. Not mighty like an elephant, mind you ... but mite-y like a *mite!*" Florian held up a thumb and forefinger to his eyes. There came a scattering of polite laughter, which caused Florian to put on a look of exaggerated surprise.

"Please, good people! Small things are not always insignificant. Think of diamonds. And the gem I am about to produce for you is our world-famous midget, Tiny Tim Trimm!" There was a start of applause, but it died when Florian said loudly, "Eh?" and held up a hand to his ear. "Did I hear some Doubting Thomas ask: how small *is* this midget of ours?" Everybody leaned and looked about for the Doubting Thomas. "I'll *tell* you how small this midget is. This irreducible fraction of a man, this lowest common denominator, this midget is so very short that, even when he is standing fully erect ... when he stands as tall and upright as he possibly can ... *his feet barely touch the ground!*" Several people in the audience groaned, but the mass of them gave a burst of laughter, while Florian, with a sweeping gesture, bellowed, "We take pride in presenting ... Tiny ... Tim ... TRIMM!"

A cornet fanfare blared from beyond the back door, and

the audience quieted in anticipation. Then nothing happened.

After a moment, Florian did an exaggerated business of craning and peering, and said, ''Told you, folks. Little tiny legs that barely reach the ground. Takes him a while to get here.'' From the audience, more laugher, and it increased as Tim gradually came out into view from between the two banks of seats. He was walking frantically fast, but doing it *inside* his great boots and billows of clothes, scarcely making progress, and again blowing his fanfare, with breathless sputters and gurgles. He seemed to consist only of a large straw hat atop a heaving pile of laundry, with the cornet bell sticking out from between. Aboard the elephant during the promenade, he had been unremarkable, and in any street crowd he would have been taken only for a runt, not a midget—but now he contrived to look like a bug struggling across a pan of molasses. By the time he had flailed and floundered over the intervening ground to the ringside, the audience was roaring loud enough to drown out his horn squawking.

''Ah, there, Tiny Tim!'' Florian bawled, when the laughter began to diminish. ''You are late, my lad. Explain yourself. What kept you? We won't stand for slack here, you know!''

''Maybe you won't stand for slack,'' piped Tim, in a squeak meant to be a typical midget's voice. ''But that lady yonder does.'' He pointed to a woman on one of the front benches.

''That lady yonder stands for slack?'' said Florian, astonished. The woman looked flustered, and everybody in the stands looked wide-eyed at her. ''Whatever do you mean, Tim?''

''She was standing on the slack of my britches!'' squawled Tim, holding out a yard or two of his overalls. ''That's why I was late!'' But his last words were lost in the gales of laughter, and even the guiltless woman rocked and pounded her fists on her lap.

"I didn't mean that kind of slack," Florian protested.
"You don't understand."

"Oh, don't I? *Look* at me, man! I understand *everybody!*"

Laughter continued in gusts through the comic duologue, which played every possible variation on words like standing, upstanding, outstanding and misunderstanding— "Miss Understanding? Why, she's my little sweetheart!"— with Tim getting ever more smug and cocky in his retorts, and Florian getting increasingly exasperated at being the butt of them. When the audience seemed to tire of laughing at the wordplay, Florian began slapping the little man every time he made one of his smart-aleck remarks— "Smart? I'm smarter than liniment!"—and the laughter got properly loud again. The slaps looked gentle, but they resounded—*thwack!*—and every one made Tim reel and fall and lose his hat. The spectators would howl at that, and go on howling, because Tim, scurrying for his hat and impeded by his swaddle of clothes, every time would kick it farther from his reach. When finally he retrieved it and returned to Florian, he would deliver another drollery and receive another slap, and he would fall again and have to repeat the fumbling for his hat.

Even Edge, looking on from the sidelines, was grinning, but not at the hilarity of the performance. He had just perceived something that he never had before, when he'd watched other such knockabout acts. Florian was not hitting the little man at all; his slaps never touched Tim's face. The loud *thwack!* was made by Tim himself, at the precisely right instant, by clapping his own cupped hands together—and that small fakery went unnoticed by those who saw only his violent recoil from the apparent blow.

Florian seemed to have some kind of gauge inside his head that alerted him to the exact moment when even the funniest act began to pall. The next time Tim demolished him with a witticism—"You can't hurt me! I don't have far to fall!"—Florian did not slap him, but waved his arms

in despair and cried, "Enough of this! Let's have somebody with some intelligence out here!"

"Right!" squeaked Tim. "Right as a fellow with his
left arm off! You go away, you dummy, and send in an
animal!"

"We'll do just that! Let's let the young folks say what
it will be. Sing it out, kids! Which animal do you want to
see?"

The resultant shout was commingled of "Lion! Elephant! Horses!" but Florian pretended to hear a consensus.

"The elephant it shall be! Give us a fanfare, Tiny Tim!"
Over the cornet's brassy arpeggio, Florian went on, "Ladies and gentlemen, I invite you now to sit very still. Do
not move. You will feel the seats beneath you—the very
earth beneath you—tremble to the thunderous tread of that
mighty pachyderm I now have the honor to present . . . *Big
Brutus, Biggest Brute That Breathes!*"

"Mile up, Peggy," was audible from the back door.
Then the bass drum was heard—loud *boomp!-boomp!* and
ominous *rumble-rumble*—in time and countertime to the
elephant's steps as she strode into the tent. It was a masterly conjuncture of the program. The elephant made Tim
Trimm look even smaller than he had seemed until now,
and Tim made the elephant look even bigger than she really was. The turbaned drummer seated on her said,
"Peggy, tut," and she halted at the ringside. She stood
with patient dignity while Florian indulged in some more
of his flapdoodle:

"You heard, ladies and gentlemen—*peggitut*—one of
the mystic Hindu words with which only the great beast's
master, Abdullah of Bengal, can control the bull elephant's
unimaginable power and gigantic size. To get some idea
of Brutus's immensity, ladies and gentlemen, try to con-
ceive of this. All of you together do not weigh as much
as this single titanic pachyderm! To subdue a behemoth of
such size and strength is an art known only to the natives
of the far-off land of Bengal. Not I, not any other white
man, could tame such a monster as Big Brutus, and teach

him the performing skills which you are about to witness. Only a genuine Hindu, like Abdullah here, has the knowledge of those secret words of command . . ."

He went on for some while in that strain, then finally relinquished the arena to the performers and came to stand with Edge and Yount near the tent's front door. Brutus stepped delicately over the curbing into the ring, raised her trunk and one knee, and Abdullah did his lithe descent of her, from neck to trunk to knee to ground, bringing the drum with him. From then on, he seemed to have no need of his mystic Hindu commands, but only tapped the drum now and again to cue the bull from one pose to the next. Edge knew that even that was unnecessary, since he had seen Brutus go through her repertoire entirely unprompted.

She did the same things now. Abdullah ran to bring, from under the stands, a piece of equipment that Yount recognized as the circus's washtub, and upended it in the ring. At the *thump* of the drum, Brutus slowly raised and placed one foot on it. Suspenseful pause, then *thump*, and she took that foot down and put up the other. *Thump*, and she gathered herself, gave an exaggeratedly mighty heave and got both front feet up on the tub, her body at a steep slant, and stuck her trunk out stiff and blared triumphantly. The Negro spun around to give the whole audience a grin, and raised his drumsticks in the high V sign that everyone recognized as the signal for applause, and they clapped delightedly. Abdullah gave the same high sign every time Brutus did something else spectacular— sitting on her haunches like a dog, then sitting up like a dog begging, front feet pawing the air—and every time the audience responded with vigorous applause. When the elephant hesitated, and she did that at intervals, cannily aware that it made each new pose look more difficult than the last, Florian would dash into the ring and give a brief, edifying lecture.

"There are many curious things about an elephant, ladies and gentlemen, which Abdullah would wish you to know, but he speaks only Hindu. So allow me to inform you, while Big Brutus ponders the difficulty of his next feat. Among the peculiarities of the elephant, it is the only creature on this planet that has a knee in every one of its four limbs. Observe and count them, ladies and gentlemen—four knees!''

When the time came for Brutus's crowning achievement, she stood for a minute or two and frowned at the washtub—in the manner of Ignatz Roozeboom, frowning without any eyebrows—while the Negro gently thumped his drum again and again and made pleading, encouraging gestures. Again the elephant put both four feet on the tub, then reluctantly, cautiously hunched her massive body to bring one of her rear feet stepping up there, too. The audience rustled and whispered anxiously and waited. Florian bounded forth.

''While Big Brutus gathers his every muscle for this most arduous attempt at balance and precision, allow me to point out another unique thing about the elephant. You have all known your horses to get mired in the mud, I am sure. An elephant, though twenty or thirty times heavier, never does. Its tremendous feet have spongy soles; when the behemoth puts his weight on a foot, it spreads like a supporting mat. When he takes the weight off, it contracts. And so—but *hark!*'' Abdullah had given a ruffle of his drum. ''Let me not distract you, ladies and gentlemen. You are about to witness a feat that is not given to many to see and marvel at.''

Brutus waited for him to shut up, then lifted her fourth foot, so all of her was standing atop the tub, feet bunched together like those of a cat on a newel post. She trumpeted gleefully, and Abdullah danced around, alternately pounding his drum and throwing up his arms in the V sign, as if he had at last accomplished his whole life's purpose, and the audience was lavish with applause and approving shouts.

''And now,'' boomed Florian as the elephant daintily got down again, one foot at a time, ''you have seen the extraordinary agility and grace of this mammoth creature.

I invite you now to see his strength—I challenge you now to *test* his strength for yourselves. I call the ten biggest and burliest men among you to come forth and pit your combined muscularity in a contest of tug-of-war against this single specimen of the grandest mammal in all God's Creation!''

There could not have been ten really ablebodied men in all of Lynchburg, unless they were deserters or early retirees from the war. But there were at least some fat men and some fairly fit old farmers. After they had ducked their heads and said aw-heck and been prodded by their neighbors on the benches, ten men clambered down and bunched bashfully in the ring. Abdullah meanwhile fixed Brutus's leather collar around her neck, and Monsieur Roulette ran in with a length of the heaviest tent rope. It was hooked to the collar and the men took overlapping hold of its other end.

Tim and Abdullah played ruffles and flourishes, and the men—at Florian's "Heave *ho!*"—leaned back and dug in their heels and tugged mightily and Brutus eyed them humorously and never budged. The ten men took fresh hold and this time leaned back almost horizontal, and Brutus eyed them humorously and never budged. Florian said, "Very well, you've had your try. Abdullah, give the secret Hindu command." The Negro called, "Peggy, taraf." She began walking slowly backward, drawing the men as easily as a tent peg. Tim swung into a waltz tune on his cornet and Brutus walked faster, almost dancing as she dragged the ten men around the ring, one after another of them falling down, while the crowd rocked in convulsions that threatened the seating.

Florian cried again, "Big Brutus, Biggest Brute That Breathes!" and the elephant and Abdullah, pounding the drumheads near to bursting, exited to the loudest applause yet. So Florian's next announcement was audible only in fragments: "Monsieur . . . engastrimyth and ventriloquist . . . amaze you . . . voice projection and insinuation . . ."

Rouleau came in leaping, bounding, turning cartwheels, bouncing end over end. He stopped in the ring, upright, and immediately, but without moving his mouth, began barking like a dog—a sort of muffled barking, like that of a dog with its head in a sack—meanwhile pointing meaningfully to the still upturned washtub on the other side of the ring. He stood there and barked for some time, not getting much attention, then went and, with much theatrical posturing, tipped over the washtub to show there was no dog underneath.

It was just as well that the audience wasn't very attentive, because Monsieur Roulette's voice throwing was something less than prodigious. At one point, he began wailing like a hungry infant, with his mouth still immobile, then moved it to shout in his own voice, "Feed your poor child, madame!" and jabbed an imperious finger at a woman in the crowd who held a blanketed baby in her arms. She shouted back, "I'm a Christian woman! I ain' go' give tittie in public!" The spectators went into convulsions again, and Roulette, no doubt realizing he could never top that for audience appreciation, bowed and went bounding end over end out of the tent.

Florian hurried to cover his retreat, though again the new act's introduction was only fragmentarily to be heard: ". . . Late of the Boer Irregulars . . . against the Zulus . . . Hotspur!" The crowd finally quieted enough for all to hear: ". . . To thrill you with his spectacular reenactment of the Saint Petersburg Courier!"

Instantly, from outside, there came the noise of pounding hooves, together with Tim's blowing of the cavalry "Charge!" and Abdullah's beating of his drum, and a sound like repeated gunshots. Captain Hotspur must have started his run from a good way up the backyard, because the horses were at full gallop when they erupted into the area. The white and the dapple careered side by side around the space between the ring and the stands, the purple-uniformed man standing on them, one foot on each horse's back, their reins gathered in his left fist, his right

cracking a viciously long sjambok whip. The audience
cheered as the trio made several thunderous circuits of the
tent, the horses authentically wild-eyed and foam-lipped,
as if they really were bearing an urgent message across the
Russian steppe.

"Actually, in the classic Saint Petersburg turn," Florian
said to Edge and Yount, whom he had joined on the sidelines, "the rider next forces his two steeds apart, so other
horses can pass one by one under his legs, and he snatches
up their reins, until he is driving a whole herd. Unfortu-
nately, we do not have a whole herd."

The captain brought his two horses skidding to a stop,
and they reared handsomely, their necks arched by the
check-straps. Hotspur nimbly dropped to a sitting position
astride the white horse. Clover Lee was suddenly present,
to take the dapple's reins and lead it aside, while Hotspur
neatly jumped the white over the curbing and inside the
ring. There he bawled, "Mak gauw!" kicked it to a canter,
circling the ring, and, as it went, he began to leap off the
horse's back and on again. His wide-awake hat flew off,
and Clover Lee ran to snatch it out of harm's way. Next
Hotspur hung head downward from the horse, supported
by one foot inside the girth band. Then he sat up long
enough to leap off again and run alongside, then vaulted
astride again, to work his way completely around the
horse's underside, by way of the girth, while it continued
unconcernedly to canter. The spectators admiringly applauded each new feat. Almost every one of them had
owned at least one horse, and knew horses better than any
other mode of transport, and could descry good
horsemanship better than, say, good Hindu elephantman-
ship. Their approval inspired Captain Hotspur to repeat
every trick he had done, until the sweat flying off him
sparkled visibly in the sunbeams.

"It's called the voltige, that violent sort of circus riding," said Florian.

"Called gander pulling in the cavalry," said Yount.

"It also put a word into the formal English language,"

said Florian. "The word 'desultory' comes from the Latin. And in the ancient Roman circus, a 'desultor' was a performer who leapt from horse to horse."

As Captain Hotspur brought the white horse again to a rearing halt, Florian said, "It's time now for the Pete Jenkins." He strode into the ring, where Hotspur was taking bows. Clover Lee brought the captain his hat, and he carefully mopped his sweat-beaded bald head with a rag before he put the hat back on.

Florian called to the audience, "While Captain Hotspur takes a well-deserved pause for breath, I have an announcement to make. One of our patrons just a minute ago informed me that we have a birthday lady in the house." The crowd made noises of interest, and began to lean and look about. Florian consulted a scrap of paper. "And a very *significant* birthday—her seventieth! The biblical three score and ten!" The crowd made noises of being impressed. "Because of the coincidence—her celebrating such a momentous birthday on this Circus Day—I should like the lady to stand up and let us all wish many happy returns . . . to Mrs. Sophie *Pulsipher*, of Rivermont Avenue!" He began clapping and the crowd joined in.

"I thought he said Pete Jenkins," murmured Edge.

"Must of been a Pete Jenkins that told him about her," said Yount.

"Come on, Mrs. Pulsipher!" Florian urged. "Don't be shy. Come and take a bow!"

"Hyar she be! Hyar!" shouted several voices. Florian shaded his eyes with a hand to peer up into the seats. In one of the upper tiers, a woman awkwardly fumbled to find footing to stand. The men around her gently helped her down the boards to the tent floor.

"Here she comes!" cried Florian. "Let's hear congratulations, ladies and gentlemen, for Mrs. Sophie *Pulsipher!*"

All previous applauding was surpassed now, and the crowd sang as well, when Tim began tootling "For He's a Jolly Good Fellow," and the kerchiefed, shawled, gnarled little woman hobbled to the ringside. Edge and

Yount would have suspected it was the old circus gypsy
doing some kind of impersonation, except Magpie Maggie
Hag now came from the other side of the tent, carrying a
tiny cupcake on which stood a single candle. At that, Mrs.
Pulsipher turned to flee from the attention she was getting,
but Florian had hold of her arm. Some of the spectators
stopped singing to call, "Blow out the candle!" "Make a
wish!"

Mrs. Pulsipher wavered, hesitated, leaned over and—
after several weak attempts—blew out the candle flame.
"Wish! Make a wish!" cried the people. Florian smiled
encouragement at her and bent his ear to her lips. Whatever
she said seemed to surprise him; he gave her a very odd
look. Then he laughed and shook his head in a firm neg-
ative. The audience, intrigued, went quiet and waited. Still
shaking his head, Florian quietly said, "No, no," but
everybody could hear him. "Mrs. Pulsipher, I thank you
for confiding your wish, but no—that could not be permitted."

Several of the spectators yelled, "Tell! Tell!"

Florian looked a little perplexed. "Well . . . heh heh . . .
this dear little old lady . . ." he paused, then reluctantly let
it out. "She says she never in all her long life rode on a
bareback horse. Heh heh. Can you believe this, ladies and
gentlemen? Mrs. Pulsipher would like to go once around
the ring, riding pillion with Captain Hotspur." The captain, inside the ring, also looked astounded, wrinkling his
eyebrowless brow.

The women in the stands crooned things like, "Aw-w-w,
the precious ol' critter . . ." and some young rowdies
yelled, "Hey, let her do it! Let's see her ride!" The rowdies swung the vote; others took up the call, "Let her! It's
her birthday wish! Let her ride!"

Florian looked even more as if he wished he had never
started this. Mrs. Pulsipher stood visibly quivering, while
Florian went and conferred with Captain Hotspur, who
looked annoyed and impatient to get on with his act. But
the two of them came back to Mrs. Pulsipher, and the

crowd began cheering and clapping happily.

Clover Lee led the white horse close to the ringside.
Florian and the captain gingerly lifted the old lady over
the curbing onto Snowball. There was a good deal of awkward scrabbling, and even the horse looked back in inquiry, as they got Mrs. Pulsipher on to a sidesaddle
position. Florian held her securely there while Hotspur
made sure her hands were clasped on the girth band in
front of her. Then he effortlessly vaulted up behind her,
wrapped his arms about her waist and nodded to Clover
Lee. The girl led the horse by the bridle, walking it very
very slowly. Even so, the old lady teetered considerably,
and let out a high giggle that had a tinge of hysteria. The
audience laughed at her, and began applauding again, as
if she were performing some trick that outdid Hotspur himself. Tim blew a bray of fanfare.

The tent suddenly rocked to a mixture of women's horrified screams and men's hoarse bellows. The audience
leaped to its feet, and Florian and Magpie Maggie Hag—
even Edge and Yount—lunged toward the ring. At the
blare of the cornet, the horse had started violently. Captain
Hotspur, caught unprepared, slid off its rump, which scared
the horse even more. It bolted, and flung Clover Lee
sprawling, and now the horse was galloping madly around
and around the ring, with Mrs. Pulsipher clinging for her
life to the girth band, but the rest of her fluttering like a
sheaf of rags from one flank of the horse to the other. The
horse was terrified further by being chased by Florian,
Edge and Yount, so it went even faster, while the tent's
seating boards clattered as the men in the crowd tried to
get down to ground level and lend help.

But before the consternation and uproar could get any
worse, the old lady somehow got her legs bent under her
and onto the horse's back, and she was whizzing around
the ring in a kneeling position. Everybody else in the tent
stopped and froze in silent astonishment. Then Mrs. Pulsipher let go of the girth band entirely. In one limber bound
she was on her feet atop the runaway horse and she was

shedding into the air a litter of flying shawls, kerchiefs, skirts and other haberdashery—and stood revealed as a shapely and pretty woman, glittering and smiling and riding easily upright.

"Ma—DAME *Soli*-TAIRE!" boomed Florian at his very loudest.

The spectators let out another roar of pleasure at the metamorphosis of old lady into spirited woman, now striking one graceful pose after another, as serene and confident as if the galloping horse were a parlor carpet. She balanced on one leg, she swooped and pirouetted, she made figures like a swan flying, and every time the horse carried her through one of the shafts of sunlight, her sequined bodice and white tulle skirt lit up the tent's twilight like a flare of summer lightning. Edge had seen players in spangled outfits before, but he had never previously noticed how the spangles reflected upward. Solitaire's face was iridescently dappled by their light and made mysterious, as might be the face of a naiad under rippling water.

The crowd settled back to the seat boards, the extraneous circus people cleared out of the ring, Yount and Edge retired to where they had stood before, near the front door. Florian joined them there, beaming in vast satisfaction at how well the imposture had gone over. They watched as Madame Solitaire continued and elaborated her lissome dancing on her moving perch.

Yount muttered, almost grumpily, "You said that act was called Pete Jenkins. How come?"

"Damned if I know," Florian said cheerfully. "Somebody by that name must have been the first to do the turn."

The white horse slowed to an easy lope. Tim began to play a melodious tune—he had hung his straw hat over the cornet's bell to mute it—and Madame Solitaire threw flirtatious smiles to the men in the stands, while at ring center Monsieur Roulette sang, in quite a good tenor, a most moving song:

As I sat in the circus and watched her go round,
I thought that at me she was smiling,

And smiling so sweetly, this fairy completely
The heart from in me was beguiling.

The spectators tilted their heads from side to side, to the
lilt of the anapests. In the ring, suiting their actions to the
lyrics, Solitaire now waved to the men while Roulette
wrung his hands together and thumped them at his bosom.

She waved to the audience—I knew 'twas to me,
And the heart in my bosom was gay,
Solitaire is the Queen of all riders, I ween,
But alas! she is far, far away!

When the song stopped, so did the horse. Madame Solitaire jumped down, as lightly as any fairy, and flung up
her arms in the V appeal for applause—which came generously—while Monsieur Roulette and Tim slipped out of
the tent. Florian came running to give the lady a paternal
hug, and shouted facetiously, "Mrs. Sophie Pulsipher
thanks you, ladies and gentlemen!" Laughter from the
crowd, and from Solitaire, too, as she departed, leading
her horse.

Florian asked for, and got, a round of applause for the
ring horses, then said, "Now . . . to make the moments
pass pleasantly while we prepare the ring for the next
thrilling spectacle on our program . . . here again is our own
Merry Andrew of Tom Foolery and Joe Millerisms . . . the
ever popular *Tim Trimm!*"

Tim arrived quickly and bouncily this time, no longer
encumbered by the oversized farm garb. What he had been
wearing under it, and was wearing now, might have been
snatched off some household clothesline. It had originally
been a boy's flannel combination suit of underwear, but
was disguised by having enormous polka dots of various
colors daubed all over it. He was also carrying Abdullah's
drum instead of the cornet. He came in pounding on it and
skipped spastically around the ring, while he told—in his

normal loud voice, not the midget squeak—some of the oldest jokes known to mankind.

"The boss of this-here circus didn't want us to get this-here drum, you know!" Boomp-boomp. "He said the noise would upset him." Boomp-boomp. "So we promised him we'd only play it when he was asleep!" Ba-*boom!* Maybe some of the children in the audience laughed. So Tim set down the drum and tried a different theme "Our boss is a furriner, you know? You got to be careful how you say things. When I told him I was hungry as a hoss, you know what? He tossed me a pitchfork of *hay*!" Not even the children laughed.

Meanwhile, Captain Hotspur, Abdullah and Monsieur Roulette were manhandling the lion's cage through the front door of the pavilion, and maneuvering it through the gap in the ring curbing. More people were watching that procedure than were attending to Tim, as he doggedly kept on:

"So the boss said eat up that-there hay, Tim, it'll put color in your cheeks. And I said who wants to look like a *high-yaller?*" No laughter at all, so Florian trotted out to his rescue, saying jovially and without preamble, "I hear you're thinking of getting married, Tim, my lad!"

Tim looked grateful for the new subject. "Well, I don't know, boss. After all, what does ma-tri-mo-ny mean? A *matter o' money!*"

Evidently a few men in the audience caught it. Anyway, a few men laughed.

"Yes!" boomed Florian. "You must look for a good wife, and a good wife should have certain qualities. A good wife should be like the town clock. She should keep punctual time and regularity."

"No, sir, that would be a bad wife! She would speak so the whole town can hear!"

By now, the cage wagon was positioned at ring center, so Florian tossed out just one more line: "Furthermore, a good wife should be like an echo. Speak only when spoken to!"

"No, sir, boss. A bad wife, that! She'd always have the last word!"

"Aargh, get along with you!" And Florian sent a kick to his backside. It did not connect, but it sounded so, because Tim hit the drum at the proper moment. He threw himself asprawl, got up and scuttled out of the tent.

"And now, ladies and gentlemen!" Florian shouted, waving toward the cage wagon. "You have all had an opportunity to look closely at that beast yonder. You have seen the size of him, the sharpness of his dread fangs. You have heard his heart-stopping roar." Captain Hotspur poked the end of his sjambok in through the cage bars. The cat batted at it with a paw, and obliged with a coughing grunt and growl. "Now you are about to see a brave man actually get into the cage with that vicious predator, to demonstrate man's mastery over the brute creation. I ask you all please not to applaud or make any other sudden sounds, for if the lion is at all startled, or the lion tamer's concentration even for an instant distracted—well, the result could be horrible beyond description. So I beg for silence and without further ado . . . I give you the daredevil *Captain Hotspur* . . . and the King of the Great Cats, the lion MAXIMUS!"

The crowd obediently ceased every whispered conversation. The captain dramatically flung away his curly-brimmed hat, then flung off his epauletted purple jacket to reveal a brawny bare chest and arms. Coiled whip in one hand, he cautiously undid the latch of the cage door. Maximus growled in what could have been a tone of malice and menace. Slowly, Captain Hotspur put a foot up to the cage entrance and, still very slowly, levered himself into the doorway, stepped slowly inside and swung the door latch behind him.

He and the big tawny cat stood facing each other inside a barred area only four feet by ten. The captain let his sjambok uncoil and flipped the tassel end of it close to Maximus, who again batted at it and curled his lips to display his formidable teeth. "Platz!" commanded Hot-

spur, in a voice as gruff as the lion's and, after a surly
hesitation, Maximus lowered his rear end and sat. Someone in the stands involuntarily clapped twice, but Hotspur
threw a glare in that direction. Next, he twitched the tassel
to flick Maximus under the chin, and commanded,
''Schön'machen!'' The cat again balked and grumbled and
looked gloomily about, as if for escape, but then sat up on
his haunches, forepaws lifted.

The captain put the lion through its repertoire of not
very sensational tricks—after all, there was not room in
the cage for him and it to do very much—making Maximus jump over his whip (''Hoch!'') and then lie down and
then play dead (''Krank!'') supine with all four paws in
the air. Then he backed the lion to the far end of the cage,
and himself backed against the other end, and held them
apart with the extended whip, while Florian reappeared to
announce:

''Now, ladies and gentlemen, Captain Hotspur will attempt the most daring and death-defying feat of all. He
will demonstrate his total power over the lion by opening
its jaws with his bare hands . . . and putting his unprotected
head into the killer animal's *jaws of death!* Let us keep
silence . . . and let us pray!''

''Platz!'' barked the captain, and Maximus again grumblingly and reluctantly sat down like a house cat. The spectators made not a sound, but their very breathlessness was
almost evident, as Hotspur stalked step by step toward the
lion, then dropped to one knee before it. Actually, he did
not have to pry the animal's jaws apart; Maximus opened
them as boredly as if in a yawn. Captain Hotspur turned
his head sideways—he did have an admirable head for the
purpose: bald and smooth—and put it between the lion's
gaping jaws, and from there grinned hideously out at the
enthralled audience. After a moment, he extracted his head,
stepped away from the lion and bounded upright. There
was no room for him to raise his arms in the usual V.
Instead, he theatrically threw out toward the lion the hand
that held his coiled whip, and insouciantly stuck his other

hand in his trouser pocket—and so stood beaming in the storm of applause and cheers and whistles.

Then, again, the applause suddenly became screams and yells of horror—as Captain Hotspur's grin turned to an agonized rictus and his body contorted. Maximus had abruptly reached out his still-open jaws and closed them around the captain's bare forearm. Grimacing and writhing, Hotspur managed to yank the arm loose from the enclosing teeth, yanked his free hand out of his pocket and clamped it around that arm, and blood spurted from between his fingers.

The spectators were vociferous in their commotion as a number of circus people ran to help. Roulette and Abdullah and Tim Trimm got into the ring first, but stopped in their tracks when Captain Hotspur yelled, through clenched teeth, "*Bock! Stay bock!* Not yourselfs in danger poot!" To the lion he said firmly, "Zurück! Stille!" and stuck out the whip to keep him at bay.

Maximus was not pursuing the attack; he stayed where he was and looked more bemused than maddened by the taste of blood. Hotspur, with his uninjured arm holding the sjambok steady and the lion in place, thrust through the bars the arm smeared and dripping with blood. Abdullah quickly stooped, tore a long strip from the hem of one of his several robes, stepped close to the cage and deftly bound the rag about the protruding arm. The spectators' cries diminished to sobs and gasps and noises of admiration, as the staunch Captain Hotspur eased himself backward, step by slow step, to the cage door. Monsieur Roulette leaped to unlatch it and, when the captain had jumped backward out of it—reeling giddily as he landed— Roulette emphatically slammed and fastened the door again.

Though clearly unsteady on his feet, the captain insisted on a proper close to his turn. He raised both the whip arm and the bloody-bandaged one in the V, and got the applause he deserved—from most of the audience, anyway. Numerous women had swooned and collapsed, and were being fanned with the hats of their male companions.

"Have you ever noticed," Florian said to Edge, as Roulette and Abdullah helped the captain totter out of the tent, "how a woman never faints until there is nothing more to see?"

"Well, *you* don't seem to mind the sight of blood."

Florian looked mildly surprised. "Not when it's the blood of a jackass. You saw it being collected and saved. The captain had a bit of it in a sausage skin in his trouser pocket."

And, waving his arms, Florian went into the ring again to quell the crowd's agitation.

"Ladies and gentlemen, we regret the terrible accident, but I am happy to report—our company physician assures us that the gallant captain was not badly injured by the man-eater's assault. The captain will be with us again, just as soon as the wound is properly dressed and he has taken a short rest. So we shall now declare an intermission. The program will resume after half an hour, during which interval our talented musicians will render various popular melodies for your delectation."

On cue, Abdullah and Tim struck up "What Is Home Without a Mother?"

"You are welcome, ladies and gentlemen, boys and girls, to leave the pavilion and stretch your limbs with a stroll along the circus midway. At our Mobile Museum of Zoölogical Curiosities, I shall personally deliver an educational lecture on some little-known facts about the rare specimens of fauna to be seen therein. Adjacent to the area, you will be able to observe the recently captured Wild Man of the Woods . . ."

Most of the people were already climbing stiffly down from the benches, talking among themselves and gesticulating excitedly.

"If some of you ladies would prefer to remain in your places upon the grandstand, you may there avail yourselves of the prognosticatory and divinatory arts of the all-seeing clairvoyante, Madame Magpie Maggie Hag, who will move among you during the interval. At your request, she will accurately foretell what lies in your future, give sage advice in matters of love, health, money and marriage . . .''

After all the people who were leaving the tent had gone, Edge and Yount helped Abdullah and Monsieur Roulette haul the lion's wagon outside, and a considerable crowd of rubes collected around the cage to watch Roulette throw to Maximus a meal of jackass meat as his reward for having performed so nobly. Yount loitered there on the lot—what he had regarded only as ''outside the tent,'' but Florian had grandly called the ''midway''—to listen as Florian expatiated on the ''little-known'' aspects of the extremely well-known creatures stuffed and mounted in the museum wagon.

''. . . May *look* to you like an ordinary woodchuck. But in truth this is the *very* woodchuck that inspired the poet who wrote that immortal lyric of rustic humor: 'How much wood would a woodchuck chuck, if a woodchuck could chuck wood?' . . .''

Inside the tent, where Magpie Maggie Hag was at the moment tête-à-tête with a plain-faced but shining-eyed young woman, Edge sidled close enough to overhear the gypsy saying, ''You want your man fall in love with you, juvel? What you do, you take long piece of string. Wait until he stand in sunshine, but where he no see you. Take that string, measure his shadow, cut string that long exactly. Remember, he must not know. Put string under pillow while you sleep. Masher-ava! He fall in love with you. Five cents.''

Outside, the Wild Man of the Woods capered about at the end of his chain, gibbering and scratching himself in intimate places under his covering of animal skins and dirt and campfire char, while Florian informed the watching crowd:

''Since nothing remotely like him has ever been discovered before, the savants are unable to accord the Wild Man a specific native country. However, by examination of his peculiar dentition—that is to say, by comparing his teeth to those of known mammals—the scientists *have* concluded that he is part-bear, part-human. The conjecture from that can only be that he was miscegenetically sired by some deranged mountain man upon a she-bear. Or, even more horrendous to contemplate, that the Wild Man is the offspring of a he-bear which somehow . . .'' Florian left that one dangling, and the eyes of the women in the crowd got wide and speculative. "As you would expect of a bear, the half-ursine Wild Man likes his meat raw. So perhaps some of you ladies would prefer to avert your gaze, for it is now the creature's feeding time.''

None of them looked away. Monsieur Roulette threw to the idiot a jackass thighbone, which Maximus had at some earlier time picked clean and almost polished. The Wild Man seized it avidly and, with a delighted mooing, began to rattle his dentition up and down it. The rubes muttered among themselves, and Yount muttered to Roulette. "I think that's purely awful. Using that poor idjit so.''

"Pourquoi?'' said Roulette. "He enjoys it. He is happier here, being admired, than he was at home with his family, being despised.''

"Still, it don't seem right.''

Roulette said, somewhat tartly. "You and your ami ought to restrain your habit of chiding people for doing what they can do best instead of what you think they ought to be doing.''

Inside the tent, Edge listened as Magpie Maggie Hag told a middle-aged but still handsome woman, "You maybe want get rid of old, rich husband, be merry widow! What you do, take string, measure shadow of him standing in sunshine, but not let him know. Roll up string, sneak it under his pillow while he sleeps. Soon—mulengi!—he be dead. Ten cents.''

"Shit!'' said Madame Solitaire, outside the tent, where she was examining the gear of her white horse.

"Is something the matter, ma'am?'' asked Yount. He thought she might be cussing her own gear, for she had changed clothes since she had left the ring, and this outfit

was even more sadly shabby than what she had worn earlier. There were more bare patches among the sequins
sewn on her bodice, the tulle skirt was more frayed at its
fringe. But that wasn't what was bothering her.

"I just noticed. Snowball's check-strap is about worn in
two. Right here, see? And he's a great one for throwing
his head back. If he does it while I'm a-straddle and bent
forward—which is when he'll do it—I get a busted nose.
I've had enough busted noses for one lifetime."

"When do you go in the ring, ma'am? Can't it be fixed
afore then?"

"I'm a fair hand at sewing, Obie, but not through
leather. I'll have to ask Ignatz, but he's going on any minute." The cornet was playing "Wait for the Wagon,"
which meant that Florian was herding the rubes back into
the tent. "The first turn is Clover Lee doing the garters
and garlands, and Ignatz works with her."

Yount scratched in his beard. "If there's time, and if
you've got an awl and a piece of waxed twine, I can fix
that strap for you, ma'am. Us cavalrymen get to be pretty
good at harness work."

"Oh, that's gentlemanly of you, Obie. Come on." They
took the strap and went to the prop wagon. "There's Ignatz's tool kit. While you're working, I'll go and see what
kind of barter Florian took in—what kind of peck Maggie
and I can make of it after the show." She went away,
leaving the wagon door open to give him working light.

". . . And now, ladies and gentlemen," Florian wound
up his introduction to the second half of the program,
"here she is—cousin to the brave General Fitzhugh Lee,
grandniece of our beloved General Robert E. Lee—riding
her horse Bubbles, which you will easily recognize as a
son of Traveller, General Lee's own famous gray—and
herself renowned as the world's youngest, most talented
équestrienne, Mademoiselle *Clover* LEE!"

Tim and Abdullah blared and boomed into "The Erie
Canal" and Clover Lee rode in, smiling radiantly, seated
sideways on the bare back of the dappled horse. Captain

Hotspur and Monsieur Roulette trotted in on foot and went to the center pole. Florian departed to the sidelines, where Edge said:

"How can you spout such flummery? That child's no more kin to Uncle Bobby and Nephew Fitz than I am."

"You know that, and I know it, but do these yokels know it?"

"If they know that Traveller is a gelding and never sired any get, they might doubt the rest of your rigmarole."

"They're not here to seek Clover Lee's hand in marriage, only to see her ride. But if it's even barely possible that she comes from a family they know, they'll be more kindly disposed to cheer her on."

The horse loped around the inside of the ring and Clover Lee bounded to a stand on its back, but her movements were rather less graceful and fluid than her mother's had been. When Tim and Abdullah swung into the chorus of the tune ("Low bridge, everybody down . . .") Captain Hotspur ran to the outside with a garter, merely one of the fluffy pink ropes Edge had earlier seen. One end was attached to the center pole and Hotspur held the other above his head to make a barrier in Clover Lee's way. The horse went under it and the girl cleared it with a bound, to come down safe on the horse's back again. Then Roulette ran out with a second rope ("Low bridge, for we're goin' through a town . . .") so, next time around, Clover Lee had to make two quick bounces.

When she had repeated that trick several times, the men dropped the pink garters and Captain Hotspur stood on the ring curb holding a garland—one of the hoops fringed with pink paper ruffles—out in her path. Clover Lee jumped, somersaulted through it and landed standing on the still-loping horse beyond it. Again Roulette stepped forward, with a second hoop, and now the girl was no sooner landing from one somersault that she had to throw another. It was a pretty sight, and she got tumultuous applause when she finally hopped down from the running horse. Bubbles was also applauded when Florian reminded the crowd again of the animal's distinguished lineage.

"And now, direct from Paris . . . where his astonishing agility amazed the Emperor Louis Napoléon and the Empress Eugénie . . . that master of tumblers, foremost of gleemen, the most accomplished of parterre gymnasts . . . I give you *Monsieur* ROULETTE!''

The man's acrobatic turn was immeasurably better than his voice throwing had been. Indeed, Edge thought it stupendous, and he could honestly believe that even emperors and empresses might well find it amazing to watch him. As Tim Trimm variously tweedled softly and blasted rollickingly, Monsieur Roulette did leaps and twists and turnovers that seemed to gainsay his having any bones in his body or any obligation to the law of gravity. He Frenchified every trick by crying "Allez houp!'' before he began it and "Houp là!'' when he succeeded, and occasionally even explained in French what he was about to do: "Faire le saut périlleux au milieu de l'air! Voilà!''

After an unassisted display of several-in-a-row forward and backward somersaults and numerous midair cartwheels and flip-flops, he ran and got from ringside the short ladder Edge had seen him fetch to the tent. He stood it upright in mid-ring, not leaning against anything, merely balanced on its two legs—and climbed swiftly up one side and down the other, the ladder somehow just standing there. He did all kinds of posturings and balancings on it, himself sometimes standing up on the rungs and sometimes horizontal to the ladder, held only by one heel against and one toe under the rungs, while the ladder teetered and swayed, but miraculously always stayed erect.

Then he scurried to the top of that standing ladder, stood up on its two uppermost points and walked the thing, like a pair of hobbled stilts, around the ring. Next, without ever getting down, with the ladder still vertical, he stood on his hands on those two upper stubs and again walked the thing around the ring. During much of Roulette's performance, the audience had sat silent, as if afraid to make a noise

that might topple him. But that latest feat brought a tremendous burst of clapping and cheers and whistles.

Out in the property wagon, Yount was busy with sail
twine, leather palm and curved needle, when Clover Lee
suddenly breezed in past him and, not even closing the
wagon door, began to undress, right down to the buff.
Yount was too confounded even to turn politely away, but
frankly stared and finally stammered, ''Girl, what are you
doing?''

''Changing for the closing spec—the closing promenade. Sweat is worse than moths for eating holes in
clothes. Got to rinse them out right away. What's the matter, Sergeant Obie? Surely you horse soldiers know what
sweat is?''

''Well, uh . . . sure.''

''Ah. Then maybe you never saw a female naked before.''

''Well, uh . . . not free gratis, no, miss.''

''Enjoy it, then. I don't give anything else away for free.
That I'm saving for when I'm grown, when I meet a duke
or a count to give it to, over in Europe.'' Yount stared
even more unbelievingly. ''Meanwhile you go ahead and
look all you want at what little I've got to show.'' Then
she laughed, as she realized the object of his gaze. ''Oh,
you're looking at this thing.'' She held up the small pad
she had just removed from inside her discarded tights.
''Every circus artiste wears one. Men, too—only in their
case it's to make the bulge at their crotch less noticeable.
For us females it's to cover our little cleft, so it won't wink
at the audience. It's called a cache-sexe. That's French.''

''I might of knowed.''

She tucked the cache-sexe between her legs, swiftly
slipped into clean clothes from the skin out and flitted out
of the wagon. Yount wonderingly shook his head, finished
the strap mending and went to take it to Madame Solitaire.

Inside the tent, Monsieur Roulette brought to the ring
the thing Edge had thought might be a child's teeterboard.
It turned out to be simply a slant short ramp for Roulette

to run up and jump from. He did that several times, the board giving him extra altitude and a longer parabola in which to do his fantastic capers and head-to-toe backbends and legs-apart splits in mid-air. Meanwhile, Abdullah led Brutus into the tent again, and the climax of Monsieur Roulette's act consisted of taking a run at his board, giving a mighty bounce on it, sailing high and far into the air, turning a succession of tightly tucked somersaults over the top of the elephant and coming down lightly on his feet on the other side of Brutus—''Houp là!''—and the crowd nearly lifted the tent roof with its acclaim.

After Abdullah had taken the elephant outside again, he bounded into the ring anew and Florian introduced him this time as ''The master of those *other* Hindu secrets known in the Hindu language as the Art of the Hannibal-tyree. That tongue-twister Hindu word, ladies and gentlemen, means a worker of wonders. And here to *show* you what it means . . . is *Abdullah* of BENGAL!''

The Negro at first seemed to be empty-handed, but when he began moving his hands up and down, an onion suddenly appeared in one of them. It was flipped to the other hand, but that first hand somehow still held an onion, and that one was flipped into the air, but each hand still held an onion . . . and so on. Faster than the eye could follow, Abdullah produced onions out of nowhere and sent them arching from hand to hand in patterns so fast and quick-changing that their blurred trajectories looked to be an insubstantial cat's cradle being woven and remade and made ever more complex. Then the number of onions began mysteriously to lessen, until the individual onions could be seen flipping from hand to hand. There there was only one of them, and Abdullah was tossing it idly up and down and grinning at the audience. He gave it one last toss, higher than before, got his head under it as it came down, caught it in his mouth and took a loud, juicy bite out of it.

Over the applause, Florian said to Edge—and to Yount,

who had just joined them—"To think, friends, that boy used to shine shoes!"

Tim Trimm ran in and handed Abdullah three lighted torches—sticks with bundles of pitch-pine splinters burning at one end—and Abdullah juggled those for a while, making them spin end over end while they were flying high over his head, from hand to hand, and they made a fine spectacle in the tent's twilight. When he had finished with those, catching all three in one hand and blowing them out, Tim ran in again, with a stack of what Edge and Yount recognized as the sort of bowls they had supped from the night before.

Abdullah sent them flipping back and forth between his hands, almost negligently, and this time Tim stood close by. He was playing the clown again, watching the act with an expression of imbecile-Reuben vacuity. He began to make broad gestures of imploring, and Abdullah responded with an inviting nod. So Tim got alongside him, and Abdullah abstracted one dish out of the number in the air and handed it to him. When Tim only gaped at it, Abdullah had to snatch it back from him to keep up the continuity in the air. So Tim repeated the business of imploring, and Abdullah again slipped him one of the soup plates, and Tim flung it at once, and Abdullah had to scramble half across the ring, juggling all the while, to get it into his stream of plates again.

The audience giggled at that, and then they guffawed, and before long were laughing constantly, as Abdullah and Tim rushed hither and yon, colliding, falling down, though still somehow keeping the dishes aloft. Finally Abdullah made a broad gesture of disgust and quit the whole affair—while the soup plates were helter-skelter high in the air—folded his arms and stood aside. Tim managed to skitter about to catch and hold the things as they came down, but there were too many for him, and he could hold only so many in his clutching arms—and the last one fell on his head and shattered to pieces, and the spectators howled and pounded their knees.

Tim looked contrite, then vexed, then indignant. He suddenly gave a yowl of rage—and the audience stopped laughing to duck and dodge. Tim had flung one of the soup plates so it whirled upside down, straight at the bank of seats farthest from him. But oddly the dish slowed in its discus flight and then paused, spinning above the masked and ducking heads—then reversed its direction and sailed back into Tim's waiting hand. The people straightened up again, astounded.

"Now you know why Tim acquired that pie tin," Florian shouted to Edge, over the renewed laughter and applause. "To gaff the mimic-juggling turn."

Tim and Abdullah went off, bowing, and immediately grabbed up cornet and drum to provide a fanfare for the reentrance of Captain Hotspur and Madame Solitaire and the two ring horses. The captain again stood straddled between Snowball and Bubbles, but this time the pretty lady stood right behind him, one hand lightly on his shoulder, the other raised in greeting to the crowd. Hotspur wore his purple uniform jacket, so no one could see whether he was still bandaged, but clearly he had full use of both arms. Their horses went side by side around and around the ring, while the man and the woman assumed various artistic poses, sometimes both of them using both horses, sometimes one of them on each horse, sometimes both on one.

Most the tricks consisted of Madame Solitaire's being assisted by the captain to an otherwise impossible position—as when she stood on Snowball's withers and bent backward, Hotspur from his stand on Bubbles extending an arm to support her, and she continued arching backward until her hands rested on her horse's rump, both the horses galloping like fury the whole time. The most impossibly perilous pose was of course saved for last. Hotspur knelt atop his horse, and the woman climbed up his back to sit astride his shoulders. The captain slowly stood upright and shifted one foot so he again stood upon both horses. Then Solitaire carefully lifted one foot at a time to Hotspur's shoulders, and unfolded herself so she was *standing* up there, holding onto nothing, her arms outstretched like wings, she and the captain leaning inward as the horses pounded around the ring. When the horses were slowed and she and Hotspur dropped lightly to the ring in their arms-up V stances, the cornet and the drum were drowned by the applause.

"Madame Solitaire and Captain Hotspur thank you, ladies and gentlemen!" shouted Florian, when he could be heard. "And now, before the Parting Salute of the Grand Closing Promenade, we have a very special treat for you, an addition to our regular program. Because you have received us so warmly, our wagon-train escort—Colonel Zachary Plantagenet-Tudor of the British Grenadiers—has volunteered to entertain you with an impromptu exhibition of pistol sharpshooting!"

"Why, the son of a bitch!" Edge exclaimed.

Tim Trimm immediately began a spirited rendition of the "British Grenadiers" march. Florian beckoned to Edge while he continued his blatant falsehoods: ". . . A fact little known, but our stalwart British sympathizers seconded some of their most expert marksmen to our gallant Confederate Army during our recent struggle against the Yankee invaders . . ."

"Colonel Tooter," said Yount, highly amused, "you better get out yonder, afore he runs out of guff."

"Let him, the presumptuous windbag. I'm damned if I'll go out there and make a fool of myself."

"You'll look more of a fool if you cut and run."

"God *damn!*" Edge looked almost frantically about and saw that everybody in the seats nearby was eyeing him expectantly.

Florian was still beckoning and still spouting: "However, since our show has already run overtime, Colonel Zachary will make only a single demonstration of his marksmanship. Therefore, I shall ask him to shoot just once—to put out a flame while I personally hold it up. That is how much confidence I have in the colonel's keen eye and consummate skill."

He took from his vest a match, bent and plucked a splinter of pitch pine from one of Abdullah's discarded torches, lit that and held it at arm's length.

"Christ," muttered Edge. "He's not only crazy, he's suicidal. Obie, quick, you got a worm handy?"

"Uh huh." Yount took out a formidable folding knife and opened from it a small corkscrew.

Florian went on, "To overcome the colonel's very British reticence, let's give him a welcoming hand!" and the people obediently started clapping.

"Damn it to hell!" growled Edge. He handed Yount his pistol. "Quick, Obie, pull one of the balls." And he went out into the ring.

"Colonel Plantagenet-Tudor!" bawled Florian, waving his little flame. "Not in British red coat now, but wearing the good honest gray of our beloved Confederate Army!" The applause got even louder. "Take a bow, Colonel Zachary." Edge did so, stiffly, and gave Florian a baleful glare. Then he strode again to the sidelines where Yount, with a nod, handed him the big revolver.

Edge glanced at the front of the pistol's cylinder, and gave the cylinder a slight turn as he stepped again into the ring. The crowd quieted, and the oily triple click of the gun's hammer being cocked was clearly audible. Edge stood with the weapon down at his side until Florian raised and held steady the tiny flame, ten feet away. Edge moved sideways so he had Florian between him and the tent's back door, empty of people. Then he raised his arm, seeming not to aim at all, and pulled the trigger. Even in the considerable expanse of the Big Top, the shot was a concussive *blam!*, and several people jumped. But Florian did not wince, and the flame at the end of the pine splinter puffed instantly out.

The people clapped heartily, but Edge did not do any V-posturing or even stand still to be admired. He simply turned and went back to his former place by the front door. As if the gunshot had been their signal, the circus troupe and animals came parading in again. Florian stayed at ring center, turning as the parade went around him, as if his extended hand, holding his top hat, were directing it.

Edge commented, ''They've most of them changed clothes, just to do this walk around.''

''Sweat ruins their costumes,'' Yount said authoritatively. But then he gave due credit. ''That girl Clover Lee told me so. Hell, she changed clothes right in front of me. These circus females've got about as much modesty as so many Injun squaws. You know what else that kid told me? She's saving what she's got atween her legs, until she meets a count or a juke over in Europe.''

''I hope there are enough of those to go around,'' said Edge. ''Her mother's got somewhat the same idea. I wouldn't be surprised but the old gypsy woman does, too.''

''I mean to say,'' said Yount, ''when I was that kid's age, I didn't know I *had* anything atween my legs, except a spigot to pee from.'' He paused and reflected. ''Hey, maybe I ought to save my thing, too, for some countess or—Zack, is there such a thing as a jukess?''

''Duchess. And I believe countesses and duchesses only get that way by marrying counts and dukes. Sarah or Clover Lee might have a hope of snagging a title, but you wouldn't. Obie, are you seriously thinking of joining this bunch?''

''Well, I ain't saying I ain't. Hell, I'd never even get to *see* such a thing as a countess in Tennessee.''

The troupe had completed two or three circuits of the pavilion. Now Tim muted his horn and swung into the most popular ballad of the day, and Madame Solitaire and Mademoiselle Clover Lee sweetly sang it as they rode:

> We loved each other then, Lorena,
> More than we ever dared to tell . . .

The lyrics of ''Lorena'' were woefully lugubrious, but the tune was as beautiful and bittersweet as that of ''Auld Lang Syne,'' and the spectators hummed or sang along with it as they began to clamber down from their benches and make for the front door:

> It matters little now, Lorena,
> The past is in the eternal past . . .

Since Edge and Yount were the only apparently circus people in their path, several folks stopped during the come-out to give them a word of thanks for the entertainment.

"I don't reckon," said an elderly gentleman, "we should exactly be celebrating the *way* this war ended. But it's a comfort to have it over with. And you folks, coming along just now, have made us feel a lot better about things in general."

"Yes," said an elderly lady. "Thar ain't nothin' like a circus or a good rousin' camp meetin' to lift the sperrits."

"And y'all's is the fust circus to come since the waw begun," said her elderly lady companion.

"Maw and me'd been keepin' our jar of canned peaches," said a middle-aged man with a middle-aged wife, "for a slap-up dinner whenever our boy come home. But last week we got word he ain't a-comin' home. So we're glad we swapped them peaches for y'all's show. Maw and me, we made out like Melvin was with us, and we enjoyed it a whole lot. Bless you folks."

6

"OUR TAKINGS, our profit, our plunder!" exulted Florian, standing in the door of the tent wagon where it was piled. He began to tally the acquisitions out loud, for the benefit of his colleagues gathered about the cooking fire. At any other time or place, the takings would have been accounted a pathetically paltry treasure.

"Foodstuffs first. Well, there are the eggs and sausage and mushrooms, some of which Mesdames Maggie and Solitaire are cooking this very moment. Homemade sau-

sage, said the lady who brought that, and I gallantly refrained from inquiring what went into it. We also acquired
the onions you saw Abdullah juggle, and quite a quantity
of other root-cellar produce. Potatoes and carrots and turnips and parsnips and some black walnuts. Two good-sized
sacks of corn meal and a can of lard. *Four* combs of honey.
At least twenty jars of preserved goods—um, let's see—
tomatoes, snap beans, peaches, squash, plums, pickled wa-
termelon rind. A fair-sized sack apiece of dried pinto beans
and black-eyed peas and goobers in the shell. From the
kids, three hefty strings of suckers and catfish. Ladies, I
don't think we ought to let those lie around too long un-
cooked.''

''We had fish for breakfast,'' said Sarah. ''Now we're
going to have eggs and sausages, with mushrooms and
corn cakes, and honey for the cakes. *And* coffee. Well,
parched-peanut coffee, but it's the first of any kind we've
had in ever so long.''

''If some of you would prefer another beverage,'' said
Florian, continuing the tally. ''We have spruce beer, persimmon beer and scuppernong wine. None of them tainted
with the demon alcohol. *However*, for those who are not
teetotallers, we also have here two stoneware jugs of what
I was told is Lynchburg's own best brand of white lightning.''

All the males except the idiot immediately handed up
their tin cups or china mugs to Florian. He poured liberal
tots of whiskey all around, including one for himself, and
went on:

''Of plunder not edible or potable, but still useful—let's
see. We have about a lifetime's supply of Lynchburg's
prime product, tobacco in shag, plug or even leaf, if anybody wants to roll a cigar. Here, Abdullah, take a plug and
give Brutus a treat right now. We also acquired a quantity
of mixed tableware, including those dishes for juggling.
Some nails and screws and clothespins. A small mirror and
some candles and a can of coal oil and lamp wicks. A
couple of not too threadbare horse blankets, a box of

horseshoes of mixed sizes, and three or four nose bags, in case we ever get some grain to feed the poor brutes. Various townswomen contributed lengths of ribbon and braid and some paper flowers. Madame Hag, I'll let you determine what decorative use may be made of them. We also have various odds and ends of military uniform that we can dye and even got some pots of copperas and sassafras and sumac dyes." He paused to refresh himself with a sip of the corn whiskey. "It's almost more fun to do business like this than the orthodox way of just taking money. Never know what you'll come up with. For example, this."

He held up a six-string banjo, in good shape except that it had only the chantarelle and two of the long strings.

"If we can procure three more strings, one of us will have to learn to play it. But I also got a musical instrument for *me*." He stuck a tin whistle in his mouth and blew a shrill blast. "I've been without one too long, and an equestrian director without a whistle is like an orchestra conductor without a baton."

He tucked it carefully in his vest pocket, then went on with the catalogue.

"Here's a nice portable library for us. Six or seven copies of *The Camp Jester* magazine and three Beadle dime novels. Let's see—*Nick of the Woods, The Indian Wife of the White Hunter* and *The Forayers*—ha! that's us! From the youngsters I took in a whole heap of these little 'comfort bags' their Sunday Schools were supposed to have sent to the troops. I think we can discard the tracts against drinking and cussing and such. But the bags do contain useful items like pins and needles and thread." He sipped again at his whiskey. "And now, last but not least, the actual cash money we took in. I am happy to announce the grand total of four dollars, eighty-seven and a half cents in good Federal silver and copper, eight *hundred* dollars in Confederate paper. Now I call that a pretty good take!"

All the circus folk applauded as exuberantly as the paying audience had done, but Edge spoke up:

"I reckon I'm as Confederate as they come, Mr. Florian, but I frankly don't understand why you're continuing to accept those shinplasters."

"I may be wrong," said Florian, "but I strongly suspect that we'll meet diehard Rebels, somewhere along our way, who will actually refuse to accept Yankee money in exchange for whatever we might want to buy."

"If you say so," said Edge, and subsided.

"Maggie," Florian called down to her. "How did you make out with the rubes in the interval?"

She looked up from her cookery to say, "Seven dollars."

That rather dampened Florian's glee. "Why, Mag, you used to do better than . . . why, I'd have expected . . . Hell, Mag, that's only worth about seven *cents* in genuine—"

"Not paper." She gave him a gap-toothed but very satisfied grin. "Real money."

"What!" Now Florian was stunned. So was everyone else. "Why, that's almost as much as *all* we took in at the red wagon, Federal and Secesh together."

Magpie Maggie Hag set down her cooking implements to feel about among her layers of skirts and underthings. She extracted a cloth bag that jingled richly and handed it up to Florian.

Jules Rouleau asked, "How in the world did you come by it, Mag?"

"Women," she said, and spat contemptuously. "Come war, come misery, come Doomsday, *all* women magpies. Sneak away penny at a time, hide away little nest egg. Any woman can pilfer good as any gypsy. She maybe won't spend for food, shoes for family, even frippery for herself. But she give nest egg to have her dream or her palm dukkered, if she think it maybe dukker affair of love. A man if she got none, a new man if she already got one. *Women!* Now come, everybody. Supper ready. Good supper."

It was a good meal, and a welcome one, not to say a necessity and long overdue, and the fire made a bonny gathering place in what was now the no longer warm dusk of the day. Only the Wild Man unmannerly slobbered and gulped his share of the meal and then drifted away. The others enlivened their dining with amiable chatter in the various jargons of their several arts.

Hannibal Tyree said to Tim Trimm, "Would it be easier for you, when you horn in, if I was tossin' a shower 'stead of a cascade?"

"Don't matter. But next time, after I throw the tin and skeer the rubes, we ought to give 'em a laugh to relax. So you kick me into the tub and roll me around."

Clover Lee said to Ignatz Roozeboom, "I think, instead of just a hop-down at the close, I should do a back lay-out from my last somersault to the ground."

"Ja, gut. But if you stop den, you sway, look unsteady. From dot lay-out, go into a one-hand round-off."

Edge leaned over to say to her, "I remember, mam'selle, that you called your tights 'fleshings.' But you call the other garment some foreign name?"

"A léotard. I don't know why it's called that."

"Shame on you, Edith Coverley," said Florian. "The man who designed it and gave it his name is the greatest trapeze artiste alive, Jules Léotard."

Rouleau said, "I hear that all kinds of things in France have been named in his honor—rissole à la Léotard, pâté Léotard—just the way we have the Jenny Lind bonnet, the Jenny Lind polka and so on, over here."

"How lovely!" said Clover Lee. "Maybe, when I get famous in France, they'll name something after me."

Edge turned to Magpie Maggie Hag, who was frying another batch of sausages, and said, "Ma'am, I hope Lynchburg is well supplied with string. Do you tell every woman that's the way to get a man—or get rid of one?"

"Why not, gazho? *You* ever try measure man's shadow with string, and him not know it? That can take a long time to do. In long time enough, man going to fall in love with *somebody*. Likewise, sometime man going to die. Give it time, string *always* works.''

"Hey, horse sojer," said Tim Trimm. "You axin' us questions, I want to ax you one. How come you don't wear a beard? Your sergeant does, and so does practic'ly every other sojer I've seen. You think your face is too pretty to cover up?''

Edge said equably, "Is that why you don't wear one?''

"Shit, no. Circus men don't grow beards 'cause they kin git caught in the riggin' or somethin'. Dangerous. One of these days, old Ignatz here is gonna git his walrus mustache snagged on that old lion's teeth. And you'll be in trouble, won't you, Dutchman?''

Roozeboom only shrugged his mustache. Edge said to him, "I hope, if you do get in trouble, the whole troupe doesn't think you're play-acting, like that trick with the bogus blood.''

"That's called gaffin' the act," Tim explained. "To give it a toot. A li'l extry flash and dash.''

Roozeboom chuckled. "Ven I was a jong, first learning, my old Baas he told me: de trick is not to piss, it is to make de foam.''

Edge laughed, too, and turned again to Tim. "Me, I shave my face so the fleas and lice will have one less place to roost.'' He added reminiscently, "All through the war, we had those daguerrian artists following us around with their camera boxes and cabinet wagons. Every time I'd see one of their pictures—of a bunch of heavy-bearded generals in war council or whatever—I'd wonder how in hell the generals sat still long enough for the man to catch their picture. I knew damned well they had to be itching and frantic to scratch.''

Tim said grudgingly, "There's one thing I gotta admit, sojer. You done some nice shootin' back yonder. Can you do that every time?''

"I don't know," Edge grunted. "I haven't had much experience shooting at toothpicks.''

He and Yount, having finished eating, emulated the others in the matter of disposing of their used implements. The wooden washtub—which had, in this one day, variously served as a washtub for persons and for soiled costumes, as a thing to be sat upon and as a ring prop for the elephant to perform on—was again right side up and full of river water, and the troupers swashed their dishes and cups around in it before giving them to Magpie Maggie Hag for more thorough scouring with sand. Edge and Yount then packed pipes and strolled about, smoking with great gratification. Yount paused where Hannibal sat, still eating, and asked him in all seriousness:

"Boy, do you really talk Hindu to that elephant of yours?"

Hannibal giggled and said, "Lawd, nossuh. 'Mile up' and 'tut' and them words, they jist circus-elephant talk I talks at ol' Peggy. Mas' Florian, he *tells* the rubes it be's Hindu, and they don't know no different. They ignernt."

"Oh," said Yount. "Then I reckon I am, too."

"Then we all are," said Florian, overhearing. "Hell, I don't even know if there is such a thing as a Hindu lingo."

"I'm surprised," said Edge. "In the little time we've known you, I've heard you spout at least three other languages. How many do you speak?"

Florian reflected, then said, "Fluently: French, German and American colloquial English. Well enough to get by: Dutch, Danish, Italian, Hungarian and Russian. That's what? Eight. Nine if you count the Latin I acquired at the lycée. Ten if you count Circus."

"Godamighty!" Yount exclaimed. "Why don't you dump the rest of this outfit and just charge people admission to admire *you?*"

"How did you come by so many?" Edge asked.

"Partly by accident of birth. I am from the Alsace, in the middle of Europe. Do you know it?"

"I know more or less where it is."

"To the west of it is the French Lorraine. To the east, the Duchy of Baden, which is a German-speaking land. They continually compete for the possession of Alsace, so we Alsatians grow up speaking both French and German, just in case. Meanwhile, the rest of the world never knows to whom the Alsace belong. Witness, you foreigners prefer to call our Alsatian sheep dog a German shepherd, and our Alsatian water dog a French poodle. Anyway, my knowing French enabled me fairly easily to pick up Italian. Knowing German made Dutch not difficult. As for the others, I was once married to a Danish woman, and another time to a Hungarian, and yet another time to a Russian. If there's any better way to learn a language than pillow talk, it's mutual vituperation.''

Yount murmured, ''Well, I'm damned.''

''So was I, fluently and frequently. Speaking of Europe, how did you enjoy playing the British Grenadier, Zachary?''

''Well, I had determined that I wouldn't even speak of it, for fear that I would get to cussing, but since you broach it . . . For one thing, grenadiers don't shoot pistols. They throw grenades.''

''Is that a fact? Yes, of course. I was being 'ignernt.' Thinking the word signified a corps d'élite. Well, I was sincerely trying to do you proud.''

''I'd be more gratified if you didn't do it again. This time, since you hadn't given me any advance notice— whether you truly wanted to commit suicide—I wasn't sure whether to oblige you or not.''

''Come, come. I had every confidence in your marksmanship. Are you suggesting that I was in some peril?''

''Not just some. It's a good deal easier to shoot a man than deliberately *not* to shoot him. Even if I were the world's champion pistolero, my first round might be a badly cast or badly seated ball that could go slewing off sideways. Now, a miss wouldn't matter much if I was shooting to *hit* a man; I've still got five more rounds to plug at him. But if I'm deliberately aiming left, where you held the torch, and that bad ball chances to go right . . .''

''Good heavens,'' Florian said faintly, looking at Edge's holster with new respect and some misgiving. ''But—heh

heh—it did not, after all. And you did shoot straight. You hit the flame."

"I didn't have to. Any wind would blow it out, and that's all I shot—a puff of wind. Obie pulled the ball while you were introducing Colonel Fancy-Pants."

"But—but there are professional shootists. If a gun can't be trusted . . ."

"Oh, this one's trustworthy. Remington 1858, calibre forty-four, six-shot percussion. None better among handguns. I was talking about the loads. If I were a trick shooter, I'd make damn sure about the loads beforehand. That is, if I was notified beforehand that I'd be called on to do some trick shooting."

"Yes, yes. See your point. Foolish of me . . . impetuous . . ." to take Edge's sardonic eye off him, Florian pointed at the pistol again and asked, "Standard issue, that?"

"To the Yankees," said Yount, with a snort. "All *we* was issued was permission to go and snatch any that we could."

"And you did."

"More than once," Edge said dryly. "The first pistol I took from a Yank was the Colt forty-four. But it doesn't have the top-brace across the cylinder, and it begins to feel loose and rickety after a while. So next I went for a Yankee that had one of these."

"I'd think any forty-four would do to stop a man in his tracks. But I couldn't help noticing: that carbine on your saddle is bored like a young cannon."

"Fifty-eight calibre. That's for stopping a charging *horse* in its tracks."

"Ah, of course. Another bequest from the Yankees?"

"No, that one's pure Confederate. Made by the Cook brothers down in New Orleans. Well made, too."

The talk of the tools of his trade appeared to have mellowed Edge's mood, so Florian dared to say, "I realize I pulled a low trick on you, Zachary, but the audience was clearly pleased with your impromptu performance. And you brought it off with admirable savoir-faire. Are you really going to carry a grudge about it?''

Edge made a sour face, looked over at the Big Top and finally said, ''Oh, hell, I reckon it wasn't too mortifying.''

''Well, then!'' said Florian, with a gusty sigh of relief, but he did not pursue the matter. ''Tell me, what is the next nearest town of any size?''

''There purely ain't any,'' Yount put in. ''Not this size, not in this end of Virginia. Lynchburg's the third biggest in the state, and the other two are 'way over east in the Tuckyhoe country.''

Edge said, ''If you want to take the shortest way north, up this piedmont side of the mountains, Charlottesville is the next town big enough to fill a shirttail. Or you can go north up the valleys, and the nearest town will be Lexington, where Obie and I are headed. But that's fifty or so miles from here, and westward beyond the Blue Ridge.''

''A two-day run, and over the mountains,'' mused Florian. ''If we were to go where you're going, friends, could we still have the loan of your horses and your companionship on the way?''

Edge and Yount exchanged glances and said they wouldn't mind.

''Then that's preferable to the easier route without your animals to help,'' said Florian. ''We'll go with you to Lexington.''

''We'd figured on going tomorrow,'' said Edge.

''Yes. Tomorrow. We'll start the teardown right now.''

''You don't give any night show?'' Yount asked. ''Seems to me that other circuses do that.''

''In big cities, and when we have lights enough, Obie, we do, too. But never in farm country. Folks have to get up at cockcrow, so they go to bed early. And this may be a city of some size, but it's still a farm town full of farm folk. And I rather suspect that we already have milked the town for all it's worth.''

''I ought to warn you,'' said Edge. ''Lexington is only a little college town, and it got raked over by General

Hunter's Yankees less than a year ago. Poor pickings for you, I'd estimate.''

"A college town. I assume that's where you intend to settle down as a schoolmaster. Where your military academy is.''

"Was. VMI and Washington College, too. David Hunter looted and burned them both. The rest of the town exists only to peddle goods to the professors and cadets and students, of which there likely are not any, so the whole place may be deserted. It could turn out that *I'm* foolish in heading there, but I'm not responsible for a herd of other people dependent on me. You are.''

"Ah, well. One must have a destination, however illusory or—what's that?'' They had been interrupted by a thrumming, strumming sound. It went on, at first just a disorganized jangling, but then resolving itself into an attempt at music.

''Look yonder,'' said Yount. ''It's the idjit. He found that busted banjo you took in today.''

"Not only found it,'' said Florian. ''He's playing. Like he knows how.''

They walked over to where the Wild Man sat on the ground, his back against a wagon wheel. Without missing a stroke, he looked up and gave them a looselipped grin, his tongue protruding through it.

"Listen,'' said Florian. ''You can make out what he's playing, by damn!''

"Uh-huh. 'Lorena,' '' said Yount. ''And not too bad, with only half the strings. Lucky one of 'em is the thumb string.''

Florian knelt and stopped the Wild Man's hands momentarily, gave him an encouraging nod, then whistled to him the first few bars of ''Dixie Land.'' The idiot listened, gave an even more sloppy grin and began to pluck and strum the identical notes.

"Oh, hell,'' said Yount. ''Every least nigger knows 'Lorena' and 'Dixie.' ''

Florian stopped the young man's hands again and whistled something that neither Edge nor Yount could name. The Wild Man again listened and immediately played the same melody.

Florian straightened up, with a look of mixed triumph and awe. "Not many Negroes know that one. 'Partant pour la Syrie.' "

"What?" said Yount.

"The French anthem. Well . . . I've heard of such things, gentlemen, but he's the first I ever encountered. An idiot savant."

"And what's that?"

"What you're looking at. And listening to." The Wild Man was playing that scrap of anthem over and over. "An idiot totally devoid of intellect and capability, except in one area where inexplicably he excels—without ever having been taught, and probably without having the least notion of what he's doing. Sometimes it's mathematics— an idiot savant can do sums and calculations that would confound a whole roomful of professional accountants. With this one, it's music." Florian lifted his hat to scratch his head. "By holy Hades, I thought I was humbugging, but I bet the scientists *would* like to get hold of him. We could ask a substantial price . . ."

"We-ell," Yount said thoughtfully, "I don't know about scientists. But if there's colleges and professors in Lexington . . ."

Florian bounded erect and snapped his fingers. "You've hit it, Obie! So! We have a destination and a reason for going there. Zachary, we'll give your VMI first bid on the creature."

"Jesus! I go back to my old alma mater bearing an idiot for sale. Mr. Florian, you are determined to mortify me, aren't you?"

But Florian didn't hear; he was striding off, alternately blowing ear-splitting blasts on his new whistle and shouting names: "Hotspur! Abdullah! Roulette! Hop to teardown. We're blowing the stand early in the morning."

"Reckon I'll lend a hand," said Yount. "You, Zack?"

"Oh, hell. I reckon."

The teardown was pretty much the setting up done in reverse order, except that it went a good deal faster, even in the now near-totally dark night. Magpie Maggie Hag, Sarah and Clover Lee all got lanterns from the wagons, lit them and went inside the Big Top to hold and aim them while the men bent to their work. That commenced with the dismantling of seats. Gathering up the unfastened bench planks was a quicker job than laying them in place had been, and so was the knocking loose of the sapling jacks and the toe pegs and the notched stringers they supported.

Edge found this operation more interesting than the daytime work had been, simply because every person and every thing looked somehow larger and grander in the dim lamplight than in the radiance of forenoon. The lanterns held by the women threw the shadows of men and equipment up onto the sidewalls and the canvas ceiling high above, making them gigantic and black and almost mysterious in the swift, well-practiced movements they made.

When the last of that lumber had been hauled out and stacked in the property wagon, all the men and women vacated the tent to work outside. The moon had not yet risen, but the lamplight made things even more eerie than moonlight would have done. The night's slight chill was bringing up a ground mist, so the lanterns threw not beams but a diffused, foggy, dreamy sort of light—and it was given a fairy flutter by the hordes of moths that followed the lanterns around and flickered like sparks detached from them and added their twinkling little shadows to the greater ones the lanterns flung about. Every man cast a tremendously long and attenuated shadow, either high on the tent's roof or from his feet across the lot into the far distance where the shadow was absorbed into the night, and when he walked the long shadows of his legs scissored like an immense, black, insubstantial pair of shears trying to trim the lamplit weeds off the lot.

Tim again shinnied up one of the poles, then clambered

up the billowy slope of the Big Top, along one of its seams, to undo the lashings with which he had secured the bail ring at the top of the center pole. And he slid down again, and again into Roozeboom's waiting arms. Meanwhile, Hannibal had put the leather collar on the elephant and was leading her around the staked perimeter of the pavilion's side ropes, followed by Clover Lee carrying a lantern. They stopped at each stake, Hannibal whisked around it a loop of the rope attached to Peggy's collar, the elephant merely leaned back and the stake—which three strong men had sledgehammered three feet deep in the ground—came up and out as if it had merely bobbed up from underwater, and they moved on to the next one.

Florian picked up one of the removed stakes and judiciously examined its pointed end, its arm-thick length and its hammer-splayed top end. "I suppose they'll do for a while longer," he said, as if to himself. But Yount was working nearby and threw him a questioning look. Florian explained:

"We usually cut new staubs every year, while we're in winter quarters, and we cut them five feet long. By the end of a season of setups and teardowns, they'll have worn down to useless nubbins. In Wilmington there weren't any new ones to be had, but there it didn't matter, because we weren't moving. Now—you see—these staubs have already been beaten down to some four feet long. I must remember to keep a lookout for every good stand of saplings where we can cut new ones."

Yount nodded solemnly and went back to what he was doing, which was helping Roozeboom and Rouleau to unrope and unpeg the sidewall sections of canvas, and roll them up and lug them to the tent wagon. But suddenly all work stopped as Florian blew another commanding blast on his new whistle. All over the lot, the men and women paused in their several occupations and looked to him, puzzled.

"Lads and ladies," Florian called. "You're all toiling away as morosely as if this were season's end. But we've had a straw stand, and we're on the road again tomorrow for new horizons. Why aren't we hearing a good rousing heeby-weeby?''

He blew the whistle again and waved his arms like a choral director. The troupers all laughed and, as they went back to their chores, began chanting:

> Heeby, weeby!
> Shaggid, taggid, braggid,
> Maggie *moo*-long!

''If that's a work chantey,'' Edge said to Florian, ''it's one I never heard before.''

''You'll hear it from the canvasmen on the ropes, some version of it, every time a circus sets up or tears down. A prosperous circus, that is. These poor folk haven't had much esprit de corps for a long time. But maybe today marks the start of better times—and higher morale. Maybe from now on they'll sing without my prompting.''

Right now, anyway, they were repeating the chantey, over and over, in unison, and seeming to do it cheerfully. Edge listened closely, but finally said, ''I give up. What are the words?''

Florian sang along with them, but carefully articulating:

> Heave it, weave it!
> Shake it, take it, break it,
> Make it *move* along!

Edge took it up himself and, chanting, went back to what he had been doing, which was helping Tim Trimm undo the guy ropes from the uprooted ''staubs,'' then flicking the loop ends of the ropes of the top spikes of the side poles, then neatly coiling the ropes. As they progressed around the guys, Tim also gave the side poles a kick, so they fell outward from under the tent roof eaves, but he left every sixth pole unkicked and upright. So, by the time the workers and the elephant had gone once around the pavilion, there was nothing left of the Big Top except the center pole and the tent roof depending from that to the few remaining side poles—a roof no longer trimly conical but sagging in wrinkled scallops from its high peak. Hannibal ran into the darkness under it and emerged with a single rope end. He stood holding it and looking alertly at Florian.

"Everybody clear?" called Florian. Then he put his whistle to his mouth and blew once more. Hannibal yanked his rope end. It evidently loosed some crucial hitch or warp among the many ropes and pulleys of the center pole, because the bail ring came with a rasping rush down the length of that pole, and the whole vast extent of roof canvas came with it. Everybody standing around felt the swoosh of wind from under it, and was pelted with blown dust, grit, bits of weed, straw and paper and other trash left by the audience. The tremendous canvas continued to belly and billow as it settled, and its eave edges fluttered quietly against the ground as the trapped air sighed out.

Edge and Yount followed the other men as they ran onto the canvas—being careful to step only on the lapped-together edges of the several sections—tramping down the last pocket of air. Still chanting the heeby-weeby, they quickly undid the ropes at the bail ring where all the canvas pie-slice points converged, then undid the lengths of the seams down to the eave edges. They did not bother to unlace the ropes from the grommets one by one, as they had so painstakingly laced them together, but simply pulled a rope end so it whipped out of a series of grommets in one yank.

"But don't pull *too* fast," Rouleau cautioned Edge. "In dry weather the friction could set the rope afire. Or the whole canvas."

When the sections were all separated, the men rolled them into bundles and tied them with the ropes that had just been removed. There remained only the center pole, standing rather precariously now, supported only by the spike in the gumshoe base. Hannibal again brought Peggy, attached her collar to one rope, the men took hold of another and—at Florian's whistle and shout of "Lower away!"—they tugged (*"Heeby!"*) to bring the high pole tilting to one side. On its other side, Peggy took the weight as it leaned (*"Weeby!"*) and moved to let it gently down toward the ground, the gumshoe careening over with it. When it was down (*"Shaggid!"*) Roozeboom ran to pry the gumshoe spike out of the pole's interior. Rouleau quickly (*"Taggid!"*) took off all the pole's pulleys and ropes and coiled them. Then (*"Braggid!"*) all the men combined their strength to slide the separate sections of the pole out of the uniting metal sleeves. When all the bundles of canvas, pieces of pole, pulley blocks and coils of rope (*"Maggie MOO-long!"*) had been stowed in the tent wagon, nothing remained of the Big Top except the heaped-up circle of the earthen ring curbing.

The cooking fire was only embers now, but sufficient for Magpie Maggie Hag to warm up the pot of parched-peanut coffee and give everyone a restorative mug of it. She and some of the men lit up pipes and passed around one of the jugs of moonshine, and Peggy got a chew of tobacco. Then they all jumped as Florian blew yet another whistle blast.

"Damn it all!" said somebody. "Wish you'd never got that gimmix."

"I was sounding curfew," said Florian. "Early day tomorrow."

He, Trimm, Roozeboom and Rouleau went to climb into their bunks in the prop wagon. Edge was unrolling his thin old pallet and blankets under that wagon—so were Yount, the Negro and the Wild Man—when a lantern shone over his shoulder and a voice sang softly at his ear a revised version of the ring song he had heard earlier:

As you sat in the circus and watched her go round,
    You knew that at you she was smiling . . .

He turned and looked up into Sarah's lamplit face. She grinned mischievously and whispered, "It's been *such* a good day, oughtn't we to celebrate?"

"Not much privacy here," Edge whispered back.

"We'll move 'way over by the railroad sheds. Combine our bedding."

So they went over there, made a bed, undressed and, after a while, Edge remarked, "Obie was right. He said you circus women are shameless."

"Oh? What have any of us done to shock Obie Yount? What in God's name *could* anybody do that would shock a sergeant of the horse cavalry?"

"He said something about Clover Lee undressing in front of him."

"For Christ's sake, this is the circus. We don't have any privacy, so we cultivate the good manners to ignore such things."

"What you call good manners, I suppose some people would call not very good morals."

"Let them, and be damned to them. Manners are a lot more important than morals."

"That's an interesting theory."

"It's not a theory, it's the plain truth. What you and I are doing right now, most people would consider immoral, but—"

"I wasn't *complaining*."

"—But we're doing it in private, where it can't possibly bother anybody. We people with bad morals don't parade them. But bad manners, why, they're right out in the open, where they can offend and upset everybody."

Edge said, "Then I don't know whether you'd consider this bad morals or bad manners, but I'll tell you something. When you were doing your act, up on that rosinback horse, and you did that backbend—where you curved all the way over backwards—you know what I was thinking then?"

"Hell, yes. I know very well," she said, pretending exasperation. "You gawks are all alike. Never admire the skill and grace and perfection of the pose. You just think *hey*, I never tried it in *that* position.''

''Well . . . I never did. Did you?''

''No. I doubt that anybody ever did. It's not exactly an easeful position for me alone. It ought to be damned uncomfortable for two.''

He said playfully, ''Let's find out.''

She laughed again, but eased out from under the covers and cast a wary glance over toward the distant circus wagons. The moon was up now; she could see nobody stirring. So she stood erect, naked, glowing in the moonlight, and easily arched over backward into a bow, her hands and feet on the ground.

''Well?'' she prompted, looking at him upside down.

''I'm admiring you,'' he said truthfully. ''Your skill and grace and perfection.'' In her backward-arched position, the uppermost part of her was her blonde little pubic escutcheon, and it gleamed in the moonlight like a night-blooming pale flower.

After a wary look about, Edge also got out of the bedding. There ensued a period of awkward movements, trials and retrials, whispers of encouragement and mumbles of frustration, and finally he confessed defeat. ''I reckon you're right. Nobody ever did.''

''One of us would have to be built different, or both of us,'' she said. ''Can we resume the old, tried-and-true ways?''

After another while, when they were resting, Sarah said, ''Now let me ask you something. Did you ever watch a klischnigg?''

''Jesus. I don't know. What is it?''

''Just another name for a circus posture-master, a contortionist. It's the word Florian uses. I think Klischnigg was the name of some old-time artiste. There are other names—india-rubber woman, human serpent, boneless lady. Anyway, it's a woman who does impossible wriggles and contortions with her body.''

''Then no, I never saw one. Why?''

"Well, now that I know your secret tastes"—she gave a mock-melancholy sigh—"when you meet a klischnigg, that's when I'll lose you."

He laughed at that, then said, "You'll still have Florian."

"I told you. If I'm nevermore to be wanted, I would like at least to be needed. He doesn't need me very often."

"Well, there'll be all those dukes and counts. They can probably buy everything they need. So, when you captivate one of them, you'll know he really wants you."

She sighed and said she would hope so. "But until then . . . as long as I'm needed . . ." and she burrowed close beside him, and after another while they went to sleep.

7

THOUGH IT was still very early, next morning, when the rockaway carriage lumbered off the lot and the other wagons followed, some of the local children were already "playing circus" in the abandoned earthen ring and the flattened weeds of what had been the Florilegium's pitch. Hannibal and the elephant again trailed at the end of the train, and the Negro kept running back and forth across the street, to peel off as many as he could of the pasted-up circus posters to keep for future use.

Florian said to Edge, on the seat beside him, "You overslept again," delicately not alluding to the fact that Edge and Sarah had come from the far margins of the lot just in time to partake of Magpie Maggie Hag's breakfast of cornmeal mush, preserved peaches and counterfeit coffee. "So you probably don't know—and I'll tell you, before you throw another tantrum about our cruelty to dumb animals—that I had Captain Hotspur shoot the other jackass and skin it out for Maximus. It also prevents our having to drag the poor creature over the mountains to no purpose."

"It also means," said Edge, "when Obie and I part

company with you folks, you'll have one heavy wagon with not even a single jackass to hitch to it.''

"Oh, I wasn't angling for sympathy—or charity. We can employ Brutus if nothing else offers. As I've said, I don't like to put a valuable bull in road harness. But, as always, we'll have to work things out as we go along.''

Florian was keeping to Lynchburg's less hilly riverside streets. The few adults abroad at that hour stared in surprise or waved familiarly as the train went past, and the many children abroad at that hour frisked and capered behind the elephant. They came to Seventh Street and the city's one rickety wooden bridge across the James. When they had crossed, and all the children turned back for home, Edge pointed for Florian to turn west along the River Road.

"If these were normal times,'' said Florian, as he turned the horse, "we'd be following a route sheet made up by our advance man, telling us two or three weeks ahead of time where to be on what date. He'd know the condition of the roads everywhere, and what kind of ground we'd find at every pitch—good, bad, tolerable. He'd know, in every factory town, exactly what day the workers get paid. In farm country, he'd know when the farmers are plowing or planting and couldn't take time off to see us. And he'd know when they get their harvest in, and how good a harvest, hence how much money the yokels would have in their pockets. He'd know any places ravaged by flood or drought, and he'd route us around them. He'd know every local law and license imposed, and he'd either comply with them or he'd do what we call patch. Useful word, patch. It covers every kind of means to cut red tape and dodge blue laws and save unnecessary expense or trouble. Our advance man would also know the route of every other circus and minstrel show and medicine show, so we wouldn't find ourselves going day-and-date against any rivalizing outfit.'' He sighed and repeated, "If these were normal times.''

"Well I'm sorry I can't do any of those things for you,''

said Edge. "I can only take you through the easiest pass
in those Blue Ridge Mountains yonder. It's called Petit
Gap, where the James flows through, and this road hugs
the river level a good part of the way. It has to skirt aside
and climb a little way up a mountainside here and there,
but none of those places is a rugged haul. If we don't stop
for any midday meal we ought to make the other side of
the mountains, where the North River runs into the James,
right about camping time."

The day was fair, with big whipped-cream clouds float-
ing about in an azure sky, and the scenery was splendid.
To the left of their way, the wide brown river slid majestically along, dividing now and again to accommodate a
green island in midstream. All around were the mountains
of the Blue Ridge, not craggy and forbidding peaks, but
gentle wooded swells and hollows and soft rounded ridges,
voluptuous as women's breasts and bellies and buttocks.
Any mountain near the road was all vivid green spring
foliage and colorful wild flowers. But when the vista
opened out so a mountain was visible at any distance, it
was an all-over soft, misty blue.

"It's not the distance that makes them look so," Edge
explained. "Of their millions of trees, maybe a third are
pines, all breathing out a mist of resin. It hangs in the air
and gives that pale blue tinge to everything."

The circus train made the fine day's journey with no
trouble—except once, briefly, when Tim Trimm, again
driving the museum wagon, got careless and let a hind
wheel drop into a narrow roadside ditch. For all Tim's
strenuous sawing back and forth, inching and pinching,
and turning the Blue Ridge bluer with his profanity, the
horse Bubbles could not hump the wheel out again. So
Hannibal brought Peggy up. She had only to lean her great
forehead against the wagon's back panel and give the mer-
est nudge to put the wagon back on the road.

When the mountain hollows began to fill with twilight
and a chilly mist began to rise from the river, Florian suggested to Edge that they could stop anywhere along here,

since there was ample camping space and wood and water. But Edge said to keep on, and before long his reason was clear. For they came out of the Blue Ridge into a verdant and hospitable valley, where the sun was just now setting beyond another mountain range far to the west, and the air was still warm and golden.

"The Valley of Virginia," said Edge, as the wagons wheeled into a riverside meadow. "To the south it's the valley of the Roanoke River, to the north the valley of the Shenandoah."

"It certainly is a pretty place," said Florian.

"Even the old-time Indians thought so. The Catawbas, the Onondegas, the Shawnees—they were all rival hunters, and usually at war with each other, but they made a treaty. They agreed that this valley was so almighty beautiful, so full of game and other good things, that they would all hunt here, but never fight here." He added somberly, "We white men didn't have such good sense."

"You have fought here?"

"Not on this precise spot. Down the valley, several times. All the way to Gettysburg in Pennsylvania, once. But long before that, I lived hereabout. This is Rockbridge County, and I was born just a few miles farther on from here."

"No, is that so? What's the name of your hometown?"

"It wasn't a town, just a place in the bottomlands, and it wasn't called anything but Hart's Bottom. The house is long gone, and my folks long dead. But I lived here in Rockbridge until I was seventeen or so. Worked in the Jordan iron furnaces and forges. You'll see them as we go along the North River yonder. That river used to have coal and ore bateaux forever going up and down it."

While the women gathered wood and lit a cooking fire, Roozeboom fed Maximus another chunk of jackass, then went about the wagons, examining all the horses' shoes, before the men unhitched them and turned them loose to graze and drink. Night had fallen by the time the troupers sat down to their own meal. But it was a balmy and starry night, and the meal was another good one: fried fish, corn-cakes, turnips and beans, with pickled melon rind for the sweet. The imitation coffee was getting low, so Magpie Maggie Hag decided to save that for the next day's breakfast. She found in the meadow some of the minty plant that the local folk called Oswego tea, and brewed up a pot of that. After supper, the men all lit up pipes and passed around one of the jugs of corn whiskey. Florian came to where Edge and Yount were sitting, and said, with a sigh of well-being:

"Yes, sir, Zachary, you picked a fine valley to be born in."

Yount grunted. "You won't think it so fine when you get a ways north of here. The whole damn valley, from about Staunton clear to the state line, was a wasteland last time we seen it, and that was only last fall."

"Big battle up there?"

"Big and plenty of 'em. But worse—the Burning. When the Devil and his inspector-general decided to relocate Hell in the Shenandoah Valley."

Florian cocked his head and said. "Setting conundrums, are you? I know Ulysses Grant is called the Devil. But I didn't think he had ever set foot in western Virginia."

"He didn't," said Yount. "He sent Little Phil."

"Now, that's Sheridan, am I right?"

Edge said, "The Shenandoah Valley was our army's commissary, so to speak. Grain, timber, garden truck, herds of cattle and sheep and horses. Grant sent Phil Sheridan to wipe it all out. We've even seen a copy of his actual orders; it said something like, 'Leave that valley so bare that even crows flying over it will have to pack their own rations.' And Sheridan did. That's why he's not so fondly known around here as the Devil's inspector-general."

Yount added, "But he didn't just grab the herds and the eatables. He burned the pastures and the forests, farm-houses and barns and mills. Left the *civilians* without roof or food or a rag to wear—old folks, women and children—

and with winter coming on. That wasn't a soldierly thing to do.''

"So you lads were among those who went to stop Sheridan?''

"Went to try,'' said Edge. "Lee sent every man he could spare. But the Yanks outnumbered us two to one, and they came armed with the new Henry repeater rifles. Obie and I were with the Thirty-fifth Virginia Cavalry in those days.''

"The Comanche battalion, we called ourselves,'' said Yount. "Never been whipped, not in any engagement during the whole war. Until then.''

"And how did that happen?'' Florian asked.

Both men went stony-faced, and looked away into the night, and were silent for a while. But then Edge hoisted the jug, and apparently found in it some resolution or consolation or absolution or something. He said grimly:

"Sans peur et sans reproche, that was the Comanche Battalion. Until last October, at a little stream called Tom's Brook, down the valley, near Strasburg. We were riding as part of the Laurel Brigade, advancing in support of some infantry moving against Custer's division. Then we were caught by flanking fire. That was no novelty; it never stopped us before; so there's just no explanation for what happened. Our advance became a retreat—no, a rout—running for the rear. What's worse, the whole Laurel Brigade *kept on running*—three or four miles from the fight—and there were no Yankees chasing.''

"Hell,'' said Yount. "Velvet-Suit Custer and his Yanks were busy, grabbing onto all our artillery pieces and supply wagons and caissons that had been left unprotected.''

"When the remnants of us finally got rounded up,'' said Edge, "our Colonel White called the roll. It didn't take him long. Company F had deserted entire, and the other five companies could muster, in total, about forty men and six officers. We'd started with a hundred and fifty men. In less than an hour, what had been one of the proudest cavalry outfits in the CSA had lost two-thirds of itself, and pissed all over its fine reputation, and demolished its morale beyond recovery. Those few Comanches who were left didn't want any more association with it. Colonel White did eventually put together a whole new Thirty-fifth out of replacements, but it was never again trusted to do anything worth mentioning. Meanwhile, we others got parceled out amongst other outfits. Obie and I were posted to Second Corps—over east, with the others of what were called Lee's Miserables, holding Petersburg against the siege.''

"Ah, well. The fortunes of war," said Florian, to put a merciful end to their recollected misery. Then he said, "What goes on here?" and stood up a little unsteadily, to ask, "Is something wrong with Maggie Hag?"

The gypsy had disappeared, and only Sarah and Clover Lee were cleaning up after the meal.

Sarah said, "Something's got her out of curl, yes. But I don't think she's taken ill. She all of a sudden mumbled that a bad thing was happening somewhere, and she would have to consult the spirits."

"Oh, Lord," said Florian. "Did she say *what* might be happening?"

"No, but I can vouch that she's consulting the spirits. You can almost smell them from here. She took one of your jugs into the wagon with her."

Florian flapped his hands helplessly. Since Edge and Yount still had possession of the other jug, he sat down with them again, and explained, "Mag has these spells every so often."

Yount asked, "She really got second sight? She ever see anything worthwhile?"

"Hard to say. Sometimes she suggests that we take some different road than the one we're on. And we always humor her, so of course we never know what might have happened on the other road." Florian took a long swig of whiskey, and changed the subject. "Tell me, Zachary. How did a hillbilly—such as you claim to be—manage to get an education and learn languages and wind up a field-grade officer, instead of remaining just another hillbilly bump on a log?''

Edge thought about it for a while before saying, ''Curiosity, mainly. I remember, when I was a boy, my papa used to sing me that song about 'The bear went over the mountain, to see what he could see . . .' It goes on for about twenty monotonous minutes, the bear climbing all the time, and finally it finishes, 'The bear got over the mountain, and all that he could see—' ''

'' 'Was the other side of the mountain,' '' said Florian. ''Yes, I've heard it.''

''Around here, folks take it for gospel. What's the point in going over the mountain, when there's nothing yonder but the other side of it? I didn't believe that. So it was mainly curiosity that took me away from here—and dissatisfaction, too. I wasn't eager to spend my whole life toiling in old John Jordan's ironworks. That's why, when the Mexican War came along, I went for a soldier. Cavalry, of course.''

''That was when me and Zack met up,'' Yount said proudly. ''On our way to Mexico.''

''Well,'' Edge went on, ''I didn't figure to toil my life away as a trooper, either. But I turned out to be good enough at it that our Colonel Chesnutt took notice of me. And, when the war ended, Jim Chesnutt very graciously drew up all the applications and recommendations to get me into VMI—as what they call a State cadet, meaning free tuition and board and uniforms and books and all.''

''Me, I just plugged along as a trooper,'' said Yount.

''Being a State cadet puts you under an obligation,'' said Edge. ''When you graduate, you have a choice: take a military commission as a second lieutenant or go off to some country school and teach for two years. So, when I got out in 'fifty-two, I put on the cavalry blue-and-yellow again and was sent out to the Kansas Territories.''

''And there at Fort Leavenworth,'' said Obie, ''me and him met up again.''

"Peacetime garrison duty?" said Florian. "Now that I *would* call drudgery."

"Not in the Plains, not in the fifties, hell no!" said Yount. "That was when the Territories came to be called Bleeding Kansas. All the border wars, you know—Pro-Slavers ag'inst Free-Staters. And whenever the wars simmered down, we could count on some kind of Mormon outrage against decency or some Injuns raiding an emigrant train that we'd have to go and make 'em sorry for."

"One of my fellow lieutenants out there was a fellow named Elijah White," Edge went on. "After a time, he retired from the army and came to Virginia to be a gentleman farmer. But when the War for Southern Independence started, Lije began raising his own company of Rangers for the Confederacy. It was about that time that I resigned my USA commission, and Obie his enlistment, so we came and joined Lije White. When his horse company was formally mustered into the CSA as the Thirty-fifth Cavalry. I got the grade of captain, with Obie as my troop sergeant. You know the rest. That's my life story. All resulting from curiosity—and dissatisfaction. Oh, and lot of luck, too."

Florian firmly shook his head. "Considering where you started from, you've come a good way, and I'd wager you'll keep on upward. But luck means the aces that life deals you. Everything that's come to you, Zachary, you went out and did it yourself, or earned it, or had the gumption to take it."

Edge said, with a straight face, "I wasn't being maidenly modest about the thundering success I've made of my life. Hell, anybody can step up and admire that for himself. How I've worked my way up from hillbilly obscurity to this pinnacle of being an unemployed soldier, on the brink of middle age, living on handouts along the road—and with all the rosy prospects of a Free Negro running for elective office in Mississippi." Then he dropped the sarcasm. "No, I was being honest about the luck. And grateful. One more war is over and done with, and I'm still alive. That's aces enough. Now, this jug is done, too, and I'm sleepy. Good night, gentlemen.''

The next day's journey, alongside the North River, was an even easier one for the circus train, because the road rose and fell in only undemanding grades over the valley's undulations. Magpie Maggie Hag rode inside the tent wagon, in her bunk and still nursing her jug, evidently still unstrung by whatever had spooked her the night before. The idiot rode strumming his banjo, playing over and over the last two tunes he had heard, regaling the countryside alternately with the national anthems of Dixie and France. That was enough to give notice of the train's approach to the few riders and other wagons they met on the road, but Florian, up front as always, was careful to call out, ''Hold your horses! Elephant coming!''

Once, when the road detoured a good distance from the river, as if deliberately to take every wayfarer through a glen floored with white and yellow crocuses and daffodils, walled and perfumed with lilacs, Edge idly mentioned to Florian, ''This is Hart's Bottom, and I was born over yonder.'' He indicated some crumbling stone foundations where once had been a house and maybe a barn or a stable. But he showed no inclination to stop and meditate on the scenes of his boyhood or commune with any lingering ghosts.

In midafternoon, the wagons crossed a log bridge over a smaller stream and then had to climb the one rather steep and very long hill on the day's route. From the top of it, they were looking out and down, across meadows and woods, at a tidy little town a couple of miles distant—neat brick business houses, pillared or porticoed residences and some rectitudinously tall and sharp church steeples—all clustered rather close together, considering how much empty land lay about.

''We're on top of Water Trough Hill,'' said Edge. ''It actually does have a spring and a trough down at the bottom, for the sake of the horses that make this pull. That's

Lexington yonder, and those jagged black things you can see on the near edge of it used to be the walls and towers of the VMI buildings. Out the other side of town, past the cemetery, there's a fairground that's probably the best place to pitch the circus, if we're allowed.''

They went down the hill, let the horses and the elephant thankfully take on water at the trough, then continued along the road and came to a mill dam and covered bridge of brand-new, yet unpainted wood. It took them across the North River and past the ruins of the military academy. As if the circus had been expected, all the local children immediately congregated to troop and dance along with it, or to run ahead crying warning of the elephant to everybody with a horse. The adult residents also collected on both sides of Main Street to watch the train's entrance—and these people were not dressed in everyday overalls and calico. The men wore hats and suits and even cravats; the women were in hooped skirts and flowered scoop bonnets—mostly old-fashioned clothes, and showing their age, but clearly the townfolks' best dress. Florian reined Snowball to a halt and tipped his own hat to a gentleman so respectably stout and fullbearded—the beard even scented with bay rum—that he had to be one of the town fathers. Florian politely inquired about the availability of the fairground for a circus performance on the morrow.

"Tomorrow!?" exclaimed the respectable man, as scandalized as if Florian had asked permission to undress and expose himself. "No such thing would ever be allowed on any Sunday, sir!''

"Oh, I do beg your pardon," said Florian, flustered. "I had been keeping track of the date, but not the day. We would never dream of profaning the Sabbath.''

"Not just the Sabbath, sir. Your calendar must be seriously out of kilter. Tomorrow is Easter Sunday.''

Edge said, "So it is. Palm Sunday was a week ago. Day of the surrender. We stacked arms on Monday. It seems longer ago than that.''

The respectable man went on, "Truly there is ample

reason for special jubilation and rejoicing tomorrow, as there has been today. But the celebration will be done devoutly and with dignity, not with theatrics. And in church, not in a circus tent.''

''Er . . . special rejoicing?'' Florian asked. ''Has something occurred, sir, that outshines the Resurrection?''

''Where *have* you been, man? The joyful news must be resounding up and down every road throughout Virginia. The despot Abraham Lincoln is dead!''

''What!'' blurted Florian. ''Why, he was younger than I am.''

''He did not die, sir, of natural causes. The government at Washington tried to contain the news, but every telegraph wire has been humming the day long. The tyrant was shot last night and died this morning.''

Florian rocked backward on the seat of the carriage. From inside it came the stunned gasp of the listening Coverley women. Edge breathed, appalled, ''Good God.''

''God *is* good, sir,'' said the respectable man. ''He helpeth those who help themselves. And it was about time, too, if I may say so without seeming to criticize the Almighty. The dispatches report that the perfidious Secretary Seward also was attacked last night, but his wound has not yet proved fatal. Wherefore the churches have been full all day, of supplicants praying that Mr. Seward may speedily go to join his—''

Edge cut him short, demanding, ''Do they know who did those outrages? Did they catch him?''

''Outrages, sir?'' said the man, raising his bristly eyebrows. ''If I mistake not, you wear Confederate gray.''

''That's why I'm anxious to know, damn it! Was it a southerner that shot Lincoln?''

The man said stiffly, ''Profanity uttered in public is a breach of the peace. And on Easter Eve—''

''Was it a Southerner?''

''One sincerely hopes so!'' the man barked back at him. ''The reports have been only fragmentary, but that is the assumption, yes. It would be a sad reflection on Southern manhood, sir, should the champion prove to be only some disaffected Yankee blackguard.''

"Why, you sanctimonious imbecile—!'' Florian jabbed a sharp elbow into Edge's ribs, and in the same motion flicked his reins to start the horse moving again, saying over his shoulder to the affronted and angry gentleman:

"We thank you, sir, for imparting the news. I have no doubt that everyone in our train will be joining tomorrow's churchgoers in their thanksgivings.'' They had left the man behind by then, and Florian turned to Edge. "You said you wanted to settle here. That's a fine way to court a welcome. What's the matter with you?''

"Settle here? If that pietistic old vulture was telling the truth—if Lincoln really is dead—there won't be *any* Southern place worth settling in.''

Florian said incredulously, "Surely you had no personal fondness for Father Abraham?''

"No. Are you as dense as that damned driveler we just talked to? If Lincoln is gone, there goes any hope of a soft peace. Especially if he was assassinated by a Southerner. That'll be the excuse for Stanton and Seward and all the other no-mercy men in Washington to trample and gouge the South, the way they've wanted to all along. And if that drunkard Johnson is President, he'll be just their pawn. Lincoln talked reconstruction. What we'll get now will be retaliation, revenge, reprisal.''

"Well, don't despair until we have more news. Maybe *everybody* in the Washington government is dead.''

"I'll ask around, see what I can get.'' Without waiting for Florian to pull up, Edge swung down from the rockaway seat. Inside the carriage, Sarah and Clover Lee looked shocked and pale as they rode past him. He waited in the street until the tent wagon came along, Yount on its driver's seat. Edge walked briefly alongside to shout the news up to him, adding, "I'm going to look for any old acquaintances I might be able to find. Learn more, if I can. Join you later at the fairground.''

That fairground and, next to it, the Presbyterian Ceme-

tery, occupied most of the crown of a small hill. When the
wagons turned onto it, everybody got down and looked
back the way they had come, where most of Lexington lay
spread out before them. On the town's farther side were
the black and broken remains of the buildings, barracks,
armory and magazine of the Virginia Military Institute.
Closer in, some once-fine residences were also burned-out
shells, and even some of the substantial brick business
buildings had holes in their roofs or chunks torn from their
walls.

"Done by General Hunter's cannonballs," said Yount.
"He bombarded the town for a while before he marched
in. Then he done the looting and burning—all of VMI, the
homes of some prominent people, the science building and
library of Washington College—which is what got him the
name of Vandal."

"Still, with all the damage," said Sarah, "Lexington is
a pretty place."

"Let us pray," said Jules Rouleau, with nonchalant ir-
reverence, "that the handsome town treats us handsomely."

It was well after dark when Edge got back to the circus.
He found the Big Top set up and faintly glowing with
lantern light inside, where the men were putting up the
seat stands. Florian emerged from there, saw Edge and
hurried to meet him, jerking a thumb to indicate the pavilion.

"Partly just to give the boys something to do. Partly to
advertise our presence in the town, since I don't want to
plaster posters around at such a time as this. Come and
eat, Zachary. Maggie is up and working again, she saved
you some supper. Have you learned anything more?"

"Yes," Edge said glumly. They went to the fire, and
all the rest of the troupe gathered to listen, solemn-faced.
Magpie Maggie Hag gave Edge a plate of beans and corn
bread, and he talked between forkfuls.

"I found a man I used to know: old Colonel Smith, who
was superintendent of VMI. He still is—what there is of

it to superintend. He's General Smith now, and I gather he gets to read all the telegraph reports of the scouts and spies that are still reporting. Lincoln is as dead as a wedge, that's certain, and it's a Maryland man to blame. But there seem to have been a number of others in it with him, all ex-Rebs or Rebel sympathizers."

"Just what you were afraid of," said Sarah.

"Yes. What it amounts to is that they've broken the word of honor of Robert E. Lee. A week ago, General Lee downed arms—no more killing. So did Grant—no more killing. And then, goddamn it, *one of us*, in the most cowardly way possible, shoots Abraham Lincoln in the back. I wish *I* could catch the son of a bitch. I guarantee you, he has made 'South' a dirty word—far dirtier than it ever was before. And I can also guarantee you, the whole South will suffer for that."

Florian said, "I take it your General Smith feels the same way you do. Not gleeful, like that lout we met on the street."

"Francis Smith has good sense. He even broke out a bottle of prime Monongahela rye—and he's no drinking man—so we could drink our condolences to the South. Thank God, not everybody in Virginia has the jackass mentality of a clodhopper or a counter-jumper."

"Rooineks, ve call such asses back home," Roozeboom said helpfully.

Clover Lee said, "Will you still be settling here, then, Mr. Zachary?"

"No, miss," Edge said, with a sigh. "I kind of hinted to General Smith that I could be coaxed back to VMI, but he threw cold water on that." He looked around at the troupe. "You know what he told me? He said this state isn't even the Commonwealth of Virginia any more. From now on, officially, this is nothing but Federal Military District Number One, and it'll be under an appointed governor, and probably under martial law."

"Ça va chier dur!" exclaimed Rouleau. "We'd better

get north in a hurry, then, before we're trapped. Be worse getting stuck here than in Wilmington.''

Yount said, ''But Zack, none of that ought to interfere with schoolteaching—what you figgered on doing.''

Edge gave a wry laugh. ''The Institute may survive, but it'll be one hell of a long time before it can call itself a military school, or its students cadets—or teach them military subjects, or dress them in uniform again. No, General Smith and the other remnants of the faculty are going to have a hard enough time fending for themselves. They don't need any added handicaps, like me.'' He said sardonically to Florian, ''And they won't be wanting your idiot savant, either.''

''What *will* you do, Zachary?''

''Well, General Smith says a lot of ex-Rebel officers are going to Mexico, to fight for or against Maximilian, whichever side will hire them. But, hell, I've already served a hitch south of the border.'' He looked up from his plate of beans. ''Europe sounds better all the time. If your offer still holds, Mr. Florian, you've got yourself a shootist.''

''Well, now!'' said Florian, with vast delight.

''And a strongman,'' said Yount. ''And two good horses.''

''Well, now!'' Florian said again. ''Welcome, gentlemen!''

''Welkom, meneers,'' said Roozeboom.

''Bienvenue, mes amis,'' said Rouleau.

''Bater, gazhe,'' said Magpie Maggie Hag. ''You now first-of-May.''

Yount said, ''It's still April, ma'am.''

''First-of-May is circus language,'' Florian said jovially. ''Meaning any new recruit or temporary performer. Because we can get plenty of would-be's in clement times, when the season is well along, but only real troupers hit the road while the weather is still chancy. You yourselves will soon be greeting other newcomers as 'first-of-Mayers.' ''

''Well, you can consider me as green as any new recruit," said Edge. "I may be a veteran at shooting, but I've never done it theatrical style. You're going to have to show me what part you want me to play."

"Me, too," said Yount.

"Gladly, gladly," said Florian. "But start by getting the terminology correct. Only actors *play*. Circus artistes work. We'll commence lining out an act for each of you as soon as—"

But he was interrupted. Six or seven soberly dressed townsmen came onto the fairground just then, and expressed a desire to have a private conversation with the owner of the establishment. So Florian and they went off to one side of the Big Top and talked long and earnestly. Then there was a lot of handshaking all around, the gentlemen departed and Florian came back to the fire, looking pleased.

"Fortune continues to smile upon us. Or perhaps I should say Providence—even Heaven—since those gentlemen were all preachers. Inasmuch as our pavilion will not be in use tomorrow, they have requested the loan of it for an ecumenical tent meeting."

Most of the troupers made exclamations of surprise or inquiry, but Tim Trimm said sourly, "Something smells fishy. I bet I've been saved in every kind of church there is. And there ain't no such a church as Ecumenical."

"The word means all-embracing, Tim. Various different sects getting together for a special occasion. This occasion being, of course, the spectacular coincidence of Easter and the assassination. The pastors expect to have a big turnout tomorrow."

"There's churches all over this town," Trimm persisted. "Why do they need a circus top?"

Florian said patiently, "True, the established sects all have quite imposing edifices. But the men who came calling are the pastors of congregations not so well endowed. They meet in each other's front parlors or empty shops or whatever. Adventists, Dunkers, Evangelicals, Quimbyists, Premillenarians—I forget what all of them are. But they expect an attendance tomorrow that would strain any of their facilities. So they asked for our Big Top, to accommodate a day-long, maybe even night-long service, one congregation after another. Possibly overlapping, truly ecumenical.''

''And you said *yes?*'' Sarah asked incredulously. ''A rock-ribbed unbeliever like you?''

''My rock ribs enclose a gut, Madame Solitaire, just like the gut of the most devout, which requires occasional nourishment. Those services will each conclude with an offertory. I asked a rental fee of half the take. They proposed one-quarter. We compromised on one-third.''

''Don't count on a largesse that will bulge your rock ribs,'' said Rouleau. ''Not if I know those fence-corner cults.''

''They won't make us wealthy, no,'' said Florian. ''But it beats having a Big Top full of nothing but air.''

Yount said hopefully, ''Well, whether it brings in much money or not, a nice religious service ought to lend the tent some holiness.''

At that, all the troupers laughed, and Clover Lee said, ''Mr. Obie, if that canvas gets any holier, it won't keep off the dew.''

''No matter,'' said Magpie Maggie Hag, addressing Edge. ''I told you already, gazho, la tienda es un tabernáculo. Soon you *abide* in tabernacle.''

''Yes,'' said Florian. ''Let us to bed now, and tomorrow—Zachary, Obie—we shall commence the making of you into artistes. *Artistes*, my lads!''

8

IN THE morning, the circus women made use of the pump and troughs provided by the fairground to wash every piece of costume and spare clothing the show owned, including a quantity that had been long laid away in the

property wagon's trunks, so the new artistes Edge and
Yount would have articles from which to assemble costumes of their own. Roozeboom strung a line, zigzagged
back and forth between the tent wagon and the prop
wagon, where the wet clothes were hung to dry. They
made a spectacle of variegated color and glitter in the April
sunshine: spangled léotards, diaphanous skirts, flesh-tinted
tights, garish tailcoats and frock coats, faded drawers and
combinations and stockings and an assortment of underwear, including the little trusses called cache-sexe.

Then Sarah and Clover Lee dressed in what Sunday-best
civilian clothes they owned—outdated bonnets and gowns
so old they were stiffened with crinolines instead of hoops,
but the Coverleys looked surpassingly pretty in them—and
went off to Easter services at the massive stone Presbyterian church just across the cemetery beyond the fairground.
Most of the men also donned clothes nattier than overalls
and also went to church: Trimm to the Baptist, Roozeboom
to the Methodist, Rouleau to the Episcopal—that being the
closest thing to Roman Catholic in Lexington—and even
Hannibal went seeking a black congregation of some de-
nomination.

By that time, the first tent-meeting pastors had arrived
at the fairground, bringing in a wagon a portable rostrum
and lectern and even a small footbellows organ to place
inside the Big Top. Shortly afterward, the worshippers began coming, on horseback, afoot, in a variety of vehicles.
Long before the preachers had drawn straws to determine
who would lead off, the Lexington fairground was much
more crowded than the Lynchburg circus lot had been.
Though the people were of various religious persuasions,
they seemed to have come not only to hear their particular
preachers, but to stay through the services of all the others.

Florian kept the museum wagon shuttered and the lion
wagon and the elephant positioned out of sight on the far
side of the pavilion, so they should not be savored by the
nonpaying public, but he could not very well chain up the
Wild Man all day. Anyway, the idiot wasn't wearing his

smudges and tattered furs, so he was given his banjo and
bidden only to stay out of people's way. That satisfied him
just fine. He went and sat outside the tent on its far side.
Every time the organ inside laid out a hymn, he had only
to hear the first couple of bars and, about simultaneous
with choir or congregation breaking into song, he would
start to strum—in perfect tune and time—so he was an
addition to the music, not a distraction.

While the townsfolk and folk from the countryside all
around continued to come from Main Street across the fairground and into the tent, Florian, Edge, Yount and Magpie
Maggie Hag sat together in the shade of the tent wagon.

"Maggie is our wardrobe mistress and chief seam-
stress," said Florian. "But before we talk about what dress
we'll put you into, let's talk about what you're each going
to do. You first, Zachary. Now, you have a sabre, a carbine
and a pistol . . ."

"There's not a lot I can do with the sabre, all by myself."

"You can whip it out as you ride in during the opening
spec, and wave and flash it about."

"All right. Then, the carbine, it's only single shot. So
most of my act will have to rely on the pistol."

"I've never owned a six-shooter. I'd be obliged if you'd
explain the workings of that thing."

Edge took it from his holster. "It loads just like that old
buggy rifle of yours, except that you load these short
chambers in the cylinder, so you don't have to shove powder and wad and shot down the whole length of a barrel.
You start by pouring your powder charge into the opening
of each chamber."

"Since I don't imagine you got instructions from its
Yankee owner, how did you find out how much to pour?"

"When I first got the gun, I worked out the best load
by firing over snow."

"Over snow?" Florian and Magpie Maggie Hag said
together.

"Stood in a snowbank and kept firing, using a little

more powder each time. When I saw unburned specks of black powder on the white snow, I knew I was overloading, so I cut back to the proper load.''

"Ingenious," said Florian.

"But now, for performance shooting inside that tent, I figure to use only a light charge of powder. Just enough to give me reach and accuracy, but not enough that the ball will keep on going full range."

Yount said, "So as not to bring down somebody's cow off beyond the lot."

"Next," said Edge, "I put a lead ball here on the opening of the cylinder chamber. The ball is just a hair bigger than that hole, so now I unlatch this rod from under the barrel. It swings down and—you see?—it's a lever pushing this plunger set here in the frame. The plunger seats the ball well inside the chamber, just like a ramrod. When you've got charges and balls inside all six chambers, you pinch a percussion cap onto each of these six nipples around the back of the cylinder. Then cock the hammer and pull the trigger, and it shoots. Exactly like your rifle, only here each cocking of the hammer brings a new chamber around, and you've got six shots before you have to reload again. I always—after loading—I always let the hammer down easy, so it rests between two of the nipples. Prevents it going off until I want it to."

"A beautifully made piece of machinery," said Florian. "It's even an elegant thing to look at." He stood up. "Excuse me one moment. There really are so many people, and still coming, I'd better go and see how the seats are holding out."

Yount strolled with him, and they peered around the front door opening of the Big Top. The tiered planks were close to capacity, mainly occupied by old folks, hoopskirted women and girl children. Since there had been no ring built, the younger men and boys sat on the ground around the rostrum. The crowd had just finished singing, to organ and banjo accompaniment, "Shall We Gather at the River?" They were now settling back, spangled with roundels of sunlight from the holes in the canvas overhead, to hear the preacher say:

"Brothers and sisters, this has been a month of Sundays. Just two Sundays ago, we got the dreadful news that General Lee's lines in the east had broken, that our President and Cabinet and Congress were refugeeing from Richmond and abandoning our capital city to the enemy. A week later, only last Sunday, we got the even more terrible news that General Lee was surrendering his entire Army of Northern Virginia. The noble war against Northern tyranny was ending here in the Old Dominion, and our gallant Confederacy would soon be no more."

The people moaned and there were a few sobs. The preacher raised his voice, and his tone rose from somber to exultant.

"Those were the darkest Sundays in many a year, but today is a brighter one. For this day, this Easter Sunday, while we sing hosannah that the Christ Jesus has risen from the tomb, we can also praise the Lord because Satan's chief emissary on this earth—known while he was here as Ape Lincoln—has been gathered back to the brimstone pit he came from! Yea, brethren and sistern, the old Ape is in Hell now, pumping thunder at three cents a clap!"

The people chorused, "Amen!" with fervor.

Florian said, "Obie, do you really think that kind of blather is going to make our pavilion holier? I'll be satisfied if the deity doesn't send down a lightning bolt and tear it all to shreds."

They returned to the tent wagon, and Florian said, "Let us look over the garments the ladies washed and hung up. See if anything give us any ideas on how you lads might best perform."

Magpie Maggie Hag pointed among the array of haberdashery and suggested, "Leather jerkin?"

"Hm, a leather jerkin," said Florian. "Zachary, how about you doing William Tell's Triumph Over Gessler the Tyrant?"

"And who's to be the boy with the apple on his head?"

Edge asked. "Tiny Tim? The Wild Man? Which can you spare? Mr. Florian, even a crack shot is going to shoot a little low once in a while."

Magpie Maggie Hag pointed again and suggested, "Feathers?"

Florian said, "Yes, there's that feather cloak that Madame Solitaire hasn't used for a long while. We could pluck some plumes, fashion a feather headdress. You wouldn't need anything else but a simple loincloth . . ."

"Jesus. If you're going to rig me out as a redskin, why don't I save on lead and powder? Throw some tomahawks."

"Ah! Splendid! Could you do that?"

"No."

Florian sighed. "Oh, well. I suppose it's best that we go back to my original conception. Colonel Deadeye? Colonel Ironsides? Colonel Ramrod? That's it! That's a good one. Will you settle for being Colonel Ramrod, Zachary?"

"In a uniform?"

"Well, not that one you're wearing. You'll need that for street clothes. But we acquired quite an assortment of uniform pieces in Lynchburg. Mag, you can put together something dashing, can't you, and dye it?"

Edge asked, "Purple, like Hotspur's? I'd almost rather wear Yankee blue."

"No, gazho," said Magpie Maggie Hag. "Indigo and berry all I had, then. Now I give what color you like. Yellow? Orange? Black?"

"Black and yellow," Florian answered for him. "That sounds dashing, indeed. And while you're at it, Mag, cut up one of those vest-and-drawers combinations for Obie here. Cut it like a caveman's fur piece—you know, one shoulder strap, rest of the chest bare—and use the same dyes. Color it yellow with black leopard spots."

"Hot damn!" said Yount, grinning and thumping his chest in what he supposed was a caveman manner. "Here comes the Quakemaker!"

"Now, about your props," Florian said. "Something hefty."

"I already got some," Yount said proudly. He reached inside the tent-wagon door and yanked. One after another, three immense iron cannonballs rolled out and thudded heavily on the ground.

"Bless my soul," said Florian.

"Shells for the Yankee's ten-inch Columbiad," said Yount. "The leavings of General Hunter, no doubt about it. They burned out without exploding, or maybe they was never charged. Forty-eight pounds apiece, which is hefty enough for a strongman to play with. But if we plug up them loading-and-fuse holes, folks won't realize they're holler. They'll look like pure solid iron and a damn sight heavier than they really are."

"Where did you find them?"

"Right yonder in the graveyard. There was a heap of fourteen, piled up nice and neat. I figgered three would do me for—"

"Christ, Obie!" said Edge. "They were a monument over Stonewall Jackson's grave."

"Is that a fact?"

"He's buried right here. It's probably the most sanctified spot in Rockbridge County."

"Is that a fact? Well, if I was Stonewall, I'm damned if I'd want a pile of Vandal Hunter's cannonballs laying on my belly."

Florian said, "Just don't let any of the townfolk see them until performance time tomorrow. Then we'll be decamping before they can realize where the balls came from."

"How *do* I perform with them?" asked Yount. "Juggle 'em, like Hannibal? I'd fall down as dead as General Jackson."

"Captain Hotspur will have some ideas. He has doubled as a strongman in his time. And here he comes now."

Roozeboom, Rouleau and Trimm had returned together from their separate churches. Rouleau threw a disapproving look at the Big Top and said, "Merde alors, Florian. What are your pet preachers doing in there? You can damned near hear that one downtown."

They all listened. A minister of one of the less temperate sects was now bellowing, "The Beast of Revelation, that's what Abraham Lincoln was! It says right here in Revelation thirteen, *'And there was given unto him a mouth speaking great things and blasphemies.'* And didn't Lincoln blaspheme, brothers and sisters? Didn't he utter the abominable Emancipation Proclamation?"

Response: "Lay it out, brother!"

"Look again at chapter thirteen. *'And it was given unto him to make war with the saints.'* And didn't he make war against us? Against all our sainted beliefs and traditions and Southern virtues?"

Response: abysmal groans.

"*'And he had power to give life unto the image of the beast.'* What that refers to, brethren, was Lincoln lettin' loose the black savages from their rightful masters!"

"Kushto," murmured Magpie Maggie Hag.

"Rooineks," grunted Ignatz Roozeboom.

Edge asked, "Are the more orthodox churches ranting like these gospelgrinders?"

"They're not exactly grieving that Mr. Lincoln is dead," said Rouleau. "But the Episcopalians at least are lamenting the fact the he was *shot* dead."

"That reminds me," said Florian. "Zachary, I once saw a shootist who shot little glass globes all to splinters as his assistant threw them high in the air."

"He must have been a wizard marksman."

"Not really. The audience thought he was firing balls, but he had actually loaded his rifle with bird shot. If we can find something for an assistant to toss up, could you smash that with your carbine?"

"Using bird shot, even the Wild Man could do it. But I don't have any. Bird shot is not standard issue ammunition in the cavalry."

"No problem there. I've got some."

"But won't the audience wonder how it is that I'm not punching a new hole in the tent roof every time I fire the carbine?"

"Audiences don't cavil when they're overcome with admiration. Very well, that will be the carbine part of your act. Clover Lee can assist. Here are the Coverley ladies now. And I had another idea—remembering how you shot out that flame the other night. Clover Lee, my dear, would you stand still while Zachary shoots his pistol at you and you catch the ball in your teeth?"

"*What?*" Edge exclaimed.

"That old chestnut?" said the girl, without concern. "How about a variation? Let Ignatz catch it in his mustache."

"Captain Hotspur is not a pretty girl. No audience is going to tremble for fear he'll get a hole bored through his head."

"Now see here—" Edge protested.

"Calm down, Zachary," said Sarah. "We'll show you how it's gaffed. We won't let you kill anybody."

There came a sudden, loud and melodious singing of "Bringing in the Sheaves" from the Big Top. Florian motioned to Trimm and Rouleau. "You two get inside the pavilion where you can keep an estimating eye on the collection, every time they take one. In the meantime, Captain Hotspur, would you kindly give Obie the Quakemaker some pointers on the art of being a professional strongman?"

Roozeboom and Yount each picked up one of the General Jackson's cannonballs. "Kerst Jesus, man," Roozeboom commented. "You nee start small, do you?" They took the iron balls off to the very farthest limit of the fairground, where they could practice unobserved by Stonewall's local votaries.

"Obie, you know vas is spier? How you say . . . musskle?"

"Uh, sure. Muscles." Yount flexed his biceps.

"Ja. Now, de muss-kles of de body are of differences,

and you must learn de different abilities, if you be strongman. Some are long muss-kles, some are short, some are
broad. Long muss-kles, like in your arms, dey for t'row,
for lift. Broad muss-kles, dey for heavy strain. You know
vas is trapezius?''

''It's that swing, 'way up in the air, where the acrobats—''

''Nee, nee, nee! Trapezius is muss-kle—here.'' He
slapped Yount's beefy back. ''Broad muss-kle, trapezius,
toughest in body. Under it is splenius muss-kle''—he
slapped the back of Yount's neck—''also broad, tough.
Now to begin. You have pick up heavy t'ings before, ja?''
Roozeboom bent at the knees and got his hands under one
of the iron balls.

Yount nodded, ''I know you got to get the power of
your legs and back into it. You don't just lift it, or you
rupture yourself.''

''Ja, correct.'' Roozeboom straightened up, with the ball
in his hands. ''Now, ven you got it dis high, you can t'row
it up.'' He did so, tossing the forty-eight-pound ball some
distance in the air. Then he simply stood and let it thump
to the ground again. ''You don't catch in hands from so
high, or you break somet'ing. You catch on neck.''

''On the *neck*? Are you crazy?''

Roozeboom made no reply. He hefted the ball again,
stood upright, threw it a yard or so into the air, bowed his
shaven head and caught the thing with a meaty thud on
the back of his neck. He juggled his upper body just
slightly to balance it there for a moment, then let it roll
over his shoulder and caught it in his arms.

''Kee-rist,'' said Yount, in awe. ''I druther bust a gut
than break my neck.''

''Takes practice. You build up pad of splenius muss-
kle, it take de blow, de trapezius muss-kle takes de weight.
I show you. Bend head.''

Yount did so. Roozeboom gently laid the cannonball in
the declivity between Yount's occiput and nape. ''Put
hand, feel. Ball must land in curve between back of head

en dis first knob of backbone. Never hit dat knob or you bad hurt.''

"Jesus.''

"Takes practice,'' said Roozeboom, lifting the ball off him.

"Just how do I do the practicing?''

"First time—many times—put ball on top of head, bend head, let ball roll, catch on neck. After while, toss ball little bit in air over head, bend and catch on neck. Toss a little bit higher each time. Dat you can do by yourself, Meneer Kvakemaker. For now, show me how to begin. Pick up.'' He let the ball thud onto the ground again. Yount squatted properly, knees on either side of it, got his hands under it and stood up. "Nee, nee, nee. You do it too easy, Obie. Make believe it ten times heavier. Strain. Do some sweat.''

"Damn it, Ignatz. I can't sweat on command.''

"Sies, who knows dat? Carry rag. Wipe face, hands, shake head in doubt, despair. Looks real to rubes.'' Yount, feeling rather silly, pretended to be mopping away beads of desperation and determination. "Ja, gut. And you have big beard, looks gut on strongman. But I say also shave your head. De scalp sweats most of whole body. Shiny wet head makes look real strongman.''

"There's more to this than I figgered on,'' said Yount.

"Anyt'ing gut, worth working for. Even look ugly for. Now—you put ball on back of neck, practice balance it dere. Klaar? Walk around like dat all time, make muss-kles strong. But not dis minute. I see rubes on lot. Never dey should see practice.''

From the front door of the pavilion, some of the congregation had come trickling out, either for a respite from the humid heat in there or because the organ and banjo had swung into "Stand up, Stand up for Jesus,'' and the baskets were being sent around. The women, once outside, undid their bonnets and fanned themselves with them. Some of the men lit up pipes or cigars. The children began to scamper all over the fairground.

A woman called to two of them: "Vernon, Vernelle, y'all behave! Come away from them people's things. Come away from that-there clothesline." Then she gasped. "Oh, mercy me!" She scuttled about, collected a number of other women, and they huddled in converse together. Then they approached the group of circus folk, and the mother of Vernon and Vernelle said frostily to Florian, "Be you the proprietor of this establishment?"

"I have that honor, madame." He swept off his top hat and smiled. "The main guy, as we say in circus circles. May I do something for you, ladies?"

A very large woman said severely, "You may cease displaying your loose morals among respectable folks."

"Eh?" said Florian, bewildered.

"Look a-yonder, sir!" a sharp-nosed woman commanded. "That-there clothes-line!"

"Ah, the laundry," said Florian, properly contrite. "I grant you, ladies, Sunday should be a day of rest. But I beg your tolerance of the exigencies of road travel. We must do the necessary when we can. Surely it is a small enough sacrilege that—"

"Bad enough to be hangin' out wash on the Lord's day," said the mother of Vernon and Vernelle. "But look what's hangin' right out in the open, where mixed comp'ny can see 'em. Inexpressibles!"

Florian looked even more bewildered, but Magpie Maggie Hag inquired, "You mean underwear?"

The women recoiled at the word, but the large one rallied to say, "Yes! It is scandalous and indecent!"

Florian said, without contrition this time, "Ladies, over the years I have managed to cure myself of most of the depressing virtues. Nevertheless, I do believe that morality should consist of more than mere pudicity."

The sharp-nosed woman said, "You won't cozen us by usin' bad language at us, mister. I bid you again, look at what is hangin' on that line. Men's and women's unmentionables *together*!"

Sarah said mischievously, "Oh, I doubt they'll mate,

dearie. They're too wet and soggy. Would you, in that condition?''

All the women gasped, and the mother of Vernon and Vernelle said, ''Advertisin' your loose morals is indecent enough in front of your own girl child there, but *my* children is pure and innocent. Ladies, let's go straight to the police!''

''Fiddle-dee-dee!'' Clover Lee said suddenly. ''What makes you old biddies think children are pure and innocent?''

And just as suddenly, though she was still garbed in a full-belled gown, Clover Lee tilted sideways and turned a slow cartwheel. It let her skirt upend over her torso and bare the length of her legs before she was upright again. The women reeled away, squawking ''Lordamighty!'' and ''Disgraceful!'' and ''Worse than disgraceful! Didn't you *see*? She wasn't wearing *anything* underneath!'' and they scurried back into the sanctuary of the tabernacle.

''Shame on you, Clover Lee,'' Sarah said, mock-sternly. ''You offended the tender sensibilities of those good modest women.''

''Mokedo,'' sneered Magpie Maggie Hag. ''Good modest women built no different from any other kind. Except they more troublesome. And Clover Lee, you maybe agitate them make trouble for us.''

''Let's hope not,'' said Florian. ''Anyhow, go and take down that clothesline, Mag, or conceal its depravity some way.'' She went, as Tim Trimm and Jules Rouleau emerged from the Big Top. ''Ah, here are the basket boys. Let's see how we're doing so far.''

''It looks like a lot,'' said Rouleau, handing him a paper bag. ''But it's all Confederate torche-cul.''

Tim said, ''You know nobody's going to toss anything worthwhile into a stump collection. The preachers didn't even bother to filch any before we got our share.''

''Thousand dollars or so, it looks like,'' said Florian, rummaging through the limp and tattered bills. ''Worth about ten. Not bad, with the day half gone. And we'll make use of it somehow, lads.'' Then he looked up, past Rouleau and Trimm, and said with surprise, ''Hello, what's this?''

Hannibal Tyree was just now coming back from whatever church he had found, and he was not returning alone. The elephant was supposed to be still tethered out behind the Big Top, but here came Peggy trailing the Negro across the fairground from Main Street. The bull's trunk was draped over Hannibal's shoulder, and he was holding tight to it with both hands. Another man, a white man, was holding one of Hannibal's arms just as tightly captive. The elephant managed to look perceptibly guilty, and both men looked angry. All three marched up to the group of circus folk and Hannibal said:

''Mas' Florian''—but he said it in no servile mumble— ''hyar I goes off to services and trust y'all to keep watch on our most precious propitty, and what happens? Down de church, us has a happy shoutin' time, den de church empty out and I hears screechin' like de Debbil outside de door. I step out, see ev'ry brudder and sister scatterin' ev'ry whichaway, and dere stand ol' Peggy, waitin' for me. Now, I hopes to tell you, Mas' Florian, she could o' been shot on her way dere, or fell down a well, or—''

''Hush up, boy,'' said the white man. He was Sunday-dressed, but he wore a tin star on his suit lapel. To Florian he said, ''That big critter frisked like a goat through half the backyards in Lexington, and plucked up every green sprout from the kitchen gardens, and turned over privies, and part of the monument to General Jackson has gone missing, and I'm here to inform you that you-all are responsible for the damages. I am a depitty sheriff of this county, and *my own privy* was one that got turned over!''

Florian apologized profusely, and Edge thought it remarkable that he commenced by apologizing to the black man.

''I am terribly sorry, Abdullah, and we all stand convicted as charged. It is no excuse that we had quite a lot of other matters to occupy our attention here. Please accept my apology on behalf of us all. Go and take Brutus where she belongs, and give her a plug of tobacco to settle her nerves.''

Until Hannibal led the elephant away, Florian let the white man stand fuming, then turned to him and said, "Shades of Mary and her little lamb, eh, Deputy? Well . . ." he squared his shoulders. "Can you tell me what the damages are likely to amount to?"

"No, sir, not yet I can't. Practically the whole town was in church during that animal's foray, and half the town is still inside that tent of your'n. I won't know the total extent until everybody gets home and starts raising the dickens."

"At least let us begin by paying for your own, er, out-building.''

The officer dismissed that with a wave of his hand. "Never mind. No real damage to speak of. Except that Maw was inside it at the time. No, what I want to say is that the property damage is the least of your problems. I could swear out a criminal warrant for you-all letting a dangerous beast like that run loose.''

Florian chuckled richly. "That mild-mannered old pachyderm? Why, a cow elephant is no more of a menace than a cow *cow*.'' The other troupers had been staying carefully impassive, but at that remark Florian got sharp sideways looks from Rouleau, Sarah and Clover Lee. "You observed yourself, Deputy, that the animal is a vegetarian. Clumsy and awkward, yes. But vicious? Tut tut.''

"Well . . .'' said the deputy. "Well, there's still the matter of its committing a public nuisance. After eating up them gardens, the critter—if you'll excuse the vulgarity, ladies—the critter emptied its bowels all over them gardens.''

"What? Great Scott!'' blurted Florian. He whirled to Edge and Rouleau and Trimm. "Get shovels, men!''

The deputy blinked. "Is *that* stuff dangerous?''

"Dangerous, sir? Elephant dung is the most potent fertilizer in all Creation. Lexington would be a jungle of vegetable produce. Cucumbers climbing in your windows, corn on cobs you'd need two hands to lift, watermelons blocking the road traffic. However, we will scoop it up, it being rightfully our property. Whatever we are fined for the damage done here, we can sell that rich manure to any plant nursery along our way, for forty or fifty times what we have to pay your citizenry."

"It's that valuable, eh? Well, then, wait a minute, sir. Consider. You'll have to send your men all over town to find the sh—the stuff, and shovel it up, and fetch it back. Then you'll be detained while all the folks' damages are assessed, and then you'll have to pay. How about we settle for an even swap? Leave the elephant droppings and I'll explain to the people, and them that don't want to use it themselves can sell it to Gilliam's greenhouse, and we'll call everything square."

"We-ell . . ." said Florian. "It's noble of you to save us work and time and penalties. I think we'd do better by peddling the manure, but"—Florian took the man's hand and pumped it—"I'll accede to the agreement. And here, sir, tickets for tomorrow's performance. For you and Mrs. Deputy, if she has recovered from her, er, discomposure by then . . . for any little deputies . . ."

The man went away happy, and Florian took out his sleeve handkerchief to pat his brow. The other troupers were looking at him with mixed expressions.

"I've known you to tell some Christly lies before, Florian," said Trimm. "But making Peggy out to be a cuddlesome pet lamb would have strained Ananias."

"If some rube had poked her with a pitchfork," said Rouleau, "or some brat had thrown a stone—ça me donne la chiasse!—you know damned well she'd have done a headstand on him. We'd have needed a shovel for sure."

"Of course I know it!" snapped Florian. "And I am sincerely thankful that no such thing happened. But I refuse to fret over every *what if?* until I have to. Now, Monsieur Roulette, Tiny Tim, get back in the tent there on basket patrol. Colonel Ramrod, go get the Quakemaker, and you two report to Maggie for costume fitting. Madame, mam'selle, get out of those fancy clothes and start preparing some peck. I'll go and try to make peace with Abdullah. This may be the Sabbath day of rest and tranquillity—*hah!*—but tomorrow we have a show to put on!''

Either there were not too many rubes fearful of indecency, or else the deputy sheriff had spread the word that the circus was passably decent, because the people of Lexington and vicinity came again to the fairground next day to attend the performance. There was not the crowd that had flocked to the religious services, but at least enough to fill the seats.

"Most have paid in Secesh paper, of course," Florian said to Edge. "But some seem to realize that we fleshly mortals required more tangible remuneration then the spiritual clergy. So a fair number have paid in silver, and the rest brought good edible or usable barter. I even had one boy offer me a fistful of Brutus's droppings."

Edge laughed. "You turn him away?"

"Hell, no. I told him a mere pinch of the stuff was worth a ticket, and let him keep the rest. A good lie is always worth the effort of sustaining it."

Magpie Maggie Hag was still dealing out tickets from the red wagon, and today Monsieur Roulette was being the talker to the crowd at the museum wagon. Inside the pavilion, Tim's cornet and Abdullah's drum had been joined in their musical medley by the Wild Man's banjo.

"Among the goods we've taken in," said Florian, "are some more cheap dishes. So Clover Lee can toss one in the air for you, and you can use your carbine to shatter it. Have you worked out the rest of your turn yet?"

"I've got my pistol sighted. I spent the morning practicing with the lighter loads, shooting dead persimmons off a tree at the back of the lot yonder. I reckon you heard me."

"Yes. And I saw Obie going around hunched under a cannonball. I'm pleased that you two are taking your apprenticeship seriously."

"Well, I can't fetch a persimmon tree into the tent. So

I just sketched out a target." Edge showed it: on the back of a circus poster, with a bit of bullet lead, he had traced concentric circles. "If you'll lend me that pencil you·carry, I'll black in the rings and bull's eye."

"No, no," said Florian. "You are a straightforward sort of man, Zachary, but sincerity does not make for showmanship. No, no, a paper target won't do."

"I've got to shoot at something."

"For today, at least, we will sacrifice some more dishes. Tell you what you do. Load the carbine with bird shot for knocking one dish out of the air. Load your pistol with five balls, and only powder in the remaining chamber. Clover Lee will set five saucers on the edge of the ring curb. Shoot them to pieces, as dramatically as you can. That'll convince the audience that you're shooting genuine balls. Then I'll talk you up some more, then you'll fire the uncharged chamber at Clover Lee. She'll know what to do then."

"All right. You're the boss. Or no—the main guy, you said."

"You're learning. The name comes from those guy ropes that hold the Big Top together." He gestured to the ropes that ran from the ground stakes up to the tent roof eaves. "By analogy, every performer and crewman is also a supporting guy, and the director of the whole works is the main guy."

Roozeboom and Yount approached them, Roozeboom carrying a wooden fruit crate and Yount one of his cannonballs. Because Magpie Maggie Hag had only begun on the new costumes, Yount had contrived one of his own. He was barefooted, bareheaded and mainly clad in his own long underwear, but around the waist he had draped some of the Wild Man's spare skins. From a distance, he looked like a very pale and muscular giant, nude except for the dense hair of his kilted furs and his facial beard. As he came close, Edge realized how *very* nude he appeared, and exclaimed:

"Obie, what have you done? Just *look* how you look!"

"Shaved my head," Yount said airily, "so it'll sweat. Hey, Mr. Florian, Ignatz and me had this idea for what he calls the capper of the act. What do you think of it? He'll prop Jules's ladder against the center pole, climb up it and drop a cannonball on this-here crate. The crate'll go all to smash. Then I'll kneel down in its place, and Ignatz'll drop the ball on me. How's that sound?"

"Admirable, Obie!" Florian turned to Edge and said, "Now, see? That's showmanship. All right, everybody, get ready. I'll soon be giving the musicians the signal to play 'Wait for the Wagon' and that will signal Monsieur Roulette to turn the tip."

"Turn the what?"

"He'll cease the free show. He'll stop bragging on the museum and the lion, and turn the gawkers—the crowd, the tip—into the tent. As soon as they're all seated, it'll be time for our come-in and spec. Zachary, hadn't you better be loading your weapons?"

"I will, as soon as Madame Hag has sold tickets to those last few comers yonder. I need to borrow a little cornmeal from her."

"Whatever for?"

"I told you, I'll be using only a light load of powder on my pistol, so I want to top up each chamber with a little cornmeal before I ram in the ball."

"But don't you spray a cloud of yellow powder when you shoot?"

"No. It burns as it goes out the barrel behind the ball. And it burns out the powder residue from previous shots, so it helps keep the barrel clean. Every pistol shooter knows that little trick."

"Well, well. Live and learn."

Some ten minutes later, a tremendous blaring and booming of cornet and bass drum silenced the expectant rustle and murmur of the crowd in the Big Top. Then Florian's whistle blew a shriek.

This time the come-in commenced with Colonel Ramrod in solitary splendor. He rode headlong into the tent on his claybank Thunder and galloped several times alone around the ring, his sabre high. He still wore his old army boots, gray trousers and tunic with CSA brass buttons, but Magpie Maggie Hag had found for him somewhere a cocked hat, and stuck in it a huge plume that made him look as dandified as the notorious fops Stuart and Custer. But the crowd evidently did not see him so; it burst into appreciative applause. That, to Edge's surprise and gratification, made him feel less like a ridiculous posturer, more like a genuine performer, so he tried genuinely to perform. As he careered around the ring, he wielded his sabre in the thrust, the down-stroke, the flank and cuff cuts, the banderole, the disengage—at least as well as he could without an opponent to fight or skewer—making his blade flash and flicker, and making the audience applaud ever more heartily. Some of the men in the crowd even gave the shrill, hair-bristling "Rebel yell."

The cornet blared again outside, and Colonel Ramrod hauled Thunder to a skidding stop at the back door. Then he let the horse go on again at a sedate, high-stepping walk, and held his sabre at the "charge" to lead the Grand Promenade of artistes, horses and elephant. He even joined in the song: "All hail you ladies, gentlemen! Let nothing you dismay . . . !"

In the opening act, Tim Trimm again came laggardly to the ring, swaddled in his joey clothes, and was reprimanded by Florian: "You should get out of bed earlier, young fellow. It's the early bird that gets the worm, you know."

"Hah! Then the worm got up even earlier. I should imitate *him?*"

That and Trimm's other smart-aleck sallies drew the expected laughter. But then Florian said, "You claim you work so hard every day. I daresay you really enjoy your bed at night."

And Trimm retorted, "No, sir. The instant I get into it, I fall asleep. And the instant I wake up, I must get out of it." He leered and concluded, "So I get no *enjoyment* of my bed at all."

The audience laughed again, or most of it did. There came also some highpitched cries of "Shame!" and "Nasty!" and "Such language!"

"Christ, it's the bunch of harpies from yesterday," said Madame Solitaire, watching from the sidelines.

Florian swung a slap at Trimm for that riposte, but instead of faking the slap sound Tim ran away, forcing Florian to chase him. Tim ran clumsily in his voluminous boots and trousers, and so fell flat on his face. Then he was up again, running *out* of the boots and trousers entirely, his bare little legs twinkling under his shirttails. The audience roared with laughter again—except for the mother of Vernon and Vernelle, and her companion females. They hissed, hooted and called, "Shame! For shame!" until the other people ceased laughing and sat uneasily quiet. One of the females stood up, turned slowly to sweep the stand with a stare like a scythe, and loudly declared, "Neighbors, it appears to me like you-all are enjoin' yourselfs too much to be good Christians!" The rest of the people looked meek, as if the female had spoken true.

For once, Tim Trimm's poisonous disposition came in useful. He stopped short in his toddling run and angrily pointed at the women, who were still crying "Shame!" through cupped hands. He jumped up and down and screeched loudly. "This show ain't goin' on until them drunken men in women's clothes are made to behave!"

The audience rocked again with laughter—so did all the troupers—and many another finger was derisively pointed at the women. The females turned white with indignation, then red with embarrassment. Then they tried to sidle crabwise off their plank without standing up. But that brought catcalls from the crowd—"Them drunks is sneakin' out for a snort!"—so the women literally jumped from the stands and fled out of the tent.

Tiny Tim resumed his clown act, to laughter and ap-

plause considerably in excess of what he was accustomed
to hear. And when he finally came out of the ring, he got
an equally unusual acclamation and backslapping from his
fellow artistes.

The remainder of the program's first half was as well
received here as it had been in Lynchburg. The good folk
of Lexington were as naïvely taken in by the Pete Jenkins
act of the aged "birthday lady," and were as delighted
when she turned out to be Madame Solitaire, and were as
thoroughly horrified by the "vicious" Maximus's biting
of ass's blood out of Captain Hotspur's arm. The ensuing
intermission was something of a torment for Edge and
Yount, because Florian had scheduled them both for the
second half of the program. They several times remarked
to each other that they hoped to hell something would occur to prolong the intermission indefinitely, and then several times remarked that they wished to hell it would hurry
up and end, so they could the sooner have their début
performances, success or failure, over and done with.

As before, the second half commenced with Clover
Lee's being introduced as a near relation of Generals Fitz
and Robert E., and her horse Bubbles's being introduced
as an equally near relative of Traveller. When the act had
concluded, and Clover Lee was still taking bows to the
applause for herself and Bubbles, Florian came to the back
door of the tent, where Yount in his underwear and skins
was fidgeting, and said, "It's show time, Quakemaker.
Any questions before I introduce you?"

"Yes," said Yount and, as if he had been addled by
stage fright, he asked a question totally malapropos. "How
come you always tell the folks to clap for them horses?
They don't do no more than run around in a circle, and
I've seen corraled Injun cayuses do that."

"You're right, Obie," said Florian, answering as seriously as Yount had inquired. "Our mounts could hardly
compete with real show stock. But regard Bubbles, as he
exits now. That horse is strutting as proudly as if he'd done
an aerial ballet. Should I deny the animal a share of that

admiration all artistes yearn for and revel in?''

"I reckon not. I don't begrudge him. I just wondered.''

Florian murmured a quotation:

> Hath wingèd Pegasus more nobly trod
> Than Rocinante, stumbling up to God?

Yount asked, "Is that another poem you made up on the road?''

"No. I wish it were. Are you ready, then, Quake-maker?''

"Ready as I'll ever be.''

Whether he had been nervous or apprehensive or down-right terrified, the Quakemaker and the others participating in his act put on a very commendable show of showman-ship. To a fanfare of cornet, drum and banjo, Florian gave him a flavorsome introduction as "the tremendous human being discovered by a scientific expedition exploring Pata-gonia, which name means in the Argentinian language 'The Land of Giants' . . .'' This went on for some time. "And now, clad like Hercules in the skins of savage lions he slew with his bare hands . . . the world's strongest man, the *Quakemaker!*''

And Yount strode in through the back door with a tread almost as majestic as that of Brutus, who came right be-hind him, Abdullah on top pounding the drum. The ele-phant was hauling a rope net in which the three cannon balls dragged along the ground, clanking heavily—and Brutus took care to walk slowly, leaning forward, as if the weight were a load even for a behemoth. Ex-Sergeant Obie Yount followed all the advice Captain Hotspur had given, beginning by heaving and puffing audibly as he rolled the iron balls from the net to the ring center. He even im-proved on the advice, when he realized that taking his position directly in a sun shaft from one of the roof punc-tures would accentuate his newly shaven head.

After much rag-wiping of his hands and repeated, frac-tional, finicking adjustments of the way the three cannonballs lay around his feet, he struggled mightily—and took several minutes—to lift just one ball in both hands. While the audience ooh-ed and aah-ed, he put down the ball and did some more wiping—hands, bald head, black beard, even armpits—slowly lifted the same ball again, tucked it under one arm, stooped and with even fiercer effort lifted a second with the other hand. Eruption of applause. He swiveled that hand around to tuck the ball under that arm, so he was holding the two balls between elbows and waist on either side. That left his hands empty, and when he stooped again, just barely able to grasp the third ball with his fingertips. By the time he had struggled erect, two balls under arms, the third precariously held by the extended fingers of both hands, the Quakemaker no longer had to pretend to be sweating.

The capper went well, too. Captain Hotspur trotted in and climbed the short ladder propped against the center pole. The Quakemaker, again with many trifling little adjustments, positioned the fruit crate, then gruntingly heaved a cannonball up to perch upon the ladder ends protruding on either side of the pole. Then Hotspur and the Quakemaker engaged in a dialogue of grunts and gestures, which occasioned some more adjustments of the crate's placement. Finally, at a signal, Abdullah rumbled his drum, from soft up to loud, the Quakemaker made a chopping gesture and Hotspur pushed the ball off the ladder. The old crate crashed all to flinders at the impact. The Quakemaker again muscled the cannonball up to Hotspur at the ladder top, and then went down on hands and knees where the crate had been. He was sweating now so profusely that the beads were visible as they dropped from his face to the ring ground he was staring at, bulgy-eyed.

After some more dialogue in grunts, and Abdullah's even more prolonged rumble from pianissimo to fortissimo, the drum gave one thunderous *boom!* and in the sudden silence Hotspur let the ball fall, so that its hitting the Quakemaker's neck sounded like a sledgehammer whacking a side of beef. The Quakemaker gave a mighty grunt, perhaps not mere showmanship, but his head stayed on, his neck stayed intact and the cannonball stayed steady there. After a suspenseful moment, keeping his head bent, he erected himself onto his knees, then slowly on his feet, the iron ball staying put. He waited for the applause, which came prodigiously, then let the ball roll over his shoulder and down his extended arm. At the last instant, he flipped his hand so it was palm up, and the ball came to rest on it. He twirled the thing as if it weighed nothing, then dropped it so the audience could hear its convincingly heavy thud on the ground. Louder and longer applause, while Hotspur and Trimm rolled the balls back to the net for Brutus to drag out.

"You did it like a seasoned trouper!" Florian cried, and clapped Yount heartily on the shoulder, then ran to the ring to introduce the next artiste, Colonel Ramrod.

"I hope I do as well," Edge muttered uncertainly.

The seasoned trouper, so recently his troop sergeant, told him, "Just act like a real colonel out there, Colonel."

"Mr. Obie, you sure did sweat toward the close," said Clover Lee, and laughed. "I bet you were wishing you had left some hair on to cushion that cannonball."

"It wasn't that, miss," the Quakemaker said sincerely. "I just then realized that I'd get my neck broke for damn sure if somebody all of a sudden stood up in the crowd and yelled, 'Them is Stonewall's balls!'"

That remark so amused and relaxed Edge that, when Florian wound up his long introduction, he pranced into the ring almost as carefreely as Clover Lee did.

". . . Scourge of the Red Indians, hero of the Border Wars, officer of our own indomitable Confederate Cavalry . . . the world's premier sharpshooter, Colonel *Ram*-ROD!"

When Clover Lee gracefully assumed the V-pose, Colonel Ramrod did too, holding his brassbound carbine high in one hand, his plumed hat in the other. The audience clapped more than merely politely or expectantly, for they were applauding the gray he wore.

"As his first display of shootistic virtuosity, ladies and gentlemen . . ." said Florian, and went into another spate of superlatives. Clover Lee danced to where Ramrod's few props were stacked by the center pole, and the colonel, emulating the Quakemaker's painstakingness, frowned studiously and pretended to check over his weapon, from muzzle to percussion cap.

". . . Only one shot, only one ball," bawled Florian, "so only one chance to hit the moving target, ladies and gentlemen. I will allow you five seconds to place any wagers you may care to make among yourselves." While Florian slowly counted aloud, Colonel Ramrod felt the fixity of the crowd's gaze as if he himself were the focus of a battalion of gun barrels. "Mam'selle . . . *throw*!"

She scaled the saucer edgewise, straight up in the air toward the tent's peak. Ramrod had been holding his carbine at port arms. He almost leisurely brought its butt to his shoulder, cocked the big hammer, pretended to sight as if he were really drawing a bead on the little pale object, but merely fired in its general direction, confident that some of the charge of bird shot would hit it. So loud was the blast of the carbine that the saucer seemed to dissolve silently into atoms up there.

Clover Lee skipped about, as delightedly as if she had bet on the shot and won. Tim Trimm came running to take the empty carbine, while the big cloud of blue smoke wisped away and the crowd applauded the man in gray. The colonel next unholstered his pistol, scowled at it and examined it: twirled the cylinder, counted the caps and so on. Florian reeled off some more rigmarole, while Clover Lee took the remaining five saucers to that arc of the ring backed by only the empty back door of the tent, and stuck each saucer's rim into the ring's earthen curb so it stood upright.

"Notice, ladies and gentlemen!" commanded Florian. "Five targets, and Colonel Ramrod has only six rounds with which to hit and shatter them." Et cetera, et cetera. Ramrod settled the pistol back in its holster on his right hip, its walnut grip facing forward, the holster's stiff leather flap unbuttoned and raised. He walked to the edge of the ring farthest from the target, then held both hands a little way out from his sides, a little below waist level, until Florian barked, ''*Fire!*''

What followed happened so quickly that the pistol's *blam*! seemed to put the exclamation point to Florian's command, and the first saucer in the line disintegrated. Colonel Ramrod had flicked his left hand across his body to the holster, whipped out the revolver and thumb-cocked it as it came up level in front of his face. Then the left hand had dropped away, leaving the pistol apparently levitating there just long enough for his right hand to flash up, seize it, aim it and pull the trigger—all of that done so fast as to appear simultaneous with Florian's barked order. As the blue smoke billowed about, and the crowd applauded, and Clover Lee cavorted with pleasure, Colonel Ramrod spun the gun around his finger in its trigger guard, so it did a graceful twirl, and he plunked it down into the holster.

He could have blown to pieces the remaining four saucers as fast as he could cock the pistol's hammer—but ''make everything look real difficult,'' the Quakemaker had advised. So the next saucer he shot from a kneeling position, the next with his left hand holding the revolver, the next shooting from the hip without appearing to take aim at all. And in between, he wiped his palms on his trousers, swiped the back of a hand across his forehead, knuckled his eyes, as if the strain and deliberation were almost too much for mortal endurance. When he blew the last saucer to pieces, Clover Lee and the audience responded as joyfully as if he had just shot the last Yankee in Virginia.

''Now!'' cried Florian, when he could be heard. ''Now that Colonel Ramrod has succeeded in the next to impossible, he will attempt the *truly* impossible. Mam'selle Clover Lee, do you have faith enough in the expertness of this gentleman officer to trust your life to his skill?''

The girl looked nervous and hesitant, but for only a moment. Then she looked noble and courageous, and gave a resolute nod.

"Gallant lass," said Florian, and turned to Ramrod. "Do you, Colonel, feel that your hand and eye are still steady enough to essay this hazardous feat! Are you willing to accept the risk of being the murderer of this lovely child?"

Colonel Ramrod looked staunch and masterful, and gave a resolute nod.

"Very well," said Florian. "On your head be it. Ladies and gentlemen, I must beg you now for absolute silence and stillness. For what Colonel Ramrod will now attempt is to *shoot directly into the face* of this brave child in such a way that she can *catch the ball in her teeth*!" Several people gasped. "Please! Absolute silence. Those who cannot bear to watch are requested to leave the pavilion this moment. Also any who are liable to swoons or epileptic seizures. Colonel Ramrod must not be discomposed by any sound or movement."

Colonel Ramrod could not suppress a smile at all that taradiddle, and a smile was not his most appealing expression. The people stared at him, some perhaps taking his look for one of melancholy at the prospect of doing harm to the girl, others perhaps believing he was expressing the true maleficent nature that had led him to scourge Red Indians. Clover Lee stood with her hands on hips, her back to the tent's back opening, head erect, with a farewell-cruel-world expression on her face.

Florian asked "Are you ready, mam'selle?" She did not budge or even nod, only slid her eyes sideways to him. "Then commend your soul to God, my dear. Are you ready, Colonel?" Ramrod licked his lips, rubbed his trousers, readjusted his hat and nodded. "Very well, I shall say no more, and give no command to fire. From this moment, sir, you are on your own." And he stepped entirely out of the ring.

Colonel Ramrod spread his feet apart and assumed a

solid, tense, braced posture. He really did aim most carefully—low, so that any sprinkle of still-hot cornmeal par-
ticles would patter harmlessly onto Clover Lee's léotard.
After the longest and most suspenseful pause in the whole
day's performance, he fired. Clover Lee rocked backward
the tiniest bit, and her hands left her hips in an uncertain,
steadying gesture, as the blue smoke briefly blurred her
outline. Then she was seen to be smiling, showing her
bright white teeth, slightly parted. The crowd released its
pent breath in a whoosh. Clover Lee raised a hand to her
mouth, plucked the bit of lead from between her teeth, held
it up and danced around the ring, displaying it to the crowd
that thundered in ovation. After a full circuit of the stands,
she espied a wide-eyed, beaming, hard-clapping old man,
and tossed him the ball.

"Examine it, sir!" called Florian, and the crowd began
to quieten. "Pass it around so all may see. The ball shows
clear evidence of its terrific impact upon the fragile teeth
of the winsome lass."

As Colonel Ramrod walked backward from the ring,
sweeping his plumed hat repeatedly from head to ground,
he realized that Clover Lee had not swiped a clean ball
from his possibles-bag of ammunition and implements.
She must have picked one up from the ground behind the
saucer targets: a ball that was plausibly misshapen for
handing around among the rubes. He might be working
now with tricksters, but they were *professional* tricksters,
and good at it.

"You show promise of becoming a real artiste, Zachary,
ami," said Monsieur Roulette, at the back door awaiting
his own cue to enter. "That ugly grimace you made, just
before the capper, that was masterly. Ambiguous. Intrigu-
ing."

Edge thought back, and said, "All I did was grin."

"I asked myself—even I—does he dread the risk of
killing the girl? Or does he relish the idea, peut-être? Ambiguity is true artistry."

"All I did was grin," Edge said again, but his colleague

was gone, flip-flopping heels over head into the tent as Florian cried:". . . That swift, slippery, slithering, brisk and nimble limberjim . . . Monsieur *Rou*-LETTF!"

Edge and Yount had nothing more to do until they mounted Thunder and Lightning to ride in the closing spec and sing "Lorena" with the others. It was some time later, after the crowd had gone, while the troupers were waiting to eat supper, that Florian came to congratulate Colonel Ramrod on his maiden performance. Edge was sitting apart from the others, apparently rapt in deep study, and he murmured only an offhand thank-you for the compliments.

"What's the matter?" Florian asked. "Are the nervous conniptions just now catching up to you?"

"No. No, I'm all right. It didn't bother me at all. That's what bothers me."

"Eh?"

Edge took a deep breath. "I was wondering if I'm really cut out for this sort of career. Practically all my life, I've been a soldier, dealing with hard realities."

"So will you here. The circus life is not too different from the military. Like an army, we're frequently on the move, concerned with the logistics of living off the land. Like soldiers, we adhere to discipline on duty, but we have liberty—even license—when we're off duty. The main difference between circus and soldiering is one I should think would appeal to you. We don't operate by manuals and rigid regulations, so we have infinite scope for improvisation and ingenuity. There are not two days alike with a circus. We expect the unexpected: surprises, obstacles, setbacks, the occasional stroke of good fortune. Dealing with such things will make a man fit for any eventuality. If and when you *should* go back to soldiering, I'd wager you'd be the better officer for the experience."

"The logistical part of a circus is reality enough, I grant you. But . . . the *showmanship* part? Forgive me, Mr. Florian, I don't mean to make it sound trifling, but . . ."

"We like to think of circus as an art, and I would hardly rank art as a trifle," said Florian, but not testily. "Indeed,

ours is the oldest art there is—performing. Also the most
ephemeral of arts, I have to admit that. We strike light
across the air, yes. But, like light on air, we leave no mark,
no trace, no history. Poets leave thoughts, artists leave
visions—even warriors leave deeds. We do nothing but
entertain, and we don't pretend we're doing anything more
significant. We come into humdrum communities where
pinched little people lead commonplace lives, and we bring
them a bit of novelty, a touch of the exotic. For the space
of a day perhaps, we give those people a look at gloss and
gossamer, danger and daring, a laugh and a thrill they may
never have had before. And then, like a dream or a fairy
tale—or what the Scots call glamour—we are gone and
forgotten.''

"Well, there you are. A soldier may be just a pawn in
a game, but the game itself is not a fairy tale.''

"Warriors leave deeds, eh? You want to be remembered. We only want to be enjoyed.''

"I don't mean that either. Hell, I doubt that General
Stonewall yonder under the sod knows now whether he's
remembered or not. I just mean that an officer, even the
lowliest enlisted man, while he's alive, deals with solid,
enduring things.''

"With the eternal verities?'' Florian said sardonically.
"With immutable truths? Let me remind you, Zachary. A
few years ago, wearing the Union uniform, you were fighting against the Mexicans. If you were still in Union blue,
now that this war is over what do you suppose your army
would likely be doing next? Fighting *alongside* the Mexicans to drive the French out of the Americas.''

"All right, not eternal verities,'' Edge said, a little uncomfortably. "But, *at any given moment*, a soldier knows
where he stands. Who is enemy, who is ally, what is black
and what is white. I'm trying to say that here—in the circus—one minute you think you know and the next you
don't. Sure, you have realities, like worrying about getting
enough to eat, money to go on with. But all of a sudden
everything shifts, and you're dealing with sheer unreality.

Like . . . take Sarah, for example. I know you know about her and me.''

''No explanations necessary, Zachary, and no apologies. Long before you came on the scene, Madame Solitaire and I arrived at an understanding and comfortable arrangement. A man of my age seeks not sole possession of a love, only tranquil enjoyment of it at intervals. An autumnal love gives a man the sober splendor and gentle warmth of a September sunset, but it does not buffet him with the springtime storms of resentment or jealousy.''

''I wasn't apologizing. And I wasn't resenting your sharing her, either. What I wanted to say was—well, when she and I are Sarah and Zack, it's something real. When she turns into Madame Solitaire, it's—I don't know— she's fairy-tale gloss and gossamer.'' Edge paused, pondered and went on, ''Maybe this comes close to what I mean. This afternoon, I heard you recite that pretty little couplet about Pegasus and Rocinante. It sounded like something you sincerely believed.'' He waved toward the Big Top. ''Nothing you ever say in yonder ever sounds sincere.''

''Ah, well . . . showmanship,'' said Florian, and shrugged.

''It's not just you. It's the difference between Sarah Coverley and Madame Solitaire, Hannibal and Abdullah, Peggy and Brutus. One minute they're one thing, the next they're another. And now it'll be me, too. Zachary Edge and Colonel Ramrod. Right after I finished my turn in the ring, Jules Rouleau said he admired me for being ambiguous, when all I had done was—''

''Ah, well . . . Monsieur Roulette,'' said Florian, and shrugged again.

''It's everybody and everything. One minute it's practical business, like finding food and fodder. And sincere feelings, like yours about that couplet. And the next minute we're dealing in pure fantasticality. From real to unreal. Oughtn't even a *circus* to be one thing or the other?''

Florian meditated for some time, and finally pointed and said, "Look there."

Clover Lee had washed out her latest-used costume and was pinning it up to dry. The sun was just going down, and its level amber beams struck multicolored sparks and splinters of light from the léotard the girl was hanging there.

Florian said, "That garment is decorated with sewn-on sequins, brilliants, spangles, whatever you prefer to call them. Each of those is a thing—an entity—it exists—it is a tiny, thin flake of bright-tinted metal. In the circus ring, under sunbeam or limelight, it reflects a sharp flicker of color. And a circus audience, not being very close to the performer wearing it, sees only those coruscations of red and gold and green and blue. Now tell me, Zachary, which is more real? The flake of inert metal or the vibrant glint of color? Decide that, and you'll have answered your own questions. Furthermore, you'll be well on the way to becoming a philospher of some eminence." Florian stood up, dusted the seat of his trousers and, before he went away, said again, "Which is more real? The spangle or the sparkle?"

9

MAYBE IF the next morning had been the sort to remind a man that the realistic world is a jagged and granular place of harsh weathers, dreary duties, wan hopes and inevitable disillusionments, Edge would have waked still in his mood of perplexity, and he might have abandoned the circus then and there. But the day dawned so unrealistically spangled with light and beauty that the world seemed a pleasant place and brimful of promise. The sunrise turned the sky a rosy pink, fluffed with little clouds as white as innocence, and their shadows put dapples of emerald on the ordinary green fields, dapples of sapphire on the ordinary blue mountains. The balmy air might have been borrowed from

May, and the new-leaved trees everywhere twinkled like tinsel. Even the cemetery next to the fairground looked festive, what with the tulips, hyacinths and jonquils the people had piled on the graves two days before. And Edge felt on his face that old familiar breeze that blows always from the far places and beckons: "Come see what I have seen."

They were hitting the road early this morning. The next sizable town to the north was Staunton, some thirty miles away, and Florian wanted to make it in one day's run. So the Big Top had been torn down the night before, and the wagons packed with the heavier goods. Now most of the men were stowing the last few items and harnessing the horses, occasionally pausing to grab one of the hot-cakes and rashers of fried fatback the women cooked and handed out in relays.

"Would you mind driving Lightning on the tent wagon, Zachary?" asked Florian. "Our Quakemaker is quaking a bit."

"A bit, hell," groaned Yount. "I do believe I *did* break my neck yesterday. Damn my showing off!" With winces and grimaces and slow movements, he peeled his shirt partway down to show them his bruises.

Edge whistled and said, "Obie, you remember the sunsets on the Mexican desert? You won't have to perform any more. We can call you a panorama and charge people just to come and look."

"Not to worry, Obie," Florian said airily. "Our company physician will fix you up. Docteur-Médicin Roulette."

"What's good for a busted neck, Doc?" Yount asked him.

"Regardez," said Rouleau. "My entire medicine chest—lint, liniment and laudanum. I will use the lint to dab on the liniment while you swig some of the laudanum."

"You can ride with me on the rockaway, Obie," said Florian. "It will give you the least jolting." Then, half an hour later, he said, "I *thought* it would. Sorry, Obie." The

rockaway was truly rocking, also pitching and lurching and
bouncing, over a grievously rutted and blistered and
scabbed and chuck-holed road on which even the four-
footed Snowball was having to watch his step. "What do
they call this terrible road? And why is it so terrible?"

"This is the Valley Pike, from Lexington on north,"
said Yount, between grunts of discomfort. "Macadamized.
At least it used to be. One of the few such high-class roads
in all Virginia. Reckon we ought to be glad it's ruined. It
it was still in good condition, we'd be stopping to pay at
a tollhouse every few miles."

"Did the tollkeepers take the money and abscond? I
thought the tolls were for road upkeep."

"It wasn't neglect that ruined this turnpike, Mr. Florian.
It was the war. There's been one after another Rebel and
Yankee army charging or retreating up and down it on
wheels and hoofs for four years." He grunted at a bump.
"That's one reason I was glad to be cavalry. We didn't
have to stick to roads. We could go overland. Ride free
and wide."

"Ah, yes. I gather that the cavalrymen have always been
the knights-errant of every army."

"Well, I sure preferred ranging service to any other soldier's kind of life. It beat digging rifle pits and ditches
with the webfoots, or dodging them big iron pumpkins the
cannoneers slung at each other. All we ever asked in the
cavalry was a fair fight in a fair field. That's why the *best*
time to be in the cavalry was during the Mexican War.
Wide open spaces to fight in, no civilians or settlements
to get in the way of a charge. Best of all, you was far away
from all the headquarters brass, the wagon-dog officers,
the spit and polish."

Farther back in the train, riding with Edge on the seat
of the tent wagon, Sarah was saying, "You mustn't get
puffed up now, Zachary, just because that one audience
applauded your act. It still needs a lot of practice and
thought. You see, anybody can work up an *audience* trick
in a couple of days, like you did. To work up a *performer's*

trick may take a couple of years. Inventing and rehearsing and perfecting.''

"I won't ask what's the difference," said Edge. "I imagine you're going to tell me."

"It's the difference between the showy and the artistic. An ordinary audience will go wild over something that *looks* difficult or dangerous. But only other performers and a very few discerning spectators will appreciate a trick that *is* difficult but looks easy, because it's done with skill and grace and Jesus!" The wagon had given an exceptionally lively lurch. "Right now, we're practically doing a sway-pole act."

There came a thumping from inside the wagon. Edge stopped the horse, and the wagon's back door opened. Magpie Maggie Hag emerged, explaining that she had been trying to work on the new costumes, but she couldn't do it in conditions that would scramble an egg. So she climbed up on the seat beside them, and Edge clucked Lightning into motion again.

He said to Sarah, "I gather that a real artiste would rather perform for the knowing few than for a whole crowd's hurrahs."

"Wouldn't you?" she asked. "Didn't you? In the cavalry? Wasn't it a better feeling to have the esteem of your fellow troopers than a lot of rube civilians who would clap for a silly garrison parade?"

"I reckon. But don't forget, a cavalryman *has* to be good at his trade or he'll soon be dead."

Sarah gave a ladylike sniff and said, "Shit. You want me to start naming risky circus acts and the performers who have died doing them?"

"Well, put it another way. The cavalry's work is *necessary*."

Magpie Maggie Hag said, "Listen, gazho, people need circuses much as they need soldiers. We been around at least as long. Jugglers and joeys, no different from Abdullah and Tiny Tim, they went along on the Crusades. Temple priests in old Egypt, they only voice throwers like

Jules Rouleau, made the god statues talk. And circus people not always looked down on. Lots got up high in the world. There was daughter of animal trainer in old Rome, born and raised circus dancer. And her? She in history books as Empress Theodora.''

''And in Philadelphia right now,'' said Sarah, ''there's a freak singer called the Two-Headed Nightingale. Just a mulatto girl, she is—or they—are—but I hear she pulls in six hundred dollars a week. United States dollars. I bet no cavalry *general* was ever paid that much.''

''No,'' Edge admitted. He made no comment on the incongruity of the women's double-harnessing to their argument a Roman empress and a two-headed mulatto.

Sarah went on, ''Well, maybe I'll never get as famous as a necessary soldier like Jeb Stuart or a legitimate stage artiste like Jenny Lind. But circus is what I *do*, so I try to do it as well as I can.''

Edge nodded approvingly. ''For the esteem of your colleagues, not just the ignorant civilians.''

''Yes. Here in America, anyway. Florian says it's different in Europe. He says over there the commonest audience can tell the difference between real artistry and sheer toot.''

Magpie Maggie Hag concurred. ''American, European circus, they different as nigger minstrel show and theater ballet. One time in Spain I see limberjim *weep* when he finished his act, he brought it off so beautiful.''

Edge asked, ''Do you ladies reckon Mr. Florian really will get us to Europe?''

Sarah said, ''He'll do it or bust a gut trying. And he may have to bust a gut. Last night, when he counted up our total take so far—counting in Mag's earnings and our share of the tent-meeting collections—we've got forty-some Federal dollars and about five thousand Confederate. If he can find some way to convert that—to fifty, say, in real dollars—it's still only about a hundred all together.''

''And we're not likely to run into any more stump preachers that want to hire a tabernacle,'' said Edge.

Sarah went on, "He got out a map and decided that Baltimore is our best hope for getting a ship. And he calculated that there are ten or a dozen towns worth our making a stand in, between here and there. If they all pay about as well as Lynchburg did, and *if* he can cash in the Secesh paper we take, and *if* we can live along the way without having to lay out cash, and *if* we don't run up against any disaster that costs us money, we ought to hit Baltimore with a total of four, maybe five hundred dollars."

"I don't know much about ocean voyaging," said Edge. "But I'd think any shipping company would ask a lot more than that to ship all of us clear across the Atlantic."

"Not all of us," said Magpie Maggie Hag, "but more than all of us." Before Edge or Sarah could ask what she meant by that, she said, "Madame Solitaire, you no tell me any dream for long time now. You no have any dream needs dukkering?"

"Only the same old dream I always have," Sarah said cheerfully. "I take a fall from a horse, and there's a net that catches me so I don't get hurt, but somehow I can't get loose of the meshes."

"And I have told what it means. But still long time off."

Edge asked politely, "Does everybody relate dreams to you, Madame Hag? I don't mean the female rubes. I mean the people in the show."

"Everybody, yes. And you better learn to talk circus. Always say on the show, not in it."

Sarah asked her, "Has anybody else been having any dreams of any consequence?"

"Yes."

After a moment, Sarah said, "Well?"

"I no tell who. Or what the dreams. But from one I dukker a wheel somewhere turning. From another a trouble with a black woman."

Edge said, "We don't have any black woman. On the show."

"And nobody works with any kind of wheel," Sarah

said, reflecting. "Maggie, do you mean some of us are going to blow the stand? And is Hannibal going to marry some black wench? What?"

"No matter," said Magpie Maggie Hag. "We go to Europe, yes, and more of us than we are now."

Sarah persisted, "Then you mean someone new will be joining out?"

Deep within her cowl, the old gypsy nodded, but said no more.

Late that night, Edge said to Sarah, "Before you fall asleep, tell me, that dream you mentioned, do you have it every night?"

"No. Only now and then. I haven't had it any of the nights we've slept together, so I don't expect I will tonight. But when I do—and that's what is curious—it's always the same. I fall from a rosinback, but safe into a net."

They were again bedded apart from the other troupers, this time in a field outside Staunton. The wagon train had arrived after dark, and so they made camp without yet erecting the Big Top.

Edge asked, "And how did Maggie interpret that dream?"

"Oh, a lot of hocus-pocus and horsus-shittus. The meshes of the net, me getting tangled in them—I'm going to fall into evil ways and then be abandoned. Something like that."

"You don't believe in such things, I hope."

Sarah shrugged in his embrace. "If and when it happens, I'll believe it. She was right about Abe Lincoln being dead."

"She never mentioned any such thing. She just went early to bed—maybe with a stomachache—and everybody took it for a portent after the fact."

"Well, I hope she's right about us getting to Europe. And it shouldn't be long before we know whether she's right about us having new people on the show." Her voice began to trail away as she drifted into sleep. "I wonder who or what we'll get first . . ."

*   *   *

"Abner Mullenax is the name," said a man, seizing and wringing Florian's hand. "That show of yours, gents, was just downright dandy!" It was the next afternoon, the circus had just finished its performance, and this man had emerged from the Big Top with the rest of the crowd. He wore farmer's homespun garb, but Edge estimated him to be not over forty, young enough to be in uniform—and probably he had been; he wore a black patch over one eye. "That show was *so* dandy that I'd like to show my gratitude, gents. I'm going to make you-all an offer of something special."

Florian only murmured noncommittally. He had been grumbling to Edge and Rouleau, before the man approached, about the sparse attendance of the Stauntonians and the poor quality of goods they had bartered for tickets. He was in no mood for further disappointment. But he looked surprised and a trifle less gloomy when Abner Mullenax went on to say:

"I got a great big colored circus tent you-all can have. Big as this one here and a whole lot purtier. And no, don't ask how much I'm asking for it. Just come and look at it and if you want it, it's yours for the taking. My wagon's yonder and my place is only three mile from here. If we hustle, we can get on the way before all these other folks clog the road. You could be back here with your new tent by nightfall. What say?"

The three circus men looked at each other, more than somewhat bewildered, but their looks agreed: why not? They went with Abner Mullenax to his ramshackle wagon and climbed aboard, Florian on the seat beside him, Edge and Rouleau sitting sprawled in the bed of it, Rouleau still wearing his gaudy ring dress. Mullenax briskly slapped the reins to prompt the plow mule, and they did get away while the rest of the circus audience still milled about. They drove a short distance along the Pike, then turned off onto a minor dirt road, and except for one digression— "There's a jug under the straw back there, gents. Help yourselves and hand it up here''—Mullenax was talking up his tent the whole way.

''. . . Splendiferous thing and looks brand-spanking new. Been hoarding it all through the war. My wife and daughters wanted to cut it up, make themselves dresses and what not. Wouldn't let 'em. A thing like that, you don't want to use it up piecemeal. It belongs all together and, by God, I've kept it that way.''

Florian finally got a word in. ''Excuse me, Mr. Mullenax, but—''

''Call me Abner. Here, have a snort.''

Florian took a sip of the corn whiskey and tried again. ''Er, Abner, what circus were you with?''

''Me?'' he laughed. ''None yet, unless you count the battle of First Manassas.'' He took a healthy pull at the jug. ''You mean where'd I get the tent? I found it. After I was invalided out again. Come back to my farm and there was the tent in my crick hollow.''

''You *found* a circus tent?''

Mullenax gave him a bloodshot look with his one eye. ''You don't reckon I could *steal* a thing that size?''

''No, no, of course not. But it's almost as hard to believe that some outfit would set up its pavilion on your land and then go off and leave it.''

''Wasn't set up. Just was laying there on the ground. Couldn't hardly believe it myself. Like it might of blowed from somewhere.''

''Well!'' breathed Florian, still nonplussed. ''Blowdowns do happen. I've never seen one blow *away*, but it's conceivable. I just can't imagine the circus people not chasing and catching it.''

Abner Mullenax alternately sucked at the jug and discoursed on his brief war service during the rest of the hour or so it took to reach his farm, a place about as ramshackle as his wagon. Only a halfheartedly barking hound dog greeted them there—none of the women Mullenax had mentioned—and a penful of pigs oinked and squealed with hungry vigor. The men got down from the wagon, Mul-

lenax a little unsteadily, and he led them around behind
the barn to a haystack, which he began tearing apart.

"Took good care of it, see? Out of the weather and out
of sight. Even the two times the Yanks stopped by, they
was satisfied to grab a pig or three I left out for 'em to
find. Didn't go poking in here."

When he had scooped away enough of the hay, they
could see that it concealed another farm wagon, ordinary
enough, except that its bed was full of folded fabric and
tangled rope. Edge and Rouleau moved in to help Mullenax fling away the hay, until they could make out that
the cloth was part vermilion, part white, and had tremendous black cloth letters sewn on it. Curiously, the ropes
were more slender than the usual circus ropes, and of finer
fibre, and seemed to be a net of some sort. When the
wagon was all uncovered, three of the big black letters
were uppermost in a row. They spelled RAT.

"Ma foi!" Rouleau exclaimed in awe. "No wonder
your women wanted to cut it up. This cloth is *silk*."

Florian gave him a sharp nudge to shut him up, but Edge
was on the other side of the wagon, and couldn't be
stopped from commenting, "Yep, pongee silk. Double
thickness, besides. And these cords are linen." Then he
laughed.

Mistaking the expression on Edge's face, Mullenax
asked worriedly, "A silk tent ain't no good?"

"Oh, I'm sure we can make *some* trifling use—" Florian began, but he was overridden by Edge:

"Mr. Mullenax, this is not a circus tent."

"*What*!" said the farmer, and hiccuped. "Why, the son
of a bitch is twice as big as my whole house yonder."

Edge asked, "Did you find a sort of basket with it? A
big wicker basket?"

"Uh huh," said Mullenax, regarding Edge the way rube
women regarded Magpie Maggie Hag when she spoke or-
acles. "It's in there under the cloth. Big enough for a
couple-three men to take a bath in, if it was zinc. And

there's some other things—wood, brass, india rubber. I figgered 'em to be circus trappings.''

Edge turned to Florian, who was looking simultaneously puzzled and annoyed. "You want us to unfold some of it, Mr. Florian? Those letters will spell out *Saratoga*."

"Never mind," Florian said, a little peevishly. "I gather you've seen it before. What is the thing?"

"I never saw this one, but I heard about it. It's a Yankee observation balloon."

"Well, I'll be switched!" blurted Mullenax.

"Four years ago," said Edge, "after First Manassas, when the Rebs damn near took Washington, the Yanks got real apprehensive about the safety of their city. They laid out elaborate defense works all around, including their Balloon Corps. All the balloons had names. They had this *Saratoga* at Centreville, and a man went up in it every day, to keep an eye out for any more Rebel buildups at Manassas Station. Then a November gale came along, and a balloon can't stay up in a wind. The Yanks cranked the *Saratoga* down far enough for the observer to jump out, but then the whole thing got away from them. The norther blew it away like an autumn leaf. Nobody ever knew what became of it.''

"Well" said Mullenax, "I'm glad to know I got *something* out of Manassas. But here I've been tending it all this time like the goddam family jewels and *shit!* It ain't no use to you-all at all?"

"Mais oui!" cried Rouleau, his eyes sparkling. "A circus that can feature a balloon ascen—ouch!" He had got fiercely nudged again.

"It's not *worth* anything to us, Abner," Florian said quickly. "But I daresay we can find something to do with it. The main problem is transportation."

"Oh, hell," said Mullenax. "Leave it in the wagon where it is. I'll just go fetch the mule and hitch him to this one. Tote it right back to the circus grounds for you."

"That's very kind, but *we* don't have anything to put it

in. Our other wagons are already jammed full to the doors.''

"Goddam it, man, Abner Mullenax don't give a gift halfway. I'm giving you this-here wagon, too, and the mule to pull it. You only got to say you want 'em.''

"All right, yes, we want them," said Florian, but with a bewilderment verging on suspicion. "We just don't want to take advantage. It is a handsome offer you make, sir, but I can't help wondering . . ." he refrained from suggesting the possible influence of the whiskey jug in this unprecedented transaction. "I mean—you're not asking *anything* in return? You're giving us a balloon, which is something you'll never likely have use for. But the mule and wagon? Surely they are necessities to a farmer.''

"Only if I stay a farmer," said Mullenax, and now there was something sly in his bloodshot eye. "Can I show y'all something else?''

He led them to the ill-smelling pigsty, where a hog, a couple of sows and three piglets wallowed in the mud, making more noise than Maximus the lion ever had. "You-all ever seen a performing pig?''

"Well . . . yes.''

"You're about to see some more." A short, crude, homemade ladder was leaning against the outside of the pen. Mullenax lifted it over the fence and leaned it against the inside. Instantly, one of the piglets slogged through the muck to the ladder, fastidiously shook its little trotters as clean as it could, scrambled up the rungs as nimbly as a cat, paused proudly, turned and twinkled down again. Another piglet came and did the same, then the third. Mullenax removed the ladder before they could repeat the sequence.

"Why, that was pretty!" said Florian. "You trained them, Abner?''

"No. I won't lie and brag that I did. The thing is, you set a ladder in front of any pig—a pig that ain't got too heavy—and it'll climb the ladder, same as it'll climb a stile in any field. For some reason, they just *like* to.''

"I never knew that."

"Not many people do. I never did, either, until I found it out by accident. I just happened to put the ladder in there one day, and saw what went on."

"Bless my soul," said Florian. There was a short silence, during which Mullenax's one eye regarded him imploringly. Florian said, "I take it, Abner, you want to sell us the performing pigs as a condition of giving us the—"

"No, sir! All I'm asking is that you take the pigs along with the balloon and the wagon and the mule. *And me.*"

The circus men all goggled at him. Finally Rouleau said, "You wish to run away with the circus, mon vieux?"

"That's right. I want you to hire me and these shoats as your—whatchamacallit—your pig act. You set the wages, or we'll work for just our keep."

"Hm-m-m . . .," Florian said. "Let's see. Pigs. Boars. Wild Tasmanian Boars. Eye patch—pirate—Captain Kidd. No, we've already got a captain . . ."

"Gents, I don't like to rush you," said Mullenax. "But I got reasons for hurrying."

"Done!" said Florian. "Barnacle Bill and His Wild Tasmanian Boars!"

"*Yee-ee-hoo-ee!*" Mullenax gave the piercing Rebel yell, startling everybody in the farmyard. Even the pigs went silent.

Florian said, "You mentioned a wife and daughters, Abner. Oughtn't you and we have a word with them? After all . . ."

"They ain't here. I took 'em to see your circus."

"You drove off and left them there?"

"They'll walk home when they get tired of looking for me. Or some neighbor'll give 'em a ride. That's why I'm in a hurry. There's another road we can take, going back, so we won't meet 'em."

Edge said, "You're simply going to disappear? No good-byes? Nothing?"

"You ain't met my wife and daughters, Cunnel. If

you're lucky, you won't. If you're even luckier, you won't never have no such things of your own.''

"But aren't they sure to chase after you?" Florian asked. "We're not leaving town straightaway. Today was such a poor stand, we're staying to give another performance tomorrow. We won't depart until the next day, and even then we won't exactly whiz off over the far horison. A circus travels at a slow pace.''

"This hive of females has been *wishing* me good-bye for as long as I can remember. If me and the animals stay out of sight tomorrow, and tag along when you pull out, the womenfolk ain't likely to follow. They'll figger it was worth the loss of a mule and some pork to be rid of me. Come on, you fellers, give me a hand.''

With Mullenax at the reins and Florian, Rouleau and Edge each holding a trussed, squirming and squealing piglet, and all of them crowded together on the driver's seat, so as not to risk damaging the precious silk and linen cargo in the wagon's bed, they took a roundabout route back to the circus pitch, and they encountered no Mrs. Mullenax or Misses Mullenax on the way. During the ride, Rouleau eagerly inquired of Edge what else he knew about balloons and the technicalities of ballooning.

"Not a hell of a lot," Edge confessed. "I've seen several of them hanging up in the air. The Yankee ones. The Confederates only tried balloons a few times, I think, and I only saw one of those being actually sent up. That was in Richmond. They squirted it full of gas at the Tredegar ironworks.''

"Arrêtez. What kind of gas?''

"Damned if I know. But the Yankee Balloon Corps had horse-drawn machines to make it on the spot, wherever it was needed. I've seen them through a spyglass, but I couldn't tell you anything about them. Just a couple of big metal boxes painted light blue, mounted on ordinary escort wagons, and a lot of hoses running here and there.''

"We must learn all these things," Rouleau said decisively. "We must become aéronautes. To own a balloon and not to send it aloft, that would be a shame. An atrocity. C'est tout dire. It must fly.''

The next morning, Hannibal rode Peggy all over Staunton, pounding his drum and shouting invitingly, and Tim Trimm rode about town on Bubbles, pasting and tacking posters. Obie Yount spent the morning painfully but doggedly practicing with his cannonballs. He had persuaded himself that yesterday's poor crowd was his fault because he had been too sore to appear as the Quakemaker—and he was undissuaded when everybody in the company pointed out to him that Staunton could hardly have been expecting a Quakemaker. The rest of the troupe more enjoyably occupied the morning by unbundling the balloon from its long confinement and unfurling it across the field to admire it. Abner Mullenax stood to one side, looking proud, and breakfasting from a jug—he seemed to have an unlimited stock of them—while his new colleagues paced up and down beside the awesome length of limp fabric, ropes and wicker basket, making comments variously laudatory, calculating and yearning.

Sarah read the name lettered on it and said, ''*Saratoga*. I did the nude 'Mazeppa' ride in the convention hall at Saratoga Springs one time. Blow this thing up and it would be twice as high as that hall.''

Roozeboom said, ''Ja, verdomde big bag.''

Florian felt the cloth and said, ''It has some kind of an elastic varnish all over it. Makes it leakproof, I suppose.''

Edge said, ''My grasp of geometry has slipped some, but I figure we're looking at something like twelve hundred yards of double-weight pongee silk.''

''Mishto!'' said Magpie Maggie Hag, licking her thin lips almost lustfully. ''How *many* nevi dress I could make. Nevi for everybody in the show.''

''Jamais de la vie!'' Rouleau said severely. ''This is not a linen closet, madame, this could be the making of our fortune.''

"Not unless we can contrive some way to inflate it," said Edge.

The object of their regard was, even in its detumescent state, a formidable thing indeed. The cloth part, laid out flat, was fifty-five feet across at its widest—"Inflated, that will be a thirty-five-foot diameter," said Edge, working his geometry again—and it was more than twice that long, a pear-shaped affair of alternate vermilion and white gores, the seams between them meticulously lapped, gummed and reinforced. The narrow end of the pear tapered to a hollow tube that ended in a brass cock, with a bright blue cord and a bright red strap dangling beside it. The blue cord went clear up through the interior of the balloon, connecting to a large and elaborate valve contraption, made of mahogany, brass and india rubber, sewn into the very top of the balloon's bulbous upper body.

"The red strap seems to go all the way up inside, too," said Florian. "But I'm damned if I can tell what it does."

"I think I see," said Magpie Maggie Hag, to everyone's surprise. "One gore, at top, only lightly lapped and sewn."

"Ah, bien entendu!" said Rouleau. "When one has used the blue cord judiciously, to open the top valve to descend and land, one then pulls that red strap to rip that panel loose. It spills all the remaining gas to collapse the balloon, lest the basket be dragged around on the ground. Then it must be resewn before the next ascent."

The upper half of the *Saratoga*'s red-and-white body was enveloped by a lozenge-meshed net of linen cord, loose and lank now, but it would closely embrace the bag when that was inflated. The linen cords' lower ends were gathered beneath the balloon, where they were firmly affixed to a stout suspension hoop of wood about five feet in diameter. From that, on fewer but heavier ropes, depended the oblong wicker gondola, commodious enough for two persons but a snug fit for three. Edge drew the onlookers' attention to the fact that an iron sheet had been fitted in the bottom of the basket.

"Armor plating," he said. "So the observer wouldn't

get shot in the—uh—between the legs—by riflemen on the ground. He wasn't in much danger, though, except when he was first going up or nearly down again. In the air, he was beyond rifle shot.''

"The silk has survived its storage undamaged,'' Florian noted. ''But I notice that some of the linen network has frayed and parted here and there. Since that is what holds up the aeronaut, it had damned well better be secure. Captain Hotspur, I'd be obliged if, in your spare time, you'd do what splicing is necessary. And Mag, stop looking so deprived. Somewhere we'll find you some other pretty cloth to work with. In the meantime, you've already got the dress to finish for Obie and Zachary. And we'll want a piratical outfit for our new artiste, Barnacle Bill.''

So Magpie Maggie Hag, though grumpily, took Edge away from the balloon and Yount from his strongman practice, for a fitting of the costumes she had by now basted together, and also took Mullenax away from his liquid breakfast. Florian, Roozeboom and the Wild Man began refolding the *Saratoga* to bundle it back into its wagon. While Colonel Ramrod and the Quakemaker were trying on their new clothes, gingerly so as not to burst the temporary seams, the old woman gave Barnacle Bill a close scrutiny and decreed that he already possessed the most necessary item of a pirate's equipment, the eye patch. She simply gave him a gaudy gypsy bandana to tie around his head and a faded green-and-white striped jumper to replace his denim shirt, and declared him costumed. She also dismissed Edge and Yount, after she had done some tucking and pinning of their new garments, and Yount went grimly back to his cannonballs. Edge wandered idly into the Big Top, and saw in use a piece of circus apparatus he had not previously seen.

From halfway up the center pole stuck out, at an angle, a second and slimmer pole, like the boom arm from a derrick mast. It was fixed there by a loose iron circlet that enabled it to swing freely around the center pole. The boom reached about midway across the ring and had a hole in its outer end. From the top of the center pole, a rope angled down and through that hole; its far end was tied to a leather belt worn by Clover Lee, who was standing on Bubbles as the horse loped easily around the ring. Ignatz Roozeboom, standing in the ring, was guiding the horse and occasionally tapping it with the tassel of his long whip. With his other hand he clung tightly to the other end of the rope that came from the top of the center pole.

"Is called rope-fall, dis t'ing," he said, when Edge asked. "I hold dis rope, see, it goes over pulley up top de center pole, comes down to boom end, den to mam'selle's safety belt. If she fall off horse, I t'row my weight dis end, she no hit ground. Rope-fall is for practice new or hard trick."

"I'm trying to teach Bubbles to do a left and right hand," Clover Lee called to Edge. "You know, frisk a little to the left and right, while I'm jumping the garters and garlands. Add a touch of toot to the trick."

She demonstrated. Roozeboom, still holding tight to the rope-fall end, flicked his whip. The horse, not slowing his lope, did a cross-leg to the left while Clover Lee bounded into a somersault, landing lightly and safely on Bubbles' rump. Then Roozeboom flicked the whip again, the horse did a cross-leg to the right, but this time awkwardly balked while Clover Lee was in the air, so he was not in the right place when she came down. Her feet skidded off the horse's rump, Roozeboom leaned into the rope, and the girl dangled in the air, laughing, still going around and around the ring some six feet off the ground. Roozeboom eased off on the rope and lowered her gradually as she slowed, until her feet touched earth and she skipped gracefully to a halt.

"Damned old rosinback just doesn't like cherry pie," she said.

"I never knew a horse that did," said Edge. "But what's that got to do with anything?"

Clover Lee gave him a look of patient toleration. "In circus talk, cherry pie means extra work laid on. Because you're supposed to get *paid* extra, but you usually don't. Anyhow, you can't be truly circus if you're too lazy to work. You might as well blow the stand. That means pick up and leave.''

Edge left the tent, cogitating. He was aware that Clover Lee had not been chiding *him* as a shirker, but he was also aware that the girl was going to great pains to perfect a nuance of her act that would not even be noticeable to most of the rubes who watched it, and that meanwhile the Quakemaker was in the circus's backyard getting in shape to return to work, while he himself, Colonel Ramrod, was loafing. So he began trying to think of ways to improve his own act. And just then a little black boy came along the road, carrying a basket of dried and colorful gourds.

"Buy a gourd, massa? Make y'self a dipper?"

Edge gave him two tickets to the afternoon show, probably an extravagant overpayment, and got the whole basketful. The gourds would shatter when shot, as impressively as did the saucers, but they were a lot showier and, being all of different sizes and shapes, they would look to the crowd as if they were harder to hit. Colonel Ramrod felt quite pleased with his notion.

He used the gourds in his act that afternoon. The crowd, though still nowhere near the tent's capacity, was gratifyingly larger than that of the day before, and it was properly appreciative of Colonel Ramrod's shooting. Among the loud applauders, two small black boys clapped loudest, and one was heard to shout to the other, with profound pride and glee, "Them's *my gourds* he busted!" Florian of course did not put Barnacle Bill and his Tasmanian Wild Boars on the bill that day, lest they be recognized and reported to the abandoned Mullenax women. Abner watched the show from concealment under the stands and said it was all right with him, not performing on his first day in the company.

"I got plans for them pigs," he confided to Edge. "Now that I've got 'em away from the distractions of farm life,

I'm gonna teach 'em a lot more tricks than just going up and down a ladder.''

Edge was slightly amused that a neophyte, who had not even been in the ring yet, should already be eager to contrive an act new and astonishing to the world. But Edge was to discover that no circus performer, however old in years and experience, was ever satisfied that his act was beyond perfectibility—and also that a circus director was never satisfied that the sequence and variety of his program was beyond improvement.

Now that Florian had the Quakemaker and Colonel Ramrod on his bill—and Barnacle Bill waiting in the wings—he told Monsieur Roulette, that afternoon in Staunton, to omit his bit of wretched ventriloquy. The decision was greeted with no outcry. Everybody in the show, Roulette included, considered it a mercy to both him and the audiences. Not at all repining, Jules assiduously practiced, from then on, to embellish his acrobatic act with even more spectacular flights of contortion—what he called monkey jumps and lion's leaps and souplettes and "brandies." He also procured a small coal-oil lamp, and at ensuing performances made his entrance holding it alight in one hand while he turned flips and layouts and one-hand walkovers all around it.

"It impresses people," he told Yount, "to see the flame go on burning while I do that."

"Hell, it impresses me," said Yount.

"Pourquoi? If you think about it, ami, why should *not* the flame stay alight?"

"I reckon you're right. But it sure is showy." He added, "I'll have to think up some new tricks for myself, if the Quakemaker's not to be totally outshined."

North of Staunton, as Edge and Yount had said, the Shenandoah Valley was pitifully war-worn. What should have been farmhouses, barns, stables, silos, fences and even stands of timber were now only crumbled stone, charred wood and stumps. The sprinkling of livestock to be seen consisted mostly of old, crippled or windbroken horses left behind by one army or another. In many places where the Valley Pike was supposed to vault over a creek or river, the road simply stopped at its brink in midair, the bridge having been a victim of Sheridan's making the valley untravelable as well as untenable by other armies. Some of the gaps were easily forded, but at others enterprising country folk—usually Negros—had rigged up block-and-tackle ferry rafts, and man-powered the circus across, one wagon at a time. The charges were modest, and the entrepreneurs accepted Confederate scrip, but they never had fixed a rate for ferrying an elephant. It didn't matter. Peggy preferred to swim at every opportunity, and did so with more aplomb than was shown by the gawking ferrymen.

The Valley's towns and villages still stood, but not undamaged. Sheridan had made his march and his Burning in too much of a hurry to take time to destroy every community utterly. He had been content to demolish mainly mills, warehouses, armories, granaries and the like. So the larger towns had a gap-toothed look about them: streets missing a building here, a row of buildings there, or whole squares flattened into rubble-strewn empty lots. The buildings that were still erect were much pocked by rifle shot, many were holed by cannonballs and some had even been knocked askew on their foundations.

Where people had been burned out of their homes, they had made at least habitable domiciles from scavenged and mismatched planks or discarded army tents. Here and there in the distance, off Sheridan's route of march along the very middle of the valley—hence remote enough for the Yankees not to have bothered with them—could be seen the occasional sturdy homestead and even a few plantation houses of estimable grandeur that had escaped the Burning. Wherever there lived an ablebodied man, woman or child, the farm fields had been at least in part resown and were showing early green. Elsewhere the soft Virginia springtime was decently clothing the fallow fields, the pastures and meadows and mountain slopes, if only with wild grasses, shrubs and flowers. Throughout the valley, dogwood trees were in full blossom and they scattered their big white petals so prodigally that even the miserable road surface was carpeted like a triumphal parade route, and the wagon train's hoofs and wheels flung the petals fluttering in a continuous gentle, warm snowfall.

The valley was coming alive again, albeit slowly and painfully, and the valley's people could hope that it would revive more quickly as the younger men came trudging home from the war. So they seemed to take the arrival of Florian's Flourishing Florilegium as a welcome augury, but they had pathetically little with which to pay or barter for tickets. This led Florian to decree that, in each of these northerly-valley towns, the circus would stay for two days of performance, sometimes three, to enable all the country folk to make their way into town from the surrounding areas. Thus, although it meant two or three times as much work, the circus realized approximately as much from each town—some good silver, a lot of Confederate paper, some edibles, wearables and usables—as it had taken in with just one show in the comparatively unravaged Lynchburg.

By the time the circus showed in Harrisonburg, Magpie Maggie Hag had finished the new ring dress for Edge and Yount. The Quakemaker proudly put on and strutted around in his bogus leopard-skin caveman attire, even in his free time. Colonel Ramrod, however much he felt a dandy and a sham in his black-and-yellow uniform, at least no longer felt he was subjecting the Confederate gray to disgrace. The gypsy had even found enough woolen material to make a cape to go with the uniform. It was black outside, yellow inside, had a stiff collar that stood up around his head like a coal scuttle, and was of a length that reached the ground. The first time he wore it into the ring, he wore it only long enough to accept his entrance applause, then unhooked it and let Tiny Tim take it while he did his shooting.

"No, no, no!" Florian scolded him afterward.

"Hell, that thing's cumbersome," said Edge. "I can't have it hindering me."

"Take it off, yes," said Florian. "But don't just *take it off*. Do it with a grand flourish. Watch me."

He put on the cape and strode around the empty tent with a swagger that made the cape billow dramatically behind him, while he gave gracefully slow arm wavings and swooping bows and arms-up V-signs to an imaginary throng. Then, still striding, he unhooked the cape at his neck and, with one hand, gave it a twirl that made the whole thing a fluttery, swirling, black-and-yellow wheel that he slowly and dramatically let subside to the ground.

"That's how," he said. "Do it when you put it on, too, to take your exit applause."

So Edge dutifully went off to practice swashing his cape. Nowadays, all the troupers were practicing *something*, either their established routines or new ones they were trying. The addition to the program of the three new men had put a fresh competitive spirit into the old troupers, and that made those three first-of-Mayers work even harder to become old troupers themselves. The fact that the circus stayed now at each pitch for two or three days, instead of tearing down every other night and hitting the road every other day, gave the company ample time in mornings and evenings to work on their acts and refurbish their costumes and props.

When Hannibal Tyree wasn't in the ring or on parade as Abdullah the Hindu, he was forever practicing his juggling and balancing tricks, and with ever more numerous, more various and more outlandish props. He could now do showers and cascades of such diverse shapes and weights as a horseshoe, a posy of flowers, an empty lard bucket, a hen's egg and—after a while of that—snatch off and add to the array one, then the other, of his own shabby shoes.

Hannibal and Tim Trimm together also spent time adding to the Wild Man's banjo repertoire. They sat him down and played through every tune they used in the program, from the "Dixie Land" overture to the closing walka-round's "Lorena." They also taught the Wild Man the piece they had chosen to accompany the Quakemaker's exhibition of brute strength, "If Your Foot Is Pretty, Show It"—and, of course, "Barnacle Bill the Sailor" to go with the newest act. Abner Mullenax had never heard the song and hadn't even known there was such a thing, but he was gravely shocked when he heard the musicians working on it, because Tiny Tim sang along with the music, and he sang the bawdy lyrics to the *original* song, "Bollocky Bill."

"Ain't them words awful dirty for a mixed audience?" Mullenax anxiously asked Florian. "Me and my pigs do a clean act."

"Only the music will be played while you perform, Abner. Nobody will sing the words."

"Well, if that's so . . . all right, then. I don't want my pigs pelted with no rotten eggs."

It was not likely. The audiences were charmed by his pigs, even when, during their early performances, they did nothing but scamper up and down the ladder. By the time the circus got to Woodstock, though, Mullenax had taught the smallest and cleverest of the pigs to do something that absolutely delighted the rubes. During just a couple of practice mornings, Mullenax borrowed Roozeboom's rope-fall, tied the piglet to the rope, set it outside the ring curb and, with Roozeboom's sjambok, prodded it to a trot. It could only run in a circle around the curb, and Mullenax could make it stop simply by dropping the whip tassel in front of it. However, at the same moment he did that, he clicked one thumbnail. After only a few circuits, the little pig had learned to stop at the sound of the click, with no need of the whip at all. By the second practice session, Mullenax was working the animal without even the rope-fall attached.

Beginning with the first show at Woodstock, the piglet—which Florian insisted be named Hamlet, though Mullenax thought the name "undignified"—was the star of the pig act and very nearly the prime attraction of the whole show. Barnacle Bill would set the pig to trotting around the tent, then call out, ''Hamlet, pick the girl that likes to be kissed,'' and, in the resultant rush of laughter, nobody would notice the faint thumbnail click that made the pig halt before some pretty girl in the first row of benches and set her blushing and set the whole crowd on a roar. Barnacle Bill would touch Hamlet with the whip to start him trotting again, to ''pick the girl what likes to be kissed *in the dark*!'' and so on. At many peformances thereafter, it was hard for Florian to summon the pirate and his piglet out of the ring, for the audiences seemed never to tire of them.

After one show's extended series of encores and bows, when Mullenax finally made his exit, he said to Florian, breathing whiskily, ''Might be that I'm ready now for bigger things. Do you reckon Captain Hotspur would give me lessons in lion taming? Like he does Obie Yount in the strongman routine?''

''Presumptuous man,'' Florian said, but genially. ''Learn lion taming? You have intrinsic talent, I don't have to tell you that, but it takes a lot of other qualities. What makes you think you could learn?''

''The fact that I think I could makes me think I could.''

Florian gave him an approving look. ''Good answer, that. I'll put in a word for you, Abner, with Captain Hotspur.''

But Roozeboom already had plenty of work to occupy him, now that the competitive spirit had infused the whole troupe. When he was not practicing with one or both of the Coverley women on new tricks to do in the various riding acts, and when he was not trying mightily to invigorate Maximus out of his customary torpor so *he* might learn a new trick or two, Roozeboom was still generously helping the Quakemaker to achieve new feats of strength. On what had been the extensive battlefields around New Market, Yount had found a Yankee ''bull-pup'' cannon— half submerged and caked into a now-dry mudhole, but quite undamaged—and employed his Lightning to drag it free and haul it to the circus lot. At first sight of it, Florian was disinclined to add such a ponderous prop to the show's transportation problems, but Roozeboom joined Yount in regaling him with reasons why he should.

"Is nee so heavy as it looks, Baas," said Roozeboom.

"And it'll look *damn* heavy," said Yount, "when the rubes watch it roll right over me. Ignatz says I can lay down in the ring with two planks across my chest and legs, and—"

"Like I haff told Obie, in de chest en thighs are strongest bones. Also, Obie have chest like verdomde oak barrel en thighs like oak stumps."

"I'll have Lightning pace up the planks and right across—"

"Good God, Obie," said Florian. "That Percheron must weigh three-quarters of a ton."

"We already tried it. As long as Ignatz keeps him moving, I only feel the whole weight for just a second, when the planks tilt for him to go down the other side. But he'll be hauling this-here field piece, and it'll roll right over me, too. Naturally, I'll groan and thrash a lot—make it look good. It'll even outdo the part where the cannonball falls on my neck."

"Well . . ." said Florian, frowning. "But the damn gun is so big. We can't carry it. We'll need another draft animal to haul it."

The iron cannon itself was only four and a half feet long, but it perched atop a formidable carriage of timbers and swivel screws and dangling chains, attached to the iron-bound beam that was its trail and recoil-spade— the whole flanked by two wheels that stood higher than the gun itself.

"Shucks, big Peggy kin drag it," Hannibal said confidently. "Lookahere, Mas' Florian. Lift de trail and de whole thing balance puffickly delicate on dem two wheels. Be no load a'tall for Peggy to pull. And jist think how fine it look on de road."

"Well, all right," said Florian, spreading his hands. "Brutus is your responsibility. As long as the bull can continue to do her crew work and ring work, I can't complain. We'll keep the cannon."

By now, so many other troupers were adding so many refinements to their acts that Edge was inspired to add another to his—a trick he had heard of other shootists doing. Among the barter handed in at the red wagon, he found a woman's small handmirror, and he began to practice firing his revolver backward over his shoulder, aiming with the mirror. It would have been difficult if he hadn't gaffed the trick. He loaded four chambers of the Remington's cylinder with regular lead balls, the fifth with bird shot and the sixth, as before, only with powder tamped down with cornmeal.

In the ring, after he had used his carbine to shoot out of the air a gourd tossed up by Clover Lee, he used the revolver to shoot at the other five gourds perched on the ring curb, and disintegrated four of them with the regular balls, fired from different positions. Then, turning his back and using the looking glass to aim over his shoulder, he had only to aim approximately at the fifth gourd to demolish it with the spray of bird shot. Finally, as usual, he fired the sixth and uncharged chamber directly at Clover Lee so she could "catch the ball" in her teeth.

Florian was so taken with Edge's new flourish that he promoted Colonel Ramrod to the coveted "close" of the show—the last act on the program before the final walk-around spec. That demoted the former closing act, Captain Hotspur and Madame Solitaire, to next-to-close. But Sarah was proud of Edge, "her protégé," and Roozeboom was stolidly incapable of jealousy, so they accepted second-best stardom without protest.

"Tout éclatant!" Florian said delightedly to Rouleau, as they stood together watching the close of the final performance at Strasburg. "We've worked up a more than decent show. Now, if we had more of a midway outside. Something to bring us extra money at intermission."

Rouleau laughed. "And if the yokels could *pay* the money. Merde alors, they're paying little enough for the main show."

"I'm thinking ahead, Jules. Up the road. Up north, where they *can* pay. In the cities where the people don't go to bed at sundown, and we can put on evening performances besides these matinées. And Europe, where we can really spread ourselves. Let the poor think us rich; let the rich think us risqué-tout."

"Bien, a balloon ascension would be just the thing for the midway. If only I can find out how to do it. All along the road, I have been inquiring of everybody that looks like a soldier-come-home—asking if he ever served anywhere near the Balloon Corps. You can imagine the kind of looks I get. Mais, sous serment—somewhere, some way—I am going to learn how to get that aérostat into the high blue sky."

"Well, until you do, I think what we need at intermission is a proper sideshow. The Wild Man and the museum aren't enough. We need the real freaks—a Human Skeleton, a Fat Lady, an Intersex, things like that. While you're asking around about balloons, ask if anybody knows of any creatures of that nature available."

However, shortly after teardown that night, the circus discovered that it no longer had *any* resident freak. Tim Trimm was the first to notice. They were all eating supper around the fire when Tim said, "Has the idjit finally got tired of his nigger-fiddle? He ain't serenading like usual?"

They all looked at each other, then roundabout. Sarah said, "He was here just a few minutes ago. He got his supper, all right. Nobody could miss noticing when the Wild Man eats."

"Well, he sure ain't anywhere around now," said Yount, after the troupers had scattered through the darkness to the farthest reaches of the lot and then regathered at the fire.

Magpie Maggie Hag said darkly, "One gazha woman today, she ask me dukker her palm if she ever have baby.

This woman got wild eyes, like loco, so I tell her yes for certain she have shavora. But I don't tell her I think she damned old for begin family.''

Florian looked mildly astounded. "Mag, are you suggesting that some woman, desperate for a child, has abducted the Wild Man of the Woods?"

The gypsy only shrugged.

"Shit, she could of had me," said Tim, with a giggle. "Serve her right, when she finds out she's adopted a fizzlewit."

"Well, she must have got his banjo, too," said Clover Lee, coming into the firelight. "I've just looked in the prop wagon and everywhere else, and it's gone."

Hannibal said wonderingly, "You know what? I bet dat boy done run off fum de circus 'cause he thinks he *is* a circus. Me and Tim shouldn't of learned him all dat music."

"It could be true," said Florian. "Even those most defective in intellect can possess a deep and devious cunning. I had a wife like that once."

"No use searching for him in the dark," said Edge. "But Obie, we'll saddle up at first light and make a cast."

They did, and Roozeboom and Sarah came with them, riding Snowball and Bubbles, so they could quarter the compass. But none of them found the Wild Man. By noontime, they had all returned to the lot, and Florian said resignedly, "I hope that childless female did give him a home, and I hope she enjoys banjo music. Now we've got a twenty-mile run to Winchester, and a late start. If you fellows will get those horses into wagon harness, we'll roll. And Barnacle Bill, I'm afraid this makes you our Wild Man until we can get another."

"What?" said Mullenax.

"Old circus saying: the newest clown has to take the water. Be the butt of every jest, the target of everything thrown. In other words, the newest man gets the dirtiest jobs. Before each show, you'll do the roaring and chain-clanking for Maximus. Then, during intermissions . . .

hm . . . I think we'll make you the Crocodile Man.''

"What?"

"Nothing intolerable about it. Abdullah used to double as a crocodile until we got the idiot. We have to work things out as we go along. You'll still do your Barnacle Bill in the first half of the program. Then you strip down to a loincloth, we pour poster paste all over you, and you simply roll in the dust. As it dries, it crusts and cracks and scales most realistically.''

"Judas Priest."

"Can't do it with your pirate eye patch on, of course," Florian briskly went on. "Lift that up for a moment, Abner, let me see the hole. Ah, ghastly, yes. Good. That will add to the frightfulness. Your Crocodile Man ought to make as favorable a hit as your pig act.''

"Jesus Christ."

While most of the men were still occupied with hitching up the wagons, Sarah said to Magpie Maggie Hag, with some awe in her voice, "You did predict that not all of us would go to Europe. Now, sure enough, we've lost one.''

"But got another," said the gypsy, indicating Mullenax, who was moodily kicking at the dust he would soon be wearing. "We still same number. More yet to lose, more yet to come.''

10

IT WAS a Friday night when they arrived in Winchester and found a place to set up, near the Negro Cemetery. So they showed on Saturday, to a fairly good crowd, then had a lazy layover day on Sunday before performing again on Monday. Most of the troupers had chores or practicing to occupy their off-time, but some of them ambled up Loudoun Street to have a look at Winchester.

A whole block of buildings near the courthouse had been razed, and the emptied square was now being used

as an open-air market, full of farm wagons, barrows and
makeshift stalls displaying handscrawled signs—Produce,
Fish, Baked Goods, Notions and so on—but only the fish
stalls had much to sell. Edge, Rouleau and Mullenax were
strolling together and paid not much attention when they
were passed by a small black girl in a flimsy calico frock,
hurrying to the market with a basket nearly as big as she
was. But they did notice when the same girl passed them
again, coming away from the market with her basket
heavier on her arm, because she was suddenly accosted by
a sinister-looking white man. Or a man who was mostly
white. The three circus troupers had stepped into the doorway of an empty shop, out of the breeze, to light up pipes,
so it chanced that they witnessed the scene unobserved.

"Little girl, let me see," said the man, stopping her and
peering into her basket. "Loaf of bread, two fish, some
packets of miscellaneous. Right. Exactly what you were
sent to fetch. Now, do you remember where you were to
deliver these things?"

"Why, sho," said the child, puzzled and wary. "I'se to
fetch 'em to my ol' Mistis Morgan. At our house, suh."

"Quite so." The man held up a finger and cocked his
head. "Now let me be sure that you are the pickanniny I
was sent to meet. That would be your Mistress Morgan
of—what street?"

"Why, Weems Street, suh, right down yon—"

"Precisely so. However, Mrs. Morgan has decided she
needs these things in a hurry, but she is going out—
visiting Mrs. Swink—and will not be in Weems Street
when you get there, so she sent me to fetch them to her
at Mrs. Swink's house instead. Here is a penny. You go
and buy yourself a sweet, and I will take the bask—"

He was abruptly surrounded by the three men. None of
them was small and none looked pleased to meet him.

Rouleau said to the girl, "Keep your basket, petite né-
grillonne, and hurry on where you belong." She obediently
ran off.

Edge disgustedly blew smoke in the man's face and

said, "That was just about the most low-down trick I ever witnessed."

Mullenax said to him, "Mister, let's you and us step around in yonder alley, where we won't bloody up the street, and discuss your ornery behavior."

The man smiled bleakly, shrugged and said, "Yes, let us do that. As well die of a beating as of starvation. And I deserve it. That *was* the lowest-down trick Foursquare John Fitzfarris ever tried."

"Hungry ain't no excuse for stealing," growled Mullenax.

"Why, it's the very best I've ever had," said Fitzfarris. "You should have heard some of my other excuses."

Rouleau said, "If you had a penny to give the girl, péteur, you could have bought at least a bun to stave off starvation."

"Alas, any tradesman would have seen that the penny is as counterfeit as I am," said Fitzfarris. "It's a Mexican centavo bit that some crook once passed off on *me*. I should have known then that I was losing my touch. Let us adjourn to the alley and get this over with."

"Wait a minute," said Edge. "You were in Mexico?"

"Well, not exactly." He glanced at Edge's uniform. "I was at the border, at Fort Taylor, when you soldier boys came marching back from down there. To sell you some of Dr. Hallelujah Weatherby's Good Samaritan Tonic. So you could cure the gleets you'd picked up from the señoritas, before you went home to your sweethearts."

Rouleau couldn't help laughing, and Mullenax asked, without growling this time, "Did it? Cure the gleets?"

"I sincerely hope so. The stuff failed me miserably as a hair restorer, pain killer, corn remover, alleviator of women's distresses—I forget what else." He turned again to Edge. "No soldier, my striking appearance doesn't date from Mexico. I had the good sense to stay out of that war. I got involved in the more recent one, however, and it was a gun's misfire that made me as picturesque as you see me now."

Edge contemplated him for a moment, then said to the others, "Fellows, I reckon we can overlook an honorable veteran's brief slippage from grace, don't you? And maybe offer him a drink and a bite?" The other two men nodded agreeably enough. "Yonder's a saloon, and I've got some of Florian's Secesh money, if the barkeep will accept it."

The taverner was willing, or afraid not to, when four such specimens bellied up to his bar. He didn't even try to foist on them scuppernong wine or pumpkin beer, the only beverages on view, but brought up from behind the bar a keg of genuine mountain mule. He also, when asked for food, went into a back room and returned with some boiled eggs and slices of gray bread spread with lard. While Fitzfarris wolfed the provender and sluiced it down with whiskey, he gave his new companions a quick sketch of his history.

"At various times, I've pushed stocks, bonds, gold shares, other sure-fire investments. I have solicited funds for nonexistent charities. I have dealt in an ointment warranted to turn black persons white. Or *some* new color, anyway. Failing all else, I have always been able to pour some fluid substance into empty bottles and paste on my Dr. Hallelujah labels. But I can't very well peddle a cure-all when I am displaying this too, too obvious affliction of my own. A confidence man, by definition, deals in *confidence*, and the surest way to arouse it in other people is to possess it yourself. But how the hell can I radiate confidence now?"

Rouleau murmured, "Hm-m," and thoughtfully sipped at his whiskey.

"Worse yet, a confidence man should have an anonymous, medium, bland physiognomy. I used to have. Ten minutes after I had sold some commodity to some client, he could not have picked me out of a crowd of his own relations. Now I'm as visible as a cannibal in a church choir. I couldn't even stoop to doing snatch-and-run. Horses would bolt at sight of me. Children would cry."

"Perhaps," Rouleau said tentatively, "you should consider some other line of endeavor."

"Well, there's always mail order," Fitzfarris said gloomily, "if the postal service ever gets dependable again. I could solicit custom with newspaper advertisements."

Edge asked, "How can you radiate confidence and all that in a newspaper advertisement?"

"Once," said Fitzfarris, "when I found myself at loose ends and low on capital, I came upon a street pitchman selling hair ribbons for two cents apiece. Nice ribbons they were, all colors, about an inch wide, couple feet long. I thought to myself: there ought to be a more profitable market for such things. So I approached him, did some haggling and bought out his entire stock at a cent and a half apiece." He paused for an egg and a gulp of whiskey.

Mullenax asked, "Then what? Sold 'em to young nigger wenches for some fancy price, I bet."

"No, sir. Sold them to young men—of what complexion I cannot say, since we dealt entirely through the mails—and sold them for a very fancy price."

"To *men?*"

"I ask you, friend Mullenax, what is the all-prevailing, all-pervading worry of all young men? It is the fear that they have made themselves unmanly, enfeebled, unfit for matrimony, through their childhood practice of—" He broke off to look about. There was no one in the saloon except themselves and the bartender, who was pretending uninterest. Nevertheless, Fitzfarris lowered his voice to a confidential whisper. "The vicious and abominable practice of self-pollution."

Mullenax hiccuped and said loudly, "What the hell is that?" Rouleau leaned over to murmur in his ear and Mullenax said, "Oh. That. Homemade sin."

"With my remaining cash," Fitzfarris resumed, "I had some printing done and also took out a couple of discreet newpaper advertisements. Invited all young men worried about the state of their virility to send in a sample of their urine, which Dr. Hallelujah Weatherby would analyze free of charge. Well, I was absolutely inundated with samples. Didn't make me very popular at the post office.''

''Nor very wealthy, as far as I can see,'' said Edge. ''What was the point?''

''To each respondent, Dr. Hal sent back a horrifying analysis—printed in advance, of course—saying, in effect, 'Yes, dear sir, your specimen shows unmistakably that you have indulged in the dread habit. You will shortly be suffering loss of hair, teeth, eyesight, fertility, potency and your mind.' Also included was a certificate, which entitled the sufferer to send in seven dollars cash money, bringing him by return post a guaranteed cure for his condition. Money back if not satisfied.''

''The ribbons?''

''One ribbon to a customer. Meanwhile, as fast as I was mailing them out, I was investing some of the seven dollarses in still more advertisements. Had quite a thriving trade going—made a satchelful of money—before I deemed it prudent to leave that dodge and that city.''

''I do not understand,'' said Rouleau. ''A potion maybe, like your Samaritan Tonic, or a pill or something. But a *ribbon?*''

''Each customer got instructions with his ribbon. Every night, he was to cross his hands at the wrist and tie them together with it. Clearly, it would be *impossible* for him to flog his—I mean abuse himself. Clearly, Dr. Weatherby's ingenious invention would break him of the pernicious habit straightaway.''

There was a long, waiting, anticipatory silence in the saloon. Finally it was the bartender who could bear it no longer, and asked:

''Did it?''

''Cure anybody? I doubt it, landlord. Did *you* ever try to tie your own hands together?''

''Well . . . but . . . then you must of got an awful lot of demands for the money back.''

''Oh, yes. Some of them in flavorful language. To every

complainant I sent another missive, directing him to read the fine print in the guarantee. His money would be returned just as soon as he sent to Dr. Weatherby three signed affidavits—one from his minister, one from some member of his own family, one from any principal businessman in his community—each affirming that the subject in fact *was* a notorious self-abuser and that, despite the professional aid of Dr. Weatherby, the wretch was *still* abusing himself. I never heard another word from—''

He was drowned out by the noise of the bartender, going into strangling and flailing convulsions of laughter. When the man had recovered, he sloshed whiskey liberally into all their glasses and into one of his own, and said:

''Here, boys, this round is on the house. I ain't had a laugh like that since before the war, when a Tuckyhoe run off with the preacher's wife. Funny part was, Preacher Dudley went chasing after 'em and *he* got struck by lightning. Here's luck, Mr.—er—''

''Ex-corporal Foursquare John Fitzfarris.''

''Tell me, Mister Foursquare, do you get anything else out of your occupation besides fun and money and lifelong enemies? Is that how your face got half blue and half normal? You look a lot like Preacher Dudley did when they fetched him home.''

''No, sir,'' Fitzfarris said sourly, but civilly enough. ''A defective gun burst and sprayed hot gunpowder over the whole half of my face. Black powder embedded under the skin looks blue. Just as neat a job as if I'd had myself deliberately tattooed, from nose to ear and hairline to collarbone.''

''Heck,'' the barkeep said, ''you can always go into circus work.''

''As a matter of fact,'' said Rouleau, ''we three *are* in circus work, I myself am a parterre acrobat. The colonel is a shootist. The pirate works wild boars.''

''Well, I'll be damned,'' said both the bartender and Fitzfarris.

''Florian's Flourishing Florilegium, presently flourishing out near the Negro Cemetery. To you, Monsieur Fitz-farris, I am empowered to offer employment. Wait. Attendez.'' he held up a hand. ''Before you strike me, hear me out. To be a Tattooed Man is at least preferable to a career of swindling small servant girls for your victuals.''

''Christ Almighty,'' muttered Fitzfarris. ''I am heartily glad that my old mother and all my mentors are dead. To think that I should come to this. Invited to be a freak in a sideshow.''

''Disdain it not,'' said Rouleau. ''A traveling circus of-fers a man ample opportunity—how shall I put it?—to exercise *all* his talents. And also, allow me to point out, it never stays in one place for very long.''

''Well, now . . .'' Fitzfarris said thoughtfully.

Florian, an hour later, contentedly smoothing his little beard, said to Fitzfarris, ''If you dislike the appellation Tattooed Man, we can bill you as—um—the Bluejay Man?''

Fitzfarris said resignedly, ''That's like debating whether to dignify your asshole as an anus or a rectum. Call me your Tattooed Man.''

And so, between the halves of the Monday program, the Winchester folk on the midway outside the pavilion heard Florian announce ''The most gallant explorer of our time! Ladies and gentlemen, meet Sir John Doe, the Tattooed Man. For reasons you will shortly appreciate, Sir John pre-fers not to reveal his true surname, for it would be rec-ognizable as one of the noblest in the English peerage.''

The people gaped at Fitzfarris, who stood blackly shrouded in Colonel Ramrod's ring cloak, both to conceal his shabby civilian clothes and to make his particolored countenance even more striking. He stood trying to look as Englishly noble as was possible with a face half face-colored and half blue.

''While daring to explore remotest Persia,'' Florian boomed, ''Sir John also dared to fall in love with one of Shah Nasir's own court favorites, the beautiful Princess

Shalimar, and actually insinuated himself into the innermost harem chambers of the Shah's palace to woo that princess. Unhappily, Sir John was surprised and captured by the harem eunuchs, and the tender affair ended tragically.''

Florian dabbed his handkerchief at his eyes. Fitzfarris looked stoic.

''The irate Shah exiled the lovely princess to a distant mountaintop, where she languishes to this day. And Sir John was punished as you see. The cruel Shah Nasir had his powerful black eunuchs hold this brave man helpless, while they scorched one half of his face with the blue flames of the terrible Bengal Fire. Now Sir John wanders the world as the Tattooed Man, unwilling to return to his own people—unable ever to return to his adored princess— bearing the ineradicable mark of love turned to tragedy.''

Florian dabbed at his eyes again, and several women in the crowd were sniffling.

''Sir John is the only Western man ever to get inside a Persian harem and come out alive. And he is prepared to tell about it. If any of you gentlemen care to spend a paltry ten cents—or ten dollars Confederate—Sir John will relate to you all the scandalous secrets of the harem, of the maidens take by force, of the mutilated eunuchs, of the concupiscent concubines. Of course, you ladies and young folks will wish to hear no such things, so if you will accompany me, we will move on to the Crocodile Man, a fearsome creature discovered on the banks of the Amazon . . .''

Evidently none of the male patrons had ten cents or dollars to spare, or had no curiosity about harem secrets. They went with Florian and the women, to look at Abner Mullenax groveling on the ground.

When the circus train left Winchester the next morning, Fitzfarris rode beside Rouleau on the seat of the property wagon. He said, ''You know, I always thought, by God, I possessed a fine line of patter. But that Florian is a nonpareil of cast-iron nerve and ossified gall and petrified impropriety.''

Rouleau laughed. "Eh, bien, I still remember, when *I* was a first-of-May, long ago, Florian told me that we must never let ourselves be bound by propriety, precedent, convention or morality; those things are recipes for banality. I think, Fitz, you and Florian are going to get along like brothers born.''

Florian in the rockaway at the head of the train, with Edge again riding beside him, said, "That fellow Fitzfarris. Which side was he soldiering on when he got that curious disfigurement?''

"Didn't think to inquire,'' said Edge. "I doubt I'd believe him if he told me. Anyway, I figure such trifles don't matter any more.'' He pointed. "Yonder's where we turn onto the Charles Town road, if you still want the shortest way to Baltimore.''

Florian steered Snowball onto the road forking eastward off the Pike. It was a firm dirt road, a much better surface than the ruined macadam they had been traveling on. But just making the turn seemed to put a finally unendurable strain on one of the wagons, because there came a splintery crash and then a spate of cussing. Florian drew Snowball to a halt and looked back. On the balloon-carrying wagon, a rear wheel had collapsed. The wagon sat tilted, stern down, its upraised shafts almost lifting the draft mule off his feet, and Mullenax was sprawled on the road, shaking a fist.

"God damn it to hell, all I do these days is roll around in the dust!'' The other men gathered to look at the damage.

Roozeboom said, "Too long das vagon vas drying out under your haycock, Abner. De spokes all loosed. I should haff giff dose vheels a good soak in some creek on de vay. My fault.''

"Well, the wheel ain't broke,'' said Tim. "Just fell apart. You can fix it, Dutchman.''

"Ag, ja. Efery vheel on dis train I haff fixed sometime.

But it means first I fix, den find creek or pond, soak it all night.''

"At least it's the one wagon we can get along without," said Florian. "The rest of the train can travel while you work on it."

A new voice suddenly spoke up. "Are any of you people Yankees?"

They turned to see a man regarding them from across a rail fence. The fence was all entwined with honeysuckle in flower, and smelled delicious. The man was gray-haired and gaunt, but well favored and even well dressed for the time and place. Behind him stretched a rising slope of ground that had once been an expanse of lawn, now gone to weed and seed and rank growth. At the distant top of the slope was visible a manorial house fronted by two-story columns and surrounded by ancient oaks.

"No, sir," Florian said. "Some of us are émigré Europeans, but the rest all staunch Southerners. Right here is Colonel Edge, late of the Confederate Cavalry. Sergeant Yount, likewise, and Corporal Fitzfarris . . ."

"I am Paxton Furfew, erstwhile adjutant of the Frederick County Home Guard, now living in retiracy," said the man, in the soft accents of the well-born Virginian. "Forgive me for having blurted a qualifier even before the invitation, but would you-all care to rest here at Oakhaven while your wagon is being repaired? Mrs. Furfew and I simply will not abide Yankees, but we're grateful for the company of more decent sorts. Perhaps the ladies in your party would like to spend a night in a real bedroom. And we set a fairly commendable table here, such as it can be in the circumstances."

"Why, that is surpassingly gracious of you, sir," said Florian. "I think, as director of this enterprise, I can say that all of us accept your invitation with alacrity and with heartfelt thanks."

"It is we who should thank you, sir. We have never entertained a circus or an elephant before. If you'll simply continue on, you will find the entry to the drive. Leave the

broken wagon where it is. Some of our darkies can take
down this section of fence and drag the wagon up to our
outbuildings. Your cartwright will find there a smithy with
a forge and all the tools he'll require.''

In some wonderment and considerable admiration, the
troupers went along the road bordering the property, turned
in through a stone-pillared and wrought-iron arch, in which
was worked the name ''Oakhaven,'' and followed a gently
winding drive between walls of untended and overgrown
shrubbery that had once been banks of flowers. The house,
when they finally got there, proved to be even bigger than
it had looked from the road, but in sad disrepair: the paint
all peeling, windows broken and patched with pasteboard,
the stucco sheathing of the wooden columns so crumbled
that they resembled Roman ruins. Mr. and Mrs. Furfew
awaited them on the veranda, and she was as pudgy as he
was lean. Though she was equally well turned out—clad
in a voluminous hoop skirt and a profusion of furbelows—
and though she had the same magnolia voice, her speech
was as rustic slovenly as his was precise.

''Ain't none of y'all Yankees, you claim,'' was how she
greeted the guests.

''And mighty glad not to be, madame,'' said Florian.
''Those of us who were not actually fighting for Dixie
Land at least endured with her throughout the entire war.''

''It's like I allus say,'' she said. ''The Yankees may
hold the ground now, but that's all they got. They ain't
defeated the sperrit of the South. Ain't that what I allus
say, Mr. Furfew?''

''Always, my dear,'' he murmured. Then, to the troupe,
''Won't you-all come in, refresh yourselves? The stable
boys will see to your animals. They will show your own
darky to the quarters, too.''

A number of black men, mostly barefoot, all clad in
much-worn homespun, all acting as subdued and obsequi-
ous as if they had never heard of Emancipation, came to
take most of the reins. But, muttering and walling their
eyes, they left the elephant and Thunder with the lion

wagon for Hannibal and Roozeboom to lead around to the stable yard. As the other troupers got out of and down from the vehicles—the females trying to step as queenly and daintily as if they were descending from barouches at a court ball—Mrs. Furfew continued to fulminate.

"Us bein' right smack on the enemy border here, we done already seen more'n we'll ever want to see of Yankees ever again. Them scoun'erls just about ruint our Oakhaven. Tell 'em, Mr. Furfew."

"The Yankees just about ruined Oakhaven," he patiently repeated, as he led the way into an entry hall that was immense but unfurnished. "They looted and smashed and—"

"And what them scoun'erls couldn't pilfer, they ruint. Tell 'em about the chandelier and the pitchers, Mr. Furfew."

He waved vaguely toward the ceiling and walls. "Here in the hall, there used to be a pendant chandelier of crystal lusters and prisms, and a gallery of the Furfew family portraits. The Yankees—"

"They drug down the chandelier, and what dangles didn't break they hung on their horses' harness for pretties. Then they got a pot of tar and dobbed mustaches on Mr. Furfew's Grandmaw Sophronia and Aunt Verbena and all. Just ruint 'em. The men ancestors in the pitchers already had mustaches, so them Yankees took their bayonets and slashed 'em to ribbons. Tell about the clocks and the books, Mr. Furfew."

He sighed. "They carried off all the clocks except the tall case clock. It was too big to haul, so they toppled it down the stairway to destruction. They burned all our books, including a hundred-year-old Bible that chronicled all the Furfew births and deaths and weddings. They burned all the other family records, land deeds, slaves' titles, everything on paper. Now, my dear, perhaps you'd show these ladies upstairs and have the maids bring them wash water."

Mrs. Furfew looked as if she'd rather continue reciting

grievances, but she shepherded Sarah, Clover Lee and Magpie Maggie Hag up the long and curving staircase. That would have been an elegant feature of the hall, except that it was missing many of its banister posts and even some treads and risers.

"You must forgive Leutitia's stridency, gentlemen," said Mr. Furfew in an undertone. He gestured toward his wife as she climbed the stairs behind the other women. "Look at her shoes. Satin, you think. Yes, but the satin is of pieces carefully peeled from old notions boxes. That black blouse she is wearing was originally an umbrella covering. Ah, the pitiful little pretenses and brave little graces of destitution. If she seems obsessed with Yankee-hating, she has had provocation, God knows."

"Well, I suppose you ought to congratulate yourselves that you still have a house," said Florian. "Not to mention servants. I am surprised they didn't run off with the Yankees."

"I think they are all too afraid of Leutitia," said Mr. Furfew, with a chuckle that was not entirely humorous.

Fitzfarris asked, "Which Yankees was it, sir, that you got overrun by?"

"Just about any of the regulars you can name. McClellan's, Banks's, Shields's, Milroy's. Banks quartered his officers here, which is doubtless why the house didn't get burned. And of course, we did get to see an occasional one of our own Confederate commanders—Jackson and Early have dined at our table. Most recently, since that damned Sheridan pulled out, we've had bunches of bummers come looking to sack anything that the regulars might have left. The last straggle of rogues, a week ago, not finding anything they could use, despoiled what they could not. Look at this."

He had led them into what must once have been the drawing room, though its only piece of furniture now was a massive imperial-size grand piano. "This is a Bösendorfer with Erard action," he said. "Or it was." He lifted the tremendous lid and they looked in. The latest bummers had used the remains of the tar that had earlier been daubed on the Furfew family portraits. They had poured it all over the piano's strings and hammers.

"Fils de putain," muttered Rouleau. "Totally ruined."

Edge said, "I believe you mentioned, sir, that you'd been with the local Home Guard."

"Yes, damn it. Too old and rickety to serve. Didn't even have a son to send. And about all I could do in the way of Home Guarding was to give our neighbors the benefit of our own sad experiences. Very early on, we tried to preserve Leutitia's jewels, the family silver, other such things, by burying them about the yard. But the Yankees already knew that trick. They didn't even bother digging up the whole yard. They just went about jabbing their rifle ramrods deep in the ground until they hit something. Then they made our own darkies do the digging up. So the next time Oakhaven had a surcease from occupation, and any things worth keeping, we put them under the privies—very deep under—and the stable-yard manure pile. We managed to save a fair quantity of canned goods, root vegetables, even grain, and I advised our neighbors to do likewise. Oh, by the way, I've told Cadmus to grain your animals. They look as if they could use it."

"Oh, my dear sir!" Florian exclaimed. "You'll spoil the creatures. But it is a kindness beyond hospitality. Do let me pay you for that."

Mr. Furfew looked uneasy, and threw a glance at the hallway. "In God's name, man, if you're carrying Federal specie, don't dare show it around her. I mean around here. We've sworn to spend and accept only Confederate money until there is absolutely no other recourse."

"As it happens, I can pay you with some of that."

Mr. Furfew waved dismissively. "One day, a crippled Yankee happened by and, when our little black boy gave him a dipper of water, the soldier gave him a penny. Leutitia snatched the coin and threw it at the man. Then she birched the boy nearly bloody for accepting it." He sighed. "But, as I say, she has had ample provocation."

"It *is* so provoking, the war and all," Mrs. Furfew confirmed, when they all sat down to a midday dinner around an uncovered and improvised trestle table, eating off an assortment of tin and wooden plates with an even sketchier assortment of utensils. "I feel like Oakhaven has been *defiled*. Do you know—when them filthy Yankee officers was quartered on us?—they had the gall to bring their wenches from Washington to stay with 'em! Them *hard* and *coarse* Yankee women! Naturally, what bedding and linen them officers didn't steal when they left, we took out and *burned*. So it's poor pallets we're giving you, ladies, but if they look a little gray, think of it as *Confederate* gray."

Edge sneaked a look at Sarah and Clover Lee, those hard and coarse Yankee women, but they were keeping their eyes demurely on their plates, and he suspected that neither of them had said so much as a "damn" since they had come into the house.

He also saw how grotesque the circus troupe looked, sitting around a table in at least passably civilized surroundings. There were two glossily bald-headed men, one with a fierce walrus mustache, the other with an even fiercer black beard; the trim and dapper, silver bearded director; a slat-thin, high-shouldered yokel who would be a typically Virginian bumpkin except for his sinister black eye patch; two fairly good-looking younger men, but one with his face in permanent blue half-shadow; a runt whose head barely topped the table; a pretty blonde woman, a pretty blonde girl and a hag whose nose and chin, though barely visible inside the hood she wore even to meals, nearly scissored every time she chewed. And then there was himself, Zachary Edge, whatever he looked like. Small wonder, he thought, that the little mulatto girl waiting on the table was warily goggle-eyed as she served them pots and platters.

Florian swallowed a mouthful of the succulent stew on his plate and said, "I sympathize with all your deprivations, madame. But I must say you have coped well with them, and made the most of what provender you've managed to hold onto. This meal is delicious."

"Thank you, monsewer. Yes, our Aunt Phoebe can do wonders with little provisions. I just wish she could learn her high-yaller brats some manners." She raised her voice to the girl who was at the moment spooning stewed tomatoes onto Yount's plate. "You, miss! You're serving that gentleman from his right side. That's the wrong side! Come here, hussy!"

The girl, no older than twelve or thirteen and no darker than fawn color, rolled her eyes and wailed, "Mistis, I ain' nebber knowed. How kin de right side be de wrong side?"

"Hush your mouth!" Mrs. Furfew's face turned the color of eggplant, which made her rather darker than the mulatto. "I said *come here*, you sassy critter!"

The girl sidled reluctantly around the table to where Mrs. Furfew could reach and out and give her a hard slap across the face. The girl flinched and started away, but Mrs. Furfew snapped, "No, miss, that won't do. I want to *hear* it. You puff out your cheeks, like I've learnt you." The girl puffed out her cheeks, making them an even paler tan, and Mrs. Furfew slapped her again, this time producing a *whap!* as resounding as any Tim had ever achieved in the circus ring.

When everyone else sat silent in some embarrassment, Mr. Furfew relieved the strain. He turned to ask Florian what was the destination of the northward-bound circus train.

"Baltimore, sir, on this side of the water. We intend to take our Florilegium on to Europe—if we can convert our Secesh money to pay for passage." Florian saw Mr. Furfew wince, and quickly said placatively to Mrs. Furfew, "We have to recoup our fortunes, but we are determined *not* to do it by touring Yankee land."

She had not turned purple, and indeed nodded approvingly. "Them's my sentiments, too. My dear brother lost his life in Tennessee. But I've done stopped grieving for him. I envy Henry now, I really do. He fought for the

cause, and that was more'n any of us women could. We
could only try to manage, try to keep on.''

"At Petersburg," said Yount, "the city ladies used to
come out, during lulls in the fighting, and visit the lines
to *inspire* us soldiers." He said it acidly, but Mrs. Furfew
did not seem to notice. "They used to bring us tracts.
Them was to persuade us not to gamble or cuss or do
improper things. Only fight and kill, like we ought.''

Mrs. Furfew again nodded approval. "Yes, our work
was to inspire. There was little else we frail women could
accomplish. That's why I envy Henry. He at least got to
die for what he believed in.''

Fitzfarris spoke up, lazily, "What was that, ma'am?''

"Why—why, the *South*, of course. For the Southern
culture and principles and morality. Henry must feel proud
and good about having died so. Don't you expect, Corporal?''

"I don't know, ma'am. I saw many a dead man, and
none of them looked proud to be that way. I imagine Henry
just feels glad to be lying down and resting. And· not
having to be shot more than the once.''

"He was not shot, Corporal. His colonel. sent a nice
letter of condolence, and said Henry died of dysentery.''

"Ah! Then I'll wager he feels even more glad to be at
rest. I had the scours once myself, and—''

Mrs. Furfew suddenly flared up. "Listen at you! Oh, a
live man can afford to run down a dead one—can't he?—
and throw off on the glorious cause. *All* you men may
forgive and forget the whole war, because it was you that
lost it!'' She had gone eggplant again. "But the cause will
not *ever* be forgot by us Southron women. *We* never surrendered, we never quit, and we never will!''

"My, my," said Florian, again hastening to placate.
"Fruitcake for dessert. Will wonders never cease? As
toothsome as everything else of the meal. Your cook is a
real treasure, madame.''

Mrs. Furfew's color ebbed, and she grudgingly accepted
the change of subject. "Yes, Phoebe makes a right tol'able

fruitcake, considering that all she's got to put in it is persimmons and hickory nuts and peppercorns."

"I think I shall go in person and compliment the lady chef," said Florian. "If I may?" He waited for Mrs. Furfew's condescending nod, then fled from the table to the kitchen outbuilding.

But the hostess threw no more tantrums, and the dinner party disbanded without further unpleasantness. Mrs. Furfew insisted that "all us ladies" follow the inviolable Southern-belle custom of retiring to their rooms for an afternoon nap. Roozeboom went off to the smithy to work on the broken wagon wheel. The other men went out on the veranda for a smoke, there breaking up into groups of two and three.

Mr. Furfew was discoursing to Trimm and Edge, ". . . Yes, Jeff Davis was much criticized. But, gentlemen, President Davis knew the temper of the South. He knew that, if there was ever to be amicable accommodation between us and the North, the South must win the war. Or, if she could not win, she wanted to be whipped—well whipped—*thoroughly* whipped."

"Well, she was," grunted Tim.

"Yes, we lost. But *ah!* was it not a most magnificent fight?" Fitzfarris said to Rouleau, "Our host is a cultivated gentleman and she's no better than a swineherd putting on hoity-toity airs. How do you suppose those two ever got together?"

"Tiens, I am inclined to suspect that they met in a forest," Rouleau drawled, "when he took a thorn out of her paw."

Mullenax said to Yount, "That woman is rattling the shingles on her garret. I hope every female in Dixie ain't gone as crazy."

Yount growled, "If such women want to carry on the war after it's over and done with, I say let 'em. Miz Furfew may be short on shoes, and holding a grudge about that. But I ain't seen any women lacking *legs*, not even in Petersburg."

"Nor eyes," said Mullenax. "No denying it was us men

that lost the war—but we lost a lot else besides. I'm with you, Obie. The damned old biddies can *have* the god-damned war.''

In the kitchen shanty, which was separated from the main house by a covered breezeway, Florian had fulsomely complimented the cook, Phoebe Simms—a large, plump, glossy-black woman—and had proffered some further pleasantries, and now, a gleam in his eyes, was pursuing a line of seductive inquiry.

"Haven't you thought of traveling, Aunt Phoebe, now that you're free to travel?''

"Ain' no place special callin' me to come,'' she said good-humoredly, as she washed dishes. "An' I got obligations hyar.''

"Surely you feel no overwhelming obligation to Madame Furfew. I've seen the way she treats her help.''

"Least she feeds 'em.''

"You feed *her*, Aunt Phoebe. There are folks who would better value your services, and treat you better, and give you the respect your deserve. *And* let you be something more high-toned than help.''

"Whut dat?''

"You could be a circus artiste. A star attraction.''

She giggled and jiggled all her adiposity. "Hee hee! Me wear tights, Mas' Florian, an' jump around? I seen a circus onct, an' I marbled at dem pooty ladies. But laws-a-mussy, I be's black an' I be's fat.''

"Exactly why I want you. I offer you a position of dignity. No funny dress and no jumping around. You'd simply sit on a platform and be admired. The one and only Fat Lady in Florian's Florilegium. I will even ennoble you with a title—*Madame Alp!*''

"Ain' nobody go' call no nigguh Ma'am. Anyway, shoot! I ain' much fatter'n ol' Mistis.''

"But far more impressive. Your being so magnificently black adds to the impressiveness. You'd be fairly paid and—''

"*Paid?!* You means cash money, Massa?''

"Why, assuredly. It might be scanty for a while, until we get up north where the real money is. But yes, you'd be paid, and you'd get to see new country almost every day, and you'd have all the rights and privileges of a Freedwoman."

"Lawsy, lawsy . . ."

"And we would not neglect your other talents, either. You can cook for us, just as you do here. I guarantee it will be better appreciated than it is here. For one thing, you'd eat *with us*, not off in a corner. Everybody in a circus is one of the family. You can ask our own respected black companion, Hannibal Tyree."

"Wull . . . him an' me did talk some," Phoebe admitted, "when I guv him a dab o' dinner. He do talk mighty happy an' high an' mighty fo' a nigguh."

"Well, there you are, then. What more need I say?"

"But . . . how 'bout my chirren, Mas' Florian?"

"Eh?"

"My pickaninnies. Sunday, Monday, Tuesday an' Quincy."

"Is that how she spells Wednesday?" asked Edge, when Florian excitedly broke the news to him.

"The boy's a different litter. He's only eight years old. But the girls—"

"Mr. Florian," Edge said tolerantly. "I've had a look at that Aunt Phoebe. You've already got the world's tallest circus midget. Now you want to have the world's puniest Fat Lady? Hell, down in Rockbridge County, every third woman bloats up bigger than Phoebe Simms, just as soon as she's hooked herself a husband."

Florian waved in the elegantly dismissive manner of Mr. Furfew. "Maggie Hag can pad her out to hippo dimensions. Europe has probably never seen a *black* Fat Lady. But listen to this, Zachary. The three girls are all thirteen years old—*identical triplets!* And handsome, too. You saw the one that waited on table. I really had no idea what a splendid coup I was in fact engineering. We not only get a Fat Lady, but also three good-looking mulatto wenches who are triplets. No other circus can claim such a show-piece! The boy Quincy is blacker than Abdullah, but we can always find use for another Hindu.''

''Curious. How did the woman come to throw a whole litter of yellow roses and then a single blue-gum black?''

''I wasn't so rude as to inquire too closely. But she used to belong to a different master, and maybe she herself was smaller and prettier in those days. He must have been a handsome man, to judge from the result. It probably would have gone unremarked, even by the man's own wife, if Phoebe had dropped just one half-breed daughter. But *trip-lets*—the whole neighborhood would have been a-buzz. So he sold her and them in a hurry. Little black Quincy dates from since she's been here at Oakhaven. I'd guess that that stable man Cadmus is the father.''

''Well,'' said Edge, ''I can't accuse you of taking up slave stealing. They're all free darkies now. But don't you feel you're ill repaying these people's hospitality?''

''Oh, indeed I do feel bad, on Mr. Furfew's account. Phoebe's cooking must be the only delight he has in life. But to deprive the *mistress* I think justifies the crime.''

''I can't gainsay that,'' said Edge. ''Even a gypsy life will be better for those pickaninnies than growing up here. How do you intend to do this?''

''The Simmses don't own more than the clothes they're wearing, so they're not coming freighted with luggage. All they'll have to do—right after breakfast tomorrow—is slip away to the farthest roadside corner of the property and hop the fence. We'll pick them up there. And now that we've got the balloon wagon, we've got something for them to ride in and sleep in. We'll just throw a protective canvas over the balloon. I only hope we can make some distance before they're missed and we're pursued.''

''No problem there,'' said Edge.' ''Make eight more miles or so and we cross the●border into West Virginia. Even if the Furfews had any legitimate claim, no Virginia lawman can press it there.''

"Ah, good, good!" Florian exulted, rubbing his hands together. "Seldom has Dame Fortune so concatenated her blessings on our behalf. Why, with all these Negroes, we can even have our own troupe of Ethiopian Minstrels— no, no, no—every show calls them that." He pondered briefly. "Aha! The Happy Hottentots! How does that strike you, Zachary?"

Edge only sighed and said, "Nothing surprises me any more."

Nevertheless, something did, the next morning after breakfast. The troupers were dispensing thanks all around and making ready to depart, when Mrs. Furfew drew Edge aside and said:

"Colonel, seeing as how you're the ranking Confederate officer amongst this crew, I want to show you something. I'd like your Monsewer Florian to see it, too. And you might want to fetch along a pry bar, and somebody strong to use it."

Wondering, Edge went and collected Florian and Yount. After Mrs. Furfew had made sure nobody else was paying any attention, she led the three men around behind the house, beyond the outbuildings, across a long-fallow field where they stumbled over old corn stubble. They came finally to a copse of trees that had been left growing to conceal what would otherwise have been an unsightly rubbish dump: all the boulders, stumps, deadfall branches and other trash removed when the fields were cleared.

"Monsewer," said Mrs. Furfew, "you said you wanted to convert some Confederate money to Yankee dollars." She gestured to Edge and Yount. "Start shifting them stumps and things, and see what you find in yonder."

Still wondering, they obeyed, and after some labor they uncovered the rear end of a blue-painted, metal-sheathed wagon of unusual configuration. Edge stepped back in amazement and exclaimed:

"That's an Autenrieth wagon! All fitted out inside with compartments and pigeonholes. The Yankees used them mostly for ambulance wagons. But look, Obie—the initials on this one: P.D. Not Medical Department, by damn, but Pay Department! Ma'am, I don't know how this got here, but this is the wagon of some outfit's *paymaster*."

"That's right," she said. "Can y'all get it open?"

"You knew it was here? You knew what it was?" said Edge, as Yount pried at its padlocked door with his iron bar.

"Course I did. I had Cadmus and some of the other boys hide it here. Please don't let Mr. Furfew know about it. Now, Monsewer, about that money of yours—"

"But where did you get it?" Edge persisted, in bewilderment.

"From Little Phil Sheridan. Anyhow, from whatever part of his army it was that left here last, going eastwards, back in February. It sprung a wheel rim and the rest of the column went on without it, until it could be fixed and catch up. The Yankees ordered me to give 'em dinner while Cadmus worked on it. There was a driver, a lieutenant and two clerks that wore spectacles. I reckon Sheridan's looking for 'em, or got 'em listed as deserters, but they're there in the trash pile, if you want to see 'em."

"What?!" exclaimed Edge and Florian together. Yount glanced around, wide-eyed, but went on working at the door.

"Phoebe fixed 'em a meal and I brung it from the kitchen myself, but I come by way of the potting shed and mixed Paris green in the food."

"Madame, that is arsenic!" said Florian, horrified.

"Well, it kills garden vermin, so I figgered it'd kill bluebelly Yanks, and it did. After they ate, they was in the smithy watching Cadmus work, when they fell over and started squirming. Mr. Furfew thinks they went on and caught up with the others. I'd sooner that he keeps thinking so."

"Ah . . . um . . . yes," said Florian, in a strangled sort of way. There was a loud twang, as the paywagon's hasp and staple yielded to Yount's levering, and then a rusty screech as he forced the metal door open. "But why, Madame Furfew, do you disclose the secret to us?"

"You got some Confederate money. I'll buy it from you."

"Christamighty, she can, too!" cried Yount. He was inside the wagon, in the narrow aisle between the banks of shelves and drawers. "There must be a whole division's whole month's pay here! All in U.S. greenbacks!"

"I congratulate you, madame," said Florian. "That should go a long way toward restoring Oakhaven from the damage—"

"May the Lord strike me dead if I spend a penny of it," she said firmly. "The storekeepers hereabouts know I won't pay in nothing but Confederate paper. That's why I want yours."

"I'll be happy to accommodate you, madame. Were you thinking of paying the official exchange rate or the prevailing one?"

"I'll give you dollar for dollar."

When Florian found his voice, he breathed a prayerful exclamation in one of his native languages, something Edge and Yount had never before heard him do:

"Ich mache mir Flecken ins Bettuch . . . Er, I mean to say, madame, our exchequer comprises quite a *lot* of Confederate dollars. Something in excess of nine thousand. Were I to exchange them for Federal dollars anywhere else, they would be worth only about ninety . . ." Mrs. Furfew had begun to turn eggplant color again, so Florian ceased his protesting and said, "Excuse me, madame. If you'll allow me a brief consultation with my colleagues . . ."

Florian, Edge and Yount moved a little way apart from her, and Florian confided in a mutter, "This creature belongs in a cage. I've done some underhanded things in my time, but I do hesitate to take advantage of a sanctified and certifiable lunatic."

Edge murmured, "Nine thousand real dollars would sure get us to Europe, and probably with some left over to pay wages."

"Yes, but . . . ill-gotten gains? And blood money, at that?"

"Listen here, Mr. Florian," Yount growled. "I ain't often insubordinate, but let me say this. *I* got no scruples about skinning this particular old sow. You run and fetch that worthless paper of ours while I help her start counting out the greenbacks from them drawers in yonder. And if it still bothers you, *I'll* do the handing back and forth when you get it here."

So that is what they did, and then, at Mrs. Furfew's command, the three men piled the rubbish over and around the wagon again. When they returned to the house, Florian's frock-coat pockets were visibly bulging—with nine thousand, two hundred and twenty-four dollars in genuine, spendable, United States cash money—and none of the three men was able to meet the honest eyes of Mr. Paxton Furfew when shaking his hand in farewell.

The circus train maintained a sedate pace going down the drive and along the road as far as it bordered the Oakhaven property. But where the fence left the roadside to turn at the Oakhaven boundary, Phoebe Simms and her four little Simmses were waiting, as scheduled. The train paused while Mullenax helped the Negroes scramble onto the canvas-covered bed of the balloon wagon, then Florian called:

"Now let's make tracks!" He flapped his reins and put Snowball to a canter, and all the animals behind hustled to keep up. "Never," said Florian to Edge, beside him on the rockaway, "never have I done so many dirty dealings in just one morning. Ha-ha! And never have I felt so downright happy in my unregenerate sinfulness."

"I have to agree. The money's a fine thing and, now that I've seen the Simmses climb aboard, I think they were worth acquiring, too. The boy's only a little ink blot, and his mammy's no sensational freak, but the three yellow roses do look as much alike as peas in a pod."

"Wait until we get them in spangles, Zachary—and

now we can afford to. They'll look as pretty *as real* yellow roses. If only we can get clean away.''

''If the Furfew place was pestered by Yankee bummers just a week ago, it argues that there isn't much law around this border area.''

''Hell, I'm not worried about lawmen now. I'm purely terrified that *that woman* might come after us.''

''She'd starch and iron us, all right. But any place where you don't have to worry about law, you sometimes have to worry about outlaws. Maybe you've noticed that we haven't passed anybody else at all on this particular road. Looks like the common folk avoid it.''

They rode a couple more miles at the canter. Then the road began to slope gently uphill, so they eased the pace to the usual walk, and Edge spoke again. ''We're climbing up toward Limestone Ridge. It marks the state line and the international boundary. Once we cross it, we're in West Virginia.''

''Newest of the United States,'' mused Florian.

''Yep, a whole new state,'' said Edge, and shook his head. ''I've seen many a change made by this war.''

''Nonsense,'' said Florian. ''That piece of land ahead may have changed its name, but it's still the same piece of land. You've read history, Zachary. Name me one war that ever made any change on the face of the earth that stayed visible or significant for more than maybe a century or two.''

''Put it that way and, just offhand, I can't.''

''No, the things that *do* cause changes—and irreversible ones—are usually less dramatic and more insidious. I can show you two of them right here and now. Look at that railroad running parallel to us over there, and the telegraph wires strung above it. Swift locomotion and far communication, they're already changing the world. When people can get quickly and easily from one place to another, every damned place worth going to will be overrun and overflowing with people. When they can talk by telegraph to anybody anywhere in the world, you can damned well bet they *will* talk. And pester and peddle and harangue and preach. Within your lifetime, Zacharay, there will hardly be a place on this planet where you can find privacy from people and the yammer of people.''

Edge said he was probably right, and it was a sobering thing to think about. They rode in silence for a while, and then he said:

''Time was, I did my best to *stop* the spread and straddle of railroad. Back when Obie and I were with the Comanches, the battalion used to tear up railroads to interrupt the Yankees' supply lines. We'd pry up the rails, make a big bonfire of the cross-ties, lay the rails across the fire until they got hot and soft, then wrap them around trees to cool solid. We blew up bridges, too, but that was more sport than practicality.''

''Why so?''

''Well, it seems that every iron bridge in America is made in Cleveland, Ohio. And some engineer in Cleveland figured out how to build portable bridges—in small sections that the Yankees could carry and bolt together and make a bridge wherever it was needed. So they replaced the bridges about as fast as we knocked them down.'' He laughed and added, ''One time, we blew up a railroad *tunnel*. Did a good job of it. Brought the whole hill thundering down into it. But when the dust cleared, one of our boys said, ''What the hell, them Yankees'll just fetch another tunnel down from Cleveland, Ohio.''

Florian laughed too, but stopped laughing when he noticed what Edge was doing. He had unsnapped the flap of the holster on his right hip. Now, without taking out the revolver, he cocked his hammer with that familiarly ominous triple click. Then he let the pistol stay there, snug in the holster, its butt facing frontward as usual in the cavalry-carry position, but with his right hand resting on that butt.

Florian said, ''I thought you always carried that thing with the hammer down for safety.''

''It's another kind of safety I'm concerned about now.

I said this might be lawless territory here. I had Obie carry
my carbine handy, too, just in case. And I might as well
tell you: ever since we got a little way from the Furfews'
place, there've been three riders keeping pace with us, over
the fields yonder to the right of the road. They've stayed
well off behind the trees, so I've only caught glimpses of
them, but they're still with us.''

"And you never said anything? You must not be very
worried about their intentions.''

"We'll likely get an idea of their intentions when we
breast the top of Limestone Ridge—when we're going our
slowest. I figure they'll be waiting on the other side of the
crest.''

They were. The men had dismounted and left their three
horses to block the road, so the wagons could not have
made a dash past them in any case, but one of the men
raised his hand and called amiably, "Hold a minute, folks.
Like to have a word with y'all.''

Florian said bitterly, "I should have known we'd had
too much good luck. Here's where we lose it all.''

Edge quietly advised, "Just rein in slow, so the other
wagons come to a stop close behind us.''

The three men in the road looked sufficiently ugly to be
bummers or bandits or any other kind of undesirables.
They were dirty, their beards had been trimmed by the ax-
and-stump method, and they were dressed in a motley of
Yankee and Rebel jackets, boots and forage caps, plus derelict items of civilian attire, belts and bandoliers of modern
cartridge ammunition. Only in two respects were they elegantly fitted out. Their horses were prime animals, though
wearing battered, old-fashioned Grimsley saddles. And
each of the men, in addition to a belt pistol, was carrying
a new-blued Henry repeater carbine. Holding those weapons casually, but with their hands ready on the levers and
triggers, the men fanned across the road. One stayed directly in front of Snowball, another slowly approached on
Florian's side of the rockaway, and the third came toward
Edge, saying:

"Stay sittin' just like you are, sojer. I don't want to see that left hand sneak across towards your pistol holster."

"We don't mean to sound unfriendly," said the man on Florian's side, in a wheedling way. "But these are hard times, and you meet some hard characters on these roads."

"What can we do for you, gentlemen?" Florian asked levelly.

"We seen y'all leave that plantation a few miles back," said the man, moving closer to him. "We been there ourselfs, and we left as poor as we arrived. Folks not hospitable a'tall. Tightfisted as homemade sin."

"Yeah, damn 'em," said the man on Edge's side of the carriage, moving closer to him. "And the only female yonder was so ugly she'd skeer a dog out of a butcher shop. Hyuck hyuck." He spat a stream of tobacco juice.

"But you-all," said the other to Florian, stepping still closer, as if preparing to pounce. "Y'all come ridin' spry out of thar, like you'd just got drunk and got laid and got prosperous, all at onct."

"Yeah," said the other to Edge, spitting amber again. "We kinda wondered if we might of missed somethin', and mebbe y'all got it instead. Anyhow, you got a couple mighty purty passengers in this-yer rockaway . . . Say! Don't I know you, sojer?" He stood right before and below Edge now, and stared up at him. "I'll be a son of a bitch. Hyuck hyuck. Ain't you Zachary Edge, what used to be a Comanche?"

Edge said, just as bogus-cheerfully, "Sure am. Hyuck hyuck. How've you been, Luther?" and shot him in the belly.

Edge had not made any sudden or overt move, and actually had fired his revolver upside down. With his right hand resting on the backward pistol butt, and that hand's ring finger inside the holster, on the trigger, he had only to twist the holster a trifle upward and fire through its open narrow end. Before Luther finished sprawling backward in the road, there came the heavy *boom!* of the Cook carbine from Yount's wagon farther back in the train, and the bum-

mer on Florian's side of the carriage did an abrupt pirou-
ette and also fell down. Meanwhile, the recoil of Edge's
own gun had squirted it backward, free of the holster. It
was in his hand, right side up, the hammer thumbed back
again, before the third of the men, farthest up the road,
even grasped what was happening—and Edge had time to
aim and shoot him in the breast. The three rapid gunshots
were echoed by a few weak feminine shrieks, from Clover
Lee and two or three of the Simms females.

When Edge jumped down from the driving seat, through
the hanging cloud of blue smoke, Sarah Coverley was
leaning out of the rockaway, her eyes wide.

"My God, Zachary," she said, half-awed, half-appalled.
"They hadn't so much as threatened us."

He gave her a look. "Sometimes it's advisable to soothe
a man a little before he gets to the threatening stage."

His Remington cocked again and at the ready, he went
cautiously to stoop over each of the men. The one he had
shot in the breast and the one Yount had shot side-to-side
through the rib cage were already dead. But Luther, flat
on his back in the road, was still alive, opening and shut-
ting his mouth like a fish. When Edge bent over him, he
said crossly: "I swallered my damn tobacco. Don't never
swaller yer chaw, Cap'n Edge. It makes yer stummick hurt
like hell."

"You deserve to hurt, Sergeant Steptoe. You never were
worth a damn as a soldier, and you haven't improved any
as a road agent. You'd have died a better death at Tom's
Brook."

"Shit, I warn't the only one what turned tail at Tom's
Brook, and you ought to know that better'n—*ow!*—
Christamighty, but that tobacco's gripin' my poor stum-
mick!"

"I'll ease it for you," said Edge, and shot him again.

The other men of the company had got down from the
wagons and now came to gaze at the victims, occasionally
casting sidewise glances of genuine respect at Edge and
Yount.

"Well, I'll be double damned," said Yount. "Pittman and Steptoe and Stancill. I thought they was dead long ago, so this is what they come to."

"How do you happen to know them?" asked Florian, his voice somewhat unsteady.

Yount said, "We told you about that battle where us Comanches got scattered. These three was among the men that never regrouped. They must of been bumming around the vicinity ever since." He paused and considered, then said, "I'd almost like to ride back and tell Miz Furfew, so she could share out some of that blame she puts all on Yankees."

Rouleau said to Edge, indicating the late Sergeant Steptoe, "Did you have to shoot him twice, ami? Might not that one have lived?"

"No. In a minute he'd have been screaming and writhing. A man gut-shot can take hours to die. Would you want to sit and hold his hand that long?"

"Well, do we just let 'em all lay?" asked Mullenax. "For the buzzards to deal with?"

"Better not," said Edge. He scanned the horizon. "These could be just outriders of a bigger bunch somewhere. If so, and if these are found—well, we're the only other people who've passed this way, so their bummer chums might come looking for us."

"Anyway, Mr. Florian, you've got three good remounts," Fitzfarris said. "None of them is wearing any brand, army or otherwise. Throw away the saddles—they're worthless old things—and chances are nobody will ever recognize the horses as anything but circus stock. We probably can find employment for these weapons too. Zack, you want to use a repeater Henry in your act, instead of your single-shot. The revolvers are two Colts and a Joslyn."

"Fine," said Florian, taking command. "Sir John, you collect the arms and ammunition. Captain Hotspur, unsaddle the horses and tie them on lead, one to each of the first three vehicles. Monsieur Roulette, bring some of our old pieces of canvas. We'll wrap the cadavers and stow them in the tent wagon. Then let's roll.''

When they were again under way, Florian said to Edge, ''Well, it *has* been a lucky day, thanks mainly to you and Obie.'' When Edge said nothing. Florian gave him a look. ''Are you feeling remorse, my boy? I gather that those men were never exactly your bosom comrades, but I realize they were at least old acquaintances.''

Edge shook his head. ''They'd have been shot by firing squad after Tom's Brook, if they had been caught. Shameful as a retreat is, it's no capital crime—but those three kept on running. They were deserters, renegades, and it's obvious that they'd become even worse things since then.''

''Um, yes,'' Florian said thoughtfully. ''After seeing what they did to the Furfews' fine piano, I can guess what they'd have done to Sarah and Clover Lee.''

''The bastards figured they had us cold, and I wasn't inclined to sit idle until they really did. I don't feel any remorse at all. How long do you intend to play pallbearer for them? In this warm weather, they won't keep very well.''

''We'll bury them when we get to Charles Town.''

''That could cause some questions.''

''I didn't mean we'd do it ceremoniously. No, there's an old circus way of disposing of potential embarrassments. When we're preparing the ring, we'll plant the departed under it. After two or three shows, with the horses and elephant pounding over them, the rogues will be well tamped down. Unlikely they'll ever be resurrected, to cause any questions.''

11

AT CHARLES TOWN, they found the old racecourse ground available for a pitch, and Florian put the men to work right away, erecting the pavilion in the twilight and then, in the dark, preparing the ring. It had to be spaded and forked deep, to accommodate their detritus of dead bummers, and then firmed flat again before the curbing could be heaped up around it. When the troupe finally sat down around the campfire to eat, they ate well, for Phoebe Simms had already taken over the cooking job, and she did wonders with the circus's scant supply of provender, as she had done with the Furfews'. After the meal, the men and Magpie Maggie Hag lighted pipes and Abner Mullenax passed around one of his ever-present jugs, and Florian said, "Gather close, everybody. I have an announcement. Today is salary day!" and a cheer went up from the whole company.

Florian found an old shingle on the ground and, with his mason's pencil, did elaborate calculations on it, then began peeling off greenbacks from the wad he'd got from Mrs. Furfew. The artistes who had more recently joined out were paid in full, and consequently were not paid very much. Edge and Yount, for example, were owed for only some three week's work, and so were handed just twenty-two dollars apiece. The original troupers, dating back to long before Wilmington, got paid considerably more in lump sum but considerably less than they were due. Florian acknowledged that, and apologized for it.

"However, if our luck holds—and the attendance—I ought to be able to whittle down the deficits bit by bit. In the meantime, old friends, you understand that the greater part of our treasury must be kept by, for passage money."

At any rate, everybody had been paid unequivocally hard currency, so nobody complained. Indeed, Sarah Coverley declared her intention of strolling downtown to buy for herself and Clover Lee something in the line of sheer frippery, just by way of celebration.

"Restrain yourself, my dear Madame Solitaire," said Florian. "In case our luck should *not* hold, I would suggest to all of you that you tuck away at least part of your wages in the good old traditional grouch bag." Sarah shrugged and sat down again. Florian went on, "Now that our Florilegium is to some degree approaching solvency, and has burgeoned in numbers, we must give some thought to the best utilization of our company. If anyone has any suggestions, I shall be happy to hear them. Anyway, I have some of my own on which to solicit the company's opinions." He looked around. "Comments?"

"Well, first off, what's a grouch bag?" asked Mullenax.

Sarah said, with a grin, "It's what your wife would wear, Abner, if you still had a wife."

"Eh?"

"A grouch bag is all *I* had when the late Mr. Coverley ran out on me. When there's a woman in a team of performers—especially if her man drinks much—she'll put away what money she can. Some women buy a teensy little diamond now and then, to carry in a chamois bag on a neck chain. Diamonds are easy to carry and they're sellable anywhere. So a woman's always got grouch money when she needs it."

Mullenax mumbled something about "uppity females," then avowed that he didn't drink so doggoned much, then took a pull at his jug.

"All right. Now my suggestions," said Florian. "First for you, Madame Alp."

It was a moment before Phoebe Simms realized it was herself that was being addressed. She said, "Oh . . . yassuh," and laughed delightedly. "Take a while t' git used t' not bein' called Aunt or Mammy."

"Well, among ourselves, we'll call you whatever you prefer."

"Don' matter," she said, with another laugh, this one slightly rueful. "I bin called darlin' honey and I bin called nigguh hussy. But I be's always me, and I knows who I am."

"Would to God more folks did! Anyway, as of your first appearance on the show, in public you'll be Madame Alp. But, first thing in the morning, I want you to take this money and go to market. Stock our larder with all kinds of staples and groceries—get some fresh horsemeat for the cat, as well—and get every kind of cooking and serving utensil you think we need. Buy plenty of everything because, once you're Madame Alp and a celebrity, you can't run around and give every yokel a free look at you.''

"Yassuh. I go to market.''

Florian turned to Magpie Maggie Hag. "Madame Wardrobe Mistress, I'd like to you to get started right away on padding a tremendous dress for Madame Alp. Have her rigged out for showing as soon as possible. Also, think about some kind of dress-up for the triplets. I know I'm putting a lot of work on you, Mag, but at least those three all have the same measurements. And here's shopping money for you, too. Go and buy every gaudy piece of cloth and trimming you can find in Charles Town. You've been making do with scraps for too long.''

"Next—Colonel Ramrod. Will you look over those new horses we acquired? See if they'll work in harness.''

"They ought to," said Edge. "Considering who's been using them, they've probably done every kind of work. But I'll make sure.''

"Then we'll need extra harness to equip them, Captain Hotspur.''

"Ja, Baas. I go buy vas ve need.''

"I have another job for you to attend to at the same time, Captain. Since you are also our boss rigger, I want you to do some *rigging*. Here is ample money. While you are in town, buy us some lights.''

"Kerst Jesus!'' Roozeboom exclaimed. "You mean it Bass? Ve make night show now? I can buy *everyt'ing*? Chandelier and all?''

"All. You decide what we need, and you get it. Tomorrow, ladies and gentlemen, for the first time in this touring season, there will be two shows—afternoon and night. Mam'selle Clover Lee, here is my pencil and here is a stack of our posters. Start adding at the bottom of each one—'Evening performance, eight p.m.' and Tiny Tim, I want you out early tomorrow, posting that paper. Abdullah, you and Brutus do the usual rounds, as well, but yell to folks now that there will be both daytime and after-dark shows.''

''Yassuh, Mas' Florian.''

''Abdullah, Abdullah, I am still *Sahib* Florian to you. And to your apprentice Hindu, too. Impress that on little Quincy. No—Quincy doesn't sound very Hindu. Ali Baba, that's it. From now on, professionally he is Ali Baba.''

Roozeboom said, ''Baas, now ve got Mevrou Alp en dem klonkies, dey can't ride alvays in open ven it rains. Ve going need 'nother vagon.''

''Hm. Yes, I daresay you're right. Very well, procure one. As sturdy but as cheap as you can find. Thank goodness we've at least got enough draft animals now for all our wagons. And one of the new horses can take over the job of dragging that cannon, so Brutus doesn't have to do it.''

''Ja, Baas.''

''Everybody else on this show doubles or triples, and so should those new horses. Colonel Ramrod, do you think you could train them in some ring tricks? Since we now have more horses than equestrians, could you possibly work up a liberty act?''

''Possibly, if you'll tell me what a liberty act is.''

''Horses working by themselves with no riders aboard, with no controlling harness, only decorative plumes and such. You make them do drill and parade maneuvers on command. Or better, with unobtrusive signals of hand and whip, so they look like they're really doing it ad libitum.''

''I can give it a try.''

''Good. Do so. Do it well enough, Colonel Ramrod, and you will be promoted to one of the posts I now hold— equestrian director—what the rubes call ringmaster.''

''Whoa, now,'' said Edge. ''I don't have your gift of blarney.''

''Oh, I'll still be the talker. But you'll wield the whistle and a whip. Get the acts on and off in proper order— including your own—and in good order. Find a way to cover up when things go wrong. Decide when to pull an

act off early or let it run long. Things like that. You'll
learn. And, as soon as I can afford it, I will double the
pittance I am paying you at present.''

Rouleau asked, ''Florian, mon vieux, are you preparing
to abdicate? Going to grab your grouch bag and run?''

''Au contraire. We have come some way toward being
a real circus, not any longer just a mud show, and now the
main guy must delegate some responsibilities to others.
Which brings me to you, Sir John.''

There was a moment of general puzzlement, everybody
looking at everybody else. Then Fitzfarris gave a start and
said, ''Oh, yes. That's me. Shucks, it's been so long since
I was called anything but Aunt Mammy or honey darling . . .''

''Sir John, you *can* tip off the blarney, so I'd like you
to take over complete supervision of our growing sideshow. Build it into a real annex to our main program. For
now, I will still introduce *you*, and relate your tragic history, so you won't have to brag on yourself. But then I'll
step aside and you'll be the talker. Explain the lion feeding, expatiate on the museum of Zoölogical Wonders, tell
how the Crocodile Man was captured, introduce Madame
Alp and her—what?—the Three Graces?''

''No, no,'' said Fitzfarris. ''If I'm to be responsible for
the sideshow I want *curiosities*. How about the Three
White African Pygmies? Would you object to that, Madame Alp?''

''Dey still be Sunday, Monday and Tuesday to me, and
I still be's Mammy to dem. But dey good gals, dey do
whatever you want.''

''All right,'' said Fitz. ''And let me suggest one other
thing, Florian. You talked about not letting the public get
free looks at Madame Alp, but everywhere on the road
people are looking at the lion for free.''

Florian said, ''Well, a lion says *circus*. It's an allurement.''

''You've got the elephant for that. I say let's put sidewalls around the lion's cage while we're traveling.''

"There's not much allurement to a blank-walled box, Sir John."

"There could be. That wagon's got just an ordinary brake lever now. Ignatz, couldn't you take that off and whittle a great *big* one; near as hefty as a tree trunk, to put in its place?"

"Ja. But for vhy?"

"People see this closed cage rolling along the road. They see this monster brake lever sticking up beside the driver. They wonder what in Christ's name could be so big or so strong or so dangerous inside that box that it needs such a safeguard. Now *that's* allurement!"

Everybody around the fire stared at him, and finally Rouleau said softly, "Par dieu, this man *has* got circus blood."

Florian said, with admiration, "I wish to hell, Sir John, I could send you out ahead of us as our advance man. By God, you could get us talked about and newpapered like P. T. Barnum. But there—I'd be giving folks free looks at our Tattooed Man." He turned to the others. "Well, the other main item that's concerning me right now is that I sure wish we had some more music to go with the show. Does anybody here have any talent on any instrument?"

Phoebe Simms said, "Sunday can pick some on a pianner. Ol' Mistis used to show her."

"No! Well I'm damned," said Florian. "That old dragon actually once did a good deed?" He looked at the three ragamuffin Simms girls, who had sat all this time in a row, moving only their eyes to gaze in concert at whoever happened to be speaking. "Which of you is Sunday?"

"Me, suh," said one of them, otherwise indistinguishable. They all wore identical garments: shapeless, frazzle-hemmed frocks of colorless homespun, apparently with nothing underneath, and none of them had shoes.

"Sunday, my dear, do you remember what you used to play?"

"Yassuh. A pianner."

"I mean the names—the names of the pieces that woman taught you."

Sunday looked blank. "I played music, suh. Music ain't no *thing*. It cain't hab no *name*.

"Could you perhaps *hum* to us something you remember playing?"

Sunday walled her big brown eyes like a frightened colt, but then began shyly to hum, and gradually hummed louder, until it was audible.

Florian said, " 'Ah, vous dirai-je, maman.' That's what it is."

Yount said, "Sounded to me like 'Twinkle Twinkle, Little Star.' "

"Same song," said Florian. "It may not be great music, but it's international. Monsieur Roulette, maybe you can work her up into something. Any person that can play a piano can play an accordion, n'est-ce pas?"

Rouleau scratched his head. "I would guess so. Just have to learn the squeezing. I'll see if I can find one cheap in a pawnshop. Sunday and I between us can have a go at it. I will at the same time work on her abysmal dialect and diction."

Florian said, "I also want the children to become something more than sideshow curiosities. Madame Solitaire, you take first try at the girls. See if they have any gift for equitation. We'll all have a try at them and see where their talents lie. Monsieur Roulette, regard the little boy there— Ali Baba. Isn't eight years about the right age for starting klischnigg practice?"

"Contortions? Oui. Before that age, the bones are too easily broken. After that age, the ligaments soon get inelastic."

"Would you undertake to teach the posture-master's art to Ali Baba?"

"I can get him started. Crack the instep. Begin the side practices."

"Hoy!" little Quincy cried faintly, but he was ignored.

*   *   *

Roozeboom was the first back from town next day, driving the new wagon he had bought—another slab-sided, closed van, similar to the tent wagon, and about as dilapidated—and he commandeered Mullenax to help him unload from it his other purchases. There were torch poles wound with turpentine-dipped wicking at one end, and fully forty small coal-oil lanterns, each with a tin reflector attached.

"And what the Jesus is this thing?" Mullenax asked, grunting under the weight, as they manhandled the largest piece of new equipment out of the wagon.

"Is a chandelier," said Roozeboom.

"Hell, I was expecting something fancy, like what Mr. Furfew said he used to own. All glass and bangles."

"Dis I made myself at a carpenter shop. Made it in fast hurry."

"It looks it."

A lot of rough, unpainted two-by-twos were nailed together to make a pyramid of square frames of diminishing size, with an iron hanger ring attached at the pinnacle.

"Komt u, klonkie!" Roozeboom called to the nearest of the Simms triplets. "You fix candles on here, ve vork on odder t'ings." He produced a tremendous box full of cheap tallow candles, and showed her how. He lighted one candle and used it to soften the bottom end of another and another, sticking them upright around the perimeter of the top chandelier frame. "Stick dem close togedder, und as many as you can on dis sqvare. Den move down to next frame, do de same. It ought to hold maybe t'ree hundred candles."

The two men went to distribute the pole torches, and Mullenax discovered that the four upper corners of the lion wagon and the museum wagon were already equipped with sockets for them. Roozeboom stuck other torches in the ground in a line, as guide lights from the street to the front yard, and a couple on either side of the Big Top's front door.

Inside the pavilion, Roozeboom showed Mullenax how

to affix the small coal-oil lamps at intervals all the way around the lowest tier of seat planks, their reflectors positioned to aim their light at the ring. While Mullenax was doing that, Roozeboom went to the center pole and undid various hitches from various cleats, to let the boom angle out just a bit from the center pole and dangle its pulley rope. When the Simms girl had finished studding the wooden chandelier with a thicket of candles, the two men carried the big thing into the tent and attached its ring to the rope-fall. Roozeboom struck up the ''heeby-weeby'' chant while they hauled it up to the boom end, some twenty-five feet above the floor and necessarily a little off-center of the ring.

''Tonight ve let it down, light it, send it up again,'' said Roozeboom. ''Be pretty. You vill see. Now—I also bring from town vagon spokes, hubs, shims, strip iron, axle grease. I go fire some charcoal, get my hammer en anvil, you en me start repair en true all our vagon vheels.''

They were sweating at that job when the other troupers returned from town, with a wail and squawl of music. Jules Rouleau was jauntily perched atop one of the wagons and working an accordion, wheezing out ''Frère Jacques,'' not very well but very loudly.

''It's almost a pleasure to be here in Yankee Land,'' Yount declared to one and all. ''Charles Town ain't no hub of all Creation, but it's better stocked than the whole of Dixie.''

''Yes, indeed,'' said Florian, who was wearing a new high hat. This was a beaver, much richer-looking than his old silk one. ''I decided, by damn, Monsieur Directeur, you're owed a treat, too. Voilà, le chapeau!'' He gave it a juggler's twirl along his arm, then flipped it back onto his head.

''Nice, Baas,'' Roozeboom said dutifully, then anxiously, ''You got meat for Maximus?''

''Half a horse, damn near,'' said Edge. ''And for us, some beef, Not dried, not salted, not smoked. Real beef!''

Yount said, "I'm just about herniated from carrying Aunt Pheobe's grocery purchases."

That lady announced, with vast self-satisfaction, "I 'spect I done cleaned out eb'ry market in dat town."

"And Maggie every draper," said Rouleau. "There's no great tonnage of cloth goods to be found, but what there is, she got it."

"And I see you got your musical squeeze box," Mullenax said to Rouleau. Then he turned to Fitzfarris. "How about the squeezin's I asked for?"

"Yessir, yessir, three jugs full," Fitz sang cheerfully. "In that crate there with all *my* bottles."

Mullenax took out one of the jugs, uncorked it, took a drink, happily smacked his lips and handed the jug around the circle of men. "How come, Fitz, you bought me full jugs and yourself only empty bottles?"

"They won't be empty long. They're for my tonic. And I'd like to ask a favor, Abner. Can I pour just a dab of your whiskey into each bottle? It'll give some authority to the other contents."

"I reckon. Just a dab, mind. What else is going in?"

"Mag says she's got some tincture of ipecac I can have. That's pretty authoritative, too, in its way. And Clover Lee says she's just washed out some red tights, so the wash water is a nice shade of pink. I shouldn't need anything else."

"Jesus. Dirty water and upchuck root and a dash of chain lightning. Is this the gleet-cure tonic you talked about?"

"Oh, no. I've got a new and splendid crocus to peddle." He turned, as Magpie Maggie Hag plucked at his sleeve.

"You come, get ipecac. Get something else I got for you."

"And you girls come try on these shoes I bought for you," said Sarah to the triplets. "Then we'll introduce you to Snowball and Bubbles. See how you like them and they like you."

"And then, Sunday—" said Rouleau, "Whichever one

of you is Sunday, you and I will go off and learn the
accordion together.''

So, as everyone else drifted away, Mullenax retrieved
his jug and took it to where Roozeboom, resting from his
exertions, sat leaning against a wheel of the cage wagon.
Mullenax plopped down beside him and proffered the jug.

"Dank u, nee," said Roozeboom. "Not so soon before
show time."

"It ain't often I can catch you not workin', Ignatz, and
I want to ask something. Everybody else around here is
gettin' up new acts. I'd like to broaden my own edjication.
Florian said you might be willin' to learn me lion taming."

Roozeboom jerked a thumb over his shoulder. "Dere is
a lion. Go tame him. Gelluk en gezonheid."

"Oh, crap, man. That old hearth rug is already tamer'n
my gran'daddy."

"You t'ink so. Stand up dere close en say hello to hearth
rug."

Mullenax got up and put his face close to the cage bars.
Maximus immediately showed his yellow teeth and roared
menacingly. Mullenax backed away abruptly, sat down
again, took a restorative nip and said, "I reckon that signified he's in a bad mood. How do I know when he's in
a good one? Does he purr?"

"Nee. Lions cannot purr. Of all de big cats, only chee-
tahs en cougars can purr. En *dey* cannot roar. A tiger, now,
a tiger makes a noise only tigers can make. A rough sort
of chuff-chuff—means good humor, same as purr."

"That's right interestin', Ignatz, but it don't help me
much. All we got is a lion, and all he's done is roar."

"To trainer, roar don't mean much. Lion could be cross,
hungry, playful, anyt'ing. Some say ven cat lashes tail he
is angry. I say vatch—ven cat goes stiff, rigid, *den* he is
dangerous. I say also, ven you vorking cat, remember alvays you are looking at five mouths. Vun full of teeth,
four full of talons. I tell you, Abner, vunce you get in dat
sqvare cage, you don't never be bored."

"Tell me what I *do* do. Ain't there some rules, like ABC's?"

"Dere probably are ninety-nine rules for cat trainer. None of dem can be trusted. But I recite you some of dem, sure. Eerste, Abner, never approach or touch cat timidly, alvays firmly, en never unexpectedly, never from behind."

"Well, I learned that much on the farm. Touch even a hog unexpectedly, he'll near jump out of his skin."

"Touch so a cat en he peel you out of *your* skin. Remember also, if a cat bite you, he can let go. But if he claw you, he *nee* can let go. His paw is made so by God Himself. Ven cat reaches to grab somet'ing, de tendons extend en *fix* dem in hooked positions. So, even if cat grab you by accident, en he is sorry, ven he pulls paw avay he vill rake hunks out of you."

"All right. That's rule one to remember. What's second?"

"Tweede, grow yourself another eye."

"Eh?"

"Only vun eye, Abner, means you nee can judge distance too good. You should know alvays exactly how far you are from cat. Also many cats—like people—be righthanded or left-handed. Got to learn each cat, so you know vhich paw to keep eye on. A man vit only vun eye . . . en so much to look out for . . ."

"I can't grow another one. I'll just have to take my chances."

"Derde rule: *never* take chances. Vierde rule: stay avay from dat stuff." He indicated Mullenax's jug. "A cat vatches for every veakness, take qvick advantage."

"Aw, hell, I've always worked better with a little Dutch courage."

Roozeboom said dryly, "In Dutch, ve call it drunk courage, meaning don't rely on it. But come, Abner. Stand here vit me." He got up and stood close to the cage bars. "Let Maximus see us togedder. Soon he accept you as friend. Ve go in cage togedder."

Mullenax set down the jug and the two men stood at

the cage for a time, Roozeboom occasionally reaching in
to scratch the lion's head. After a bit, Mullenax was en-
couraged to do likewise, and the lion permitted it. After
another while, making no sudden moves, the men edged
around to the barred door and opened it. Maximus roared,
but only in an absentminded way. Roozeboom went inside,
talking softly and persuasively, then went close and affec-
tionately ruffled the lion's mane, while Mullenax also sidled inside and prudently stayed at the far end of the cage.

That whole procedure was observed with great interest
by one of the Simms triplets, standing a little distance
away. In her absurd garb of ragged homespun frock and
bright yellow brand-new high-top spring-heel shoes, she
looked rather like a pretty duckling. As she watched
Roozeboom and Mullenax cautiously enter the cage
wagon, she wore a dreamy half-smile, and every time the
lion rumbled her whole body trembled.

She in turn was being watched by Sarah, Rouleau and
Florian. The latter remarked, ''The girl is frightened.''

''No, she's enjoying it,'' said Sarah. ''She's a peculiar
child. When I plunked her up on Bubbles, bareback, nothing to hold onto but his mane, and let him walk with her
around the ring, I'd have thought that would scare her at
least a little. But she said, 'This feels good,' and got that
same funny smile on her face and that same tremor all
over.''

Florian shrugged. ''Maybe she is a born équestrienne.
Which one is that, anyhow?''

''That one's Monday. You'll soon be able to tell them
apart. Sunday is the quick and lively and intelligent one.
Monday is this dreamy one, kind of strange and contained.
And Tuesday, well, she's a plodder. She'll tackle anything,
and probably do it dutifully, but without any spark or sparkle.''

''That is approximately my summation, too,'' said Rouleau. ''So we have pronounced our expertise upon them;
now let us decide how to employ them.''

Florian said, ''Well, naturally we'll show them as a trio

in the sideshow. But in the ring, I think we ought to scatter them somewhat. Make our troupe look more numerous and various.''

''Bien,'' said Rouleau. ''Sarah, you and Ignatz take Monday and Tuesday for riders, and I will keep Sunday and Quincy. The boy holds promise as a contortionist, and I can start the girl with the same basic instruction, then bring her along to parterre acrobatics, eventually even to aerial, if we ever get any such rigging.''

''I'm agreeable to that,'' said Florian. ''Meanwhile, is the girl's piano playing adaptable to the accordion?''

''We have not got beyond 'Vous diraij-je.' But I think that girl Sunday could learn anything. She told me that she hopes to *be* something in this world, something better than her mammy. I suggested she could start by referring to her 'mother,' and now she does.''

''Aunt Phoebe will be flabbergasted,'' said Sarah.

''I further suggested that speaking good English is a good way to get ahead in the world. So she *axed* me if I would *learn* it to her. I began by drilling her in the pronunciation of 'ask' and the difference between learn and teach. And she grasped them, à l'instant.''

''Bless my soul,'' murmured Florian.

''I will teach that child to read and write, too, while I am teaching Clover Lee. French as well as English. All three of those little mulattoes are handsome chabines, Florian, but in that Sunday girl, you have made a real find.''

They were interrupted by the voice of Magpie Maggie Hag, calling, ''Olá, Florian, look what I bring you!''

They turned and, when they saw the stranger approaching with her, they put on polite smiles of greeting. Then, as the man came closer, their smiles changed to looks of incredulity.

''Well, I'll be damned,'' murmured Florian.

''I do declare,'' breathed Sarah. ''Sir John Doe.''

''Maggie Magicienne, you've worked a miracle!'' said Rouleau.

For the first time since they had known him, Fitzfarris's

face was all the same color, and that color all human. Not until he was standing right before them could they discern the cosmetic appliqué.

"However did you do it, Mag?" asked Florian.

"Barossan, you remember that toby clown we had on the show, long time ago, back in Ohio? Billy Kinkade? He leave me some his face paints when he blow the stand. I keep ever since. This color here, Billy the Kink called 'complexion ointment.' Always he put it on first—not zinc-white muck like most joeys—before he start with bright colors. I decide I try, see how it work on Sir John."

"It works wonders!" said Sarah. "Fitz, you're a good-looking gentleman."

"And do you know what this means, Sir John?" Florian crowed. "You can be our patch!"

"Patched is what I am, all right."

"No, no. Our advance man, our advertising agent, our fixer, our patch applier."

"Ah," said Fitzfarris, comprehending. "In my former trade, it was called a soap specialist."

"You'll have to scrub off the good face to appear as our Tattooed Man this afternoon and evening. But our next pitch will be Harper's Ferry, only six miles along the road. Tomorrow morning, you can put on the good face again and ride over there to start the publicity mill to grinding."

From the direction of Charles Town now came the boompty-boom of Hannibal's drum, and Tim Trimm rode onto the lot on the smallest of the new horses, carrying only his paste pot and brush.

"Looks like Tim has got this town all papered," said Florian. "And yonder comes Brutus leading the first of today's crowd. So let us get ready for show time. Monsieur Roulette, would you help Maggie open the red wagon for business?" He turned and called to Mullenax, who was just then descending from the lion's cage, "Barnacle Bill, ahoy!" Mullenax shambled over, looking slightly sweaty but extremely proud of himself. "I'm afraid you'll have to go on doing the Crocodile Man until we've got our other curiosities costumed for showing.'' Mullenax stopped looking proud.

''And hey, Abner,'' said Fitzfarris, ''I'll make a celebrity of you and some publicity for us. When I ride over to Harper's Ferry tomorrow, I'll spread the word. The circus is coming, and it'll be grateful if everybody will keep a lookout, because its Crocodile Man has *got loose*. That'll raise some noise and interest, you can bet.''

The others regarded Fitz with dazzled admiration, but Mullenax only muttered, ''Jesus,'' and went off to get into his pirate dress for the first half of the program.

The crowd at the afternoon performance was of estimable size, and paid more in currency than in barter— good Yankee coin and paper—and was properly appreciative of the show. Phoebe Simms was not yet accoutred to appear as Madame Alp at intermission, but Florian and Fitzfarris decided that the triplets were worth displaying even in their duckling-looking garb of threadbare old homespun and big new shoes. After Florian introduced Sir John Doe and recounted the woeful tale of how he had come to be a Tattooed Man, Fitz took over:

''And now, ladies and gentlemen, allow me the honor of presenting to you my companion unfortunates in this Congress of Curiosities and Abnormalities. First, cast your wondering eyes upon these three identical White Pygmies, discovered by missionaries traveling through deepest, darkest Africa. No one knows how these white women chanced to be there, among the black and savage pygmies of the Congo. But these are adult and full-grown white women, only disastrously pygmified and negrified— stunted of growth and given a dusky tinge to their skins— by the terrible environment from which the mission fathers rescued them . . .''

He spouted fictitious facts about every dusty and dubious marvel in the museum wagon, and prattled lies all during the lion's feeding, and made the Crocodile Man sound even worse than he looked—''cast up on the banks

of the Amazon, just as you see him now, scrabbling on all
fours like any other saurian beast, crusted all over with
reptilian scales, except for that hideous gap in his face,
where he was struck by the dart from an aborigine's blow-
gun. And that concludes our display of Wonders and Phe-
nomena. But, gentlemen, when the ladies and children
have departed, perhaps you will linger to hear one last
announcement *for your ears only . . .*"

The females obediently moved away, children in tow,
and a few dragged their men along with them. But Fitzfarris was left with quite a surround of male adults, variously grinning and looking skeptical.

"Gentlemen," Fitz said, in a just-among-us voice.
"When I escaped from Shah Nasir's harem, I brought out
one other thing besides this blue disfigurement. I stole the
secret formula of the potion which enables that monarch
to satisfy the nightly lusts of his sixty-nine young wives
and four hundred beautiful concubines. And, using those
same rare herbs and spices and extracts, I have compounded a limited supply of that powerful invigorating
fluid, to offer to a few of my fellow men the veritable stag
and stud virility it can give them."

He reached behind him, under the museum wagon, and
dragged forth a crate clinking with half-pint bottles of all
shapes, containing a rather vividly pink liquid.

"It is called in Persian the Potentate's Resurrection
Tonic, but as you see I take care to put no such label on
the bottles, so the compound is not susceptible to pilferage
by womanizing scoundrels or—heaven forbid—by small
boys, who might be impelled to molest their little girl
schoolmates, or even their very school-marms."

"Mister . . . I mean Sir Doe," said a voice, in a fair
imitation of the local drawl. The man was slouch-hatted
and dressed in overalls, so none of the rubes recognized
Jules Rouleau. "A pow'ful pecker bracer like that-there
must be almighty scarce and hellaciously expensive. Kin
folks like us afford it?"

"Sir you cannot afford *not* to possess it. True, in the

Orient, this manhood-enhancing medicament is dispensed only in tiny phials, and exchanged only for its equal weight in twenty-four-karat gold. However, I will frankly confess that it is only for the motive of avenging myself upon the hated Shah Nasir that I offer you his long-guarded secret *not* for gold, not for ten dollars—nay, not even for five. Take the Potentate's Resurrection Tonic, gentlemen, for only *two* dollars the bot—''

He was almost swept off his feet by the surge of them.

The night show was the first in a long time for all of the Florilegium's veteran troupers, and a novelty for those lately joined out. Edge had been worried that the poor light might adversely affect his shooting, but he found that, though the little reflector lamps and the cheap candles were individually feeble, all together they were ample for everybody's work. Hanging high above the crowd, where the crude wood frame was unnoticeable, the chandelier's constellation of some three hundred candles looked really splendid. They did, however, create a minor nuisance: a steady drizzle of wax pellets, melted up there and congealing on the way down. A drawback to the candles and lamps alike was the horde of moths and other insects they attracted—flickering like bright confetti around the lights, and sizzling and popping and giving off wee puffs of smoke whenever they hit the flames.

"I am particularly pleased to have the footlights," Florian said to Edge. "See how even more beautiful they make Madame Solitaire and Mam'selle Clover Lee appear out there. Set low, shining upward, casting a warm and gentle light, the footlights soften the jawline, enhance the forehead, make mysterious the eyes and merry the mouth. They accentuate the cheekbones and almost vanish the nose. I have never known a woman, Zachary—even the most gorgeous woman—to be entirely satisfied with her nose. Yes, I firmly maintain that mother Nature never provided any light so flattering to a woman as the man-invented footlights."

In an unbusy interval, Edge stepped outside the pavilion to admire the look of the circus lot by night. Across the darkness of the racecourse grounds, the double row of torches outlined an avenue leading to the cage wagon and the museum wagon—also ruddily illumined by their corner torches—and to the front door of the Big Top. The peaked canvas that was drab by day, now lighted from within and glowing ivory-white against the night, was a thing so soft-bright and immense that now it might well be called a tabernacle without disappointing anybody who expected a tabernacle to be an imposing edifice. When the performance concluded, and the people dispersed from the light into the darkness, they discussed the show as appreciatively as any daylight audiences had done, but less raucously and more reverently, as if the entertainment had also constituted some sort of devotional service.

The next morning, Fitzfarris, with his cosmetic face applied and with a roll of circus posters tied behind his saddle, rode eastward to Harper's Ferry. Magpie Maggie Hag sat down, with Phoebe Simms helping, to work on the costumes for Madame Alp and the White African Pygmies. Tim and Hannibal got out some newly bought buckets of paint and began to turn the balloon wagon and the newly acquired one from their weathered gray to cobalt blue. Sarah took Monday and Tuesday to the ring, to give them their first riding lessons, and Yount accompanied them to lend his weight on the rope-fall when it was needed. Rouleau took Quincy and Sunday to start their acrobatic training. Edge, assisted by Clover Lee, began breaking-in the three new horses for a liberty act. When Roozeboom and Mullenax had finished refurbishing all the wagon wheels that needed it, they went again into Maximus's cage to continue the lion-training lessons. Florian circulated among all those arenas of activity, contributing advice, criticism or encouragement as required. There was not an idle person on the lot.

"That's all it takes?" said Clover Lee, with admiration.

"Just tap the horse like that, Mr. Zachary?"

"Well, you've got to do a lot of gentling first," said Edge. "Stroke and caress him, get him nicely soothed. Then you strap up his off foreleg, like I just did. Then take the whip and tap him gently just below the knee, on the leg he's standing on. After a little, to stop his being tapped, he goes down to both knees. It looks to the audience like he's taking a bow. Caress him some more, to show him he did the right thing. Then stand off to one side, pull the reins gently toward you, and he'll ease over sideways and lie down. Caress him some more. Pretty soon you've only got to touch him just barely, to make him do either move."

"I've never had to learn much about horses except my own work on top of them." She added, with unconcealed jealousy. "Now that we've got those buffalo gals studying riding, too, I'm going to have to add some more toots and flash to my own act."

"Let me show you another trick I'm teaching them," said Edge. "Look, I take this pin and just barely prick this fellow here at his withers." The horse whickered in surprise and reared up on his hind legs. "Now I prick him again, back here on his crupper." The horse made another surprised noise and kicked up his hoofs behind. "Pretty soon I throw away the pin, just touch him back and forth, both places, and he imitates a rocking horse."

Clover Lee exclaimed, "That's as pretty as can be!"

"Ow!" cried Quincy Simms. Then quickly, penitently, "I'se sorry, mas' Jules, but dat hurt."

"It's supposed to," said Rouleau. He held one of the boy's bare, black, mauve-bottomed feet in his hands, and was bending the toes under and backward, toward the heel. "You must keep doing this yourself, just as I am showing you, and do it every chance you get. Every time, do it until it hurts so you can hardly stand it. And each time, the instep will bend a little farther and more easily. It is the only way to perfect the pointed toe, and that is essential to any limberjim. Now let's have the other foot."

"Ow-oo!" howled Quincy. "Sorry, Massa."

"Crybaby," Sunday said loftily. "And de man don't be's massa, he be's Monsieur Jules."

"He *is* Monsieur Jules," said Rouleau through gritted teeth. "I *am* Monsieur Jules. There is no such word as 'be's.' "

"Hoy," said Quincy, bewildered. "Dem ain't bees yonder?" He pointed to the ones buzzing about a nearby clump of clover.

"J'en ai plein le cul," Rouleau muttered to himself. "Why do I let myself get saddled with eight jobs at once?"

"He talkin' Eur'pean at you, Quince," Sunday said brightly. "J'en ai plein le cul. I say dat right, monsieur?"

'Exactly right, chérie. And I expect you will say it often in times to come. Now take off those foolish stiff shoes. We've got to start cracking your instep, too."

He manipulated her fawn-colored, pink-soled feet, and she bravely resisted crying out at the pain. Florian came ambling by, and asked avuncularly, "How go things here?" He started slightly, and Rouleau burst out laughing, when Sunday piped up joyfully:

"J'en ai plein le cul, Monsieur Florian!"

"Before anyt'ing else, Abner," said Roozeboom, "must know *care* of cats. Poor Maximus here, he has learned to eat anyt'ing nearly. But now ve can afford skoff, he vill eat ten or tventy pounds of meat each day. Feed alvays lean meat; fat giffs lion boils. Also, alvays feed meat vit bones in, so cat has to eat slow, not gulp it down en get indigestion. Vun day each veek, no feed at all, let belly empty out. En vun day each month, giff him *live* skoff—chicken, kid, vun of your piglets, maybe."

"Hey, them pigs is my livelihood, Ignatz. At least until I'm a genuine lion tamer. Tell me about the *taming* part."

"Vell . . ." Roozeboom tugged at his walrus mustache. "Dere is taming . . . en dere is training. Here in America, most cat men imitate Thomas Batty—show off de tamer's mastery of de animals. In Europe now, many imitate de Hagenbecks—show off de animals' beauty, grace, de routines dey haff learned.''

"Well, Maximus ain't no beauty, but he's beautifuller than me. I'll let the folks admire him and his tricks.''

"Nee, cat never learns a *trick*—cat don't know trick from man in moon—cat learns a *habit*. En only two t'ings make it possible a man can train a cat to a habit. Vun is dat a man has patience, a cat has greed. Oder is dat a cat nee realize he is stronger dan a man. So you use his greed, your patience, to make him a habit. Say you lay broomstick across inside his cage. He valks, steps over it, you giff him bit of meat. You raise stick inch each day, he must step higher en higher, you feed his greed each time. Vun day he vill have choice: make little chump over or creep under. You say, 'Springe!' ''

"Why not say jump over?''

"Alvays giff command in Cherman. Is tradition, is also good sense. Sometime you buy cat from oder show, you nee have to vunder: does dis vun speak French, Zulu, Chinese? All cats obey Cherman.''

"All right. I say 'Springe!' Then what?''

"Ven he chump, you giff bit of meat. Raise broomstick higher each day, he chump higher. In time, he make big high chump every time you say 'Springe!' ''

"Wait. Back up. That first time he has to choose—suppose he chooses to creep under the stick?''

"You scold, sound angry, crack whip, giff no meat. Hit him if necessary, not to hurt, only to show you angry. Never do cruelty. Cat is dangerous enough, you nee vant make him enemy besides. If you must, start over from beginning. From broomstick down on floor.''

"Jesus, such a simple trick. Does it have to take so long?''

"You de superior human, nee? You have de patience, you must use it. Get cat in a habit, he vill repeat it over en over. Die gewente maak die gewoonte. But if ever *vunce* he refuse, you must insist. He must never get idea he can disobey en get avay vit dat. He must never suspect he stronger dan you, in villpower or in muss-kle. If ever a cat scratch you, don't flinch, don't get angry, don't let cat know it *can* hurt. Klaar?''

"That's kind of a tall order, asking a man not even to flinch.''

"Chust get out of cage soon as you can. Voetsak! Is best idea, anyvay, go get carbolic en bandage. Cats are clean animals except in mouth en under claws. Alvays bits of old meat dere, rotting. Small bite or scratch giffs you mortal infection. Also remember, if cat attacks you, de most tender spot on him is his nose. You nee can beat off a cat by main strength, but hit him on nose, he maybe back off.''

"Maybe.''

"Vatever happens, Abner, try stay on your feet, even if whole cage of cats go crazy. On your feet you taller dan dey are, you still superior. But you fall down, you look to dem like fresh kill of gazelle, laid out to eat. Dey vill eat you.''

Mullenax swallowed. "You mean . . . if a tamer falls down even once in his career, he's a goner?''

Roozeboom shrugged. "Try to fall face down. Ven a cat kills in de vild, first t'ing, he eats is entrails. You lie on stomach, he vill paw at you, try roll you over, get at your belly. Maybe dat giffs time for somebody come running en help.''

"Maybe,'' Mullenax said again, looking at old Maximus with a new respect and apprehension. "Well, we're talking about cats already sort of tamed—and me in the cage with 'em. But suppose I was to get a new one, or a whole herd of 'em. How does a man *begin!* What's the *very first* thing you do?''

"You sit for long time at a distance en you vatch.''

"Watch what?''

"Vas dey do. Kerst, Abner, you already know dat. You vatched pigs on your farm, you saw dey like climb ladders. You made act of pigs climbing ladders.''

"That's it? That's the secret? Find something the animal already knows how to do?"

"Or likes to do, en can do better. Cats all playful. Lions, tigers, some as kitty cats. You vatch dem play, maybe you see vun dat chumps backvard, or vun dat likes to roll. See vas de cat does naturally, encourage him to exaggerate dat, make a habit of it. After vhile, you haff cat dat can make big backvard chumps, or roll like a barrel. Rubes t'ink you vunderful, make cat do somet'ing *un*natural."

"Well, I'll be damned. Here I was, learning lion taming in my own backyard, and never suspected it!"

"I cain't let folks see me lak dis!" wailed Monday Simms.

"Laigs all hangin' out!" wailed Tuesday Simms.

"Dey's right, Miz Maggie," grumbled Phoebe Simms. "Bad 'nuff I looks big as dat tent yonder. My gals looks *indecent*."

Magpie Maggie Hag had finished basting together the dresses for Madame Alp and the White Pygmies, and had commanded a try-on. Madame Alp's blouse and skirt, voluminous to begin with, were now so padded inside they bulged at the buttons and seams, and the skirt needed no hoop or crinoline to make it stand out all around. For contrast, the wardrobe mistress had made the girls' garb slim and sylphlike, mere tights that fitted like paint on their narrow torsos and willowy limbs. She had chosen cloth of a tan color that matched their own—so on these girls they were "flesh-colored"—and decorated them only with bursts of glittery sequins around their chests and loins: red for Monday, yellow for Tuesday and a blue-spangled outfit set aside for Sunday.

"Cain't even bend to sit down!" wailed Tuesday Simms.

"An' *I* cain't hardly stand up," growled Phoebe Simms.

The old gypsy did not argue; she went to fetch Florian. At his approach, the two girls squealed and hid behind their mammoth mother.

"Forgive me for speaking bluntly, Madame Alp," he said. "But I fail to understand the complaints about the children's fleshings. Since I've known the girls, they've been running about in nothing but a shift. At least now their bottoms are—"

"Dem gals is jist 'bout old 'nuff to start havin' der flars. I keeps 'em unkivered on dat account."

"Der flars?" echoed Florian.

"Their flowers," Magpie Maggie Hag translated. "The curse of Eve."

"Oh," said Florian. "Ah. Um. Well, ladies, I'll leave it to Madame Hag to explain to you about—ahem, napkins and clouts. I will say only that circus tights are called tights because they are *deliberately* tight. Those fleshings are not made for sitting, they are made for freedom of movement in your work, and to show off your legs and rumps while you do it."

"Mas' Florian, dey looks *buck nekkid!*"

"Madame Alp, I have seen more countries than you have seen counties, and nowhere in the world have I ever seen anything more beautiful than a beautiful woman naked."

"Ain't *decent.* To show demselfs like dat afore white folks."

"You've seen both Madame Solitaire and Mademoiselle Clover Lee wearing tights. It white women can parade their bodies, your girls have every right to do the same. Anyway, at their age, they don't have enough curves to be ashamed of showing them. By the time they do, they'll show them proudly. Now, let me hear no more complaints. And by the way, allow me to compliment you, Madame Alp. You look alpine, indeed. Maggie, try to have these dresses finished in time for today's intermission."

She did, and made the Simms females wear them, and Fitzfarris was back from his advance run just in time to take his own place in the sideshow, and to do the talking.

"Next, ladies and gentlemen, observe this living mountain of flesh . . . The market scale registered seven hundred and fifty-five pounds before it went wild and broke . . . Requires the elephant Brutus to lift her from ground level into her specially stout-sprung traveling wagon . . . Any lady in the audience may assure herself of Madame Alp's genuine obesity by pinching one of her massive ankles. In the interest of good manners, gentlemen are kindly requested to refrain . . .''

And the Simms females were so gratified at being made to sound so special that they abandoned their prudish grousing and self-consciousness, and settled back to enjoy celebrity and the crowd's massed eyeballs.

''I was lucky,'' Fitzfarris told Florian, as the rubes headed back into the Big Top for the rest of the program. ''I hit Harper's Ferry just as the newspaper man was preparing to run off this week's issue. Got him to tear the paper apart and put in the warning about the savage Abner Mullenax on the loose. It should be on the streets right about now. Here, I brought one.''

The Harper's Ferry *Herald* was printed on the blank side of old and faded sheets of wallpaper. And this edition had elbowed into corners the news of the week to make room for the galvanizing headline CROCODILE CREATURE ESCAPES FROM LOCAL TENT SHOW! and a story obviously set in type directly from Fitz's dictation.

Florian read it, smiling, handed it around for the other gathered troupers to admire, and said, ''Sir John, that's the first time we've been newpapered in I can't remember how long. Wilmington got tired of writing and reading about us long before we left there.''

''I've also got darkies putting up our posters all over town. And I've engaged a decent lot between Bolivar and Camp Hill. Cost me a handful of tickets, all told.''

''Very good. Listen, everybody. This will be an overnight run. We'll tear down right after tonight's show and hit the road. Everybody who is not driving, try to get some sleep on the way. And Barnacle Bill, stay in your crocodile crust.''

''Aa-argh!'' cried the creature, despairingly.

''No—better yet—slather on another coating of it before we leave here. Then bunk down on your balloon wagon; Fitz will drive for you. We'll have to pretend you got recaptured somewhere along the way, so we may have to produce a Crocodile Man on demand.''

12

THE CIRCUS train was still half a mile from the Harper's Ferry peninsula, climbing the road that led between Bolivar Heights and the Shenandoah River, when Florian, in the lead, saw what appeared to be the lights of town reflected in the sky, unaccountably bright for this hour just before dawn. He was puzzled. Then he was startled, as the light rushed upon him and became a mob of men carrying torches, lanterns, shotguns, pitchforks and clubs.

''Y'all the ones that lost that crocodile critter?'' bellowed a bearded man at the front of the throng. Snowball, terrified, reared in the carriage shafts. ''We aim to keep it out of our town, by God!''

The drivers of the vehicles behind all hauled on their reins to keep from colliding with the ones ahead of them, and from inside the wagons could be heard squeals and curses from the troupers rudely awakened by the pileup. The mob poured down both flanks of the train, thrusting their torches and lanterns into the drivers' faces, and the horses all shied, snorted and danced in consternation. Fitz-farris had been dozing on the balloon-wagon seat, so he failed to halt his draft mule and it tried to dodge around the vehicle ahead. That dropped the balloon wagon's off-side wheels into a ditch beside the road, and the whole wagon tilted. Fitz merely fell sidelong on the seat. But Mullenax, who had been sound asleep on the canvas wagon cover, awoke to find his blanket unwinding, twirling him into the road. He lit on all fours—among the legs of a crowd of men and full in the light of their torches—

blinking his one good eye, dazed, but snarling bestially. Whatever the men had aimed to do, they did not do it. Instead, they recoiled, milled and cried in a clamor of voices:

"Jesus God!" "*Look!*" "It's loose!" "*Run!*"

And all the men on that side of the road leaped the ditch, flung away most of their lights and weapons, and took off through the cemetery that abutted the road there. Having come suddenly awake among a gang of grown men looking appalled and screaming and running, Mullenax gave a hoarse cry of his own, scrambled to his feet and took off in the direction they had gone, vaulting the ditch and doing a broken run among the graveyard stones and mounds. Although still half asleep and totally confused, although considerably impeded by his Crocodile Man encrustation, he ran creditably. Among the men running in front of him, a few faces turned back, turned ghastly-looking and bawled, "Christ!" "It's after us!" "Git a move on!" The retreating mob retreated even faster, and Mullenax, disinclined to turn to see *what* was after everybody, gave another hoarse bellow and accelerated his own run. His pumping arms and legs shed flakes of dried mud and poster paste that joined the other discard of guns, forks, torches, hats and chews of tobacco.

Those Harper's Ferry men who had been on the other side of the train when all this commenced, now simply stood there gaping into the darkness in which half of their company had vanished. So did the circus people. They all stood and listened to the scattered, distant shrieks and shouts getting ever more distant down the hill.

"Son of a bitch . . ." murmured one of the townsmen, in awe. "When they all hit the river at that speed, it's gonna part like the Red Sea."

"Lookahere!" growled the bearded man who had spoken first of all, again addressing Florian. "We tried to corral that monster. Now, if'n it kills or eats any of our fellas, somebody's gonna get strung up. And I don't mean just the monster."

"Not to worry," said Florian, thinking fast. "We thank you for flushing the creature. We had been seeking it all along the road. We have the one and only means to subdue it. Abdullah!"

The remaining townsmen gave a start as the elephant suddenly shouldered into the torchlight.

"Take Brutus and give chase," Florian commanded pointing riverward. "Bring back the Crocodile Man. Er— dead or alive," he added, for the crowd's benefit. As the bull loped off into the graveyard, merrily kicking aside tombstones, Florian pulled a sheaf of tickets from his pocket and began dealing them like a round of cards. "Nothing to fear now, gentlemen. We'll catch the monster for you. And if we capture him alive, you can come and see him this afternoon, safely chained. And meanwhile, congratulate yourselves that you did *not* encounter that savage creature without an elephant to hold him down."

"Christamighty, I'm gettin' more like a crocodile all the time," Mullenax said sullenly, dripping wet mud, river weeds and slime, when Hannibal and the elephant brought him to the lot where the troupe was just starting to set up. "But at least I stopped when I fell off the riverbank. Them other fellers swam right on. They must be rampagin' through the Chesapeake Bay by now."

"Why in the world," said Sarah, giggling, "did you chase those poor men, Abner?"

"Chase em?! Lady, I woke up and seen the whole world runnin' like hell, everybody yellin' 'It's done got a-loose!' I thought they meant the *lion*."

Not surprisingly, with so many tickets given away, the Florilegium had a straw house at the afternoon performance. But so many people came back again and again— the men of the vigilance committee returning to gaze repeatedly at the Crocodile Man and his elephantine subduer, and bringing their families and friends and remotest relatives to show them the monster and recount the horror story of That Night—that the pavilion was filled during every one of the four shows it gave in Harper's Ferry.

After the first day's performance, while all the other troupers tried to catch up on lost sleep, Florian drove his rockaway downtown. The circus awoke to find that he had brought back to the lot a well-dressed gentleman who was assembling an immense camera on a sturdy tripod, and a good deal of other paraphernalia.

"Mr. Vickery is a photographic artist," Florian introduced him. "He is going to prepare for us some slum to sell during the sideshow. Madame Alp, if you and the Pygmies would get into costume, please . . ."

So the Curiosities and Abnormalities sat to the artist: Sir John Doe in full face closeup, then the White Pygmies in trio, then Madame Alp in solitary majesty—sitting for nearly a minute, trying not to move or to squint in the light of the setting sun—while Mr. Vickery twiddled knobs, racked his bellows back and forth, slid plates of glass in and out of the big black box, took the cap off the staring lens and put it on again.

"Whuffo' we do dis, anyhow?" Madame Alp asked Florian.

"To make yourself some extra money. You're not just a waxworks for people to ogle, like the objects in the museum wagon. Folks will appreciate having a memento of you. Mr. Vickery will go back to his studio and print not just one picture of you, but a hundred, on little cards. What are called in Europe cartes-de-visite."

"Cartes-de-visite," Sunday repeated to herself.

"You and the girls and Sir John will offer those cards for sale to the circus patrons at four bits apiece. After my, ahem, considerable investment is recovered, those four bits will be yours to keep."

Mullenax said, "I'll be damned if I'll leave anybody a reminder of me in crocodile getup."

"No, Barnacle Bill," Florian said genially. "I think you have done your utmost on the Florilegium's behalf. This town will see your last appearance as the creature."

"Well, thank the little Lord Jesus."

The next night, as Captain Hotspur was defying death

and tedium in the lion-taming act, Florian said to Fitzfarris:

"During intermission, you might want to speed up the sideshow presentation a little. Then put on your traveling face and ride out straightaway for our next stop. Frederick City is twenty-five miles away, and you'll want to snatch some sleep when you get there. That will leave you most of tomorrow to do your advance work before we pull in tomorrow night."

"All right. I still need Mag's help with the face. I hope she's up to it. Says she's not feeling well tonight."

"Oh, Lord. She must be having one of her oracular spells."

"Is that what it is? She mumbled about something bad coming on. Across the water, whatever that means. Anyhow, I'll ride out right after the intermission. Any special instructions?"

"Same as before: stir up as much anticipation as you can. But, please, nothing in the escaped-monster line this time."

The next day, the circus train crossed the pontoon bridge over the Potomac River into the state of Maryland. The arrangement was that the troupe would find Fitzfarris waiting, when they entered Frederick City that evening, to guide them to the lot in that town. So Florian was surprised when, six or seven miles before they got there, Fitz came cantering up to the rockaway.

"I rode out to meet you," said Fitz, breathing hard, "because maybe Maggie Hag's premonition is coming true. I had darkies pasting our paper all over town this morning. But when I went out walking to admire their work, I found that somebody had been pasting other posters *over* ours. Another circus."

"Well, I'm damned," said Florian. "And tearing paper, eh? It's an old trick. I suppose we ought to be flattered that somebody thinks we're competition. But I'm amazed there's any other show at all working this territory. Whose is it?"

"Some Yankee, I take him to be, from his name," said Fitz, fumbling inside his shirt. "Here's one of his posters."

"Treisman's Titanic," muttered Florian, when he had unfolded it. "He's a flimflammer I never heard of, and I've heard of all that matter. Some parvenu just trying to get a start, I'd guess. He probably heard of the straw crowds we've been pulling and decided he'd make a stab at pilfering a piece of our good fortune. Go up against us, day and date."

He handed the poster down to Sarah and Clover Lee, who, in curiosity, had got out of the carriage. Sarah scanned it and said, "It's all balls, Florian. Here I was hoping we'd meet some old kinker friends, but there are no names at all. Just the acts—Wondrous Wirewalkers, Antic Acrobats . . ."

"Shows that he hadn't even hired artistes when he printed them up," said Clover Lee scornfully. "A pure piss-ant amateur. A professional would have *invented* some names, at least."

She passed the poster up to Edge, sitting beside Florian, and he read aloud, "TREISMAN'S TITANIC TENT SHOW, *an Omnium Gatherum of Truly Asiatic Splendor* . . ." then skipped to the bottom of the sheet. "It says they're pitching on the Liberty Turnpike."

"I went to have a look," said Fitzfarris. "Nothing there yet. I've got us a much better situation—right in the middle of town, little park on a creek—but they've got a bigger lot, if that means anything."

"Probably sheer posturing," said Florian. "But you haven't encountered their advance man?"

"No. He must have dashed in just long enough to hire a gang of paperers, then out again."

"Good. Here's some extra cash, Sir John. You go back, take a plentiful batch of posters, hire his crew in addition to your own, tear all his paper and post ours."

When Fitzfarris had cantered off toward town again and the circus train was moving on in his wake, Edge said to

Florian, "You don't seem unduly perturbed."

"Oh, this is old stuff to any veteran showman. Why, in my time, I've known two shows to get so stubbornly rivalizing that they'd play a whole *season* day and date, one town after another. Sometimes they'd cut their own prices, sometimes they'd cut each other's tent ropes. And sometimes, if neither show could trump the other, one owner would just buy out the other, entire. Maybe that's what will happen here."

"Come on!" Edge scoffed. "That's crazy. You'd never sell this show. I've seen you work too hard and lovingly—"

"Heavens, no! I meant I might snatch Treisman's away from him."

"That's even crazier. I've learned enough about circusing to know that what money we've got wouldn't buy one elephant."

"Remember," said Florian, smiling, "when in a fix . . . bluff."

They were pleased, on arrival at Frederick City, to find it posted all over with only Florilegium paper, and they found Fitzfarris waiting for them at the municipal park. They hurried to set up the Big Top, and then Florian carefully brushed the road dust from his new beaver hat and his old frock coat, and started to climb onto the rockaway again.

"Hold on," said Edge. "There's plenty of muscle and weaponry here that you can take with you. And me, I wouldn't miss this."

"I had intended only a scouting expedition first. But you're right. We might as well make it a show of solidarity. Who wants to come?"

"Me and Obie and every other man, right down to Tiny Tim. What else would you expect?"

"We cannot leave the lot and all the ladies unprotected. The hostiles may get the notion of making a similar foray."

"Ignatz and Hannibal are still working on the ring, and

Ignatz wants to do some bareback practice with the new girls. He and Hannibal ought to be enough of a garrison. Abner, fetch your balloon wagon. We'll all pile into that, Florian, and follow your carriage.''

Fitzfarris rode with Florian, to direct him to the other lot. Night had fallen by the time they got there, but the other circus's crew was still laboring, by torch and lantern light, to put up its tent. They also had only a single elephant to help with the heavy work, but their Big Top was half again as big as the Florilegium's, boasting two center poles. Edge also noted that the men raising it were shouting a variant version of the work chant:

> Heeby, hebby,
> hobby, holey,
> *go*-long!

In no respect except tent size was the Titanic show visibly superior to Florian's, or even much different. Here, as at the Florilegium's lot, a considerable crowd of Frederick City folk had gathered to watch the setting up, and those lot lice appeared to be pressing too close for the comfort of one of this troupe. A man who could have been a grocery-store clerk—bespectacled, harassed-looking—was fluttering his hands at the onlookers to shoo them farther away. Florian dismounted from his carriage, approached that nervous individual—who shooed ineffectually at him, too—and inquired in a voice that carried over the noise of the lot:

"Have I inadvertently arrived at the city dump, sir, or could this possibly be what is advertised as Trashman's Trivial Tent Show?"

The clerk said, in a thin, peevish way, "*Treisman's* . . . *Titanic*! Are you simply insensitive, sir, or are you deliberately defaming my worthy—?"

"*Yours*, sir?" boomed Florian, with contemptuous astonishment. "Are you the *proprietor* of this squalid establishment?"

The clerk opened and shut his mouth several times, unable to make words, but two other voices squealed girlishly:

"That talk! That style! It could only be Florian!"

"Florian, love! Macushla!"

And two strikingly pretty, orange-haired women burst out of the darkness of the lot to fling themselves upon Florian in affectionate embrace, complete with loud, smacking, wet kisses.

"Florian! It really is himself!"

"It has been so long, kedvesem!"

The clerk Treisman watched, with visible vexation.

Florian, laughing, disentangled himself long enough to say, "Pepper! Paprika! My hot-spice beauties! What a wonderful surprise!"

"But what are you doing here?" demanded the one he had called Paprika. "Ürülék! Surely you do not seek a job on this trash pile."

"No, no. I still have my own show. No trash pile, that."

"You are seeking artistes, then!" cried Paprika.

"Faith, you came looking for us!" exclaimed Pepper.

"Well . . ." said Florian.

The clerk's vexed look turned to one of alarm.

"We have so much lamented leaving you, Florian."

"But when you never came north again, we thought you must have perished in the war."

"No, we all survived. Come and meet some old friends—and some new ones." He led them to the balloon wagon, ignoring the clerk's grimaces and feeble protests. Tim Trimm and Jules Rouleau immediately bounded from the wagon, and they and the women rushed together.

"Paprika, you Viszla bitch hound!"

"Jules, you dear old auntie!"

"Brady Russum, ye evil little leprechaun! How awful—ye've not grown at all, at all."

"And Pepper, the Irish washerwoman! Still doing the pole? Which one of you is on top these days?"

"Arrah, how dirty ye make it sound."

Florian introduced the other men—Edge, Yount, Fitzfarris and Mullenax—all of them looking dazzled by the onslaught of beautiful women and the tumult of insults and endearments.

"These carrot-tops, gentlemen, are Pepper and Paprika. In civilian life, Rosalie Brigid Mayo, of the county of the same name, and Cécile Makkai. Or Makkai Cécile, as she would properly be called in Budapest, where she was often called improper names. It was I, myself, gentlemen, who brought them to bless America with their beauty and naughtiness. Pepper and Paprika are the best perch-pole act in the business. I assume, my dears, you do still do the perch."

Paprika, the brown-eyed one, said, "I'm doing the trap, too, since this show has the rigging. And Pep does a hairhang."

Pepper, the green-eyed one, said, "But sure and what *are* you doing here, Florian? Heading north again?"

"Heading east, mavourneen. From Baltimore, we sail for Europe."

"*Europe!*" they exclaimed together, brown eyes and green eyes shining. Pepper said, "Yez're really going beyant?" and Paprika said, "Európa, igazán?"

"Európa, idenis," said Florian. "I am sorry you are already engaged."

"Engaged here we may be," said Pepper excitedly. "But married here, sure we're not!"

"Make us an offer," said Paprika.

"*Any* offer," said Pepper. "This creature Treisman, he's as tight as a nun's nooky."

"Oh, the hell with haggling," said Paprika. "Come on, Pep. Let's get our gear."

The clerk let out a wail. "Now, wait a minute, you people!" He wrung his hands at Florian. "Mister, you can't do this. Pepper and Paprika are my star attractions."

Pepper gave him a look of disdain. "You said it. The rest of your show is bozzy-makoo. Let's go, Pap." They started off.

The clerk showed enough spirit to snarl spitefully, "You touch that trapeze rigging, I'll have the law on you."

"Izzy, you can take that bar and bugger yourself," said Paprika. "The perchpole rig is ours. Jules, come and lend a hand."

The clerk turned back to Florian and spat again, "You can't do this, mister. I'll have *you* up in court. First defamation and now . . . and now . . . alienation of affections!"

"Sir," said Florian, aloofly examining his fingernails, "I made no slightest enticement."

"This is unethical! This is illegal! This is criminal!"

Rouleau and the girls returned, he and Paprika carrying between them a theatrical trunk and a long apparatus of metal and leather, Pepper carrying an armload of spangled clothing and various other feminine belongings. As they piled the goods into the balloon wagon, the clerk made one last tearful try:

"What's this crook going to pay you? I'll better his top offer!"

Pepper said, "He can pay us anything or nothing, if he's taking us back to Europe. Piss off, Izzy. Let's roll, boys!"

When the rockaway and wagon got back to their own lot, there was another joyous scene of old friends reuniting, for the orange-haired girls knew all the others of Florian's original troupe. "Clover Lee, is it? But you were just a *baby*!" They even stuck their hands fearlessly into the lion cage to fondle "Macska" (as Paprika called him), and embraced as much as they could reach of "big old Peig" (as Pepper called her), while the elephant trumpeted and waggled her trunk in happiness at seeing them again. Then the two girls were introduced to Phoebe Simms, to Quincy, to Sunday and Monday.

"A twin act it is yez are, then?" said Pepper.

"They're not even twins," Florian said smugly. "Wait until you see the rest of the set. Where is Tuesday?"

Hannibal pointed to the Big Top, dimly glowing in the

night with only a single work light inside it. "She still wukkin' wid Ignatz in yonder."

"Come, my dears" said Florian. "You haven't greeted your old friend Captain Hotspur."

"Jaj. I knew someone was missing," said Paprika. "The Dutchman."

Almost the entire troupe accompanied them to the pavilion, all chatting and laughing companionably. As they got near, they could hear Snowball's hoofs thudding rhythmically and patiently around the ring. They crowded through the front door, and Pepper brightly gave the traditional call of the Irish come visiting, "God and Mary to all here!"

Then she and the others stopped abruptly where they were, uncertain of what they were seeing. In the flickery light of the one basket torch bracketed on the center pole, the trotting Snowball cast a giant shadow that swung around and around the empty benches and billowing canvas walls. It must have been heavy work for the horse, and it must have been quite a while since he had been given the command to trot. Tuesday was astride him, gripping with her legs as hard as she could, and lying forward on the horse, as well, her hands twisted tightly in his mane, holding on with all her strength. Her face was wet with tears, contorted with fatigue and terror and the strain of long crying unheard for help. She still wore the leather belt of the rope-fall about her waist, and the rope still connected her to the boom above, which creaked as it swung around and around the center pole. But the rope was stretched taut by an additional weight upon it.

Midway between Tuesday and the center pole, the rope was kinked about Ignatz Roozeboom's neck. Its tension held him almost upright and dragged him backward around and around the ring, so that his boots flipped and kicked and flopped as if he were playfully running in reverse. The bootheels had worn a fairly deep circular groove in the earth. The torchlight made his bald head glow healthily pink, and his eyes were open and his eyebrowless eye-

brows were raised in an expression of mild surprise, but he
had been dead for some time. The ex-soldiers were the
first to unfreeze. Fitzfarris ran to stop the horse, Edge to
free Roozeboom from the rope, Yount to lift Tuesday
down, Mullenax to unbuckle her rope-fall girdle. Then the
women came running to coddle and mother the girl while
she hoarsely sobbed and wept.

"Strangled, did he?" Florian said sadly, watching Edge
gently lay the dead man on the ring ground.

"No, sir. He'd be bloated and discolored in the face if
he had. And Ignatz could have got himself loose before he
choked. His neck is broken. It must have happened
damned suddenly."

Tuesday, though terrified and incoherent, her voice
weak and croaking, was able to tell them enough to con-
firm that it had been sudden indeed. She had been standing
on Snowball, Captain Hotspur behind her, kneeling on the
horse's rump so he could adjust her hips to some particular
angle of balance, when one of her feet slipped. She recovered, but only to feel a violent yank as the rope caught
Rooseboom and flicked him away. The abrupt pull had
made her drop prone and hold on, and she had been riding
that way ever since—for hours, she thought—with the
broad leather belt so constricting her that she could only
feebly croak and wheeze for help. And the horse, having
once been instructed by Roozeboom to trot, would trot on
until Doomsday, waiting for Roozeboom's permission to
halt.

"Get the child down to the fire," Sarah said. "Give her
a hot toddy of Abner's whiskey. She's had a bad time."

"Better make toddy for everybody," said Rouleau.
"Her sister looks just as bad."

Clover Lee, Quincy, Sunday and Monday had stayed
outside the ring. Three of the youngsters looked on with
wide and wondering eyes, but they were standing still.
Monday was trembling all over and perceptibly chafing her
legs together, and the expression on her face was as fixed
and distant as the one Roozeboom now wore.

"Run all the kids out of here," said Florian. "Pity they had to see this. Maggie, would you attend to the laying out?"

There was no answer. Magpie Maggie Hag had not accompanied them to the tent. "Remember?" Sarah whispered to Edge. "She predicted that somebody on the show would have trouble because of a black woman. Tuesday's not black or a woman, but she's Negro and female." They found the gypsy still by the cooking fire, industriously sewing away on some purple garments.

"Mag," said Tim Trimm. "We got some bad news to—"

"Yes," she said, and looked past him to call, "Barnacle Bill!"

"Ma'am?"

"I made smaller the waist, made longer the legs." She held Captain Hotspur's old ring uniform up against him. "I think it fit you now."

Then she went to a wagon, got out some old canvas, and slowly, by herself, a tiny figure darker than the darkness, went to the Big Top.

"She'll clean him and shroud him," said Florian. "We'll bury him as soon as it's light."

"Where?" somebody asked.

"In the ring, of course."

"What?" blurted Yount. "Plant a good man and a good friend the same shameful way we did them dirty bummers? And then we give a show on top of him? Dance on his grave?"

"It is the ring he shaped himself," said Florian. "The ring is where he lived, where he was most alive. Captain Hotspur would wish no different interment. And his soul, if there is such a thing, will enjoy being present at one last show."

Pepper said softly, "There's only now the tellin' of the bees."

"Yes," said Mullenax. "Can I do that, Mr. Florian?

"You are the one who should."

So Mullenax went off to break the sad news to Maximus the lion, and to keep him company for a while in his bereavement. The others went to comfort the children, and to take a drink with which to toast their late friend, and then went to their beds.

The next morning, while Tim and Hannibal on cornet and drum quietly played and ruffled a dead march, the troupers took turns dropping light spadesful of earth into the hole that had been dug for Ignatz, right under the ring chandelier he had built himself. Then Yount and Rouleau began filling the grave. Phoebe Simms said plaintively, "Ain't y'all go' say some wuds fum de Scriptures?"

Florian pondered, tugged his little beard and at last said, "Saltavit. Placuit. Mortuus est."

Pepper and Paprika, hearing Latin spoken, sketched the sign of the cross on their breasts. Rouleau, the other Catholic in the company, looked up from his spade work, slightly amused and said, "I don't believe that is from the Scriptures."

Florian shrugged. "I read it somewhere. Epitaph on a Roman circus performer. It serves."

They all waited, and when Florian did not translate, Edge did: "He danced around. He gave pleasure. He is dead."

As show time approached, the park got crowded with carts and wagons and a few carriages, and a lot of people afoot. They were not just lot lice; most were buying or bartering for tickets. Seeing them, Fitzfarris was inspired to take a horse and ride across town. He returned to report with pleasure to Florian that, perhaps because Treisman had lost his two leading artistes—with three different acts among them—The Titanic had folded its tent. "Like the Arabs," Fitz quoted, "and as silently stolen away."

"Well, I'm glad he got to steal *something*," said Florian, laughing. "But a real professional, even after his bluff was called, would have played out the hand, even if he played to empty seats. Proof enough, this fellow is small potatoes. Doomed to failure and oblivion.''

"He left heading westward," said Fitz. "I asked around. So we won't be finding him in Cooksville."

"And after Cooksville, Sir John, you'll have only one more advance run to do on this side of the Atlantic. Now, come inside for a treat. You're just in time to see our new artistes perform."

Pepper and Paprika were taking what had been Captain Hotspur's place as the closing act of the program's first half, for Mullenax declared that it would be some while before he would feel confident enough to perform in the lion cage in public. Since the Florilegium possessed no apparatus either for Paprika to do her trapeze swinging or for Pepper to do her hair-hanging, the two were doing only their perch-pole performance. That pole was a twenty-foot metal column, rather dented and discolored, which splayed at the bottom into a padded leather yoke, and at the top end bristled with vestigial metal spokes and leather loops. The two girls wore only fleshings splashed with sequins— Paprika's as orange as her hair, Pepper's as green as her eyes—and the sequins were distributed in patterns to emphasize the girls' curvaceous bodies, though those needed no enhancement.

When Edge had whistled the girls into the ring and Florian had grandiloquently introduced them, the two men helped Pepper hoist the yoke to her shoulders and balance the pole at the vertical. The top-mounter Paprika climbed up her under-stander's body and on up the twenty feet of the pole. While Pepper kept her gaze aloft and her feet ever shifting, her body ever swaying, to maintain the balance, Paprika stood unsupported on the metal nubs at the pole's tip, then did handstands on them, then put one hand in a leather loop, one foot against the pole, and struck various graceful poses. Then she put a foot in the loop, let herself fall until one hand gripped the pole, and did the same poses upside down. Then she scurried to the top again, stood on her hands again and did a series of upside-down contortions, backbends, center splits, when she spread her legs horizontally from side to side, and stride splits, when she spread them fore and aft.

"Well, here's where I lose you to a klischnigg," said Sarah to Edge, as they watched together. "Not only can they both twist like reptiles, they're at least twelve or fifteen years younger than I am."

"I don't think you have to worry," said Edge, with good humor. "Pepper was giving little Sunday some acrobatic lessons at noontime, and I heard her warn her, 'Never fall in love. It ruins your sense of balance.' I have a suspicion those girls are not much interested in men."

"You suspicioned right. They're toms. Fricatrices. They've never fancied anybody but one another. Still, some men find a tom a challenge." Sarah sighed. "God, but men are lucky. Women have to get old, and men never even grow up at all."

"I'm not men, I'm me," said Edge. He took his eyes off the ring long enough to give her an affectionate glance. "And you sure are not any Maggie Hag yet, by a long shot." Then he had to run into the ring, for Paprika slithered down the pole and Pepper had nonchalantly let it fall clattering to the ground. Edge and Florian took a hand of each girl and all four threw up their arms in the signal for applause.

When Florian began to talk the crowd out of the stands for the sideshow, Obie Yount found himself in close proximity to Clover Lee, and both of them being rudely jostled by two ladies from the audience. The women were portentously shaking their heads and saying in exceedingly refined voices:

"Shameful!"

"Yes, disgusting!"

Clover Lee threw a conspiratorial grin at Yount and stayed close to the women as they bustled out of the tent, so Yount did likewise. The ladies continued exchanging what were patently opinions of the act just concluded.

"Unfit for Christians to see!"

"So absolutely true!"

Yount whispered to Clover Lee, "What ails these old sows? That was a purely clean act, and them girls is purely beauti—"

"Ssh!" said Clover Lee, and kept close to the critics.

"Probably Eye-talian, those trollops."

"I wager you're right. No Christian lady would let herself be seen in that heathenish condition."

"Two grown women—*unshaven under the arms*!"

Clover Lee, grinning more gleefully than ever, lagged back now, and let the ladies go on unattended. Yount eyed them and her with puzzlement, scratched his cue-ball head and said:

"Well, I never. Nobody'd give a damn if *them* two females sprouted *quills*, but they have the gall to criticize girls as gingham-pretty as Pepper and Paprika. Still, you seemed mightly interested, mam'selle. You reckon you learned something?"

"I don't know," Clover Lee said, giggling. "But if good Christian women disapprove of something, it's got to be pleasurable in some way."

And she ran off to change for the second half of the program.

The loss of Ignatz Roozeboom had deprived the show not only of the lion act, for a while at least, but also of Captain Hotspur's participation in the riding acts. Edge volunteered to replace him at least to the extent of taking over the voltige turn. Since he and Thunder had often, in garrison times past, engaged in the cavalry's sporting contests of gander pulling, he was even better at the voltige than Roozeboom had been. With Thunder going at full gallop, Edge would bound off and onto the horse, swing himself under its belly and up to the saddle again, lean down at full speed to snatch things from the ground, fall off the horse's rump, seize Thunder's flying tail, let himself be dragged bodily around the ring, scramble to his feet at a pell-mell run and vault onto the horse again. In taking on that act, he took on yet another new identity. Florian insisted on his doing that turn as "Buckskin Billy, Dauntless Reinsman of the Plains," and Magpie Maggie Hag hurriedly sewed together a new costume of shirt and trousers that consisted predominantly of fringe.

Meanwhile, Roozeboom was also much missed during the teardown and setup of the Big Top, and on the road as well. The Florilegium now had more rolling stock than it had adult males for drivers, because Fitzfarris was always out ahead of the show and Hannibal, at the rear of it, had to guide both Peggy and the horse drawing the bull-pup cannon. Pepper and Paprika and Madame Alp all disclaimed any ability or desire to handle horses' reins.

So, when the circus rolled into Baltimore, late on a gray and rainy afternoon, Florian was still up front on the rockaway, but inside it the two redheads rode in leisurely comfort. Sarah Coverley was farther back in the train—and out in the wet—driving the balloon wagon, with Clover Lee on the seat beside her. Rouleau drove the tent wagon, and Edge drove the new box van with the whole Simms family inside. Mullenax, with Magpie Maggie Hag sitting beside him, drove Maximus's cage wagon—now shuttered from the public gaze by wooden panels fitted around it, and fancied up with the eye-catchingly massive brake lever that Roozeboom had fashioned.

Baltimore was the biggest city some of the troupers had ever been in, and the only real city Mullenax and the Simmses had ever seen. So there was much rubbernecking and peering out through wagon doors, as those troupers gaped more avidly than did the few people on the wet streets watching them roll in. Not that Baltimore was much to look at, or to smell either. The circus train came into town along the Old Liberty Road and, as soon as that road became a paved street with brick houses and other edifices along both sides, it also became a running open sewer, and the reek of it became first offensive, then revolting and soon nauseating.

"Jesus, it's worse'n I ever smelled around pigs," Mullenax said, his voice thick, because he was holding his nose.

"Some must come from the steam mills," said Magpie Maggie Hag, drawing her cloak's hood close around her face.

"Uh huh," grunted Mullenax. He looked at the profusion of immense and ornate signs, and mused, "I wonder how you bottle steam. Or print on it."

They were passing huge brick buildings that proudly advertised themselves as Steam Bottling Houses, Steam Printers, Steam Laundries and Steam Boiler Works, not to mention the Sulphur Match Works, Tanneries, Lard Refineries and Guano & Bone Dust Works that did not claim to have anything to do with steam. But it was evident to any nose that much of the prevailing stench came from the residential houses' backyard "earth closets," leaking the essence of their contents into the drainless streets.

Only one person in the circus train found something immediately to admire about Baltimore. Jules Rouleau stood up on the tent wagon's driving seat to call it to everyone else's attention.

"Voilà! Look! There is a thing we never saw in Dixie. Not even new Orleans has it. Gaslight!" The other troupers looked, without great interest. "Gas! We can send up the balloon!"

It was true: the central portion of Baltimore sported on every corner a modern gas lamp standard, its glowing globe casting a lovely peach-tinted white radiance on the grimy factory walls, on the sickly streetside trees, on the slimed and scummy cobblestones—and on Florilegium posters put up by advance man Fitzfarris. Many of those were beginning to peel or melt in the rain, so Florian hurried the train along through the dusk, because the posters marked the route to the circus's allotted setting-up place. The gaslight, for all its pearly beauty, did nothing to mitigate the other gases in the local atmosphere. And the farther Florian followed the route into town, the less he was inclined to do so, because the stink got more and more

noxious. Finally, at Pratt Street, where the train crossed a
bridge over "Jones Falls"—in actuality, a putrescently
burping and belching sump of black water—Florian decided that downtown Baltimore was simply intolerable. As
soon as he could find an alley opening, he swung Snowball
left into it, then left again, to lead the train back the way
he had brought it, some two and a half miles, up Eutaw
Street to the cleaner heights of Druid Hill Park. When he
stopped his rockaway on a wet greensward there, he addressed the company.

"I don't know what place the city fathers in their wisdom picked for our pitch. But I'll be damned if I'll set up
any closer to that terrible town than right here, even if I
have to pay double fees. We've got breathing room here,
and yonder's a pond for fresh water. Will you boss the
setup, Colonel Ramrod, while I follow the posters again
and see if I can find Sir John? If he's still downtown, he'll
probably be in some saloon getting drunk to numb his
olfactory sense. Anyway, he and I will see about getting
a permit to pitch here."

"Suppose the city fathers *won't* permit it," said Edge.

"This is a right swanky park," said Yount. "Band-
stands and all."

"Possession is nine points of the law," Florian said.
"You get that pavilion up and it's pretty possessive-
looking."

Setting up in the rain was no easy job, since the canvas
got wet and ponderously heavy as soon as it was out of
the tent wagon, and the wet ropes were limp and difficult
to put through grommets, and the tent stakes were so easily
hammered into the wet ground that their holding power
was suspect. But the men made sure that the seam-binding
ropes were reeved only loosely, and the guy ropes left
slightly slack. So the tent, when it was finally up, looked
despondently saggy and wrinkled. But, if and when the
rain ceased, the canvas and ropes would dry and tighten
and the pavilion would assume its proper perky shape all
on its own. Edge gave Hannibal the responsibility of stay-

ing awake all night, in case the rain stopped before morning, to keep watch that the shrinking ropes did not yank
the surround of stakes right out of the ground.

The work was done and Phoebe Simms was cooking
supper when Florian got back. He did have Fitzfarris in
tow, and Fitz was perceptibly drunk, in a mild state of
maudlin euphoria.

"I got a lot t' learn 'bout bein' advance and patch," he
declared, with hiccups. "Here I come t' town and argue
and wheedle and spread palm oil around, and ever'body
in City Hall just sits dead as flies on a sheet of tanglefoot.
The best I c'n get 'em to give me is the back lot of Wea-
ver's Coffin Manufactory. *Wouldn't* that be a dandy place
to set a circus! But this fella Florian comes along an' hunts
up the city clerk an' prattles at him in sauerkraut lingo,
an' by God we get a permit for this fine park."

"No great art to it," Florian said modestly. "I merely
happen to be aware that every Baltimorean of quality or
position is of German descent. You talk to a man in his
preferred language, and you have a better chance of talking
him into or out of almost anything. I did, in fact, get us
more than this pitch. Monsieur Roulette, écoutez. The city
folk are all buzzing about the surrender of the very last
Confederate Army, down in your Louisiana, a day or three
ago. The word just came in. So I persuaded the authorities
that the city ought to celebrate, and that a fitting celebration might include—"

"Une ascension d'aérostat!" Rouleau cried.

"That very thing. There'll be some men from the city
gas works up here tomorrow to see about inflating the
thing. Now, you must give them the impression that *you*
know what's to be done."

"Trust me, I shall act l'aéronaute comme il faut. In return, I give you a gift. My protégée Sunday has at last
mastered the playing of 'Vous dirai-je, maman' on the accordion, and her sisters and brother have learned the English words to sing along."

"Splendid," said Florian. "The perfect accompaniment

to the balloon ascension. The Happy Hottentots caroling 'Twinkle, Twinkle, Little Star' as you mount into the blue empyrean.''

"Is this really a good idea?" asked Edge. "The *Saratoga* blew away from its keepers once before, and they *did* know what they were doing. Jules, wouldn't it be better if you sort of practiced the first time or two in secret, not in public?"

Rouleau wagged a finger at him. "Ah, you are being reasonable, ami, not circus. I quote at you Pascal. 'Le coeur a ses raisons que—' ''

"I know the line, and it's a winsome one. But damn it''—he appealed to Florian—"you made me the equestrian director, responsible for the troupe's safety. I say this is not safe.''

"I'd be inclined to agree," said Florian, "except . . . tell me this. Just how *would* one practice in secret with an object nearly as big as Baltimore's landmark Shot Tower downtown?"

"Well . . .''

"And Monsieur Roulette cannot simply slip the balloon's snout over a street lamp and twiddle the gas cock. He'll need the assistance of the technicists.''

"Well . . .''

"Zachary, if I am to be exploded," said Rouleau, "or whisked off the planet forevermore, do you suppose I wish to do that *in secret?* Mais non, I want a great crowd and loud cheers as I go.''

"Well . . .'' said Edge yet again, and shrugged in resignation. "Abner, fetch a jug. Let's get an early start on the cheers.''

13

THE BIG top did not collapse during the night, and the morning brought sunshine that would soon put it in proper shape. Edge delegated Yount to keep an eye on it, and he climbed into the rockaway to go downtown with Florian and Fitzfarris. They found the smell of the city slightly less offensive by daylight—or maybe, they speculated, some of the stink had run off with the rainwater. Fitz got out at the offices of the Baltimore *Sun*, to promote the newspapering of the circus's presence and the imminent balloon ascension, and also to order the job printing of special posters to proclaim that event. Right around the next corner of the street, Florian espied the offices of the Baltimore & Bremen Shipping Line. He and Edge went in, but Edge merely stood about while Florian conversed in German with the agent. He came away from the man's desk looking rather cast down.

"Their ships do go to Bremen, and to Southampton on the way," he told Edge, as they left the office. "But there's none due in port here in the near future, and Herr Knebel did not thrill at the prospect of transporting a circus aboard a passenger line. He recommended that we apply to a freighting company called Mayer, Carroll—'out on the Point,' wherever that might be."

They drove to the waterfront and made inquiries. Baltimore's inner harbor, they learned, was reserved to the shallow-draft bay and coastal packets. To find the docks of the larger, oceangoing vessels they had to drive an extremely long way around the basin and out to Locust Point on the other side of the harbor. The wharf area, in any other seaport, would have been the foulest-smelling part of it. But Baltimore's waterfront smelled sweeter than its toniest residential districts, because here were all the city's coffee packing plants, exuding the rich aroma of Brazilian coffee beans being roasted. When Florian and Edge finally found a dingy dockside warehouse bearing the sign MAYER, CARROLL over its office door, they were somewhat nonplussed to see that the company described itself on the same sign as "Shippers of Cumberland Coal to All Foreign and Domestic Ports."

"I think we've been misdirected," said Edge. "Or do the words circus and coal sound alike in German?"

"Zirkus und Kohle," muttered Florian. "Well, as long as we're here . . ." he got down from the carriage seat, and Edge followed.

Florian and the gentleman in charge of the office conversed in German while Edge stood about some more. But this time the colloquy went on for quite a while, and Florian looked pleased by what he had heard. He waited until he and Edge were outside again before exclaiming happily, "All'Italia!"

"To Italy?"

"Did you know that the United States' chief export to that new nation is coal? Neither did I. But Herr Mayer has a shipment of it leaving for Livorno in Tuscany three days from now. Perhaps you have heard of Livorno—called Leghorn in English. And what better place for us to go than Italy? It was the home of Saint Vitus, and he is the patron saint of traveling showmen. Also it will be autumn by the time we get there. The climate will be much more clement on the Mediterranean than up around the North Sea. Furthermore, from Livorno we will have only to go straight inland to reach Firenze—Florence, the capital of that just recently united kingdom."

"But . . . Florian . . . we're going on a *coal barge*?"

"Good heavens, no. On a modern steam collier. So very modern that it is driven by a screw propeller, not paddlewheels. Let us stroll around the warehouse to the waterside and have a look at it. The merchant ship *Pflichttreu*, how does that sound?"

"If you can pronounce it, I can ride it."

"A very good name. It means loyalty, dutifulness. And I should think that a fully laden collier will give us a nice, stable ride."

They came around to the loading dock, and Edge said, "Is that it? I thought you said it was new."

"Well . . . modern, not necessarily new."

A ship that carried coal all the time was bound to get dirty and battered, Edge charitably supposed. But he was glad to see that it had masts and rigging for sail, in case

its newfangled screw propeller was as beat up as the rest
of it. And it had loading derricks fore and aft that Edge
hoped would serve to lift Peggy the elephant and the heavy
circus wagons aboard, because the only gangplank the ship
had was an ordinary wooden ladder leaning from the dock
to the deck. Edge asked wryly:

"Tell me, what is this elegant pleasure cruise going to
cost?"

"Ahem. Herr Mayer and I have not yet fully discussed
that aspect of the matter. It will first be necessary to present
ourselves to the *Pflichttreu*'s Kapitän Schilz, and persuade
him to consent to take us along as deck cargo and passengers. After all, a circus is not his customary freight."

They went on board and Florian inquired. A uniformed
personage appeared and, after some converse in German,
Florian said in English, "Colonel Edge, recently of the
military—Captain Schilz of the good ship *Pflichttreu*."

"Nein. Master I am," the man said gruffly, as he and
Edge shook hands. "Kapitän a courtesy title only is, except
in navy." His breath smelled faintly of schnaps. "You
gentlemen are pillgrumps?"

Florian said, "Er—pilgrims? Pilgerin? No, captain, I am
the proprietor and Colonel Edge is the director of a traveling circus. Wir möchten einen Seereise nach—"

"Zirkus? Nein, nein!" Schilz interrupted, violently
waving his arms. In deference to Edge, he explained in
English, "Animals all over my deck they shit!"

Edge started to remark that, having seen the *Pflichttreu*,
he doubted that its deck could be further defiled by mere
shit. But Florian simply stuck out his hand to shake the
captain's in apparent farewell, murmuring, "A pity. You
leave a brother in the craft beached on the sea sands."

Captain Schilz seemed surprised by the handshake and
the remark. His rejoinder was still mostly in English: "At
low-water mark, Bruder?"

"Or a cable's length from the shore. Es ist jammer-
schade. And all our beautiful women stranded as well."

"Beautiful women?" the captain repeated, so loudly appreciative that every deckhand in earshot looked up alertly.

"As easy as that," said Florian with satisfaction, as he and Edge went again toward the company office.

"A good thing the captain is susceptible to beautiful women," Edge observed.

"Oh, there was a little more to it than that," said Florian. "Now I hope we can settle the price as felicitously. Here, Zachary, here is a thousand dollars in paper. Slip it down inside your boot. Grouch bag, so to speak. Then I can honestly turn out my pockets in front of Herr Mayer and tell him, 'This is all I have.' "

He almost had to do that, too. Herr Mayer first commanded him to write a list of every person, creature, vehicle and piece of equipment he intended to take on board. Then the agent took the manifest and began writing a price for the fare alongside each separate item—steep prices.

"Mein Herr!" Florian protested. "Six of the passengers are mere children. Surely they should go at half fare. And only fourteen of the animals are alive—the lion, the elephant, eight horses, three small pigs and one mule. All those others listed there are dead."

"You transport dead animals?" said Herr Mayer, with distaste. "The customs house will never allow them to pass."

Florian explained that they were stuffed museum pieces. While Herr Mayer recalculated, looking annoyed, Edge said, sotto voce, "Even if you count Clover Lee a child, I can only count five children."

"We'll put Tim in short pants. Hush."

The fare still added up to more than Florian could have paid without dipping into Edge's boot. But finally, after much agonizing, he decided not to take along Mullenax's mule and Yount's Yankee cannon, and got Herr Mayer's price down to where he *could* pay it by handing over practically every dollar in his pockets. He might have gone on haggling, or deciding to leave other items behind, but it was past noon now and coming up toward show time.

They drove at a trot inland from the harbor, Florian grumbling all the way.

"Damn it, I should have *hired* that man instead of paying him. He's better at fortune-telling than Maggie Hag is. He certainly estimated my fortune almost to the pfennig. That thousand in your boot, Zachary, is going to be considerably diminished when we buy feed for the animals for the voyage. So, unless we turn a handsome profit here in Baltimore—"

"Great day in the morning!" Edge interrupted. "Look at that!"

Even though Edge had seen an inflated observation balloon before, the sight was still imposing. Indeed, he and Florian could see the *Saratoga*'s bright vermilion and white rounded top and the big black letters of its name, towering above the bulge of Druid Hill, even before they could see the treetops of the park it stood in. As they breasted the hill, they could see that the balloon was securely tethered by four ropes pegged about the ground where its basket rested. The whole circus company and a gathered crowd of Baltimoreans stood about, admiring it. The smooth, silken, pear-shaped object, clasped in its upper net of linen cord, straining against its web of cords that converged on the wooden hoop below the bag, stood almost exactly twice as tall as the Big Top's peak. The two immense cloth constructions, one bulking lengthwise on the park's green, the other upright against the sky's blue, made a fine sight.

"Une beauté accomplie. No problems at all," said Jules Rouleau, when Florian and Edge found him in the crowd. "These two gentlemen have had prior experience." He indicated the men, wearing prideful smiles and overalls stenciled BALTIMORE GAS & COKE. "They say our *Saratoga* is the most gorgeous aérostat ever seen here, but she is not the first. Anyway, that bandstand yonder is fitted with gas lights. So the messieurs had only to arrange a long gum hose from there to the appendix of the bag, as we aéronautes call it."

The younger of the gas-company men volunteered, "This-here coal gas ain't the best for ballooning with. Don't have the lift."

"Really?" said Florian. "I'd say the thing looks absolutely eager to leap up in the air."

"Aye, she'll go up," said the older of the two. "And she'll take one man, but no more. And even with no ballast she'll be sluggish. What ye really want is hydrogen gas. With that in the bag, she'll lift three men. But for hydrogen ye'll need a generator."

"Also y'all ought to take care of that beauty," said the other. "The outside varnish is weathered considerable, and the inside needs a new coat of neat's-foot oil. We took it on ourselves to put a new seal around the clack valve."

"Ah," said Florian distantly.

Rouleau explained, "So the gas will not leak until I am ready to let it out. And the messieurs were also kind enough to give me a tin of the sealing cement, left here by a previous balloonist."

"Very kind, indeed," said Florian, but then his face fell as the older man handed him a piece of paper, and said:

"Twenty-five thousand cubic feet, in round figgers. Naturally ye get a bulk rate, so I've rounded off the bill to just seventy-five dollars and no cents."

Florian said, in a strangled voice, "I understood that we were doing this performance to benefit a citywide celebration."

"All I know is that ye've got a cubic footage of gas that would light all of Baltimore for two or three nights. If ye care to argue with City Hall for your money, go ahead. But they'd likely demand to see proof of ownership of yon balloon, and the balloonist's qualifications, and surety money against any damage ye might cause . . ."

Florian made a wry face, but gave the nod to Edge to dig down in his boot. Edge brought out the wad of bills and peeled off the demanded payment. When the men had departed, Florian said reprovingly to Rouleau, "This is an expensive indulgence. That money would have bought a lot of hay and oats and horsemeat.''

''I had no idea, mon vieux . . .''

Another wagon came up the hill just then, attracted by the looming balloon, and among the family tumbling out of it came Fitzfarris, who had hitched a ride from downtown. He was carrying a large round wooden object under one arm. As he approached, Florian was saying, ''. . . Just hope the ascension brings enough extra people and extra money to offset the expense . . .''

''It will, it will!'' Fitzfarris cried gaily. To Rouleau he said, ''Be sure to make all your preparations slow and careful and long drawn out, Jules, old boy. Give the rubes plenty of time to get fidgety, so they'll turn for diversion to my interim entertainment.''

He displayed the thing he was carrying. It was like a broad, shallow drum made of plain pine, a couple of feet across but only a few inches deep. The under surface of it was solid, the upper was bored with a circle of twenty-one holes, an inch in diameter, near its perimeter. In the shallow sidewall of the thing was cut a single opening, big enough for Fitz to get his hand inside.

''I didn't have time to construct any proper wheel of chance, so I simply had a carpenter knock together this mouse game for me. No time either to get it painted nice and gaudy, but it'll serve.''

The others asked what the hell was a mouse game, but Fitzfarris had raised his voice to he crowd: ''I'll give two bits to the first kid that finds me a field mouse!'' All the children, black and white, scattered and scampered throughout the park, bent over, looking for burrows or nests. To the bewildered Florian, Fitz said, ''May I borrow that stump of pencil you always carry?''

Florian gave it to him and Fitzfarris numbered each of the holes in the drum's upper face: 0 to 20. A small Negro boy ran up, holding in his cupped hands a tiny brown and white mouse. Fitzfarris took it, thanked the boy, said briskly to Florian, ''Company expense. Pay the lad, would

you, boss?'' and dashed away to the prop wagon, to wipe
off his cosmetic face and be ready for his rôle of Tattooed
Man.

Both the afternoon and evening shows that day were
sparsely attended, obviously because most of the prospective patrons were waiting for the next day's added free
treat of the balloon ascension. But, during each program's
intermission, after the rubes had gaped their fill of the Tattooed Man, the Three White African Pygmies, the Museum
of Zoölogical Wonders and Madame Alp—and even pur-
chased a few of the cartes-de-visite—Sir John introduced
his mouse game.

"Bet a dime, folks, win *two dollars!* The most honest
guessing game ever devised. Bet a dollar, win *twenty* of
'em! It's a game of human intuition versus animal instinct.
Simply pick the hole that little Mortimer the Mouse will
run to.''

He had set his new wooden apparatus on the circus's
ubiquitous washtub. The game consisted merely of his putting the wee mouse in the middle of the board, when it
instantly scurried for one of the holes around it and ducked
into the dark interior. There Fitz's hand was waiting to
snatch it, bring it out and set it on the board again.

A cluster of rubes quickly gathered, most of them male,
and, after they had amusedly watched the proceedings for
a minute, they began to dig in their pockets and plunk
down dimes—even a few larger coins and one or two dollar bills—alongside one or another of the numbered holes.
The mouse dutifully ran for a hole every time it was exposed to public gaze, and Fitzfarris dutifully paid off every
winner, with a bellowed felicitation: "*Two dollars* to this
clever fellow! Good going, sir! A return of *two thousand*
percent on your investment!''

The noise brought others crowding around, so they had
to reach over and under the tangle of arms to place their
bets. Eventually, every time the mouse ran, almost every
hole on the board bore a stake, and there was a winner

almost every time—adding his shout of *"whoopee!"* to
Fitzfarris's own congratulatory clamor: "Mind over mammal! Absolutely the fairest game you'll ever play. And
there's *another* winner! Don't crowd, gentlemen. Give the
ladies a chance at instant fortune, too!" The mouse never
seemed to tire, and the game went briskly, the only inter-
ruptions consisting of Fitz's occasionally wiping the whole
board with a damp rag. Even with the day's scant attendance, Fitzfarris kept the intermission running over-long,
until the gamblers were either satisfied with their winnings
or unable to go on losing.

"Seventy-five dollars and forty cents clear for the day,"
Fitz said happily at the close of the evening's intermission.

"I'll be damned," Edge said admiringly. "That pays
for the balloon gas, right there."

"If we get a straw crowd for the balloon tomorrow,"
said Fitz, "the game ought to fetch eight or ten times that
much, easy."

"A marvel," said Florian. "How do you gaff it, Sir
John?"

"Gaff it, sir?" Fitzfarris looked inexpressibly wounded.

"Well, one simply assumes . . . a midway game of
chance . . . like the venerable shell-and-pea game . . ."

Fitz firmly shook his head. "Anybody can spot a rigged
game. It doesn't take detective ability. Watch any confidence man doing the shell-and-pea. He's always got one
long fingernail to hide the pea under. But my mouse game
doesn't have to be rigged. Twenty-one holes to bet on, and
I *say* I pay odds of twenty to one. Suppose twenty-one
rubes bet a dime apiece. I scoop in all the dimes and give
the winner two dollar bills. He's actually getting only nineteen dimes profit and I'm richer by one. The balance can
seesaw, of course, depending on who bets how much, and
where, but that extra hole—number zero—always gives
the edge to the house, as we say in the profession."

"Yes, of course, I see," said Florian. "I had thought . . .
that business of wiping with the rag . . . perhaps some secret preparation . . ."

"Only ammonia water. If a mouse runs to the same hole a couple of times he might afterwards follow his own scent and go there repeatedly. Some rubes can be sharp enough to notice that, and bet on it. So I wipe the board clean after every few plays. That's to keep *Mortimer* honest."

Next day, the first thing Rouleau did was to hurry to his beloved *Saratoga*. There he opened the brass fixture at the very end of the what he called the balloon's appendix. A quite copious stream of water gurgled forth, and he carefully directed it outside the basket.

"Instructions from the technicists," he explained to those watching. "The coal gas has a content of moisture, and it condenses during the cool of the night. No sense taking up more weight than I have to."

"Maybe no sense in doing anything today, kedvesem," suggested Paprika. "Maggie is staying huddled in her blankets this morning."

"Oh, damnation," said Edge. "Has she foreseen some disaster in the ascension?"

Paprika gave an expressive Hungarian shrug. "Of the balloon she says nothing. Only something about a wheel."

"Aha!" said Rouleau, relieved. "Go frighten Four-square Fitz, then. He is the only one working with a gim-mix like a wheel." He patted his wicker gondola. "I, Jules Fontaine Rouleau, am henceforth liberated from anything as earthbound as a wheel."

Paprika shrugged again and went on talking as she walked with Obie Yount to the backyard, where Phoebe was cooking breakfast. "Jules mentions earthbound. Ō jaj, I have known artistes of the most hair-raising acts to survive all manner of risks, and then get crippled or killed in a trifling and earthbound sort of accident."

"Such as what?" asked Yount, as they sat down on the ground to wait to be served. He was seated between Paprika and Pepper, and was eminently pleased to be so.

"In Paris, there was a girl aerialist who made herself notorious and acclaimed. She strung a cable between the towers of Notre Dame and danced upon it. She was famous, but the devout were scandalized, and they said Our Lady would punish her for the sacrilege. A week later, she fell off a bateau-mouche and drowned in the Seine.''

''And remember, macushla?'' said Pepper. ''That joey in Warsaw what did the humpsty-bumpsty?'' She explained to Yount, ''That's a clown what does knockabout falls and sprawls. He was forever stepping in a bucket of water and sloshing hither and yon. Never broke a bone, did he, but one day he scraped his shin on the bucket. The dye from his stocking infected the scratch and, bedad, his leg had to be sawed off.'' She crossed herself and murmured, ''Safe be my sign.''

''Say, ladies,'' said Yount. ''Since we've got to leave my bull-pup behind, I've been trying to invent Quakemaker tricks that don't need a cannon. I wondered—how about me pyramiding you two on my shoulders?''

''Not much flair to that,'' said Paprika. ''How about we stand on your shoulders and the Simms girls on ours? We can easily hold them if you can hold us all.''

''Nothing to it,'' said Yount, expanding his barrel chest to hogshead dimensions,

''It's fine with me,'' said Edge, when Yount sought him out and proposed the new bit of ring business. Then he gave Yount one of his ugly smiles and said good-humoredly, ''I've known you to get smitten by a female here and there in the past, Obie. But only one at a time. Have you got your eye now on *both* those firetops?''

Yount bashfully pawed the ground with one big foot. ''Not really. I grant that both of 'em are galuptious. But that Paprika, she's the real knee-weakener. I'd gladly tie the hitch with her and, if the opportunity comes, I'm fixing to tell her so. What do you think about that, Zack?''

''I think you'd do better, Obie, to get yourself tied to a whipping post.''

''Well!'' Yount said huffily. ''I sure do thank you for them friendly good wishes.''

''Whoa, partner, whoa. I just meant . . . well . . . red-

heads have a reputation for being prickly. God knows what
a *Hungarian* carrot-top might be like. Take care you don't
get stung.''

Yount grinned and flexed his biceps. ''That'll be a frosty
Friday, when the Quakemaker is afeared of a li'l bitty
girl.'' He strode off manfully, and Edge looked after him
with something like commiseration.

Though it was still quite early in the day, numbers of
local folk had already climbed the hill to the park, mainly
to admire the balloon, but also to peer inquisitively at what
they could glimpse of the circus's living arrangements. So
the women of the troupe made a haste to tidy up after
breakfast, to take down the clothes they had washed and
hung up overnight, and generally to make the backyard
neat. Then, one or a few at a time, they climbed into the
property wagon to change from their robes and wrappers
into ring dress. Phoebe Simms went first and took Sunday
with her, because she needed help to put on her vast costume—or rather, to construct it around herself—and while
that job was under way, there simply was not room in the
wagon for anybody else.

She emerged as Madame Alp and, so as not to be ogled
for free by the gathered gawks, went to wait in the tent
wagon, where she could be company for Magpie Maggie
Hag, still enfeebled by her premonitions or whatever was
ailing her. Clover Lee climbed next into the prop wagon,
and she and Sunday were getting into their tights when
they were joined by Pepper and Paprika. The two white
women and the white girl engaged in chatter and banter
while they dressed, but Sunday stayed silent, struggling
amateurishly to wriggle into her fleshings and trying to
stay out of the others' way. That was no easy feat in the
close-quarters mêlée of their handing bits of apparel back
and forth, doing up each other's laces and buttons, bor-
rowing and lending little pots of rouge, powders and puffs,
creams and pomades, and helping each other apply them.

The camaraderie of all-girls-together emboldened Clover Lee to tell Pepper and Paprika what she had overheard

back in Frederick City: the good Christian women waxing indignant at having seen two other women with hair under their arms. The two were not at all embarrassed or chastened by the report; they laughed hilariously, and all but fell about when Clover Lee concluded, "They said you must be Eye-talians." Pepper and Parika hung onto one another for support while they shrieked and guffawed.

"If that don't bang Banagher!" gasped Pepper. "I've near pissed me britches."

"Eye-talians, indeed!" snorted Paprika. "Ignorant old bawds."

"Well, I know you're not Italians," said Clover Lee. "But is it something you learned from Italians? Not to shave there for some reason? I asked Florian, but he just coughed."

That sent them into new paroxysms. When they had recovered, Pepper said merrily, "Colleen dear, it's sheer showmanship. Show-woman, I should say. Whenever folks see a female with bright-colored hair—not humdrum brown or black or mouse pelt—they think: aye, but is it her natural growth? Women do the wondering catty-like, of course. But men do the wondering *lustful*-like, because they seldom see aught but black or brown belly fleece on their ordinary women."

"So we make it plain that we are genuine, natural born of this flame color," said Paprika. "When the jossers glimpse the pink tufts in our armpits, they know damned well that our furbelows are pink, too. Here, see for yourself, child. It drives men wild, the imagining of that secret place. And drives their womenfolk wild with envy."

"Sure and that's why we laughed at being called Italians," said Pepper. "Faith, why would a dark dago female want to advertise that she's naught but nigger-haired all over? No offense to ye there in the corner, alannah."

"Cela ne fait rien," murmured Sunday.

"You hear her? 'Sally Fairy Ann'!" cried Paprika in surprise and delight. "By Saint Istvan, this child is no

310 G a r y   J e n n i n g s

longer a néger! Sunday, angyal, you are becoming a real cosmopolite!''

Sunday looked unsure of what that was, or whether she wanted to be it, but said shyly, ''Monsieur Roulette is teaching me to talk like a lady. In American and French, both.''

''Well, angyal,'' said Paprika, ''if you would care to further your education on the way to Europe, I will be happy to help. Magyar is hopelessly difficult, but German will serve you as well when you are in Hungary, and I can teach you that.''

Talking like a textbook, Sunday said, ''Thank you, Mademoiselle Makkai. I do desire to learn all that I can apprehend.''

Pepper looked dubious of that proposition, or disapproving, and when they all left the wagon she was intensely whispering something to her partner. Clover Lee, ever eager to overhear any secret thing she could, caught only the last few words.

''. . . Baring your bird's-nest to the one and calling the other Angel. I ken that much of Magyar.''

Edge and Mullenax were shining the hooves of the horses with stove blacking when Florian bustled up to them and said, ''Look at this mob already here, a whole hour before show time. We'll have all of Baltimore up here today. The local darkies are even setting up snack stands all over the park. Selling pork cracklings, terrapin soup, lemonade . . .''

''Well, that won't profit us any,'' said Edge, ''but it keeps the crowd in a good mood. I've told the musicians to tune up to entertain them too.''

Mullenax added, ''Every rube that's not eating or just gawking is playing Fitz's mouse game. He must be raking in the shekels for us.''

''Oh, I'm not complaining about the attendance,'' said Florian. ''It's just that there clearly will not be anybody left in town to come and see us tomorrow. And I see no profit in our showing to another bloomer stand, the way we did yesterday. So what I suggest, Colonel Ramrod, is that we simply cancel tomorrow's performances. We'll use the free day for a leisurely teardown, get everything packed good and tight, buy provisions for the voyage. That way, we won't have to hustle and hurry on the day after, getting down to the wharf for embarkation.''

Except for a few lot lice, too poor or stingy to pay for admission, the people in the park all bought tickets and took their preliminary looks at Maximus and the museum. Then, when Tim and Hannibal played ''Wait for the Wagon''—with a slightly faltering accompaniment by Sunday Simms's accordion—the people all packed into the Big Top. A good many of them had to sit on the ringside ground or stand wherever they could find room. After the intermission and the sideshow—and more mouse game— while the afternoon audience was still enjoying the second half of the program, the park outside again filled up with people come early for the balloon ascension before the evening show. They bought tickets enough to fill the pavilion once more, so, when a considerable number of the first audience decided they'd like to stay for the second show and applied again for tickets, Florian finally had to declare a turnaway. He did it with no dismay; with pleasure, actually, at having a turnaway crowd for the first time on this whole tour.

Jules Rouleau, as instructed, made his preparation for the ballooning with slow deliberation, giving Fitzfarris ample time to do a booming business with his game. Since the ascension required little more than the casting off of the tiedown ropes, Rouleau's only real preparation consisted of his fetching from the tent wagon a length of rope ladder and tossing that into the basket, for some purpose he did not confide to anybody. Meanwhile, Florian curled a circus poster into a cone and through that makeshift megaphone bellowed to the surrounding masses:

''Monsieur Roulette must await the sundown fall of the breeze . . . Such a daring feat demands absolute stillness of the air . . . Extremely hazardous even then . . .''

Between those repeated announcements, Tim and Hannibal loudly played music appropriate to a balloon ascension—"Nearer My God to Thee" and other such things—and Sunday pitched in with her accordion on every piece familiar to her. At last, when the crowd's muttering indicated the suspense was giving way to impatience, and when Fitz's marks were running out of betting money, Rouleau wetted a finger and held it in the air, gave a solemn nod to Florian to signify that he could feel no wind, then vaulted jauntily into the basket. Tim's cornet bleated a flourish and Hannibal's drum boomed a wild African tattoo and Florian shouted, "Stand by your cables!" . . . pause . . . and "Cast off!"

Edge, Yount, Mullenax and Fitzfarris all at the same instant threw off the four stake ropes, and the *Saratoga* gave a blithe bound upward. But the four men kept hold of the anchor-and-hauldown rope that had come with the balloon, already attached, when they acquired it. They paid it out hand over hand, so the balloon went up only slowly, in small jerks, and not very dramatically. To the onlookers, the taut rope might have been a stick *pushing* the contraption up from the ground. Tim and Hannibal and Sunday played, and she and the other Happy Hottentots sang—at about the same spiccato tempo that the *Saratoga* was rising—"Twin-kle, twin-kle, lit-tle star . . ." The balloon could not go very dramatically high, either, for there were only some six hundred feet of the anchor rope to pay out before the men belayed it to the stakes.

Nevertheless, the *Saratoga* was a beautiful object, and its ascent, if not exuberant, had been at least majestic, and it now hung at an altitude more than twice the height of Baltimore's Shot Tower, which was the highest thing any of the local folk were accustomed to seeing, and up there the brilliant vermilion and white silk had gone from ground shadow to where the setting sun's rays still shone, and the bag shone like a small sun itself. The crowd of watchers, after a long, sighing "Ah-h-h!" during the ascent, suddenly gave another "Ah-h-h!"—this time on an indrawn, gasping breath—for away up there Monsieur Roulette had gone insane and vaulted *out* of the basket.

Even the troupers of the ground crew were taken by surprise, for they had been busy with the belaying and had not seen Rouleau drop the rope ladder from the gondola before he leaped. He had caught onto the ladder, of course, and its upper end was secured somewhere inside the wicker rim, and now he was doing the same acrobatic poses and contortions and convulsions that he did in the ring on his wooden ladder, and the crowd was laughing and sobbing with relief, and cheering and applauding with pleasure.

Most of it was, anyway. Somebody plucked at Florian's sleeve, saying in a frigid voice, "Sir, I am told that you are the proprietor of this enterprise."

Florian turned to face a gentleman with doleful long jaw stiffly fringed with an Anglican-inch beard. "That I am, sir. I trust you are enjoying the entertainment."

"Enjoyment is not our object in life, sir," said the man, indicating the other people with him—two or three more men and several women, all wearing the same expression of pious woe. "We represent the Citizens' Crusade, and it has been brought to our notice that your so-called entertainment includes a certain wheel of chance."

"Oh, Lord," muttered Edge, at Florian's elbow. "Maggie Hag was right again."

Fitzfarris nobly spoke up. "The wheel, as you call it, is mine. And if you are here to complain, I can assure you the game is honest."

"Honesty or dishonesty is not our concern, either," said the man. "We are interested only in succoring the innocent victim of outrage and indignity."

Fitz looked bewildered. "Well, some have lost money, I confess that. But outrage? Indignity? I don't—"

"We wish you to show us this game," said a dish-faced woman.

"I don't mind," said Fitzfarris. "But right this minute

we've got our colleague dangling way to hell and gone up yonder in—''

"This instant," the woman said. "Or we can summon a constable to command you."

Florian said to Fitz, "Monsieur Roulette is all right. And he'll be cavorting for a while yet. Go get the board, Sir John."

Fitzfarris went to bring the washtub and the pine apparatus. Then he reached into a pocket and brought out his mouse, which he had to disengage from a morsel of cheese it was busy with. "You interrupted Mortimer's mealtime," he said, as he set the mouse on the board. "Now, what happens—the players guess which hole he'll run to. And Mortimer picks his own. No forcing, no trickery. See? Number seventeen this time. No earthly way this game can be diddled, doctored or deaconed."

"As we suspected," said a woman with an iron coiffure. "Cruelty to animals."

Prepared as he was to defend himself against charges of swindling, fraud or flimflam, Fitzfarris was staggered by this unexpected accusation. He said with some heat, "Lady, it was you folks who disturbed Mortimer's mealtime repose. Do you see *me* being cruel to him?"

"If not overt cruelty," said one of the men, "certainly a perversion of the animal's natural behavior and violation of its dignity."

"Dignity?" said Fitzfarris, unbelieving. "Man, this is a common, ordinary field mouse. Not some noble horse being mistreated. Just a *mouse*—doing what mice *do*—running for a hole."

"But at your bidding," one of the women said flintily. "Not of its own accord. The creature is being callously degraded."

The half of Fitz's face that was not blue had now gone red, and he seemed apoplectically speechless, so Florian intervened.

"Madame, perhaps you accord this mouse an undue amount of concern, because the mouse currently occupies, so to speak, the limelight of celebrity. But consider. If you were to find this rodent running about your kitchen, would you not regard it as unwelcome vermin? Would you not kill it, just as you would a cockroach?''

"Entirely different circumstances," said the woman, unswayed. "In that case, the animal would be pursuing its normal way of life, and taking its normal chances at survival. Here, it is being forced to unnatural acts.''

Florian also looked stunned now, and could only sputter, "Unnatural acts? . . . A field mouse? . . .''

Edge would have preferred to stay apart from this farcical imbroglio. But he realized that the zealots could easily widen their area of interest and demand the emancipation of the lion, the elephant, Barnacle Bill's pigs. Even if the meddling resulted in no worse than nuisance, it could also mean delay, and the *Pflichttreu* was sailing two days from now.

He said amiably, "Excuse me, folks. I take it you object to the use of a *mammal* in Sir John's little game. Someone just now mentioned a cockroach. Would your sensibilities be soothed if we substitute a cockroach for the mouse?''

Nobody laughed at this further descent into the ridiculous. The Citizens' Crusade exchanged inquiring glances. The man with the Anglican-inch beard scratched meditatively in it and murmured, "Hm . . . well . . . a cockroach *is* an invertebrate . . . certainly a being rather lower in the order of Creation . . .''

Edge quickly said, "Sir John, a sturdy bull cockroach would serve as well, wouldn't it?'' Then, before Fitz could reply or shriek with laughter or tear his hair, Edge as quickly said to the citizens, "There we are, then. A cockroach it shall be. And we thank you folks for helping us mend our ways. Now, would you, ma'am, care to take possession of this Mortimer Mouse?'' The woman he addressed cringed away, aghast. "Then we set him free? Very well. Sir John, let Mortimer return to his, er, natural habitat.''

Slowly shaking his head in incredulity, Fitz knelt and

tenderly set the tiny creature on the ground. It scurried off in a hurry, as Florian, Edge and Fitzfarris turned away, returning to their posts at the balloon's hauldown rope. Florian was growling, "By Christ, I'll be glad to get out of this sanctimonious, sniveling country! We have been flayed for our language, for hanging out our laundry, for not shaving under the arms, and now for giving gainful employment to a—"

He was interrupted by another concerted gasp from the crowd, and then everybody dodged as the hauldown rope came tumbling in a loose coil down among them. They all looked up—to see that Rouleau had finished his acrobatics, climbed back inside the basket and cast loose his only tie to earth. The *Saratoga* immediately soared higher aloft and drifted sideways over the hilltop. But obviously Rouleau was not going to take too much of a chance at free flight. He had immediately afterward pulled the rope that communicated with the valve on top of the balloon's crown. The bag gradually elongated from pear shape to carrot shape, and descended as it did so. Getting ever thinner and longer—and wrinkling so that its broad red and white gores became only narrow stripes—it sank to the ground some distance away, but still in Druid Hill Park. The basket gently touched the grass, Rouleau pulled the ripcord, the bag lost the last of its gas, and came billowing and fluttering and flattening out on the ground.

With more cheers and hurrahs, the crowd surged to the descension spot. Edge, Fitz, Florian and Mullenax ran, too, to prevent the crowd's stepping on the precious silk. As Rouleau wriggled his way out of the gondola and out from under some folds of the fabric, the people mobbed him with handshakes and thumps on the back. When he got free of his congratulators, he came beaming and perspiring and all but glowing, to say, "Forgive me, Monsieur le Propriétaire—and Monsieur le Directeur—but I simply could not resist one brief moment of absolute freedom."

"That's all right, Jules," said Edge, "as long as you and it are all right. It made a grand finish to the act."

"And God knows when we can afford to give you the opportunity again," said Florian. "But let's bundle up this thing, lads, before the rubes get the notion of tearing off pieces for souvenirs."

Fitzfarris and Mullenax were already straightening out the fabric and lines, and Edge went to help. Rouleau ran to bring the balloon wagon. The three men were still lapping and folding the *Saratoga* when they heard a commotion back there at the lot—a number of confused shouts and the noise of feet running about, and then a clear cry, "Is there a doctor in the crowd?"

"Something has happened yonder," said Florian, but he hesitated to leave the balloon. "Why doesn't Monsieur Roulette come with the wagon for this thing?"

Little Quincy Simms came instead, running barefoot, saying breathlessly, "Hoy! Mas' Jules done hurt he se'f. Y'all come."

"What? How? What happened?"

"He jump fo' wagon, de hoss give a start. Mas' Jules, he leg in spokes when wheel turn. Ker-rack!"

"Oh, Jesus," said Florian. The other men were already running. "Ali Baba, you stay here and guard the *Saratoga*. Don't let anybody near it." And Florian went running, too.

Rouleau was laid out on the tarpaulin in the bed of the balloon wagon. His face was stark white and his teeth were gritted, and an elderly gentleman wearing pince-nez was gently palpating the length of his left leg. Some of the troupers were solicitously peering over the wagon sides at him, others were keeping the crowd away. When Florian leaned in, Rouleau unclenched his teeth enough to give him a tortured grin and say weakly:

"I risk my bones twice a day on the ground . . . and today in the sky . . . and now, regardez. Perhaps I brought it on myself. Péter plus haut que le cul . . ."

"Chut, ami. C'est drôlement con. How bad is it, Doctor?"

The physician shook his head, removed his pince-nez and pursed his lips. Then he climbed down from the wagon

and drew Florian aside before he spoke. Edge stayed close
to them.

"Broken in three places, and curiously so, for his age.
The man must have the bones of an adolescent."

"Yes, he is exceptionally limber. That is good, right?
They will knit and heal quickly?"

"That is bad, sir. Because the bones *are* so flexible,
these are greenstick fractures, and compound. The splin-
tered ends have pierced the flesh and skin. Even if the
fractures could be properly reduced, it would mean a
month or more of complete rigidity. And during that time
of depleted blood circulation, the flesh wounds are bound
to mortify."

"What are you saying?" Florian whispered.

"I am saying amputate."

Edge blurted, "Good God! The man's a professional
acrobat!"

"You are of course at liberty to solicit a second opinion.
I suggest you make haste."

Florian wrung his beard. Edge whirled and barked,
"Abner!"

"I ain't no medic!" said Mullenax, recoiling.

"You can carpenter. Go and find some planks, at least
five feet long. If you can't get them elsewhere, rip them
off that bandstand. You there, Sunday! You and Tim and
Hannibal strike up some music. Fitz, start talking up the
lion. Florian, get the show ready to commence, and turn
the tip as soon as it is. Doctor, will you stand by while I
have a word with the patient?"

"Saint Joseph's is the nearest hospital. The quicker we
can get him there—"

"Let's at least solicit *his* opinion. I'll be right with
you."

Edge climbed carefully into the wagon, not to jounce it,
knelt and said, "There's no time to sugarcoat this pill,
Jules. You've got a choice—live with only one leg or
maybe die with both of them." Already chalk white, Rouleau went slightly green. Edge continued, "The doctor can

saw it off, and you'll be lopsided but alive. Or I can give it the treatment that once saved a good horse all intact. Say which.''

Rouleau did not hesitate. He gave again the tortured grin and said, ''If I am not as good as a good horse, ami, I deserve to die.''

''Try to bear that in mind, so you'll whinny and not screech when it hurts.'' Rouleau laughed outright before he gritted his teeth again. ''Doctor,'' Edge said, over the wagon side. ''He's decided to take his chances. We thank you, anyhow.''

''What *chances*?'' the man protested, but Edge had turned away and was shouting for Sarah. The doctor shook his head and followed the rest of the crowd to see the lion Fitzfarris was loudly advertising.

Mullenax came with an armload of light planks, a hammer, saw, nails and one of his ever-ready jugs. Rouleau drank deep of the whiskey, while Edge instructed Mullenax in the hurried construction of a shallow, narrow wooden trough, rather like a window box for flowers. It was made with one end open, so Rouleau's leg could be laid in it and his foot pressed against the closed farther end. At the bottom and on the inner side, the box was just long enough to reach from Rouleau's crotch to the sole of his foot, but the outside plank was made long enough to extend all the way to his armpit.

Edge turned to Sarah. ''You run and fetch a sack of that bran we got for the horses, and some carbolic acid, and some long, thick sticks from our stock of firewood, and some strips of cloth I can use for tying. Abner, you're going to hold Jules firm and steady while I pull on this leg and see if I can set the broken bone ends. And Jules, you're going to have to whinny like a whole herd of mustangs, because this will hurt like hell.''

Edge waited until the music and crowd noise from the Big Top was at its loudest, then started the pulling, just below the topmost break. Rouleau did more than whinny; he howled and screamed. Sarah grimaced and clapped her hands over her ears. But Edge felt one after another of the three bulges in the leg diminish, and watched the jagged ends of bone slip back under the bloodied flesh and—he hoped—fit back where they belonged. Before the job was done, Rouleau had ceased screaming and Mullenax did not have to lean on him to hold him motionless, for he had fainted dead away. Then Edge placed the sticks along the leg for splints, and with the cloth strips bound them tightly in place. He and Mullenax carefully laid the trussed leg in the new-built box, positioned the longer board up along Rouleau's left side, between his body and his arm, and bound that firmly with cloth strips running around his waist and chest.

"Sarah," said Edge, "before he wakes up, give those flesh wounds a good burning dose of carbolic."

While she did that, Edge ripped open the sack she had brought. He poured the bran into the box, packing it tightly under, around and over the leg.

"There," he said, wiping sweat from his forehead. "That'll hold it pretty near immobile, but let some air circulate around it. Sarah, you and Maggie can dig through the bran whenever you need to treat those wounds. I reckon Maggie will know how to sew them shut and what to put on them. Then pack the bran back tight again. Jules is going to have to lie still and stiff for maybe two months. But with luck he'll live, and come out of that box with a fairly usable leg. It worked with a horse, once, anyway. Come on, Abner. While he's still out, let's move him to the prop wagon where he's accustomed to sleeping."

When they had done that, Edge and Mullenax took the balloon wagon to collect the *Saratoga* and Quincy, then hastened to join the show in progress. It was the last time the Florilegium would perform in the United States of America, most likely, and also the troupe had to make up for the absent Monsieur Roulette, so the artistes exerted themselves to give their best performances. Barnacle Bill decided he had been reluctant long enough, and tonight brought the lion cage into the tent, got inside it himself and put Maximus through most of his repertoire—sit down, sit up, lie down, roll over, play dead—only stopping short of sticking his head in the lion's mouth or doing the bogus business of being "bitten."

The Quakemaker let the bull-pup cannon—because it was its last performance ever—roll back and forth over him so many times that he was almost too sore to do his new trick, but do it he did. He let Pepper, then Paprika, climb up him and stand erect, one on either shoulder. Then the Simms triplets, not quite so gracefully, climbed up him and up the women, to stand three abreast on the women's shoulders—all the females leaning sideways from their linked hands—making a three-high fan of six bodies. Florian and Tiny Tim threw local landmarks into their knockabout routine—"Ow! That kick caught me on Pratt Street!"—and when Sir John substituted for Monsieur Roulette in singing Madame Solitaire's anthem, he changed some words:

> . . . And the heart in my bosom adores.
> Solitaire is the Queen of all riders, I ween,
> But alas, she is now Baltimore's!

Magpie Maggie Hag had recovered from the prostration, now that her premonition had come to pass—whichever of the "wheel" troubles was the one she had foreseen—and at intermission dukkered a whole forest of palms. Out on the midway, Sir John, deprived of his mouse game, made elaborate and florid presentations of every exhibit, concluding with Madame Alp: ". . . and the phenomenon will now hand out mementos of her monstrosity, classic photographic replicas of herself. Yours to keep, ladies and gentlemen, for the trifling sum of fifty cents. Biggest bargain in Baltimore. You can take Madame Alp home with you for only one-fifteenth of a cent per pound!"

"Did you notice, Fitz?" Pepper said to him afterward. "When the rubes had got done buying the Fat

Lady's cartes-de-visite, there was one man—a darky—
what bought every one of them she had left?''

"No, I didn't notice. But so what? Some men admire
women who are beef to the heels.''

"No matter. Except that it put me in mind of them
maggot-brains in Europe that I've seen come slinking and
asking to rent a freak for a night or two.''

"I'll keep an eye peeled. But I doubt anybody'll *carry*
her off.''

No one did. At any rate, after the "Lorena" walkaround
and the come-out and the crowd's dispersal, Phoebe
Simms was still among the company, and already had a
hearty hot meal waiting to resuscitate them after the long
day's exertions. Sunday carried a plate to the property
wagon, to feed Rouleau, but he had kept Mullenax's jug
by him, and was feeling no hunger pangs or any other
kind. After the troupe had eaten, most of them simply lay
about in the summer darkness, chatting and smoking. Edge
took a final stroll about the lot, partly to see that the animals were all comfortable, partly just to look at the last
setup he would see on American soil in the foretellable
future. The Big Top looked metallic now, sheened with
dew that reflected the moonlight, and only palely shining
from within, where Hannibal and Quincy slept under a
single watch lantern. The tent itself seemed sleepily to
breathe, like a living creature, for the little random breezes
that wafted through it made the canvas whisper, and the
ropes and chandelier and bail ring rustled and creaked and
clinked. When Edge went to spread his bedroll in the open,
under the stars, only Phoebe and Magpie Maggie Hag were
still awake, sitting together beside the embers of the fire,
conversing in murmurs.

After Phoebe had waddled off to her wagon, Magpie
Maggie Hag stayed awake most of the night, to look in on
Rouleau at intervals. Most of those times she found him
asleep, but feverish and restless. She was reluctant to pour
laudanum into him, on top of his considerable whiskey
content, unless he should go into such a thrashing delirium

as to budge the heavy box he was tied to—and he did not. Indeed, in the morning, when Edge came in to take stock of him, Rouleau was hale enough and in good enough spirits to smile and say:

"Zut alors, those mice of Fitzfarris's have been getting their revenge. All night, they kept coming to nibble at the bran in my box. I can endure the pain and the boredom, ami, but am I to pass every night with vengeful vermin tickling up and down my leg?"

"Be glad of them," said Edge. "As long as you can feel the mice tickling, that leg is still alive, and so are you."

The teardown of the Big Top was not done "leisurely," as Florian had phrased it, but it was certainly done slowly, with now another man missing from the crew. The job took until noon, and by then the women had accomplished all the other complicated packing of the wagons, deciding what things could be kept stored away throughout the voyage, and what should be accessible for use. When everybody had had a bit of midday peck, Florian called the troupe together.

"Ladies and gentlemen, I am now going to pay out another round of salaries. Then all who wish to accompany me downtown may do so, and can pass the afternoon shopping for any items needed for the trip."

The women nodded to each other and began comparing notes on what they ought to be buying. Edge began ticking off, on his fingers, the amount of provender the animals would require. Mullenax muttered that he had better lay in a good supply of liquid refreshment and, while he was downtown, he could damn sure use some horizontal refreshment, too.

"One word of advice to you all," said Florian. "Buy no more than you really *need*, just to get you to Italy, for I can assure you that things will be cheaper over there than here."

"Mas' Florian," said Phoebe Simms. "Kin I go, too, dis time?"

"Most certainly, Madame Alp. It won't matter now if the public sees you en déshabillé."

"Well, I warn't goin' on dere. I'se goin' to Darktown."

"Mother!" Sunday murmured in embarrassed exasperation. "He meant being out of costume."

They all went except Maggie Magpie Hag, who stayed to look after Rouleau, and Hannibal, who stayed to guard everything else. And they all managed to pile into Florian's rockaway and the least loaded wagon, which was the one carrying only the balloon. They descended from the heights into the miasma of downtown and stopped at the base of the Merchants' Shot Tower.

"This edifice is visible from everywhere in the city," said Florian. "So this is where we will reconvene, at sundown."

Edge and Yount drove off in the balloon wagon, to find a feed store and a meat market. The other troupers scattered by ones and twos and groups in various directions, Phoebe Simms even going off separately from her children. And, some hours later, she and Florian were the first to reconvene. He was slouched on the rockaway seat, idly flicking his coach whip at flies on Snowball's rump, when Phoebe came plodding determinedly up to him.

"Ah, Madame Alp. Finished your business in Darktown? I see you bought a hat. That's, er, quite a hat."

"Thankee kindly. An' kin I ax you somep'n, Mas' Florian? Does de law say I be's bound out to y'all becuz I runned away wid you?"

"Why, no, of course not. There is no such thing as bound out any more. You're as free as any white woman walking this street. Good heavens, have we somehow made you feel that you're just a slave to us?"

"Nawsuh. Das why it mek me feel bad now to tell y'all good-bye."

"What?"

"I'se gettin' ma'd, y'see."

"You are getting *married?*"

"Yassuh. Dey's a fine cullud gemmun bin co'tin' me.

Mebbe you seen him. Yaller shoes an' a high-dome hat? He come to all foah shows we done give here in Baltimo', jist to marble at me. Bought all my pitchers, jist so he could talk wid me. Now I done meet up wid him at he house, an' we decides we go' git ma'd.''

"But . . . but . . . Madame Alp, you are our irreplaceable Fat Lady."

"Das whut Roscoe like. He a li'l disapp'inted, t'see I ain' really as fat as in my pitchers, but he say he go' plump me up some. He kin affo'd to do it, too. He got a high fo'man position in de Ches'peake an' Maine Dry Dock. Das a *nigguh* comp'ny here. Begun by Free Nigguhs, and all cullud dat wuk dere, an' it thrivin' fine. Roscoe he a big man dere. Got him a nice house, a hoss an' buggy . . .''

"Well, I certainly congratulate him, and the company, and . . . and you, too. But this comes as a thunderbolt. On the very eve of departure, losing you and the triplets and—''

"Nawsuh. Roscoe he ain' too fond of udder men's get. He want us start all over, hab he own.''

"Madame Alp! You would go off and abandon your children?''

"Dem gels ain' chil'rens no mo', Mas' Florian. Dey all done got der flars in de pas' couple weeks. Dey be's wimmens now, an' dey kin take keer of Quincy. You don' need worry none.''

"Woman, I'm not thinking of myself! I'm thinking of them. How they will miss you.''

"You want t' see how dey miss me, suh? You want t' see how much *anybody* evuh gets missed? Go to dat pond in dat park we at, stick yo' finger in de pond, den look at de hole it leave in de water. Mas' Florian, a mammy knows, once her chil'rens git 'shamed of her, a mammy's wuk is done.''

"Oh, come, now. If that's some tidbit of folk wisdom—''

"Das mammy wisdom. Black mammy, white mammy, make no differments. Nawsuh. Me an' Miz Hag, we done

talk dis out, an' she agree. Dem chil'rens soon be impaw-
tint folk, wid rich prospecks out ahead of 'em. Sunday she
awready talk fancier'n ol' Mistis Furfew. Dem chil'rens
won' want no ol' fat, ignernt, black mammy draggin' after
'em.''

Florian tried every argument and persuasion he could
think of, including the dangling of rich prospects for
Phoebe herself—''Why, Europe is just full of visiting African monarchs!''—but she was adamant in maintaining
that an executive foreman of the Chesapeake & Maine Dry
Dock Company was all the husband she required, and far
better than she had ever expected to find.

''Well, we've lost you,'' Florian finally sighed. ''And
we regret it, but we wish you and Roscoe all the best.
We'll even give you a wedding present. I know the Yankees promised every freed Southern darky 'forty acres and
a mule.' I don't have forty acres to give you, but when we
depart tomorrow I'll leave our mule tethered in the park.
You and Roscoe can go up and collar it whenever you
like.''

''Mighty good o' you. Mas' Florian. We be much
obliged.''

''Meanwhile—much as I'd hate losing the triplets—I
must ask you this again. Would you not wish to entrust
them to some aunt, some uncle, some other of your family?''

''I *am* leavin' dem wid fambly, Mas' Florian. You-all
is it.''

''I daresay that was meant as a compliment to us,'' Florian told Edge and Yount when they drove up later, the
balloon wagon heaped high with bales of hay, bags of
grain and slabs of smoked meat. ''But she is gone, and
how I am to break the news to those pickaninnies, I do
not know.''

''Better worry about how you're going to tell Fitz,'' said
Edge. ''Here he comes now. He's just lost a hefty hunk
of his sideshow,''

Fitzfarris, Sarah and Clover Lee came up the street together, their arms ladene with small parcels. Florian uncomfortably made the announcement that Madame Alp was off to get married.

"And from the seats," said Sarah. "To think that she'd be the first of us females to snare a beau out of the audience."

"Shit," was all that Fitzfarris said.

"Yes," said Florian. "I immediately thought of going to the local orphanage, Sir John, to see what it might have to offer as a replacement. A pinhead or whatever. But, without plausible credentials, I've always found it laborious work to convince a superintendent or a mother superior that I am a medical doctor engaged in scientism and seeking specimens for my studies. No, there wouldn't be time."

"Here come most of our others," said Yount. "I'll start perching 'em on top of that wagon load."

"Put the Simms children in my rockaway," said Florian. "And Madame Solitaire, you squeeze in there with them. On our way back up to the pitch, break the bad news to them as gently as you can. Try to convince them, as Phoebe said, that they've still got a family."

Evidently Sarah succeeded in that, or perhaps the children were by now accustomed to cataclysms occurring frequently in their lives. Anyway, they did not try to run away to find their mother, and did not weep or show any other overt signs of deprivation. Nevertheless, their elders—as soon as all had gone to look in on Rouleau and give the invalid a cheery greeting—exerted themselves to keep the little Simmses too busy to grieve. Edge and Sarah hoisted Monday and Tuesday onto horses and put them through their riding paces around the now open-air ring, and Pepper and Paprika drilled Sunday and Quincy in an exhausting routine of acrobatic exercises. The trouper most affected by Madame Alp's defection was Magpie Maggie Hag, since the cooking of supper devolved upon her, and she went about it grumblingly.

"Serves you right," snapped Florian. "You could have talked the woman out of it. You could have dukkered that her Roscoe is a notorious wife-beater or something."

"I dukkered honest—that he a good man. I flimflam rubes, yes, but never a sister on the show. Go away. Let me cook."

Florian went away, to the park pond, and squatted beside it in what appeared to be solemn meditation. Several passersby gave him looks askance, for he repeatedly stuck a finger into the water and then morosely contemplated the resultant ripples as they quickly subsided and vanished.

The steam collier *Pflichttreu* looked even uglier than when Florian and Edge had earlier seen it, for its main holds were now filled and it sat ungainly low in the water, so the grime-encrusted upper works and masts and yards were more easily visible. It also had steam up, so its tall, thin single stack exuded an ooze of dirty smoke and a steady drift of soot that did not go very high in the air before descending, on deck and dock impartially, like a sticky black snow. Though the chute loading was all done, the ship's derricks were still working, bringing sacked pea coal aboard. Their booms creaked and groaned as they swung the pallets of sacks from dockside to deck hatches, where the crewmen, as black begrimed as everything else in sight, wedged them down into the remaining hold space.

Florian brought the train to a halt at a distance from the activity and the clouds of dirt enveloping it. There were already plenty of supernumeraries and loafers crowding the wharf to see the ship off. They were presumably unemployed or off-duty seamen and stevedores, seated on rope coils or leaning on bollards all over the cobbled waterside area, all of them smoking stumpy pipes or chewing tobacco, all keeping up a running commentary—mostly derogatory—on the *Pflichttreu*'s loading procedures and its crew's competence at the work. But even from a distance Florian could notice that, notwithstanding the ship's generally repellent look, Captain Schilz had made at least one chivalrous provision for his oncoming female passengers. The only gangway from shore to ship was still the same ordinary open ladder, but it was now fitted with a "virginity screen," a strip of canvas slung below it from top to bottom, so the workers and loiterers on the dock could not peek up the ladies' dresses as they ascended.

Florian climbed down from the rockaway. "Take charge, Zachary. Make sure nobody else runs off as Madame Alp did. I'm going to the office to get a refund from Herr Mayer for her." He paused. "Now what the devil is this?"

He backed defensively against the carriage as three men sped across the cobbles toward him, gibbering in excited, high-pitched voices. They were not just running, they were gleefully leaping and bounding as they came, and pointing at the wagons and wigwagging at the elephant as though they were old acquaintances of hers. The language they gabbled was totally incomprehensible, but one locution— "kong-ma-jang!"—was recognizably repeated over and over. They were very small men, not much taller than Tim Trimm, and exceedingly skinny. They had simian faces, of yellowish-tan complexion, and were patently Orientals, but of indeterminable age; any of them could have been anything from thirty to sixty. They wore blousy tunics and trousers that had originally been of white cotton but were now mostly gray rags, and wore no shoes at all.

Arriving before the astonished Florian, they did an extravagant number of elaborate Oriental bows. Then two of them fell supine on the cobbles, in opposite directions, and stuck their legs in the air. The third man jumped straight up from the ground, curled himself into a ball in midair, and the other two began kicking him back and forth through the air between them, making him spin first one way, then the other.

"By damn!" Florian exclaimed. "Antipodists. A risley act."

"What?" said Edge, who had protectively joined him on the ground.

"Antipodists. Foot jugglers and upside-down acrobats. They're doing what's called a risley—after an old-time English performer, but it's really from the Orient."

"So are they," said Fitzfarris, also joining them. "Bunch of Chinamen, I'd guess."

"How in the world do they happen to be on a Baltimore dock?"

"The railroads out west use a lot of Chinks for coolie work," said Fitz. "I'd bet this trio booked steerage passage—or more likely stowed away—on a Chinatrade clipper they thought was bound for California. They probably don't know where the hell they are. They don't seem to know a word of English."

The Chinese, if that was what they were, had got to their feet and were again frantically jabbering and gesticulating. Whatever they were saying sounded urgent and importunate. When they pointed to themselves they said gloomily "Han-guk" and proudly "kwang-dae." When they pointed to the wagons they said imploringly. "Kong-ma-jang."

"I'd reckon that means circus," said Edge. "They can't read the words, but they recognize circus wagons when they see them."

"And I'd say they're asking to come along with us," said Fitz.

"Then so they shall," said Florian, with instant decision. "We can use a new act. We'll take them."

Edge suggested gently, "Oughtn't we to try telling them where they're going? I mean, if they think they're in California right now, what will they think when they wind up in Italy?"

"It won't be any more alien to them than Baltimore. They are obviously stranded, lost, no doubt bewildered by the local customs, out of work and desperate. We will give them employment and sustenance."

"You were just about to demand money back from Mr. Mayer. Now you're going to shell out for two more fares."

"No, sir," said Florian, still being decisive. "Fitz, strip

the Chinks naked and put them among the exhibits in the museum. Herr Mayer comes out to count noses, I'll tell him they are monkeys." Fitz and Edge made noises of appalled and amused protest, but Florian overrode them. "If he refuses to believe that, I'll convince him that they don't weigh as much all together as Madame Alp did."

So Fitzfarris rounded up the Chinese and led them to the museum wagon. He let down one of its hinged side panels, undid the enclosing wire nettings and pointed to indicate that that was where they were to ride. Then he began, with some repugnance, to disrobe one of them, and gestured to the others to do the same. The Chinese looked briefly puzzled by this, but seemed to accept it as just another California custom, and complied. Naked, they clambered in among the stuffed animals. Fitz reattached the netting, closed up the side panel and left them in the darkness.

The undressing of them turned out to have been unnecessary. Herr Mayer did emerge from his office to tally the passengers, wagons, animals and other items against the list Florian had given him. But when Florian hurried him past the museum wagon, saying, "In there are the taxidermische specimens I mentioned," Herr Mayer did not bid him open it. Neither did he volunteer to refund any money when the passenger count came out one short. Florian decided not to press his luck; he did not mention it, either.

The loading of coal sacks was finally done, so the collier's derricks were put to work to hoist the circus aboard. Edge and Yount took the job of driving the wagons one by one to the ship's side and there unhitching the horses, while the dockhands attached grapple cables between wagon and boom, and the donkeymen on deck worked a steam capstan to haul each wagon up and swing it inboard.

There was one anxious moment. When it came the museum wagon's turn, it transpired that Fitzfarris had only insecurely latched the side panel. The wagon was just at the ship's gunwale, rocking in the air, when that panel flopped open. The watching troupers held their breath, as a number of deckhands stood gaping with disbelief at the three small, wizened, yellowish, naked creatures clinging terrified to the inside of the wire netting. But all that happened was that one old seaman spat tobacco juice, imperturbably remarked to a younger, "I told ye, lad. Some quair things come in on the tide," and reclosed the panel securely.

Maximus made vociferous complaint and made the seamen look uneasy as his cage wagon was hoisted. But when a belly sling took the elephant aboard, Hannibal clung to it, too—murmuring reassuringly, "Steady, ol' Peggy, steady"—and she actually seemed to enjoy the brief ride, with her ponderous weight off her legs for a change. The elephant, with the caged Maximus for company, and two other wagons were positioned along the starboard side of the open foredeck, the rockaway and the remaining three wagons on the port side. The vehicles were all tied down and their wheels chocked, the elephant was tethered to the gunwale cleats by chains to her two right legs. Then the activity shifted to the afterdeck's derrick. The eight horses came aboard there in belly slings, but not as placidly as Peggy had. They whinnied, walled their eyes and kicked, nearly braining a couple of deckhands before they could be haltered to the gunwale.

Mullenax let his three pigs climb the gangway ladder on their own, which they did with gusto and much to the amusement of the workers and idlers looking on. Mullenax herded them to the afterdeck and left them to make their own beds in the straw spread for the horses, only taking care to caution the seamen that the porkers were *not* portable provisions for the galley. The other troupers also came aboard by way of the ladder, carrying various pieces of hand luggage. Rouleau, on his bedroll, firmed by planks under it, had been carefully removed by his fellows from the property wagon before that was hoisted. Now his sickbed was gently laid on one of the coal-loading pallets, and even the rough-handed crewmen took great care in fetching him on board and carrying him to a cabin.

The passengers had been allotted five of the four-bunk cabins in the superstructure "island" between the fore and after masts. Only Florian and Fitzfarris moved into Rouleau's, to give him as much air to breathe as possible. Hannibal insisted on sleeping on deck with his Peggy, and Quincy shared a cabin with his three sisters. That left one cabin for the four other white men, and the five white women were delighted to have two whole cabins to share among them. Fitzfarris, as soon as he could do so unobserved, sneaked to the foredeck to drop the offside flap of the museum wagon, so the three Chinese had light and air and and outboard view, and he even rearranged the stuffed occupants of the museum so the living ones had floor room to lie upon.

All the troupers, as soon as they had stowed their gear, crowded together on the after deck to observe the *Pflichttreu*'s getting under way. The idlers on shore ceased their loafing long enough to cast off the ship's hawsers from the wharf bollards, and the hands on deck hauled them in and coiled them. There was a clamorous ringing of bells and tooting of whistles and shrieking of piped steam. The stack amidships belched a storm cloud of black smoke, out of which fell a black snowstorm of oily soot, and the gritty iron deck underfoot began to throb as the engines were put in gear. The strip of fetid and trashy water between the ship's side and the wharf began slowly to widen. Then the deck settled to a steadier vibration that made everybody jitter lightly where he stood. Pepper nudged Paprika and whispered. "Look yonder," indicating Monday Simms. Her face was blissful and her thighs rubbing together. "That gal is grinding mustard again."

Nobody else noticed. They were watching the dockside clutter of Locust Point slide away from them—then all of Baltimore, the city seeming to cluster itself around the Shot Tower as it dwindled. There were various changes in the rhythm of the vibration underfoot, and varying densities of black snowfall, as the collier made various small changes of course to get into the channel. Then Fort Mc-Henry was close on the ship's starboard side, the city lazaretto on the port. Then, almost with a rush, the land swerved away on either side, and the *Pflichttreu* was out of the inner harbor, in the broad Patapsco River, and everybody on deck gave a loud hurrah. There would be a brief delay when the harbor pilot was dropped, and there would still be land visible, near or distant, on both sides, as the collier made its heavy, slow progress down the long reach of Chesapeake Bay. But they were on their way to Europe.

⊷⊶ ASEA ⊶⊷

1

WHEN THE PASSENGERS CAME on deck the next morning to see to the animals before breakfast, there was still land visible on either side of the *Pflichttreu*. Its engines were vigorously churning and its twirling screw left a foamy wake on the water behind. But, like a fat woman who walks with busy, twinkling feet but moves forward only slowly, the ship seemed to be making little progress for all its effort. Captain Schilz was on deck, watching the crew hosing water to clear at least some of the night's accumulation of grit from the plating. However, since the ship was moving at a pace so slow that it never outran its own exhalations, the soot continued to collect almost as rapidly as it was cleared.

"Guten Morgen, pill-grumps," the captain said, amiably enough. Tim Trimm immediately said, in a peevish voice, "That ain't Europe out yonder. Is this crummy bucket travelling at all?"

Captain Schilz gave him a haughty look. "Herr Miniatur, are you calling my ship slow? Not slow it is. Moderate it is."

"It also has rats," said Sarah. She turned to Edge. "Back on shore, Jules got used to the mice crawling into that box you put on him. But last night, when I went to change his dressings, he was in a state of nerves. Big, ugly *rats* were getting into the box."

The captain said, with heavy Teutonic humor, "Gnädige Frau, would you really wish to be travelling on a ship the rats had *abandoned?*"

"What I'm wishing, captain dear," said Pepper, "is that your moderate ship would at least move moderately faster than its own bad breath. Are we to be filthy and smelly all the way beyant the pond?"

"Damen und Herren," said the captain, turning pink with the effort of controlling himself. "By profession a sailing officer I was until—against my better judgment—master of this steam boiler I was made. On board a decent sailing ship, such an abomination as ein Zirkus I would not accept." His voice got louder and angrier. "You are here only because I am now a mere Mechaniker, and what miserable cargo I carry in this verdammt kitchen kettle *I do not care!*"

The artistes looked properly indignant, but dared not interrupt, as Captain Schilz went on, in a contained fury:

"To this Schmutzfink I am condemned until such day as the owners realize that no ship by steam alone to cross the Atlantic will ever be able. Ja, a collier like this—carrying four and a half thousand tons of coal—could do that, ja. But it consumes twenty-five tons each day. If all the way the engines I used, I would empty of cargo arrive in port. So no more coal will I burn than I have to. As soon as on the wide open sea we are, and whenever a fair wind we have, I promise you, I shall shut off the stinking engines and hoist good clean sail."

"We are sorry we presumed to criticize your ship," Florian said diplomatically. "You do it so much better yourself."

The captain, having let off his own steam, simmered down. "Come now, all of you, to Frühstück."

As might have been expected on a vessel under a Prussian master, breakfast was good and rich and plentiful. The Rhenish cook was known as Doc—according to Florian, all ships' cooks were so called—and he had a vile temper—also, said Florian, common to all ships' cooks. He seldom emerged from his cramped galley, where he kept up a continuous conversation with himself, consisting mainly of imprecations at his larder and equipment and wages and working hours and the unappreciative palate of the average seaman. The cabin steward, Quashee, was different. A big, black West Indian, he spoke an almost Oxonian English and served at table with the courtly manner of a professional butler.

The first and second officers and the chief engineer also dined at the captain's table when they were not on watch. They were respectively a Hessian, a Saxon and a Bavarian, but they all spoke English about as well as the captain did. Indeed, despite the fact that the ship's company included almost every nationality of western Europe, English was practically the working language of the whole vessel. Probably because Britain was the chief builder of maritime engines, almost all the ship's "black gang" and a goodly number of the deckhands were Limeys and Jocks and Taffies and Paddies. So every command, instruction, inquiry and revilement, whatever language it might be uttered in, had to be repeated in English for the comprehension of all.

Only the white folk of the circus, then or afterward, dined at the captain's table. But the urbane Quashee did not mind taking trays to the Simmses in their cabin and to Hannibal on deck, any more than he minded taking trays to Rouleau. Also, that first morning, the men of the troupe managed to pocket some rolls and pickles and cuts of cold meat from the breakfast table, and afterward to slip them to the grateful Chinese in the museum wagon. But it later became apparent that Captain Schilz regarded Chinese as no more or less detestable than anyone else connected with a Zirkus, and was uncaring whether or not their fare had been paid. So, after some days, when Magpie Maggie Hag had cut and sewn acrobat outfits for the three and they were decently covered, they were allowed out of the wagon to mingle with their new colleagues, and Quashee fed them when he fed Hannibal, and they returned to the museum only to sleep.

On the second or third day out, the circus folk who had complained about the slowness of the ship's coming south down Chesapeake Bay were given reason to wish that they had more fully enjoyed that time and had complained about it less. For when the *Pflichttreu* at last rounded Cape Charles and turned east into the Atlantic, Captain Schilz gave an order in German and the first mate passed it on to the crew in a bellow of English: "Hang out the washing, lads!"

Men scurried up the mast shrouds to unfurl the sails from the yards. When the canvas was spread and set, the captain gave another order, and there was a sudden, almost eerie silence as the engines were shut down. The passengers had got so accustomed to the continuous mechanical chuntering that to hear nothing but the normal shipboard sounds and the wind in the rigging was as startling as if they had been abruptly deafened.

Meanwhile, Florian was calling, "Abdullah, quick, go and stand ready to comfort Brutus! Barnacle Bill, run to the cage wagon to reassure Maximus! Sir John, Quake-maker, Colonel, come aft with me to hold the horses! Hurry!"

Some of them regarded him in surprise, but they did as bidden, and soon saw why. Only Florian, of the male passengers, had ever been at sea under sail, so he was the only one of them to realize what was about to occur. All the way down the bay, the heavy-laden collier had cruised as level and stable as a circus ring. But now, under canvas and in the open ocean, the *Pflichttreu*, for all its bulk and weight, gave a long, creaking lurch and leaned steeply to port. The animals had to dance to keep their footing on the slanted deck—so did the men, as they patted the animals and murmured soothingly to them—and they all had to continue fidgeting for a while to find a steady balance, for the deck stayed at that steep slope.

When the horses and pigs appeared to have adapted themselves to their side-hill posture, Edge hurried to Rouleau's cabin to make sure the man's leg had not been jarred from its immobility.

"It hasn't, thank goodness," Edge said. "And as long as it doesn't, the ship's motion ought to be good for it. Keep the blood circulating. How are you feeling, Jules?"

"I hurt," Rouleau said wearily. "But merde alors, I am in more boredom than pain. Maggie says the flesh wounds are healing. I hope the bones are, too."

"I think you're doing fine. Another week or so, we'll carry your bedroll out on deck, give you some sunshine for a while each day."

"Then let me, in the meantime, laisser pisser les mérinos. Tell Clover Lee to bring her books each day—and the other children—and we will carry on with their lessons."

The ship remained at its left-leaning cant for about the next four hours, by which time the passengers—and probably the animals—thought they had found their sea legs. But then they heard another shout, "Ha-a-ard a-lee!" which occasioned more shouting back and forth from bridge to deck:

"Bout ship!"

"Mains'ls hau-au-aul!"

"Jacks and sheets!"

"Let go and hau-au-aul!"

Canvas flapped and blocks rattled and spars clattered and the whole ship groaned, lurched and leaned steeply over the other way, to starboard, and all the passengers, human and animal, had to find new footing. From then on, during every stretch of the crossing when Captain Schilz was able to keep the *Pflichttreu* under canvas, he would hold one tack for some four hours, then come about to the opposite tack for the next four. Over the first several days, whenever that occurred, the troupers had to endure the jeers of any seamen observing them—"Look at 'em do the cuddy-jig!"—but eventually all of them, even the heavyweight Peggy and the Chinese inside their cage and Rouleau flat on his back, learned to adjust to the lurch without giving it a thought, and could do so even in their sleep.

Nonetheless, they had to develop not only sea legs, but also sea stomachs. The first day or two on the open ocean was a wretched time for practically everybody who had not been at sea before. When at one point the gunwales were draped with Mullenax, Trimm, Hannibal, Sarah and Clover Lee, Fitzfarris, Sunday, Monday, Tuesday and Quincy—all jettisoning the good food Doc and Quashee had fed them—Florian expressed some surprise at not seeing Edge and Yount in the same position and condition.

"Oh, we been vaccinated," said Yount. "The U.S. Army was kind enough to charter a steamboat to take us from N'Awleans to Mexico. The *Portland* was a side-wheeler, and pretty steady, until we run into a storm in the Gulf. We all fetched up our toenails then, I can tell you."

Florian said, "Well, it is true that one attack of mal-de-mer usually makes a person immune. You'd be doing a mercy if you went around and told the sick ones that."

By the next day, most of them had recovered and, by the day after that, all had except Tim Trimm. He turned out to be one of the unhappy few who apparently never can acquire a sea stomach. He was at the gunwale almost all of every day, and would have to bolt from his cabin at unpredictable intervals every night. He never came to the dining table any more, subsisting on ship's biscuits and water, the only nutriments he could keep down, and his dead-fish eyes began to look dead indeed.

"It's bad enough, bein' so miserable," Tim whimpered to his colleagues. "But what's worse is that sauerkraut captain comin' by every mornin' *askin'* if I'm seasick. Can't the sumbitch *see* I am?"

Paprika laughed mockingly. "If you spoke German, little man, you would realize that Captain Schilz is making a joke. He is asking only 'how are you?' but in a waggish way. 'Wie befinden Sie sich?' You see? A pun between the languages.''

''The skipper is really a decent old skin,'' said Pepper. '' 'Tis plain he despises landlubbers, but he's gallant enough to us ladies.''

''And he keeps the lesser swabbies from getting *too* gallant,'' said Sarah. ''The worst they do is ogle and leer when we show a leg.''

''Shit, I hope the gallant skipper falls overboard and drowns,'' growled Tim, and he continued to pass the days at the gunwale. But now, whenever possible, he chose the one to which Peggy was tethered, so that the elephant stood between his misery and any gloating onlookers.

The other troupers, as soon as the novelty of being at sea had given way to the monotony of being at sea, occupied themselves at their various specialties. Magpie Maggie Hag, after making the acrobats' short-legged fleshings for the three Chinese, resewed the rip panel in the *Saratoga*, then turned out extra costumes for the other performers—much better made and more bedizened with spangles than their old ones—including, for Colonel Ramrod and Barnacle Bill, new ring uniforms positively stiff with gold-braid frogs and brandenburgs and epaulettes. The circus women, more than the men, were pleased that everybody should have extra changes of clothing, because it would enable them to spend less time at the washtub. Or it would when they got ashore; there was no keeping clean aboard a collier.

The ship was a lot less besooted when the engines were shut down and the wind blowing, but even then the hold seemed somehow to exhale coal dust, and there was always at least a trickle of smoke from the stack. The deckhands who, on any other kind of ship, would have passed their free time chipping rust or laying paint, on this *Pflichttreu* had to keep up the Sisyphean task of endlessly sweeping and swabbing. So the circus costumes, old and new, were kept tight shut in the cabin trunks, and the troupers wore only derelict overalls or old and threadbare frocks. And when these got unbearably filthy, the women would launder them in the manner called by the seamen Maggie-Millering—tying them in a bundle to a rope, throwing the bundle overside and towing it through the seawater.

Some of the company were able to rehearse their routines, and work on new ones, even when the ship was under sail and therefore riding at a steep slant. Hannibal could juggle anything that came to hand, from marlinspikes to the dining cabin's best glassware, no matter how the ship was cavorting, and the Chinese could do almost as well, using their feet and toes, and Yount could do his walkabout exercises with a cannonball on the back of his bent neck. Edge, using one of the Henry repeater carbines, shot the scavenger birds that congregated whenever Doc emptied the galley slops overside.

"Why waste ammunition on fowl we can't eat?" Sarah asked him.

"Got to learn the carbine's quirks," said Edge. "The world's best sharpshooter could hardly hit Peggy with an unfamiliar weapon, even if he's always shot the same make and model. Every single firearm out of the same gunsmithy has its particular peculiarities. This one bears a tad high and to the left, but I think I've got it figured now." And to prove that, he lifted the Henry to his shoulder and neatly bagged a hovering petrel.

Under the tutelage of Pepper and Paprika, Sunday and Quincy Simms continued their calisthenics. Whatever other and more complex contortions they did, each of them was made every day to bring on deck a dining-cabin chair and, holding to its back, do the "side practice"—extending the left, then the right leg straight sideways, then forward, then backward, and holding each position for five minutes without a tremor. And they would have to do that all their working lives, said Pepper—as she and Paprika did—to assure maintaining their "poise and balance." Quincy had become, as planned, the most limber of the Simmses. He was now able to stand on even a slanted deck, do an unsupported body bend backward, and not just put his hands on the deck but clutch them to his ankles and bring his head, face forward, between his knees.

Mullenax was wise enough not to get into the lion cage to rehearse Maximus in his old tricks or try any new ones, and Pepper would not heft the perchpole with or without Paprika on it, except when the ship rode perfectly level. But it did that frequently enough. The squat, heavy and sparsely canvased *Pflichttreu* required a brisk wind, even from dead astern, to move at all, and was incapable of sailing close-hauled. So there was always a low fire kept burning under the boilers, and the watch officers and engineers had a finely developed sense of when the engines were likely to be needed and ought to be stoked. Thus, whenever a fair wind began to fade, or veered anywhere forward of the ship's beam, and the bridge officer signaled for engines, the black gang could have them going before the ship lost way.

Monday Simms was equally sensitive where the engines were concerned. After the first day aboard, she had ceased chafing her thighs together *continuously* in rhythm with the deck's tremors. Now she went into her peculiar trance only when, for navigational reasons, the bridge signaled a change in engine speed or when, for mechanical reasons, the gang below made some adjustment in the engines' workings. Whatever she was doing—harness polishing or Maggie-Millering or helping Quincy shovel animal droppings overside—Monday would sense the change in rhythm before anyone else could, and her eyes would glaze and her thighs begin going rub-rub-rub.

Mullenax was also beguiled by the ship's engines, but in a different way. As he had demonstrated by his treasuring of the apparatus that turned out to be the balloon *Saratoga*, Abner was a man interested in paraphernalia, novel inventions and contraptions in general. So, out of curiosity, he descended into the bowels of the ship whenever he had an opportunity. For some time, he never ventured lower than the catwalk, where hung the engineer's blackboard and some green-glass gauges in which the water level minutely surged and ebbed to the ship's motion. From there, Mullenax could gaze down into the long, narrow room between the coal bunkers, a place crammed with machinery—black iron, shining steel, walking-beams jerking like the legs of giant grasshoppers, convoluted and intertwined pipes and tubes encrusted with salt and furred with fungus. The room was only gloomily lamplighted except when an opened firebox door lit up the place like a glimpse of Hell. The workers in it might have been demons—half-naked, coal-blackened, sweat-glossy—as they moved up and down the walkway between the high flywheel and the spinning horizontal shaft, perpetually greasing things with their long-beaked oil cans.

Eventually Mullenax got to be such a frequent fixture that the chief engineer—a short, rotund, red-faced, balding, middle-aged Münchner named Carl Beck—warmed to him and took him down among the machinery and showed him things and explained them. "The men always greasing are, because always well lubricated the thrust block, the tunnel shaft and the stern gland must be." Chief Beck was also given to grousing about the attitude toward engineers manifested by Captain Schilz and the upper hierarchy of the merchant marine:

"The old-line officers, all once stick-and-string men were—sailing men—so nothing but poker-pushers they call us. They resent that officer rank and privileges we have. Scheisse! So masters of all the ships they still are, all the rules they make. But of the skills we must have they know nothing—the vigilance of us required—the wicked compound engines and lethal live steam to control."

"Looks to me like you do real good at it," Mullenax said sincerely. "I don't reckon steam would run a balloon, would it?"

"Wie bitte?" said Chief Beck, taken aback. "You mean Luftballon? Nein, nein. For balloon Wasserstoff you need—hydrogen gas."

"Somebody said we'd need a generator."

"Ja. The hydrogen to make. Ein Gasentwickler."

"Could you make one of them things?"

"Ich denke . . . well, different types there are. To generate by decomposition of water, ein Apparat as big as this ship you would need. A mobile generator you would wish. The action of oil of vitriol upon filings to employ. Ja, that I could build. Let me see . . ." He took down his blackboard that recorded steam pressure, vacuum pressure, feed-water temperature and so on. He wiped a clean spot on it and took a bit of chalk. "Zunächst . . . your balloon how much gas requires?"

"Twenty-five thousand cubic feet, I remember that."

Beck scribbled, then mumbled, "Sagen wir . . . seven hundred kiloliters."

"Put that way, it sounds a sight smaller."

But Beck was no longer listening; he was calculating and muttering to himself. So Mullenax went topside and sought out Florian.

"The man ought to be a prime recruit, Mr. Florian. He's purely fed up with being a lowly ship's engineer. I bet, if you offered him the job of being our balloon's gasser, he'd jump at it. But besides that, Carl rides a hobbyhorse. In private, he yearns to be a musician. Claims he can play three or four instruments."

"No! A mechanist who is also an amateur windjammer?"

"And you know what else? He's put his trade and his hobby together, and back home in Mernchin, wherever that is, he's done built himself one of them cally-opes you're always saying you'd like to own."

"I'll be damned," said Florian, his eyes shining. "Almost too good to be true. A master engineer and a windjammer and with his own steam organ. Yes, Chief Beck certainly sounds worth cultivating."

"Well, I got a suggestion about that. Another thing Carl does, he's always frettin' about the state of his liver, and how bald he's gettin', and how unsalubrious it is to work in that heat and stink and noise all the time. Now and again, I give him a dose of tonic out of my jug. But I thought maybe ... if old Maggie has some secret recipe for growin' hair ... ?''

"I'll be damned," Florian said again. "For a one-eyed man, Barnacle Bill, you often see a lot more than most of us do with two."

Meanwhile, Pepper had charmed a favor out of Stitches, the ship's sailmaker, a gaunt Welshman who might have been Florian's age, but looked much older. She persuaded him to make, at her direction, a rig for her hair-hang act: a small but sturdy thing of a heavy canvas strap, a metal ring and a metal turnbuckle. She charmed him even further by inviting him to be the one to help her test it. While Stitches freed a block and fall at the forward mast, Pepper braided her long hair into a firm plait, buckled the canvas strap around it, then did some complicated splicing of her braid, so she had a pretty chignon at the back of her head with the apparatus securely fixed in it. Stitches brought the rope end and expertly knotted it to her metal ring. Then, looking apprehensive but obeying her "houp ... là!" he hauled on the free rope end, smoothly but strongly, and she was lifted off the deck and up among the shrouds.

The troupers and various deckhands and officers had gathered by then, and cheered as Pepper, hanging some twenty feet above the deck, supported only by her own tresses—drawn so tight that she had slant eyes and a mask-like grin—did an elaborate series of poses, spins and acrobatic convolutions. When she signaled to the sailmaker to lower her again, and had taken bows to the admiring applause, she undid the chignon, shook out her hair into its customary curly mane and took her new contrivance to stow safely in the women's cabin. Then she, as Mullenax had done, made a confidential report to Florian.

"Dai's a good man with needle and thimble and palm, and he's not leery of tackling new jobs. Seeing as our poor Ignatz is gone, ye might be wanting a replacement canvas boss. I can confide that this old feller hates steam as much as the captain does, because he has so little to do nowadays. His trade is being abolished. Ye might just want to see how he'd feel about joining out.''

"I will," said Florian. "What did you say his name is?"

"Dai Goesle. One of them frightful Taffy names that looks worse than it sounds." She spelled it. "But 'tis pronounced Gwell."

Of all the troupers, Fitzfarris, with no act to rehearse or improve upon, was worst beset by boredom. So, to give both himself and Rouleau something to occupy them, he went to the convalescent's cabin and asked for instruction in the art of voice projection.

"Bien. To begin with," said Rouleau, "engastrimythism, ventriloquism—whichever word you prefer—they both mean 'talking from the belly.' But the Greeks and Romans called it that merely to impress the ancient rubes. The belly is no way involved and there is really nothing to learn, only to practice. All you do is employ a voice not your own, and keep your lips unmoving while you do it. The rest is simple misdirection of the audience's attention, by your gestures and facial expressions."

"Peter Piper picked a peck . . ." Fitz tried, and gave up. "Come on, Jules. It's impossible to say that without moving your lips."

"C'est vrai. So you do not say that. You do not say any word that has labial consonants in it. If you absolutely must utter such words, however, there is a way to fake. Say Feeter Fifer instead of Peter Piper. For big say dig. For mice say nice. No lip movement. Drop such a word into a sentence, nobody will notice. People always hear what they expect to hear. From *where* they hear it depends on your good playacting. Since you will be doing the act on the midway, you will be working closer to your audience than I did in the ring, and you should have better success. I hope so."

"Thank you, Jules," said Fitz, keeping his lips slightly apart and unmoving. "I'll go off and practice—uh—fractice."

"Oh, one other thing. Don't have animals around when you're working the act. You can persuade the rubes that you've trapped a baby under a tub, but the animals are smarter. They'll stare at you, where the baby's cry really comes from. Ruin the whole effect."

Fitzfarris went and sat in the shade of the lifeboats slung outboard of the cabins, and practiced. When a deckhand came along the row of boats, checking their davit falls, Fitz pointed and said with great concern, "Mate, I believe there's some stowaway in that boat." The seaman gave him a dull look, but then looked more keenly at the boat toward which Fitz was cupping an ear and staring intently—as a disembodied, thickly muffled voice gave a bleat of, "Oo-oo-oh, do let us out!" It took a little while, and several repetitions of pleas such as "Dying in here!" and "Good sir, fetch water!" But when the flabbergasted deckhand began hurriedly unlashing and flinging off the boat's tarpaulin cover, Fitz sauntered away, smiling.

He next happened upon Chips, the ship's carpenter, who was tacking a new tin sheathing around a hatch cover, and Fitz's eye fell speculatively on the tin scraps that fell from the man's shears.

"To make a long story short," Fitz afterward told Florian, "I convinced him that some poor soul had got shut in the hold, back in Baltimore when the hatch was closed. After Chips fell for it, and wanted to kill me, I told him he could pull the same trick on other people. To cast his voice, all he'd have to do is put under his tongue a bit of tin shaped just so." Fitz held out his palm, in which lay a piece of tin, cut in a disk the size of a fifty-cent coin and then bent not quite double, so it vaguely resembled a partly opened clamshell. "I instructed him in shaping it, and he was so grateful that at my request he cut me a whole bushel of the things. Chips is off somewhere now, practising, and I've got a supply of goods for sale. During the sideshow, I'll do my engastrimyth act, then tell the rubes they can do the same, with one of these voice projectors—"

"Swazzles," Florian said admiringly. "In circus parlance, any such bogus gadget for sale is a swazzle."

"If you say so. Anyhow, they're worth money to us. And meanwhile, Chips is our friend for life—or until he gives up on the swazzle. You got any carpentry work you want done?"

"Hm," said Florian. "I wonder if he has any spare paint . . ."

Chips did, or at any rate pretended that the blue paint he provided was dispensable stock. The men of the troupe all pitched in to patch and caulk and paint the older wagons, and they came out a near match to the two newer ones. Then Chips contributed his own spare-time labor, to paint again the legends on the wagons' sides. Some of the words stayed the same, but others Florian wanted changed. Chips proved to have considerable artistic talent, giving the red-and-yellow, black-outlined letters wondrous swashes and curlicues. He even painted the circus's name, in place of the U.S. Army's, on Hannibal's big drum. When Edge saw the neatly done and newly sparkling titles on the wagons, he looked with approval at FLORIAN'S FLOURISHING FLORILEGIUM, but looked with some surprise at the lines beneath:

Combined CONFEDERATE American Circus,
Menagerie & Educational Exhibition!

"I thought you liked to brag and look prosperous," he said to Florian. "Putting 'Confederate' in there, it'll look more like we're desperate and refugeeing."

"Not at all, Zachary. You are evidently unaware of the climate of European opinion these past years. Practically every nation and native over there was hoping the Confederacy would win the war. This will gain us sympathy and warmth and welcome. You'll see."

"You're the main guy. I'll take your word for it."

"That's another thing. I must inform the whole company. I am no longer the main guy. In Europe, I shall more properly be referred to and addressed as the Governor. And the pavilion will be called the chapiteau, not the Big Top. There are various other differences in terminology. The pitch is the tober, the rubes are flatties or jossers. The rope-fall is a lungia. The ring is the pista. A straw house is a sfondone and a bloomer house is a bianca . . .''

''It sounds like Europe got most of its circus jargon from Italy.''

''And why not? It was the ancient Romans who *invented* the circus.'' Florian sighed slightly. ''Rather a pity, that the Italians will not again found a Roman Empire. In fact, Rome—the Papal State—remains the only holdout, now that the rest of the peninsula has so recently united into one kingdom. Still . . . Italy . . . birthplace of the circus. It is only a coincidence of circumstances that is taking us first to that country. But might it not be a happy augury?''

''Hell, I'll be happy to get anywhere. Sea travel is as boring as garrison duty in flat old Kansas.''

''Pray, do not say such things. At sea, the alternative to boredom is disaster. Try not to call it down upon us. I've warned Maggie, too. She has lately been glooming and fidgeting, and mumbling something about an ominous water-wheel.''

''I think she's got wheels on the brain,'' said Edge. ''Wheels are all she's dukkered recently. And we sure won't see anything like a waterwheel until we're safe on land again.'' He looked past Florian and frowned. ''What are those Chinks up to?''

The three Chinese had discerned that Florian had no more chores to ask of the ship's carpenter, so they were presenting him with a request of their own. Chips looked alarmed as he was surrounded by the gibbering and gesticulating little men, but he relaxed and smiled when one of them pressed upon him a piece of paper and they all jabbed their fingers at the pencil drawing on it.

''Oh, aye. You want a thing like that, mates?'' He brought the paper to show to Florian and Edge. ''Your

John Chinee fellers are askin' me to build this for 'em. But you're the pilots.''

The drawing was elegant and instantly recognizable. ''A teeterboard,'' said Florian. ''For their act. Well, it's certainly all right with me, Chips, if you want to go to the trouble.''

''Depends on how big they want it.'' He consulted with the Chinese, meaning that they gabbled excitedly, took Chips's hands and held them at various measures while they pointed to the drawing's various features. Finally Chips called to Florian, ''Only a wee one. I can do it,'' and went off to the stores hold to seek materials.

Two days later, he had the thing finished and brought it on deck for the antipodists' approval. It was a broad plank, about four feet long, on a heavy base no more than eighteen inches high, and Chips had put a padded leather cushion on either end of the teeter. The Chinese were vociferous at sight of it and, two at a time, stood on the board and seesawed it. Then they vociferated some more at Chips.

''Want it made heavier, as I understand 'em,'' he said. ''With beefier hardware and hinges.''

''Damned if I can see why,'' said Florian. ''They're all featherweights. If it's troublesome, friend . . .''

''No, no,'' muttered Chips. ''I want to get it right.''

He brought it back the next day and the Chinese put it through a rigorous test. One man stood on one end of the teeter, a second jumped heavily on the other end and bounced the first, twirling and somersaulting, through the air to land standing upright on the third man's shoulders. Then that top man plunged feet first to the board, to send the man on the other end soaring even higher, with many more mid-air flips and contortions, to land on the third man's shoulders. Then they all became a sort of flickering blur, as they variously jumped on the board, flew through the air, landed on one another and jumped again, until all three seemed to be doing everything simultaneously.

When they finally slowed, and became three distinct per-

sons, and the teeterboard ceased to rock and thump, and
the watchers cheered, the Chinese stood side by side,
bowed politely, then dragged the teeterboard to where
Peggy was tethered, and began to jabber at Hannibal. After
a moment, he announced to the watchers in an incredulous
voice:

"Dey wants ol' Peggy t' get on dis rocker perch."

"Well," said Florian, after brief deliberation, "she can
stand on a pedestal, Abdullah, so let's see if she can do
this. The Chinamen seem to have encountered some such
bull act before."

Hannibal made a face of disassociating himself from the
consequences, but obediently prodded and spoke to Peggy.
The elephant's chains were long enough for her to lift all
four feet and move a step or two. When she lurched away
from the gunwale, she revealed the wretched and retching
Tim Trimm, draped there as usual. With great care but
without hesitation, Peggy shuffled slowly up the inclined
board. She looked a trifle surprised when the weight of her
forebody made the board rock and gently tilt her forward,
but it did not frighten her. After a pensive moment, and
without moving her big feet, the bull shifted her weight
slightly and the board gently rocked backward again. Turning her head, Peggy favored the company with bright eyes,
uplifted trunk and what was almost a human grin of pride
and pleasure. Then, without command, she continued shifting her weight and seesawing forward and backward.

"I'll be damned to Davy's locker," said the admiring
Chips, and he was the first to break into applause.

Thereafter, when the Chinese spent almost every day
doing their own practices on the teeterboard and evolving
ever more spectacular flying acrobatics, they would allow
a certain while for Peggy to enjoy the thing, too—but only
on days when the *Pflichttreu* was under steam and riding
level. After the elephant had got used to seesawing by
herself, she was gradually persuaded to do the same with
one and another of the Chinese on her back, until all three
of them were up there, doing poses and pyramids, and

eventually with Monday and Tuesday also up there joining
in the posturing, while the great beast happily teetered and
occasionally trumpeted with joy.

2

ON THE fourteenth day out from Cape Charles, when the
ship was somewhere in the featureless vastness between
the Azores and the Madeiras, steaming across a sunlit sea
of only frolicsome choppiniess, the voyage ceased to be
boring.

That day began ordinarily enough. The wind was out of
the east, so the *Pflichttreu* was proceeding on engines, but
the headwind dispersed most of the stack's smoke and
soot. Rouleau had been brought out on the foredeck, still
supine on his pallet and still rigidly fixed in his bran box,
but looking cheerful as he watched the doings of the other
troupers. The Chinese were rehearsing with the teeterboard
and Peggy, while Monday and Tuesday Simms waited to
join in. The Quakemaker was up in the very prow of the
ship, trying mightily to see if he could lift the massive
anchor all by himself, but not doing very well at it. Near
Rouleau's pallet, Florian and Fitzfarris sat playing black-
jack for matchsticks. When Florian took several hands in
a row, Fitz cursed mildly, shoved over his matchsticks and
cards, and said:

"A man of your talent ought to be in the confidence
game full time. How is it you got into the circus business instead?"

Florian shrugged. "Apprenticeship, the same as any
other art or profession." He shuffled the cards and looked
dreamily off toward the horizon. "The Donnert Circus
came to my hometown when I was fourteen years old.
When it departed, I went with it. Maggie Hag was on that
show then, and she took me under her wing."

"The classic runaway story. Your folks didn't chase after you?"

"No. My mother was dead. My father surely realized where I'd gone, but he may even have approved of my venturesomeness. He had always wanted me to be something better than the millhand he was, and God knows the circus was a good many cuts above that."

"Anything is. But how did you persuade the circus to hire you? Just a kid."

Florian smiled, "If by 'hire' you mean 'pay,' there was no pay. I might not even have got peck—might have had to forage for myself—if I hadn't had Mag plugging for me. As it was, I had to sleep on the folded canvas in the tent wagon. *Among* the folds, when the weather got cold. Until I took up with my first—wife, to put it euphemistically. An équestrienne, twice my age. She was not at all attractive, but her caravan was."

"I take it this was a mud show, then."

"Lord, no. Donnert's was a fair-sized and reputable circus. Still is, as far as I know."

"Did you do an act? Roustabout? What?"

"Hell, it was a long time before I could even dignify myself with the title of roustabout. I swamped out cages, I carried water buckets, I posted paper, I did every least and dirtiest job there was to do. And there were plenty of them, on a show the size of Donnert's. Oh, eventually I worked my way up to a meanly paid position on the crew, and later I did some juggling. But I thank heaven that I never had to depend for a career on either my muscularity or my performing graces. As you have remarked, my talents tended more to the, ahem, acquisitive and the annunciatory. As I moved from circus to circus—from the Donnert to the Renz to the Busch, back to the Donnert again—I was variously a talker for the midway joints, and for the sideshow, and I worked advance and patch, and I became quite proficient at horsetrading. First for mere road stock, but then for ring stock, and finally I was entrusted with buying the exotic animals. Along the way, also, I acquired various other wives, so-called, of various nationalities. Acquired and discarded or lost them. Happily, I did not lose the languages I learned from them."

"Classic success story, too, I guess. When did you strike out on your own?"

"After my second stint with the Donnert. Maggie Hag was still on that show, and it was she who prodded me to such overweening ambition. She even came with me, which was a real act of faith. It was she and I, and what small menagerie I could afford."

Still absentmindedly shuffling the cards, Florian went silent, evidently into a reverie. After a minute, Fitz asked, "Well? How did you do at it?"

"We kept a step or two ahead of starvation. And what profits there were I plowed back into the business. We gathered unto us a few more exotics, a few wagons, a few boozy or antiquated or otherwise next-to-unemployable troupers and crewmen. The one and only good act I managed to hire, toward the end, was the perchpole. Pepper and Paprika. I might not have got got *them* if they had not also just been starting their careers. They were only about fifteen or sixteen years old."

"You said 'toward the end.' Did you go bust?"

"I, sir, have never gone bust," Florian said, a little stiffly. "I meant toward the end of my stay in Europe. Maybe you wouldn't know, but, after all the revolutions, rebellions and other uproars of 1848, there had begun the great migration of Europeans to the United States. Well, this was ten years later, and both Pepper and Paprika were getting letters from relatives, friends, other troupers who had gone to America. The usual—streets paved with gold, opportunity unlimited, come make your fortune in the New World. So we decided we would try. It didn't require anything like this *Pflichttreu* to bring my Florilegium across the pond that time; we could have come in a rowboat. It was only Maggie, Pepper, Paprika and me."

"I gather you *did* do well in the States."

"Oh, passably . . . passably. Monsieur Roulette there will verify it. He was one of the first Americans to join

out with me. But then, damn it, along came *your* rebellion
and knocked everything to flinders.''

"Christ knows it did," Fitz said feelingly. "Do you
think you'd have done better to stay in Europe?"

Florian sighed. "Well, that's what we'll soon find out,
won't we?" He looked dreamily off toward the horizon
again. "I had one ambition in those days that I never got
to achieve. *The* ambition of every circus man. I have been
to Paris many times, but never—neither with my little
tramp show nor with any of the more respectable ones—
never did I go with a circus to Paris . . .''

"Arrah!" exclaimed Pepper, as she walked unannoun-
ced into the Simms children's cabin. "I swan, all you pick-
anins are queer in the attic." Sunday Simms guiltily spun
away from the washstand mirror, where she had been
studying her reflection. "The injines just changed tempo,
so your sister is doing that stand-up kerfuffle of hers. And
you—what in bejasus have ye *done* to yourself?"

"Improvements," Sunday said sheepishly.

"Improvements? Just look how you look!" Now Pepper
espied the bottles and jars Sunday had laid out on her
bunk. "What the divvil *is* all this muck?"

Sunday said defensively, "I heard the captain mention
that we'll sight the first land in maybe five days. I thought
I'd practice making myself pretty, for when we finally get
to port."

"Crown Princess Hair-Straightening Pomade?" Pepper
was officiously examining the labels. "Dixie Moonglow
Complexion-lightening Cream? Where did you get all
these nigger-swindling quack physics?"

"They're mine! I bought them, that last day in Baltimore. Clover Lee helped me pick them out."

"But whatever for, girl?"

"To make me look less like a *nigger*, that's what for!"
Sunday's language lost some of its acquired precision.
"Less like a pickaninny—that just anybody can walk in
on without knocking, and paw through her belongings!"

"Whisht, darlin' . . . easy, easy . . ." said Pepper, raising her hands in placation. "Ye're right. I had no call to do that. 'Twas only looking for Pap I was, but I had no right to barge in. And now that I've apologized, alannah, let me tell ye something. Ye've no need for that muck on your face and hair. Ye're as pretty a colleen as any white girl, only a different color."

"That's right," Sunday said bitterly. "I'm a yellow rose, a mulatto, a high-yaller, a buffalo gal, a nigger. So tell me, what would a pretty *nigger* girl look like?"

"Be blessed if I know. I never laid eyes on any such thing amongst the real black ones. But instead of trying to cover up your tan color, ye ought to play up the prettiness. Ye've got a plenty of it." Pepper again scornfully scanned the array of cosmetics. "Dixie Moonglow, bedad! Dixie Blaflum is what it is! Throw away that paleface ointment. The three of yez Simms gals have got the complexion of doe fawns, and yez ought to glory in it. Forget the hair straightener, too. Ye've not got Uncle Tom wool nor kinks, but nice wavy hair."

"Only on top," said Sunday, sniffling. "Do you remember, Pep, how you and Pap told Clover Lee about the—the other hair—down here? How men go wild about it? Well, mine—down here—it *is* kinky. Just little knots of hair. Like a sprinkle of peppercorns. They don't even begin to hide my . . . my . . . you know."

Pepper laughed heartily. "But why hide it, minikin? 'Tis the mother of all the saints, as we say. Anyhow, as I can tell you who shouldn't, there's them that *prefer* a woman's periwinkle-flower not to have foliage on it. So it's plain visible and easily accessible. For very par-ti-cu-lar attentions, which no doubt ye'll learn about in time. Now, wipe your face and wash your hair and throw all this blaflum out the porthole. Where is that Clover Lee? I've a mind to give her the father and mother of a cussing for her letting you buy these humbug things."

"Well, she bought some things, too. And she's practicing with hers, just like I was. Pap is helping her."

"Is she indeed?" Pepper said frostily, "Where?"

"One of the lifeboats is uncovered, but it's slung up too high off the deck for anybody to see into it. In there they can take off some of their clothes and have a sunbath. I don't know why anybody would *want* her skin tan-colored, but—"

But Pepper was already out the door. Fuming, she went and stood below the one lifeboat that did not have a tarpaulin over it, and listened. It sounded as if Paprika was giving Clover Lee much the same advice as she herself had just given Sunday. But the white girl seemed to be taking it more submissively than the mulatto had done. Anyway, the only voice audible was Paprika's.

"Angyal, these are semmiség—silly things. Such garbage! Mrs. Mill's Mammarial Balm and Bust Elevator! Cadmium ointment and a funny glass-and-rubber bowl." Paprika laughed. "I see. The ointment is to stimulate the titties and the vacuum globe is to suck them outwards. What foolish badarság. Clover Lee, the only way to develop yourself there is to grow normally, and you are doing nicely in that regard. Here, let me show you what an artist once showed me in Pest. What artists consider the ideal proportions for a woman's breasts. Allow me to touch you. . . ."

There came a faint noise of their bodies shifting position inside the boat. Pepper ground her teeth.

"Here, regard the distance between my two fingertips— one on your nipple, the other on your collarbone above. That distance should exactly equal the distance from one nipple to the other. It does, you see. Also, the distance between those two darling little buds should be precisely one-fourth of the circumference of your whole chest at the level of your nipples. Allow me . . . ."

There was another sound of movement.

"As nearly as I can measure with a mere embrace, angyal, you are the ideal female dimensions. And as you grow, those dimensions will keep pace. Meanwhile, it is obvious that the nipples are already most femininely sensitive. See? How they reach out to be touched some more?"

Pepper started to make her presence known, but desisted when the next sound was only the clink of glass, and Paprika went on:

"Regard this other awful ürülex you bought. Dixie Belle Extract of White Heliotrope. Jaj! It is a waste of money, Clover Lee, ever to buy manufactured perfume. I will tell you a Magyar secret, long known only to us women of Hungary. The most seductive and irresistible scent a woman can wear is her own. The aroma of her own most private precious fluid, the nemi redv, her juices of joy. What you do is take some with your finger, like this—allow me, angyal—and dab it behind your ears, at your wrists, between your breasts . . .''

Clover Lee finally and suddenly spoke. Her voice was low and tremulous, but determined. "P-please. . . . don't d-do any more of that." There was a slight scuffling noise, and the boat rocked a bit. "I th-thank you . . . for teaching me things. But I think I want to get dressed now. *Please* stop that."

Pepper snarled silently and bent to jump for the lifeboat's gunwale. But, at the same instant, the whole ship under her made a sudden movement of its own, and she was thrown headlong on the iron deck. The *Pflichttreu* had slowed as violently as if the Quakemaker had flung the anchor overboard and snubbed it. Simultaneously, there came a terrific mechanical howl and clatter from the ship's bowels, and shouts from officers and crewman everywhere: "Belay that!" and "Scaldings!" and "Shake a leg!"

Peggy had been standing on the teeterboard, tilted aft. When the ship gave that jerk, it tilted the board and the elephant abruptly the other way. Though Peggy managed to keep her feet, the acrobats on her back were spilled to the deck. Even those people simply standing about went sprawling, as well. For a few seconds, there was confusion and shouting, and men running, and the deck—the whole ship—was juddering like a coffee grinder, and the masts and derricks flailed in all directions. The tall smokestack toppled with a ringing crash and a twanging of guy wires and a voluminous eructation of smuts, rust, scales and scurfs that enveloped the ship's entire upper works in a suffocating black cloud. The vibration increased to spasm and the grating howl from the engine room rose to a roar, before it abruptly went silent and the whole ship went still, and the fallen people began picking themselves up and brushing at the grime all over them.

Then the officers and men were shouting again, even louder in the silence. Some deckhands leapt for the shrouds and climbed to the yards, others clambered to the island top to secure the smokestack before it could roll overboard, others took precautionary stations at the lifeboat davits. Before any of the passengers could begin asking what had happened, Mullenax came popping up from the companion leading below, and shouted to tell them. "Threw its propellor, it did! Shaft runnin' free, rods all jumpin'! Everybody grabbin' levers and valves to shut down. I got the hell out of the way."

"Is anybody injured?" asked Florian, his voice shaky. "Is everybody all right?"

He swept his gaze around the troupers on the foredeck. Yount was approaching from the bow, looking dazed and rubbing a bump on his bald head. Pepper and a couple of seamen were helping Clover Lee and Paprika down from their lifeboat. Those two, having been directly under the cabin eaves where the falling stack landed, were filthy with soot from head to toe. They were hastily fumbling to do up the buttons of their frocks, and were misbuttoning most of them. The scattered and hard-fallen acrobats were the last to pick themselves up, but get up they did, apparently unimpaired. Peggy remained in the position the jolt had put her in. Her four big feet were still on the teeterboard, but her bulk leaned outward against the gunwale alongside her.

"I thought I'd really made quake," said Yount. "What happened?"

Pepper took Paprika aside and, while maternally dusting her off and buttoning her properly, was also giving her a most peppery scolding, to which Paprika replied with equal heat. But they kept their voices low:

". . . Shimmy-lifting . . . scunging like an old fairy in a schoolyard . . ."

"Jealous are we, Pep? Did you have *your* eye on that one of the little tea cakes?"

"Don't come the lardy-dardy with me! The totty clearly wants none of your playing at up-tails. Instead of cherry-picking, ye could at least have the decency to try it on with somebody your own age."

"Oh, shut up! They'll hear."

But everyone else was listening to Mullenax's report on the chaotic state of affairs below and, when he had finished, Edge asked him. "What happens now?"

"Well, I know there's a spare propeller. I seen it. But how they'll go about puttin' it on, underneath the water, I'm damned if I—hey, is Jules hurt?"

They had completely overlooked Rouleau, where he lay, and only now became aware that he was frantically waving his arms and shouting weakly, "Nom de dieu, go back! Turn around! Man overboard!"

"What? Where? Who?"

Out of breath and hoarse from yelling unheard, Rouleau gasped to Edge, the first to bend over him, "Peggy . . . bumped . . . I saw . . . Tiny Tim . . ."

Edge dashed to the side, looked aft and said, "Jesus." Far astern, there was a dark speck among the choppy waves and—it was hard for him to tell—it might have been thrashing to stay afloat. The ship had seemed to come to a full stop when its lost its screw, but it actually had glided for some distance. Now it wallowed and yawed heavily, dead in the water, all momentum gone, while the officers bawled for the spreading of canvas.

Rouleau told the others, "Tim was leaning over, as

usual. When Peggy lurched, she bumped him and he went right over.''

Florian reached to seize the sleeve of Captain Schilz, who was hurrying past just then, alternately muttering curses and bellowing orders. ''Captain, we must turn back. One of our—''

''Dummkopf!'' barked the master, jerking out of his grasp. ''We have no headway, no power, the rudder loose it flaps. Until unfurled the sails are, we go no—''

''But there's a man overboard!'' several people cried.

''*Was?*'' The captain was immediately galvanized, and shouted to the men at the davits to lower a boat.

That was done as swiftly as possible, and the boat began to beat back along the ship's track. Most of the troupe stood at the gunwale, watching its progress and trying to see the speck Edge had spotted, but even he could no longer see it. Sarah spared a look at the elephant, still leaning where she had been lodged, and wearning a most mournful expression.

''Poor Peg looks as guilty as if she had done it on purpose.''

''Abdullah,'' said Florian. ''Go and attend your bull. Get her down off that teeter. Make her comfortable and console her.''

Peggy seemed reluctant to move, or even to be touched by her keeper, but Hannibal eventually coaxed her to step off the board and stand upright. So, at just about the same time that the seamen in the distant lifeboat were wagging their oars aloft—signaling that there was no sign of Tim Trimm to be found—the other casualty of the accident was revealed. When the elephant heaved her bulk away from the gunwale, Tuesday Simms flopped to the deck in a position impossible to a living body. Obviously she had fallen when the other acrobats did, but on the far side of Peggy. The elephant's leaning weight had crushed her against the rail, pinched and broken her in the middle, and she lay now like a puppet come unstrung, except that she was dripping substances no puppet contains.

Hannibal had to go away and vomit over the side, but, when he was done, he dolefully said to the others. "Ol' Peggy, she was holdin' Tuesday dere a-purpose. Peggy b'lieve anybody still alive, long as dey standin' up. She didn't want let li'l Tuesday drop an' be dead."

The double funeral, for the dead and the gone, had to wait until the *Pflichttreu* got under way again, for no seaman would willingly drop a dead body directly under his immobile ship. It meant waiting until the spare screw could be put in place, and that operation occupied the rest of this day and all of the next.

The helmsman used the rudder, and the men at the sheets used the set of the sails, to keep the ship as much as possible in one place and on an even keel. The officers directed the moving of every heavy thing in the ship's upper works as far as forward as possible, and the black gang below shifted as much coal as possible into the hold's forward bunkers. Even the circus horses were led from the after-deck and tethered with Peggy on the foredeck. The lifeboats were all unslung from their davits, hauled to the bows and pumped full of water. By sundown, the *Pflichttreu*, with every possible weight laid on its fore end, had assumed a new slant, stern up, stem down. A man at the taffrail could look down the transom and see the rudder standing half above the water, with the stub of the propeller-less shaft just awash.

Next morning, while deckhands knotted ropes to the stern rail and let them trail down the transom, stokers came hauling the huge brass spare screw top-side. Captain Schilz was growling to himself in German that if the verdammt shipowners of the world must have steamships, they could at least go back to sidewheels or sternwheels, which, if they broke a blade, could be rotated above water for repair.

"Have you had to do this before?" Florian asked him.

"Nein, Gott sei Dank. But I once watched it on another ship done. Simple enough in theory it is. However, in practice . . . down the ship's stern on a rope going, work for an Alpinist that is . . . and placing the propeller, the set-

screws underwater tightening, work for a Perlenfischer that
is. No man of this crew has ever had to do it.''

Florian felt a tug on his coattails. He turned to find the
three Chinese—all stripped naked—again jabbering and
gesticulating, pointing variously to the big screw, to themselves and down to the water. Before Florian or Schilz
could express astonishment or anything else, one of the
antipodists leapt lithely to the taffrail. He seized a rope
and, bracing himself between rope and stern plates, walked
himself backward, barefooted and surefooted, down to the
water. Once there, he simply kept going backward, right
through the surface chop, under the water and out of sight,
until only the rope's tautness indicated that he was still in
the vicinity. Florian felt another tug, this time at his vest
front. One of the other Chinese had pulled his big tin watch
from his vest pocket and was jabbing a finger at its dial.

Schilz, peering down at the dark water, murmured more
in wonderment than in anger, ''Another beschisse Dunkel
has himself drowned.''

''No . . . these two are wanting me to time him,'' said
Florian, looking from the watch to the spot where the rope
went underwater, and after a little he said, ''By damn, the
man's good at it. At least a minute already.'' When the
water heaved, splashed, and the man grinned up at them,
Florian repocketed his watch and said, ''A minute and a
half, if not nearly two. Maybe these lads *have* been pearl
fishers. Anyway, I gather that they are volunteering to do
the job for you.''

''Du lieber Himmel! To three naked apes I should trust
that?''

''Monkey see, monkey do. I'll wager that your men
would rather show them how, than have to do it themselves.''

The captain grumbled and swore, but finally acceded.
And the crewmen were only too happy to relinquish the
chore. All that was required was for Chief Beck—doing
much sign language and occasionally drawing with a piece
of charcoal on the deck—to acquaint the Chinese with the

very basic facts that the propeller had on one side a square opening to fit the shaft, and on the other a fairwater that had to point astern, and around its collar four big setscrews that had to be made immovably tight. Then the deckhands lowered the big brass thing on ropes while the Chinese went down another, one of them carrying the setscrew wrench in his teeth.

Actually, the captain's part of the job was the more ticklish. Since the rudder could not be moved while the Chinese were working about it, the *Pflichttreu* had to be held as still as possible by using only the sails. So seamen were on every yard and at every sheet and halyard, and Captain Schilz masterfully orchestrated their hauling in and letting out of canvas. He and the crew and the ship performed well enough that the Chinese manhandled the new screw onto the shaft and secured it there in no more than two hours—during which they took turns at surfacing to breathe: only one at a time and taking only a gulp of air before going under again.

When they climbed back aboard, rather less nimbly than they had gone down, they were given a rousing cheer by the ship's company. Chief Beck went down the companion and Captain Schilz up to the bridge, whence he telegraphed for engines to start. The deck began to tremble, and everyone held his breath, and then the captain signaled for slow ahead. The water beneath the transom bubbled and burbled, and the deck's vibration increased, but it was regular, not eccentric—and men who had thrown wood chips overside saw them move astern. Another cheer went up. The captain had the engines stopped and gave orders for all the heavy movables to be rearranged and the ship trimmed to its proper stance again. Not until that long job had been done—at nightfall—did he order the sails refurled and the engines full ahead, and the *Pflichttreu* resumed its voyage.

Stitches the sailmaker provided a sheet of canvas and the big curved needles with which, after Magpie Maggie Hag had prepared Tuesday's body, he helped her sew

a shroud. Once enclosed, Tuesday's small remains looked
larger than adult size, for she had at her feet a quintal sack
of pea coal to weight the pall. Then Stitches disclosed that
he was a lay minister of the Dissenter Methodist persuasion—so Captain Schilz was pleased to let him officiate at
the next morning's funeral service.

"Lord, we send Thee two small souls that have slipped
their cables," he told the sky, as the whole remaining circus troupe and all the off-duty ship's company bowed their
heads. "Jacob Brady Russolm is already on Thy crew roster, Lord, and the other is about to trudge up Thy gangplank, now just." The canvas containing Tuesday Simms
lay, secured by a single rope, on a hatch cover that had
been raised and fixed to make an inclined ramp, and at its
foot the deck rail had been removed. "We humbly ask
Thee to pipe our shipmates aboard with all fitting cere-
mony, and to kit them out in proper slops, and to mess
them always on dandy duff, and to give them only easy
duty and daytime watches, and to cuss or cat them only
seldom."

Sunday Simms was weeping, making no noise, just letting the tears run down her face. Edge, standing beside
her, put an arm down around her shoulders and gave her
a compassionate hug. Sunday looked her gratitude up at
him and her tears ceased. She even exchanged a small
smile with him from time to time, as Stitches continued
to elaborate on his salty tropes.

"We beseech of Thee, Lord, that Thy hand rest soft on
these two souls. Grant them fair weather and a clock-dial
sea and a following wind, Lord, as they crack their canvas
and set sail for Eternity."

After only a few more nautical references, Stitches bent
to the book and its far less eloquent standard service. "We
therefore commit the body of Tuesday Simms to the deep,
to be turned into corruption . . ."

When everyone had said "Amen," some of them making the sign of the cross, and Florian had murmured the
old Roman epitaph—this time in the plural: "Saltaverunt.

Placuerunt. Mortui sunt''—a deckhand cut the single line, and Tuesday, with no more sound or fuss than anyone had ever heard her make in life, slid down the hatch cover and over the side and into the sea, and in that creased and crinkled and ruffled water she left not even a briefly visible ripple.

Edge and Yount carried Rouleau back to his cabin, and Edge stayed to comment, "You look like a wet winter, Jules. Is the leg giving you trouble?"

"Non, non, ça marche—or it will eventually, I trust."

"What, then? Grief? None of us got even barely acquainted with that one of the Simms girls. And I can hardly believe you're more broken up about Tim Trimm than you were when Ignatz got killed."

Rouleau sighed. "Non . . . I do not miss Tim as Tim. But he occasionally afforded me a certain relief. I do not mean comical."

"Oh? What, then?"

Rouleau shook his head, but Edge continued to regard him with concern, so he finally sighed again and said, "Ami, on a male midget there are just two things of normal size. Les orifices des deux bouts." There was another long silence. "The reason why I had to leave New Orleans was small boys. Comprenez? As long as Tim was around, repulsive though he was, he enabled me to avoid temptations and embarrassments. Are you scandalized?"

"No," Edge said, after a moment. "No, just sorry for you."

Edge said nothing of that to anyone, but he did go looking for Florian to tell him, "Foursquare John is mumbling that he's going to land in Italy unemployed. He's got a point. First his sideshow lost its Fat Lady and now one of its White African Pygmies. When you subtract one-third from a set of triplets, you're not left with much of a curiosity show."

"Tut tut, he mustn't worry," Florian said airily. "There are plenty of freaks to be found in Europe. Hell, some of them are wearing crowns and coronets. We'll just have to work things out as we go along. What we'll have the hardest time replacing is Tiny Tim."

"Why? There must be more midgets and dwarfs in the world than any other kind of freaks."

"Oh, yes, quite. But I meant we'll miss Tim as Tim."

Edge gave Florian much the same look he had earlier given Rouleau, and said, "All right, nil nisi bonum and all that. On a funeral day, I can be as properly hypocritical as anybody. Still, that Russum was nothing but a little blister."

"And a great loss *because* he was a little blister. We must try to get another one."

"Another loathsome midget?"

"It doesn't even have to be a midget. Any kind of new performer, as long as he or she is loathsome."

"Have you gone crazy?"

"Zachary, you do not yet have long experience of managing a company of temperamental artistes. But you must have noticed that, in the main, we've all got along together quite well. Very little friction, very few quarrels. It was because we *all* detested Tiny Tim. In him, we had a focus for all our ill feelings and animosities. We could concentrate them on him, and thereby dissipate them, and therefore more easily endure the foibles and crotchets of our other companions, the slings and arrows of everyday life."

Edge considered, then nodded. "Now that I think about it, I have to concede that you're right. So . . . as soon as we land, we've got to start scouting for another despicable dwarf?"

"We need a little person, yes. And we need a clown. That's a must for any circus. And we need another abominable toad like Tim. If we can find all three in one skin, at one salary, so much the better. Better yet if he or she can also play the cornet."

Four days later, they raised the Strait of Gibraltar, and that raised the spirits of all the troupers and all but the mossiest shellbacks among the crew. As a sort of celebratory gesture, chief engineer Carl Beck came topside with a small gift he had made for the circus ladies.

"Watching you practice the other day I was," he said. "And to me it occurred: when a pretty lady does a pretty movement, up or down going, it would be good if a little musical accompaniment she had, at the same time up or down trilling."

He had collected, from his engine-room stores, eight tin oil-vent caps, all different sizes, and had strung them on a two-foot length of fishing line, graded from large cap down to small. Holding the line dangling from one hand, he could run a metal dipstick along the bits of tin, up or down, and make them give a melodious ripple of ringing. He demonstrated how they could play a slow octave, say, when Sarah unfolded swanlike in one of her bareback postures, or a quick tinkling arpeggio as Sunday spun through a fast one-hand walkover.

"Bedad, and a sweet ascending trill when I get h'isted by me hair," said Pepper, "or a descending one as Paprika comes down from the perch."

Beck said, "Aber natürlich, for more dramatic movements, big dramatic band music you should have. However, these little Kinkerlizchen, even one who is no musician can play."

"It takes a real musician, though," said Florian, "to *invent* something like that. Ahem. I should think such a musician would seek avenues in which to explore such talents."

"Ja . . ." Beck said uncertainly. "I have been thinking so . . . but I must think more." Then he spied Mullenax, and seized on him. "Herr Einäugig! I have some reading in my technical manuals done, regarding your Gasentwickler."

"Huh?"

"The Handbücher says one kiloliter of hydrogen gas it takes to lift half a kilo of weight. Therefore, I think the generator—"

"Oh, yeah. The generator. But before we discuss that, Chief, I want you to meet another little lady. Our company apothecary. I was tellin' her about your—uh—your concern for your hair. And I do believe she's concocted a remedy for that."

"Im Ernst? Wunderbar! With embraces I shall meet her."

As Mullenax swept Beck off to meet Magpie Maggie Hag, Florian smiled after them and rubbed his hands together, then went off himself to find the sailmaker. Stitches Goesle was, as usual—except when he had preached the funeral—wearing the heavy leather belt that jingled with its array of knives, awls, fids and spikes.

"Mr. Goesle, the captain was kind enough to give me some blank paper. Could you cut it into pieces small enough—and sew them into pages—to make eighteen little conduct books?"

"To be sure. But what the deuce are conduct books?"

"To show to the authorities on demand. European magistrates and constables and hotelkeepers are exceedingly suspicious of traveling show folk. Each of us must carry such a book, and put down in it our occupation and age and description and all that. Then, whenever we engage a lot or take lodgings, on our departure we must have the mayor, the landlord, whoever, write in the book that we caused no trouble or breakage, did not get offensively drunk, things of that nature. In fact, I shall ask Captain Schilz to make the first entries in our books. I trust he will give us all a good character."

It soon became evident even to the lubberly passengers that the early-autumn winds of the Mediterranean, though mild and pleasant, were maddeningly contrary, shifting from point to point on the compass. The captain, still determined to burn no more of his cargo than was absolutely necessary, called for so many and such frequent changes from steam to sail and back again that the *Pflichttreu*, which had crossed the whole Atlantic—even with the mid-ocean delay—in twenty days, took another nine to cross a mere half of the Mediterranean, from the Gibraltar Strait to the Ligurian Sea. There, on a late afternoon, Quincy Simms was the first to sight the white Livorno lighthouse, and he gave a yell, and all the passengers excitedly milled about the deck, looking at the other ships around them in the harbor roads. But then a steam launch chugged fussily out from around the breakwater, and the uniformed men aboard it waved "stay away!" gestures. When the launch was close enough, one of its crew shouted through a megaphone, in several languages, for the *Pflichttreu* to stand off.

On the bridge, Captain Schilz cursed and said, "I want to be berthed before dark. What is wrong here?" He grabbed his bridge trumpet and bawled down, "Was gibt es? Che cosa c'e?"

The launch officers conveyed that they were asking the *Pflichttreu* to delay only briefly its entry into the harbor, and they pointed to something that was occurring about a thousand yards away across the water. Captain Schilz used his spyglass to look at it, but it was easily visible, even in the waning light, to the circus folk lining the port gunwale. On the sea between them and the squat, crumbling, red Fortezza Vecchia, there sailed an immaculate three-masted man-of-war under a full cloud of canvas.

"Look you at her hard and well, mates," said Stitches, joining them. "You'll never see the like of her again. An old line-of-battle ship, vintage of Villeneuve and Nelson, two-decker, seventy-four guns. Wearing every thread she's got, from flying jib to skys'ls to spanker."

The ship also was wearing a flag, and it was not the red-white-and-green of the lately united Italy, nor the flag of any of the preunification nations. It was a pure white field with a broad, dark-blue X slashed from corner to corner.

"Russian Imperial Navy!" Florian exclaimed. "What in the world . . . ?"

"The Russian Navy does often come here on maneuvers,'' said Goesle. ''Mainly to shake a fist across the water at the Turks, I think. But it's all modern ships. I can't imagine why it has trotted out a lovely old museum piece like her yonder.''

Some other curious things about that ship were noticeable when they had watched for a while. There was not a man to be seen on her decks or in her rigging, and evidently not even a man at her helm: she moved indecisively in the capricious evening wind. The watchers realized that she was totally abandoned, flotsam adrift, and then they saw why. Smoke trailed out, then billowed out, from the open gunports all along her lower deck, and then flames belched after it, brilliant orange in the twilight.

''The thing is afire!''

''And no one is even trying to put it out!''

All around the beautiful, stricken old warship, but at a respectfully far distance, stood a flotilla of smaller craft—everything from steam launches and smart sporting sailboats to grubby fishing smacks—everything except a water-pumper steam fireboat.

''Ach y fi!'' Dai Goesle gave a cry of real pain as the fire leapt from the warship's woodwork to her magnificent plumage of sail. In a minute, the whole ship was a torch, burning far more brightly than the lighthouse lamp, which had just been lit and begun revolving. Fitzfarris was suddenly jolted as Monday Simms ran to fling her arms around his waist. She kept her blissful face turned toward the scene at sea, but rubbed the rest of herself against his leg.

In a few more minutes, the fire consuming the warship reached its magazine, and plainly that had been full loaded, for there was a tremendous booming, flaring explosion, and planks and spars flew like twigs out of the fireball. The whole air trembled, and the *Pflichttreu* rocked slightly, and the watching people's hair was stirred. Monday gave a last, hard rub against Fitz's leg, and a low moan. He reached down to disentangle her and, when she turned drowsy eyes up to him, he said sternly,

"Don't do that any more, kid. There are better games to play. Go away and learn them." Her eyes came awake, and she gave him a sad look, but went away.

From the wreckage of the warship, still afloat, came several subsequent smaller explosions, probably of powder in the cannons as they heated up. But the officials in the launch alongside evidently judged that the main spectacle was concluded, for they signaled to Captain Schilz that he could proceed.

When the *Pflichttreu* rounded the breakwater and another launch brought out the harbor pilot, Florian was the first to meet him as he came on board. A pilot, by tradition too toploftical to speak to any lesser rating than a ship's master, could have been expected to rebuff such a thing as a mere passenger, but this pilot seemed surprised and pleased to be accosted in his native language by a foreigner. He paused to reply civilly and at some length before climbing to the bridge, and Florian came to report to the others.

"I asked him what that show was all about. Damndest thing I ever heard. It seems that Tsar Alexander recently commissioned an artist to paint a picture for him—a panorama of a sea battle a century or so ago—and one of the sensational events of that battle was the explosion of a munitions ship. Well, the artist said that he had no notion of what such a catastrophe would look like. So the Tsar arranged this demonstration *just for the artist's edification*. The painter is in one of those small craft out there. He was sent down here, where that old ship has been docked, and the Russian Navy boys loaded her and fired her and blew her all to hell—all that, so the artist will get the details correct in his painting. I'll be damned if that is not *style!*"

Stitches Goesle sniffed mournfully and shuffled off to his cubby below. The troupers and a number of idling crewmen stayed on deck, looking about them with keen anticipation or old-acquaintance ennui, as the *Pflichttreu* slowly chuff-chuffed along the Molo Mediceo. That was a curving quay a couple of miles long—like an interminable high wall to those seeing it from deck level—of sea-eroded stone blocks splotched with weeds and lichens. But it was solidly built and handsomely lighted by standing lamps at regular intervals. The lamp-light cast bright squiggles on the dark-green harbor water and gave hulking immensity to the dark shapes that were moored or anchored ships. Besides the lamps and the lighthouse and the many ships' riding lights, there were numerous moving points of light, for the night fishers were just then putting to sea, and each boat carried a big, mushroom-shaped lantern bobbing at its stern. There was also noise all about—steam winches and windlasses huffing and grinding, derricks rattling, oarlocks creaking, berth and channel buoys ringing and hooting. And from the town streets at the still-distant inner bend of the harbor came an occasional trill of music or of singing or of women's laughter.

"I think I'm going to like Italy," said Edge.

"Yes, it will be a pleasant place to winter," said Florian. "Lots of people come from the chill north to do just that—including numerous circus and music-hall artistes who happen to be between engagements. So we ought to be able soon to augment our troupe."

"Abner has been grumbling that one lion and one elephant don't make much of a menagerie. He'd like to augment the animals, too."

"Hell, so would I. What circus proprietor wouldn't? But if we're to get to the rest of Europe, beyond Italy, we've got to cross the Alps. And the Hannibal we have in our company is not *the* Hannibal. Until we cross those mountain passes I'll forgo acquiring any more creatures that can't walk over them on their own feet."

"Well, you're the main—no; sorry—you're the Governor. But you never have confided what your traveling plans are, from here on."

"Simple. We'll work Italy for all it's worth, then move along. We shall aim eventually for Paris. That is the Mecca of all circus folk in Europe—in the world. Nowhere else, these days, is the art of circus so aesthetically appreciated. Mediocre shows, of course, are hooted out of there, or prudently stay away. But a good one—it can win accolades, kudos, royal command performance, even medals personally presented by Louis Napoléon and Eugénie. When that happens, the circus so blessed can pick and choose among the gilt-edged invitations it will receive from every other palace on the planet. It is an attainment more to be desired than any amount of wealth. A circus that can win acclaim in Paris can rightly take pride in standing at the acme of the profession."

"Then we don't go there until we *are* the crème de la crème."

"Right. Along the way, we must add to our troupe and our train and our menagerie and our equipment and our program."

"Along the way. You still haven't specified the way."

"I originally planned to travel from Italy across the border into Austria-Hungary—Vienna, Budapest—then up through the intervening states to France, and meander through that land to Paris. But now . . . this very day . . . I have decided not to limit our travels only to western Europe."

"Today? Why today?"

"I decided when that pilot came aboard and told me the reason for that spectacle yonder." Florian pointed astern. Beyond the bobbing lanterns of the outbound fishing boats, the horizon was still ruddy with the glow of the still-burning warship. "The pilot said—I quote his very words—the tsars of the Russias have always been splendidly prodigal in their support of the arts."

"I can believe it now. But how did that change your mind about—?"

"Zachary, *we* are of the arts. We must go to Russia. Soon or later, we must make our way to the Court of Saint Petersburg."

"You'll need these, then," said another voice. It was Stitches, returned from below, and he handed Florian a stack of paper folders.

"Ah, the conduct books, yes. Thank you ever so much, Mr. Goesle. I will have Madame Solitaire start setting down our particulars in them. But what's this? I asked you only for one apiece, and at latest count there are eighteen of us. You have made twenty."

"Two of 'em's already got writing in." said Stitches.

"Eh?" Florian riffled through them, found one that bore inked words on its first page, and leaned to read it in the light of a quay lamp the ship was just then passing. "Dai Goesle, age sixty-two, born Dinbych-y-pysgod, Wales . . . *circus canvasmaster . . .* bless my soul!"

"You're coming with us, Dai?" Edge said warmly, and reached to shake his hand.

"*And,*" said Florian, opening another book, "Carl Beck, born München, Bayern, engineer and . . . and *rigger and bandmaster!*"

"Aye," said Stitches. "We'll both come if you'll have us, Guv. We'll swallow the anchor and try a new life ashore. Him and me, we're tired of farting against the thunder. Chief Beck, he complains that his trade is too much scorned at sea; he'll never get his master's ticket. And me . . . well, yonder goes my trade." He waved toward the red glow on the horizon. "Dead as Owen Glendower."

"Why, this is tremendous!" Florian exulted. "Of course we'll have you."

"Well, there'll be no debarking nor unloading 'til morning," said Stitches. "If you will take a word of advice from a new hand, you will give those books to Captain Schilz tonight, for him to write your good conduct in. I suspect tomorrow, when his kettle-keeper *and* his sailmaker collect their pay, and he sees you make off with the both of us, the captain will be snorting fire like that man-of-war back yonder."

To be continued in
Volume II of *Spangle*

The
Center
Ring

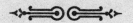

⸻⊂ Italia ⊃⸻

1

THEY ALL WAITED, WITH the wagons, animals and stacked luggage, on the vast, cobbled lungomare that stretched from the harborside to where the streets of Livorno city began. Around them, the cobbles were overlaid with tarpaulins spread by come-home fishermen, selling the night's fresh catch to housewives, domestics and even grandly attired ladies who pointed, beckoned, inspected and bargained without getting down from their carriages. Some of the troupers passed the time by walking about in small circles, awkwardly and tentatively, and occasionally stamping their feet.

"Feels funny, walking here," Yount grunted.

"You are a tenderfoot," explained Stitches. "Look you, after a long time on a smooth and springy deck, you step on the hard, unyielding land, you'll walk like on eggs for a while. Anybody newly come ashore is a tenderfoot."

They had not long to wait there. Florian emerged from the customs house looking most satisfied, and saying, "No problems at all. They may have been a little amused to find among our company three persons named A. Chink, but they made no issue of it. We are cleared to land.''

"They don't even want to count our armaments?'' asked Fitzfarris. "Examine the animals for disease?''

"No. And no quarantine. Not even a tariff to pay. I think Italy is simply too new and inexperienced at being a wholly unified nation to have had time yet to promulgate a welter of rules and red tape and tiresome petty clerks.''

"All right. What now?'' asked Edge.

"First, tov!'' Magpie Maggie Hag said firmly.

"Yes, first a good bath,'' Florian agreed. "And not in a tub of salt water, for a change. Ladies and gentlemen, I shall make an extravagant gesture, perhaps my last for some time. Follow me to yonder hostelry.''

He pointed. The Hotel Gran Duca, on the inland side of the lungomare, was an imposing three-story structure, built of stones to match the other harbor-works architecture. It had the appearance of being able to cater to any kind of traveler, by land or sea, for on one side of the main building was an extensive stable, coach house and yard, on the other a ship's chandlery and seamen's slops shop.

"I shall engage rooms for us,'' said Florian, "and order baths drawn and command that the dining room be laid for a noontime colazione. We will spend our first night in Europe in sybaritic luxury.'' All the women gave little cries of pleasure. "Meanwhile, Zachary, would you apply to the hotel stalliere and have his men run our animals and wagons into the stable yard? Arrange for feed and cat's meat—and a place for Abdullah and Ali Baba and the Chinks to bed down nearby.''

It was with some hesitancy that Edge went to the task of accosting his first Italian. But he found the hostler to be fluent in numerous languages, and so worldly that he evinced no least surprise at being asked to tend—besides eight horses—an elephant, a lion, three pigs, two black men and three yellow. When those arrangements were made, Edge went around to enter the hotel by its front door. The Gran Duca's lobby was an immense hall of rather gloomy magnificence, all dark mahogany furniture, wine-velvet draperies and upholstery. Besides the people being loudly convivial in the adjoining taproom, there were more sober ones occupying the lobby's armchairs and divans: well-dressed women chatting over teacups, well-dressed men perusing newspapers, smoking enormous cigars or just snoozing. Since Edge was wearing his only passable street attire—his old army tunic and trousers, boots and cocked-brim hat—he felt very much the country hick in these surroundings.

Then he heard a call: "Signore, per favore. Monsieur, s'il vous plaît," and he turned to see a small, very shapely young female stranger waving to him.

She was dressed all in pale yellow—full crinolined skirt, an almost naughtily low-cut bodice, pert little kiss-me-quick hat, and she was just lowering a pale-yellow parasol as she came toward him—so she gleamed like a sunbeam in the dark hall, and the bright shine of her attracted the admiring gaze of every male idler, the stony stare of every woman. She had long, wavy hair the red-brown color of polished chestnuts. The brown irises of her eyes were so flecked with gold that they looked petaled, like flowers, and there were dimples about her mouth that made it appear ready to smile at the least excuse. She came up to Edge—and she came up only to his chest in height. Also, she had the tiniest waist of any woman he had ever seen, but it obviously was not made so by any kind of corset; she moved too lithely and her breasts moved too naturally. She looked up at him with that barely contained smile lurking on her lips, and she cocked her pretty head as if debating what language to employ. When Edge doffed his hat and inquiringly raised his eyebrows, she said:

"You are Zachary Edge."

"Thank you, ma'am," he said solemnly, with a nod of acknowledgment. "But I already knew that."

She looked a trifle disconcerted at his not having said, "At your service," or some such stock rejoinder. The dimples around her mouth wavered slightly and she tried a different language.

"Je suis Automne Auburn, monsieur. Du métier danseuse de corde. Entendez-vous français?"

"Well enough, yes, but why don't we stick to English?"

She reestablished the dimples, gave her bronze curls a brazen toss, twirled her parasol in a wanton way and said in broadest cockney, "Ow, orright, guv'nor. Oy'm an equilibrist, nyme of Autumn Auburn, and—"

"I don't believe it."

"Why, 'ere 'tis in print!" she cried, and whipped a folded newspaper from under one arm. "The *Era*, see? The circus tryde-sheet. Sixp'nce a copy, but oy'll give yer a free dekko. Look there in the h'adverts. *That* cost me five bleedin' bob."

She pointed to a column, and Edge read aloud, "'A FA-THER OFFERS to managers: his young daughter, fourteen years old' . . ."

"Nar! Not that 'un." She tugged at the paper, but he kept reading, and kept a straight face:

". . . 'Fourteen years old, who has only one eye, placed above the nose, and one ear on the shoulder. Interested parties apply this paper.'" He handed the *Era* back to her. "I'd have taken you for older than fourteen. But then, you freaks often do look—"

"*Will* 'ave yer jollies, wontcher? 'Ere. This 'un's moyn." She pushed the paper at him again, and he obligingly read:

"'MISS AUTUMN AUBURN, la plus grande équilibriste aérienne de l'époque—ne plus ultra—affatto senze rivale. Frei ab August, this year.' Well, miss, I admire the linguistics. I count five languages in just those few words. But I still refuse to believe that anybody ever got christened Autumn Auburn."

She coyly ducked her head, and let her smile become a confiding laugh. "Ow, it ayn't me real nyme, o'course." She looked up at him through her luxuriant eyelashes. "But if Cora Pearl—'er wot was plyne Emma Crouch back in Cheapside—if she could myke 'er forchune in gye Paree by callin' 'erself Cora Pearl . . ." She twirled her parasol. ". . . I sez to meself, 'ow come little Nellie Cubbidge carn't do th' syme wiv a nice nom-dee-chamber like Autumn Auburn?"

"I don't believe that atrocious dialect, either. I heard enough genuine lime-juicers on the boat."

She laughed again, and said, in an English accent that was merely melodious, "Are you armor-plated against teasing, Mr. Edge? You don't even smile."

"You do it so much better, miss. I'd like you to do the smiling for both of us, the rest of our lives."

For a moment that was silent but richly reverberant, they looked at one another. Then she gave a small, come-awake shake of her head and turned hoyden again.

"Give us a job, guv, and oy'll larf me fool 'ead orf."

"How did you know who I am?"

She resumed her normal voice, but still sounded mischievous. "I know everything about you. I saw the circus carrozzoni come in, and I ran to question the portinaio. He said everybody in the troupe had gone to the baths, except the Signor Zaccaria Ayd-zhay, who apparently does not bathe. I refused to believe that anybody ever got christened Zaccaria Ayd-zhay, so I made him let me look at your conduct book. You are an American, and you will have your thirty-seventh birthday on the twentieth of September, and you are the equestrian director of Florian's Flouishing Florilegium et cetera. And all those particulars were written in a feminine hand, so you have a wife . . . or a lady friend . . ." She paused, as if waiting for him to say something, then added lightly, "I cannot imagine how you got one, if you are averse to bathing."

"Is your name really Nellie Cubbidge?"

"Crikey, would I invent that?"

"Then I'll call you Autumn, if I may. And if I'm not mistaken, an équilibriste is a ropewalker . . . ?"

"Rope or wire. Slack or tight. And I have my own rigging."

"It's Mr. Florian who does the hiring, but I'll break his neck if he doesn't hire you. Now that that's settled, may I offer you a drink of something, in the bar yonder, to seal the contract?"

"To be honest, I'd rather you offered me a bite of something."

"Well, we're all convening in the dining room for a colazione, which I take to mean a meal."

"Ooh, lovely."

"Come and help me, in case I need Italian spoken, to tell the desk clerk to add you to the dining roster. Then, if you'll excuse me just briefly, I'll abandon my lifelong aversion and go take a bath."

"Ooh, lovelier yet."

"And I'll join you at the table, to introduce you to your new colleagues."

When the company assembled, the dining-room servants shoved together several tables to accommodate them. Everyone was in Sunday-best clothes, such as those might be, and Clover Lee was redolent of Dixie Belle Extract of White Heliotrope, and Carl Beck was redolent of the unidentifiable odors of the hair-raising lotion Magpie Maggie Hag had compounded for him. Hannibal, Quincy and the Chinese, of course, were eating with the stable hands. And Monsieur Roulette was being served in his room, said Florian, adding that, after the meal, the hotel's physician would be giving him an examination. So there were fourteen at table, but Edge fetched an extra chair to set between himself and Florian, then went to escort Autumn Auburn from where she waited in an alcove.

He presented her to the troupe with the prideful air of a connoisseur who had discovered an unrecognized objet d'art in a shop of common trinkets, and Autumn good-humoredly did her best to look maidenly grateful for that deliverance. Every man in the company beamed admiringly at her. And, although Autumn was better dressed than any of them, so did the women—all but two. Sarah Coverley and little Sunday Simms had instantly read

Edge's glowing face, and they regarded the newcomer with a certain melancholy. Florian greeted her warmly, and so did most of the others. Carl Beck, when he was introduced, gazed at Autumn intently. "Fräulein Auburn, the very image you are of some other beauty I have met, or seen a picture of, but who it was I cannot think."

Sunday, on shaking Autumn's hand, merely murmured, "Enchanté." But Sarah, in her turn, lightly remarked, "Zachary, I congratulate you, but I am disappointed. Miss Auburn is not a klischnigg."

Edge said gruffly, "I decided I ought to step aside from your stampede of dukes and counts."

"A gentleman would have waited," she said, but still lightly, "until he was trampled by at least the first of them."

Autumn, whose brown-gold gaze had gone back and forth between them during that exchange, said, "Madame Solitaire, it must have been you who did the writing of his conduct book."

"Yes. And I can assure you, my dear, that he will conduct himself to your utmost satisfaction."

"Oh, my dear, you should have written that in the book. Now I shall have to judge for myself."

"Touché," said Florian. "Now, down swords, ladies. A man of any manhood abhors being discussed in the third person, as if he were a mute or a ninny or a dear departed, and Colonel Edge is none of those."

"Coo! You're a real colonel?" Autumn said to Edge, with exaggerated chagrin. "And I only called you mister."

"Sit down, everybody," said Florian. "Here is our antipasto and—not champagne, not yet—but a decent vino bianco. No doubt you are acquainted with the local provender, Miss Auburn. Are you lodging at this same hotel?"

"Not exactly," she said, as she eagerly helped herself from a platter. "In the hotel's coach house, in my own caravan. So I've been staying here at stable rates. On stable rations, come to that."

"Well, we ought to inform you, before you decide to

join out," said Florian. "This is our first lodging under
roof in a long time, and perhaps our last. But let us not
talk business until we are well nourished. Tell us how you
came to be here."

Between voracious partakings of the cold meats, pickled
mushrooms and artichoke hearts, Autumn replied with
staccato economy, "Old story. Goat show. Circo Spetta-
coloso Cisalpino. Folded on the tober here. Governor did
a Johnny Scaparey. Stranded us all. Some of us stayed.
Not much choice. Played to the summer seasiders. Passed
the hat. Hat usually came back empty. Now the season is
over. Still stranded."

The waiters brought the soup course, tureens of fra-
grantly steaming cacciucco, and started to remove the platters of antipasto. Autumn hastily said, "Prego, lasciate,"
to halt them, then said to the table at large. "Please, you
have paid for all these tidbits. If you are not going to finish
them, might I . . . ?"

"Wait you, missy," said Stitches. "There is plenty
more will come, now just. You need not fill up on the
preliminaries."

"I didn't mean for me. I thought—if I could have them
wrapped—there are some other hungry kinkers, castaways
from the Cisalpino, who'd be thankful to you all."

Florian instantly gave orders in Italian and the waiters
bowed in acknowledgment. Autumn went on:

"I'm luckier than the others. I've my own rigging and
my own transport. Actually, I had an offer to come on the
Circo Orfei, but they're away up in the Piemonte somewhere. The hotel people here have been noble about my
stable bill, but they won't let me hitch my nag to my van
until it's paid up. So I was simply hoping to survive until
the Orfei gets to this neighborhood, if it ever does."

"Orfei good show," said Magpie Maggie Hag. "Famous all over. Also prosperous. They no scarper. Better
you go with them."

Edge frowned at her. Florian gave her a painted look
and said. "Confound it, Maggie. I wanted to defer any

shop talk, but . . .'' He turned again to Autumn. "I'll concede that the Orfei family would probably pay you more, and more regularly. We can offer only part pay and promises."

"We should also confess that we don't always eat this well," said Edge, indicating the platters of red mullet and bowls of spaghetti that the waiters were just setting on the table.

"I am free, white and twenty-one," said Autumn. "Isn't that how it is phrased in your country, Colonel Edge?"

"Twenty-one," Sarah echoed faintly into her glass of wine.

"And I can make up my own mind," said Autumn. "If there's a place for me, Mr. Florian, I'll be glad to accept it."

Pepper exclaimed, "That's talkin' Irish, alannah, even if ye be a Sassenach. Hitch your wagon to a rising star." She lifted her wine glass and broadened her brogue. "In Paris we'll be toastin' ye in fine shampanny, whilst we sashay in carriages up and down the Chumps Elizas! Won't we, Pap?" When there was no immediate answer, she said sharply, "*Won't we*, Paprika mavourneen?"

"Oh," said Paprika, startled out of her contemplation of Sarah's wistful face. "Yes. Yes, indeed, Pep."

"Also, Mr. Florian," said Autumn, "if you're the only one of the troupe who speaks Italian, I might be of help in that regard, too."

"Are you fluent?" He held up a cruet from the table—a double cruet, of oil and vinegar, its two necks bent in opposite directions. "In dictionary Italian, this is an ampollina. Do you know the idiomatic name?"

Autumn smiled her dimpled smile and said, "It's the suocera e nuora, the mother-in-law and daughter-in-law. Because both the spouts cannot pour at the same time."

Florian smiled approvingly back at her. "Zachary, you have indeed found us a treasure." He turned to Fitzfarris. "Sir John, until you acquire some languages, I shall have to do all the dealing with authorities and every necessary patchwork, and all the talking on the show.''

"I'll start learning as fast as I can," Fitz promised.

"Meanwhile," Florian went on, "this afternoon I shall visit a printing shop and order plenty of new paper. Zachary, you and I must also work out a new program, to accommodate the addition of Miss Auburn and the Chinamen. Also, before anything else, I must visit the Livorno municipio, to arrange a tober for tomorrow. How long we will show here—before we move on inland—that depends, of course, on how well we do here."

He looked around the room, at the well-dressed, heartily eating and comfortably chatting other diners, as if estimating their eagerness to be entertained and their ability to pay for it.

"'If I might suggest something," said Autumn, and waited for Florian's nod. "Ask the municipio for permission to pitch in the park of the Villa Fabbricotti. Our ragtag dog-and-pony Cisalpino couldn't get it, but that park is in the most fashionable part of town."

"Thank you, my dear. You are proving more valuable every minute. Can you by any chance play a cornet?"

She laughed and said no, and Carl Beck spoke up. "Your Kapellmeister I am. A band of musicians I require, nein?"

Florian raised his hands helplessly. "We have an energetic drummer, a neophyte accordionist and a spare cornet. Im Kleinen beginnen, Herr Beck, but we shall hope to build—"

Stitches Goesle waved his fork around the room and said, "Deuce, there is all these dagos can sing like Welshmen just, and can play any instrument you put in their hands."

"True enough," said Florian. "But most Italians, except the upper classes, have a dread of traveling any distance from home. No, here in Europe . . . well . . . Paprika, Pepper, Maggie, I'm sure any of you can tell the canvasmaster."

The younger women deferred to Magpie Maggie Hag,

and she said, "Slovaks you want. Slovaks the niggers of Europe. Every circus uses. They work roustabout—teardown, driving, setup—then they play band music. So poor their country is, they leave there, work circuses all over Europe. Get money in pocket, take it home to families, come out to work circuses again."

"Upon my Sam!" said Goesle. "So much the better. Let us hire Slovaks, Carl, to be your band *and* to be my crew. Looking at your canvas I was, Mr. Florian, and I have an idea that will double your tent's capacity."

"Well, until we know what kind of crowds we'll draw . . ." Florian began, but Carl Beck spoke up again.

"Also I wish the Gasentwickler for the Luftballon to get started. Extra hands for the making of it I will need."

"Gentlemen, gentlemen," pleaded Florian. "I thought I had made it plain to you both, that we are starting this tour with pitifully small capital. Until it is replenished—"

"What can cost the Gasentwickler?" said Beck. "Some metal, some wheels, some gum hoses. No great expense. For working it, the iron filings from any smithy we can get. Only will cost much the carboys of vitriol."

"Herr Kapellmeister, right now, *any* expense is too much expense."

Beck looked at Goesle and said, "Our sea pay we have." They nodded at one another, and Beck looked to Florian again. "Ein Abkommen. Slovaks you provide, Dai and I investment make in canvas, sheet metal, Musikinstrumente, all necessary. The quicker we have good show, good band, good chapiteau, the quicker we all prosper, nicht wahr?"

"Indubitably," said Florian. "And I thank you both for your gesture of good faith. But I fear such a gentlemen's accord would not persuade any Slovaks to join in it. They are a laborer class, and thinking is the one labor they cannot do. The notion of working for shares would be too subtle for their simple intellects. They comprehend only coin in the hand."

"But they're also accustomed to the holdback," said

Autumn. "Don't you pay that way in the States?" She blushed slightly and said, "I seem to be sticking in my oar frightfully often. But our Johnny Scaparey left a crew of Slovaks also marooned here."

"The holdback, yes," murmured Florian, regarding her appreciatively. "Circuses everywhere do it, and so did I, in the solvent years of weekly salary days." For the benefit of the inexperienced, he explained, "Every new hand always had his first three weeks' wages withheld, not to be paid until the end of the season. It's an old custom, partly to discourage the good hands from defecting to some better-paying outfit, but partly also a philanthropy—to ensure that the drunkards and wastrels among the crew have at least money to get home on when the show closes."

"There you are, then," said Pepper. "The Slovaks will cost you only their keep, and glad they'll be to get that. They won't know we *can't* pay 'em. They'll suppose it's merely the old holdback. And if, after three weeks, we still can't pay 'em . . . well, we'll have worse worries than that, me boyos."

"True, true," said Florian. "And we do have funds enough for sustenance. Very well. Herr Beck, Mr. Goesle, you shall have your Slovak crew and bandsmen. You may proceed with your plans." Those two immediately put their heads together, while Florian again addressed Autumn. "You mentioned that some other kinkers had got the shove. What acts? And are they equally hard up that they might join out on a holdback basis?"

"Well . . ." Autumn said. "Now you'll think me a dog in the manger. Finding a place for myself and leaving them out. But I truly don't know that you'd want the others."

"Try me."

"The only ones that are still in town are the Smodlakas. A family act. Slanging buffers."

At least half the people at the table looked blank. Florian translated for them, "A performing dog act."

"Three mongrel terriers," said Autumn. "Nothing to look at, but jolly good they are. The Smodlakas had Serb names for them—unpronounceable, of course—so I always called the tykes Terry, Terrier and Terriest, and now those are the only names they'll answer to.''

Florian laughed, and asked, ''And what is the drawback to our hiring these Serbians?''

''Well, they include two children, younger than any on your show. A six-year-old girl and a boy of seven or so. It was for the Smodlaka family that I wanted the table leavings.''

''Are the brats mere appendages, or do they work their way?''

''They do. As exhibits. They're both albinos. White hair, white skin, pink eyes.''

''True albinos? Why, there's the beginning of a side-show for us again, Sir John! A pair of Night People to present alongside our pair of White Pygmies. Why in the world, Miss Auburn, would I *not* want such a family?''

''Because Pavlo, the father, is such an absolute bastard. Everyone on the other show detested him.''

''Aha,'' said Florian softly, and flicked a collusive glance at Edge. ''How does his bastardy manifest itself?''

''He mistreats his family. He never even speaks to the children, and when he addresses his wife he always barks, just like one of his terriers. He's been known to hit her, too. And Gavrila is such a sweet, soft person that everyone hated Pavlo for that.''

''Zachary?'' said Florian. ''Our replacement focus?''

''If you say so, Governor. When he gets totally insufferable, we can always feed him to his own dogs. We may have to. For somebody who can't pay wages, you're fixing to take on one almighty expense just for sustenance.''

''Speaking of sustenance,'' said Florian. ''Here are the sweet and the bitter to top off our meal. Zabaglione and espresso. Miss Auburn, can you find all those people for us? The Slovaks and the Smodlakas?''

''They're scattered around the city. If I might have an escort . . .''

''I'll go with you,'' Edge said, before any other man

could volunteer. "But let me take you to meet Jules Rouleau before we go. I want to hear what the doctor says
about his recuperation."

When the meal was concluded, Florian left a heap of
paper money for the waiters. Mullenax and Yount raised
their eyebrows at that, so he admonished them, "Being
poor is a disgrace only if it makes you *act* poor. Anyway,
that mancia is not as lavish as it appears. A lira is worth
just twenty Yankee cents. Which reminds me. All of you
new arrivals ought to change your American money and
begin to practice at calculating in lire."

The whole troupe went to the hotel desk to do that. The
Gran Duca's resident physician was waiting there, a Dottore Puccio, so Florian led him to Rouleau's room, accompanied by Edge and Autumn, and Carl Beck and Magpie
Maggie Hag trailed along.

"Madonna puttana," muttered the doctor, when he
lifted the sheet of the invalid's bed and saw the bran box.
"È una bella cacata." Autumn tittered at that, but did not
translate for Edge.

Dr. Puccio had reason to exclaim. The bran in the box
had been replenished from time to time, as the marauding
mice or rats or both had eaten at it. But the grain was
intermingled with the rodents' droppings and a goodly ad-
mixture of coal-fire soot. Toward the bottom of the box,
where the bran had got matted by the drizzle of the various
medicaments applied to the leg's flesh wounds, it had also
gone quite green with mold.

The leg was likewise a ghastly-looking object when he
lifted it from the box: shrunken, discolored by the bran
and wrinkled like a twig. The doctor continued to mutter—
"Sono rimasto . . . cose da pazzi . . . mannaggia!"—as he
swabbed the leg clean and then prodded and manipulated
and scrutinized it. Still, the leg was whole, and it bent only
in the places where it should, and its flesh wounds were
now only scars.

Dr. Puccio looked around at the others in the room, with
a threatening scowl, and in perfect English demanded,

"Who prescribed this lunatic treatment for the injuries? No physician, surely."

"The bran box was my doing," Edge confessed. "It worked once for a horse I was reluctant to shoot."

The doctor snorted at him, then glared at Florian. "Signore, you did not inform me that I was being called to examine a veterinary patient." He raked his gaze around the others again. "Aside from this merdoso box, what attentions were given?"

"Cleaned wounds with carbolic," said Magpie Maggie Hag. "After, used basilicon ointment, Dutch drops, cataplasms of emollient herbs."

"Gesù, matto de legare," said the doctor to himself. Then he announced angrily, "None of this should have been done. Utter stupidity, peasant remedies, horse cures, unforgivable meddling." The troupers looked contrite and Rouleau looked worried. But the doctor gave an Italianate shrug of shoulders, arms, hands and eyebrows, and continued:

"Nevertheless, it all worked. You people could not possibly know why, so I shall tell you. None of those ridiculous old-wife nostrums of yours, signora, could have prevented the fomites and miasms of corruption from getting into the wounds. This patient should rightly have died of the frenzy fever. As for this—this merda—these recrementitious husks of grain"—he disgustedly sifted a hand throught the bran—"you might as well have packed the limb in sawdust. *Except.* Surely you were all too ignorant to expect it, but the bran spontaneously generated these aspergillus fungi." He fingered the nasty mold in the box. "It is known to physicians—*but only to physicans*, not to dilettanti lay persons like yourselves—that certain of the aspergilli have a subjugating effect on the fomites of disease. This green mold, this particular green mold, this alone, healed the patient's limb and preserved his life."

"We did good, then, hey?" said Magpie Maggie Hag, and she cackled.

Dr. Puccio gave her a sour look. "Good is the prog-

nosis, at least. The leg will require frequent massage with
olive oil to restore its muscularity and flexibility. It will
be two or three centimeters shorter than the other leg. You
will walk with a limp, signore, but you will walk.''

"I am by trade an acrobat, Dottore. Will I leap again?
Jump, bound, vault?''

"I doubt it, and I disencourage it. After all, the limb
was not set and mended by a professional, but by ignor-
antes, however well-meaning.'' He gave another daunting
look around at them.

"But you have a whole new career, Monsieur Roulette,'' said Florian. "As an aéronaute extraordinaire. Chief
Beck here is about to commence the construction of a gas
generator for the *Saratoga*.''

"Zut alors! Then my accident has liberated me forever
from the dull, flat ground. I must be grateful to it. And to
you, Zachary and Mag, my ignorant, meddling amis.''

The visitors left the room and, in the hall, Carl Beck
said. "Bitte, Herr Doktor. A word of advice, if I may request? You shall already be perceiving that my hair is thin-
ning.''

"Yes. What of it? So is mine.''

"Your professional opinion of this medication I merely
wish to ask.'' Beck pulled from a pocket the bottle of
potion Magpie Maggie Hag had given him.

"Is *that* what I have been smelling on you?'' The doctor
turned to the gypsy. "What is it?''

With a good imitation of his own supercilious air, she
said loftily, "Old-wife nostrum.''

For the first time, the doctor's eyes twinkled. He uncorked Beck's bottle and sniffed at it. "Aha! Yes! Per
certo. I can distinguish the secret ingredients. But fear not,
signora, I will not divulge them. Ja, mein Herr, this ther-
apeutant should serve the purpose as admirably as anything
known to medical science.''

"Danke, Herr Doktor,'' Beck bowed to him, then to
Magpie Maggie Hag. "I was not disbelieving, I assure

you, gnädige Frau. But it is a comfort from a professional an expertise to have.''

Trying not to laugh aloud, the others departed. Edge and Autumn went on, out of the hotel, he carrying for her the ample paper sack of leftovers from the meal. Florian and Magpie Maggie Hag watched them go, and Florian asked idly, ''What do your gypsy instincts say, Mag? About the hiring of the new people?''

''I dukker yes, hire them all. All except that rakli.''

''The girl?'' Florian blinked. ''Surely you can't see any danger in Autumn Auburn.''

''No. Beautiful, loving rakli, her. Make fine artiste. For Zachary, make fine romeri.''

''Wife? Well, well, Do you foresee jealousy from—?''

''No. Even Sarah be not jealous of so good a rakli. In Autumn Auburn, no danger, only hurt.''

''Oh, damnation, Mag! Save the mystic ambiguity for the jossers. How am I supposed to interpret that?''

She shrugged. ''I dukker no more than that. No danger, only hurt.''

In the piazza, when Autumn put up her pale-yellow parasol, and the late afternoon sun shone even more sunnily through it onto her auburn hair and piquant face, Edge could not help exclaiming, ''You are the prettiest thing I have ever seen.''

''Grazie, signore. But you've been in Italy less than a day. Wait until you've seen a sampling of the signorine in these streets.''

''I'll never see them. Your dazzle is too bright. Will you marry me?''

She pretended to ponder the question, and finally said, ''Mrs. Edge. It sounds like a female sword swallower.''

''Anything is an improvement on Miss Cubbidge. But if you insist, I'll become Mr. Auburn.''

''I don't insist on anything, Zachary, including marriage. Why don't we, for a while, do what the common folk call 'practice to marry'?''

He gulped and groped for words. "Well . . . fine. But that's an even blunter proposal than mine was."

"I hope it doesn't frighten you off. I am not a wanton, but neither am I *achingly* respectable. I wanted you the moment I met you, despite the grumpy greeting you gave me."

"That was self-defense. The sight of you nearly knocked me over."

"Then we both knew from the start. Would it not be foolish of us to delay through all the trivia of flirtation and courtship and being teased by our friends and the publishing of banns and . . ."

"Yes. Why don't we go back to the hotel right now and—"

"No. I may not be righteous, but I will be fair. I will make you look at what you could be wooing instead. There—look at that lissome lass. Is she not gorgeous?"

"She's no trial to look at, no, ma'am. But I'd lay money that she'll be fat before she's forty."

"How do you know I won't? Very well—that one. You cannot fault her. The girl with flowers in her hair."

"Autumn, you have flowers in your eyes. Stop pointing out prospects. I've got the one I want."

"Ah, lackaday. Impetuous man."

"Can we turn back now?"

"Certainly not. We are on a mission for the Governor. Meanwhile, Zachary, leave off staring at me and look about you. This is your first day in a new country, on a new continent. You should be devouring the sights like any Cook's tourist."

Now that Edge and Autumn had come a considerable way inland from the harborside smells of coal smoke, steam, salt and fish, Livorno was more of a treat for the nose than for the eyes. The advancing twilight was made misty and sweet by the wood smoke that drifted from kitchen doorways. From every front garden and window box came the tart, pungent, no-perfume-nonsense smells of old-fashioned flowers: zinnias, marigolds, chrysanthemums. Autumn even showed Edge a little city park that was pure fragrance: a cool-smelling fountain in a grove consisting entirely of aromatic lemon trees. Even now in the early fall they were all still laden with fruit that was evidently public property. Numerous urchins were climbing the trees to pick the lemons, filling cans and jars with water from the clear fountain, mixing the fruit juice and the water to make lemonade to peddle on the streets.

There were beggars everywhere, even in the most elegant neighborhoods, and not all were as enterprising as the lemonade children. Most of them merely squatted or lay about on the sidewalks, their sleeves or trousers or skirts pulled up to exhibit awful sores. They plucked at the passing Edge and Autumn, and uniformly, monotonously whined, "Muoio di fame . . ."

"I perish of hunger." Autumn translated. "Don't feel sorry for them. More than half are ablebodied humbugs, and even the real cripples could find work mending nets on the docks."

So Edge gave alms to only one beggar, because that one looked genuine and because he did not pester them. In fact, he was identifiable as a beggar only by the card hung around his neck: CIECO. He wore opaque eye goggles and he was being hauled along the street by a dog straining at its leash, trotting its master too rapidly to give him much opportunity to accost anybody. Edge almost forcibly had to stop them to put a copper into the man's hand. The blind man breathlessly gasped, "Dio vi benedica," shook his head despairingly, pointed to the dog that still scrabbled to keep going, and told Edge something.

Autumn listened, laughed and said, "Give him a bit more, Zachary. He says he used to have a well-trained lead dog. It would stop of its own accord whenever it saw a good prospect for a handout, and it would wait patiently while he unfolded the sad history of how he used to be a prosperous tanner, until he fell into one of its vats and was blinded by the acid. But that dog died, and this new one is hopeless. He says, 'Now, when this dog stops, I often find myself telling my life story to just another dog.'" She laughed again, and so did the blind man, ruefully. "Do give him more, Zachary. Those coins are only centesimi. Give him a whole lire."

As they walked on, Edge remarked to Autumn that the were residing in quite a fancy district for troupers out of work. But then she led him around behind one of the mansions, and he saw that the Smodlakas were inhabiting only one end of a woodshed on the property. The head of the family, a man about Edge's age, with a great deal of blond hair and beard, was sitting on the shed's doorless doorstep, moodily whittling at a stick.

He looked up at Autumn's approach, gave no greeting, but made a wry face, hacked gloomily at his stick and said in English, "One must have something to do when one is doing nothing."

"Instead of splinters, you could at least carve a doll for the children. Pavlo, this is Zachary Edge, equestrian director of a new show that just landed from abroad. He is here to offer you a try at a place on the show."

"Svetog Vlaha!" the man exclaimed. He bounded to his feet, pumped Edge's hand and bawled greetings at him in a number of languages. Edge replied, "Pleased to meet you," so Smodlaka spoke mostly English from then on, including the command he bellowed into the shed's dark interior, "My darlings, come! Come and give welcome!

Edge was really looking forward to meeting the albino children and even the downtrodden wife, but what came hurtling out of the dark, making joyful noises, were three small, scruffy mongrel dogs. Smodlaka immediately gave orders—"Gospodín Terry, pravo! Gospodja Terrier, stojim! Gospodjica Terriest, igram!"—and the dogs began skipping around Edge, one upright on its hind legs, one walking upside down on its forefeet, the other merrily turning head over heels.

Autumn gave Pavlo a look of vexation, leaned into the shed and called, "Gavrila, children, you may come out, too."

When the first of those ventured shyly to the doorway, twisting her hands in a patchwork apron, Pavlo interrupted his commands to the capering dogs—"Woman, fetch wine!"—and she whisked back out of sight as if he had tripped a spring.

Pavlo continued to bark like a dog as the dogs, while they, as silently and efficiently as the Florilegium's three Chinese, went on with their frantic cavorting. The woman appeared again after a minute, bearing a leather wineskin and three painted wooden cups. Without command, she filled and handed the cups to Autumn, Edge and her husband, then resumed twisting her apron. From behind the breadth of that apron, one on either side, peered out faces like wax topped by hair like flax.

"My woman," grunted Smodlaka, barely inclining his head in her direction. "Her hatchlings," He clashed his cup against Edge's and took a slurp from it.

"They have names," said Autumn. "Gavrila, this is Zachary Edge. Zachary, the little ones are Velja and Sava."

"Zdravo," they all said, and shyly shook his hand.

The mother was as Slavic blonde, fair-skinned and blue-eyed as the father, and she was quite a pretty woman, in a broad-faced and chunky-bodied way. But the two children were so extremely bleached as to be indistinguishable of sex, and their waxen faces appeared almost featureless— pale nostrils, pale lips, pale brows and lashes—except for their startling eyes: red pupils centering silvery-gray irises that flashed bright pink when they caught a ray of light.

Gavrila warily eyed her husband before asking the visitors, "Have you yet eaten, gospodín, gospodjica? We have bread, cheese. We have wine. We have everything."

"We have dined, thank you," said Autumn, and handed her the paper bag.

"Here are some more goodies to supplement your everything, dear. Now we have other errands."

"But you have not yet seen my darlings' entire routine," Pavlo protested. The dogs were still frenetically do-

ing their act, now leaping over one another in a
complicated dancelike sequence.

"Take your *darlings*," said Autumn, "and your family,
and show them to Monsieur Florian at the Hotel Gran
Duca. I'm sure he will like them and engage them. Do you
know where I can find the Slovaks?"

"Prljav," Smodlaka said contemptuously. "They are all
doing beggar work at the railroad depot. Carrying bags,
hoping for mancia. Debasing themselves."

"While you sit and whittle in unblemished prestige,"
said Autumn. To Gavrila she said, "I'll hope to see you
and the children on the show tomorrow. Come, Zachary,
I know where the station is."

It was not far away. Like most railroad depots, it was
fairly new and—because a railroad, for all its noise and
dirt, was a proud acquisition for any community—had
been erected in the very heart of the city, built big and
ornate, faced with Carrara marble. It overvaulted two immense marble platforms, alongside two sets of tracks, one
incoming, one outgoing, and that area of the station looked
neither new nor proud: already begrimed with soot and
shadowed by a permanent pall of smoke hanging under the
girdered glass roof.

One train had just come in from Pisa, and the passengers
were elbowing, pushing, all but fighting each other to get
out of the compartments and dash to relieve themselves in
the depot's toilets. Edge was interested to notice that the
European locomotives were coal-fired, like the steamship
Pflichttreu. The engines puffed out less voluminous smoke
clouds than did the wood-fired American trains Edge was
used to seeing—and evidently fewer sparks; these locomotives did not wear the big, bulging spark catchers atop
their smokestacks. But their effluent of smoke and ash was
greasier, filthier and more inclined to befoul the train's
coaches, passengers, station surroundings and even the
countryside along the right of way.

After the desperate egress of its passengers, the train

disgorged an astonishing quantity of luggage they had brought: satchels, trunks, carpetbags, portmanteaux and a great number of huge, flat wooden crates. Each was of a size to contain a sizable tabletop, but evidently did not, for it required only a single porter to lift it from the luggage van to the platform. Edge looked more closely at one of the boxes and saw that it was stenciled CRINOLINA.

"Does that mean what I think it means?" he asked Autumn. "There's nothing in that big crate but hoopskirts?"

"Just one," she said. "One gown's collapsible hoop. One to each crate. How else would you expect a woman to transport her wardrobe's understructures? Ah, look. One of those porters is Aleksandr Banat."

She beckoned to a short, squat, shabby man, who instantly came to her, doffing his shapeless cap so he could tug his forelock. Autumn spoke to him in Italian, and he replied with grunts and an occasional word in the same language. Then he tugged his front hair so hard that he bowed. Then he motioned for Autumn and Edge to follow him, along the depot platform to where the tracks emerged into daylight.

"He says he and all his fellow Slovaks are living in squatters' shacks beyond the freight yard," Autumn explained. "Pana Banat is sort of the chief of them. You may have noticed that he has a whole inch and a *half* of forehead. He also has some Italian and even some grasp of English."

They picked their way over tracks and sleepers and switches and between sidelined coaches and goods wagons. On the outskirts of the rail yards, they came to a veritable township of shacks built of cast-off materials—rusty old corrugated metal, pasteboard, canvas, but mostly leaned-together CRINOLINA crates. The populace of ragged, dirty men and a few ragged, dirty women either sat about in listless boredom or stirred tin cans hung over scrap fires or picked vermin from the seams of their rags or sullenly regarded the newcomers. Banat went among the shanties and came back with half a dozen men. They could have been his blood kin, they so closely resembled him—dark, hairy, barrel-built. Banat, with flourishes, introduced them individually and effusively, but Edge could grasp only that all their names were prefixed with Pana, and all their names sounded like gargles.

"He says Pana Hrvat can play the cornet," Autumn translated. "And he himself can play the accordion, and Pana Srpen even *owns* a trombone, and Pana Galgoc and Pana Chytil can play various other instruments. Anyway, they're all eager to work. Crew or band or both." She gave Banat instructions. "Pana Banat will round up all of them—there are five or six more—and take them straightaway to meet Pana Florian."

But first Banat led Autumn and Edge out of the shanty warren, back to the city proper, so they would not have to retrace their way through the rail yard, for darkness was coming on. They found themselves in a mercantile, working-class part of Livorno, where the night and the nighttime sea fog were oozing together through the narrow, crooked streets. The municipal lamplighters were hurrying at their work, to keep apace of the darkness. The lamps they kindled shone blurrily through the mist, lighting the shopfronts and street stalls and pushcarts of knife grinders, pasta makers, coral carvers, cheesemongers, mallow gatherers, birdseed sellers, porcelain menders, all still crying their wares and services to the passersby hurrying home for the night.

Then there came down the street a considerable number of people walking together in a clump. As they passed a lamp standard they became recognizable as a crowd of beggars—all ragged and filthy, some covered with sores, others crippled and hobbling, a few actually shuffling on all fours—but there was something even more odd about the man leading the bunch and walking normally.

"It's Foursquare John Fitzfarris," said Edge, and hailed him. "We've been out collecting new troupers, Fitz. What in God's name are these you've been collecting?"

"Damned barnacles," said Fitz. "I came out for a walk, because in every new town I like to find out some of the best places''—he grinned—''and all of the worst ones. Instead, I found myself leading this scurvy beggars' parade.'' He glared at the mob of old and young, male and female. They were not plucking at his clothes or whining ''Muoio di fame''; they were simply studying him in a sort of dumb wonderment. ''I've thrown them every copper I possess, but I can't get rid of them. I think they think I'm one of their own.''

Autumn made inquiry in Italian, and a couple of the beggars muttered replies. She said to Fitz, ''They're hoping to discover how you got your face half-blue like that. It seems you're unique among the profession. No doubt they want to try it themselves.''

''Goddamn,'' growled Fitz. ''I'd like to *show* them how it was done. Serve them right. I never saw such an assembly of frauds. At times in my life, I've been on the cringe myself, so I know the real from the fake. See that one there? With all those revolting ulcers and scabs on his face and arms?''

''They look real to me,'' said Edge. ''And horrible.''

''That's the scaldrum dodge. You slap a thick layer of soap on your skin, then sprinkle it with vinegar. It blisters up, looks gruesome as hell, like advanced leprosy or something. Now, that fellow yonder, he's a bogus epilept. Falls down in the gutter, throws a fit of flailing and foaming, draws a sympathetic crowd of good Samaritans. Then that skinny woman—his wife, maybe—she slithers among the Samaritans and picks all their pockets. I'd like to hope I'm not going to have this rabble trailing me all through Italy.''

Autumn immediately gave the crowd a blistering of Italian invective. They quailed and dispersed and trickled away down various alleys. Fitzfarris thanked her wholeheartedly and said from now on he wouldn't come outdoors without his cosmetic mask, and he accompanied Edge and Autumn back to the Gran Duca. When the three made their way through the front door, they found the lobby full of people who were not the usual well-dressed loungers.

"Florian's holding court," explained Mullenax, who was looking on and smoking a twisty black Italian cigar. Its rank aroma did not quite disguise Mellenax's own ripe breath, which suggested that he had early found the hotel's bar-room and well availed himself of it. "He's been lookin' at the conduct books of all them new folks you sent, Miss Auburn. He's already done hired the dog couple, and got 'em a room here. Now he's talkin' to all them workmen."

Edge asked Autumn, "Reckon I ought to help him with the sizing up of them? You can interpret for me."

"No," she said firmly. "We have practicing to do, remember?"

So, early though it was, they said good night to Fitzfarris and Mullenax and retired forthwith. Edge had been allotted a room to himself, and they went there instead of to Autumn's caravan, because she wanted to take advantage of the hotel's bathing facilities. A maid was sent running to draw the bath, and she shortly came back to lead Autumn there and assist in the ablutions. Autumn went fully dressed, except for her hat and parasol, because she had no dressing wrapper and the bath was a considerable journey distant through the halls. For the same reason, she returned to Edge's room completely dressed.

"Not to provoke any scandal," she said to him, "I have just now had to undo all my buttons and laces and things, and then, after the bath, to do them all up again. A tiresome business, being modest."

"Then let us be immodest," he suggested, "and really scandalous. Allow me to do the next undoing for you."

For the first time in his life, Edge had the ineffable delight of undressing with his own hands a delectable woman clad in the numerous layers and elaborations of European street attire. For the rest of his life, he would never forget the novelty, the nuances, the intricacies of that night's particular preliminary to the making of love. It was like a chaste defloration to be enjoyed before the actual union—like gently loosing the petals, one by one, from a peony or a camellia or some such many-petaled flower.

While Autumn submitted to his ministrations, she wore—in addition to everything else she was wearing—that mischievous about-to-smile expression of hers, complete with dimples. She stood patiently in the middle of the lamplit room like a child being readied for bed by her nanny. Edge being no nanny, his denuding of her took quite a long time, but it was for him a deliciously anticipatory time. And, as he went about it, his combination of painstaking carefulness and fumbling eagerness seemed to excite Autumn as well. She trembled, slightly but perceptibly, whenever she felt his touch on her body.

Edge began, after some study and deliberation, by unhooking and lifting away the amber bead garniture that edged her costume's low neckline. When that decoration was removed, the pale-yellow percale beneath was loose enough to reveal the shadowed cleft between the upper rounds of her breasts. That made Edge pause and gaze in pure appreciation for a minute, and *that* made Autumn take a deep, tremulous breath, and *that* made her breasts all the more interesting to observe. Then Edge collected himself and considered the next step, and decided it was to undo the extremely tiny imitation smoked pearl buttons of her sleeves' embroidered cuffs. They were maddeningly difficult for his man-sized and inexpert fingers, but next were the larger buttons that closed the percale blouse at the back, and they were easier. However, when they were undone, something was still holding the two halves of the blouse together between Autumn's shoulderblades. She had to assist for the first time—reaching her hands behind her to show him how a hook-and-eye worked. Then, to help further, she shrugged loose of the blouse and peeled it down her arms and threw it onto the bed.

The next layer under the blouse was a complex of sateen-and-elastic straps running over her shoulders, crisscrossing her white cambric chemise to attach to her yellow percale skirt. Edge investigated and discovered that the

loops could be unbuttoned from the skirt's waistband.
Then the lacings of that band around her waist had to be
untied. Then another lacing all the way down the back of
the skirt had to be unthreaded from the eyelets of seams
concealed by a ruffle. When those things had been attended
to, Autumn unwound the yellow skirt from around her and
tossed it, too, onto the bed. She was still enveloped from
waist to ankle by the contraption that had supported the
bell skirt—horizontal hoops of stiff wire hung from each
other on tapes, graduated in size from small at her hip level
to extravagant at ankle level. But only another unbuttoning
from the arrangement of straps was required, and the hoops
collapsed around her feet in a ring of concentric circles.
She stepped out of that enclosure, kicked it to one side
and kicked off her little yellow kid slippers at the same
time.

Autumn was still by no means naked, but she was rather
more naked than most women would have been at that
stage of the proceedings. She wore no corset cover, and
no boned corset under it to pinch her waist smaller, and
no padded "dress form" to lend her a false bosom. She
did not require any such artificial enhancements. Though
she continued to stand like an obedient child being readied
for bed—and stood perhaps no taller than one of the
Simms girls—Autumn Auburn could not have been mistaken for a child. Above and below the waist that Edge
could almost span with his two hands, her breasts and hips
and buttocks were beautifully of woman proportions.

The next visible layer of dress was the sleeveless, waist-
length white cambric chemise held up by narrow shoulder
strings, and a full underskirt of tiered Valenciennes lace,
the cheap machine-made sort. When Edge untied the ribbons that bound the skirt about her waist and it crumpled
to the floor, it revealed another layer of apparel underneath.
Autumn still wore a pair of drawers—finely pleated, edged
with Hamburg lace—and garter-supported stockings of
Richelieu-ribbed lisle, rather gaudily striped blue and
white at the thigh tops, but of pale yellow the length of

her legs, and with vandyke work ornamenting the ankles.

Edge did the rolling down of the stockings one at a time and very slowly—both to enjoy the gradual, exceedingly provocative revelation of her bare legs and to enjoy the tremor his slow motion induced in Autumn herself. She was hardly trembling for shame; her legs were not anything to be ashamed of; they would have graced any classical statue of a dancing nymph. They were firm with muscle, but not muscular, most delicately molded, sheathed in peach-colored skin that was as inviting of caress as real peaches are. Edge would have expected the soles of a ropewalker's feet to be tough and callused, but Autumn's were as velvety to his touch as were her calves and thighs, and he realized they probably *had* to be kept soft—sensitive to every quiver of the tightrope.

When the stockings were off, he rose to his feet and looked her over, with both satisfaction and calculation, the next layer had to be the ultimate. She now wore only the scanty chemise on her upper body and the drawers below. When he lifted the chemise up over her head, that brought her arms up, too. So he observed that Autumn did not subscribe to the practice of Pepper and Paprika: retaining the tufts of hair under their arms to excite the male rubes. Autumn was clean-shaven and smooth there, and in each armpit was a minor constellation of auburn freckles. That seemed a trifle odd, since she had not a single freckle on her face or throat or shoulders or—as was obvious when the chemise came off—anywhere else on her upper body. Edge would later deem it an appealing feature of Autumn's, and one known only to him: that all of her few small brown freckles were neatly tucked under her arms, and no others interrupted the pearly perfection of her body. But right now he was too pleased contemplating the more evident and even more appealing features of her.

The lifting off of her chemise made her breasts bounce merrily, as if they rejoiced to be free of even that light confinement, and they were a sight to make a man rejoice along with them. But Edge devoted only a moment to that.

As he bent to take hold of the elastic waistband of the girl's last concealing garment, he bestowed a quick passing kiss on each of the auburn buds perkily upraised from its auburn halo. Then he slid the skimpy garment down past the triangle of auburn curls, still damp from Auburn's bath—and he kissed there, too, on the way—down to her pretty feet, and he kissed each of those as she stepped out of that final bit of cloth goods.

Kneeling where he was, Edge could now observe that Autumn was delightfully flower-petaled in her most secret part, as well as in her eyes. Her thighs were slightly apart, and she was aroused and invitingly open down there, and there peeked out dainty, glistening ruffles of soft pink, like the fluted edges of dew-damp petunia blossoms. After a minute or so of his simply gazing adoringly at that part of her, Autumn said in a shaky voice, but teasingly, "You did not quite finish the job. I am still not *entirely* naked." She lifted up her waves of auburn hair to show him the tiny imitation smoked pearls clipped to her earlobes.

"You can leave those on, if you want," said Edge. "If you don't want to be *entirely* immodest and shameless and scandalous."

"Oh, but I do!" she cried, unclipping the eardrops and tossing them away. "I do!" she sang, flinging herself on the bed. "I do, I do!"

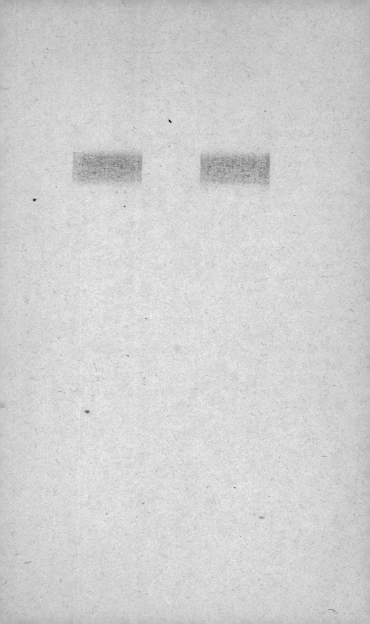